BRUCE CAEN

SUB-HOLLYWOOD

A NOVEL

FIRST EDITION 2005

 YES PRESS INC.

LOS ANGELES, CALIFORNIA U.S.A.

SUB-HOLLYWOOD ©2005 Bruce Caen

For information address inquiries to:
Yes Press Inc., P.O. Box 31369
Los Angeles CA 90031-9998 U.S.A.

THIS BOOK IS FOR SALE ON THE INTERNET AT:
Sub – Hollywood.com

Caen, Bruce, 1949-
Sub-Hollywood, A Novel

First printing, 2005. Yes Press Inc, flexibound edition 2005.

Yes Press Inc.
1734 N. Main St. Studio 3A
Los Angeles CA 90031-2517
U.S.A.
Phone: 323-222-2211
E-mail: dustyjacks@yahoo.com

ART CREDITS:
Front cover drawing by ©GARY PANTER 2005
Guillotine drawing facing title page by ©RAYMOND PETTIBON 1980
Back cover graphic art is Los Angeles street graffitti.
†©1982 'Birth' verse reprinted from NO Magazine with permission.
*©Kim Fowley, used by permission.

ISBN 0-9771571-0-5

YES PRESS INC., FIRST EDITION
SIGNED BY AUTHOR

SUB-HOLLYWOOD   BRUCE CAEN

This book is for Blanche and Dora.

Ain't It Fun

Ain't it fun when your always on the run
Ain't it fun when your friends despise what you've become
Ain't it fun when you get so high that you just can't cum
Ain't it fun when you know that you're gonna die young
It's such fun, such fun, such fun, fun, fun

Ain't it fun when you're taking care of number one
Ain't it fun when you feel like you just gotta get a gun
Ain't it fun when you just can't seem to find your tongue
'cause you stuck it too deep into something that really stung
It's such fun.

Well somebody came up to me, they spit right in my face
But I didn't even feel it, it was such a disgrace
I punched my fist right through the glass
But I didn't even feel it, it happened so fast
It's such fun, such fun, such fun, fun, fun

Ain't it fun when you tell her that she's just a cunt
Ain't it fun when she splits and leaves you on the road
Ain't it fun when you've broken up every band that you've ever begun
Ain't it fun when you know that you're gonna die young
It's such fun, such fun, such fun, fun, fun

THE DEAD BOYS (Lyrics and music written
by Peter Laughner & Richard Eugene O'Connor)

CHAPTER 1

POST-NATAL: My name is Ronnie Kale. I was born on the west coast of the United States in the summer of 1949. In my family, which consisted of my big sister, myself, my mother and father, the men didn't count for much. There were two of us men, the old U.S. Marine sergeant and me and then there was just one. Then it all ripped apart at the seams. Overall I feel that I did the best I could to keep a balance in my life and achieve some personal dignity but most of my time was spent spinning out of control. Sometimes I had the best of fun. Other times it was no fun at all, or much worse.

When I was a wee fair green-eyed boy I was an angel. I was six years old when I played a little shepherd boy in a Christmas play at our church who gave the infant Jesus a plushy toy lamb as a gift. Afterwards, all the over-perfumed old ladies came up to me and bending down, joyfully kissed me and hugged me and fawned over me. I was a pure and beautiful little soul. With the passage of so few years that they could be counted on my fingertips, my true nature was shaped and altered, essentially not for the better. By the time I reached the ninth grade in public school my prospects and demeanor did not appear so heavenly. My mother had learned year by year to lower her great expectations for me, her only son. In fact, she must have had to drastically lower them several times over the course of my childhood and adolescence because at times I was a one child crime wave. However, if it weren't for those deeply entrenched diminished expectations that she had regretfully tucked away deep down in the basement of her mind, I believe she would never have made the big bet with me at the time I was turning twenty years old. That bet cost her a little money and changed my life for the better.

In fact, my premature failure in the game of life was the real crisis that I was facing in the year 1969, a date notable to me because my father died of cancer. It was then, in that year immortalized by Iggy and The Stooges, *another year with nothing to do*, that I had just flunked out of a boring California public junior college in Los Altos with an egregiously bad scholastic record, marred even more by shamefully poor attendance, that my story starts to become interesting. I remember now that I even flunked an archery class in physical education during the final spin of our hungry planet around the warming thermonuclear sun of that decade.

Every pert and eager Dick and Jane studying in the college system was preoccupied with achieving academic credits and units that would contribute to their permanent record and lead to some kind of big whopping academic degree that would translate into gold in their piggy-wiggy banks and ultimately into property and real estate. I found the whole process very dehumanizing and frightening. Everyday I felt like jumping out of my skin as I was in the reverse process of being flushed out the back end of the system big time. Classrooms drove me crazy to the point of tears. I hated the desks arrayed in rows. I hated the instructors, their treadmill minds and their physical mannerisms. I would search for physical deformities on their bodies. Excessive hairs in, on, and about their nostrils and noses, dowdy clothing and other minor details of their physicality fed my revulsion. The packaged information that they were forcing down the throats of the eager minions was not going to enter into me, even if I tried my darnedest to absorb it. It was like giving in to rape by a warty troll and just plain bad chemistry. Who the hell was I, a flunking teenaged '60's hippie, to be critical of the almighty American college monolith? The opinion of a failing student mattered for absolutely nothing and I was tied so tightly in a knot that I was unable to express even a modestly convincing argument anyway. It should be noted that while I was recalcitrant, I was neither an active political dissident nor a participant in the social fracas of the times. I was an alienated other, a screw-up and a wash-out in the formless amoebic conurbation that contained me.

It would be redundant to mention that I wasn't keeping up with the junior college liberal arts reading schedule but I return to the subject again reluctantly because it all still festers within me like a caldera, molten below the surface. I knew that I wasn't totally stupid but the true nature of my intelligence evaded me. The grown-ups had told me when I was a kid that I had a bell ringer of a high IQ but I never really lived up to my stellar potential. In today's world they use buzzwords for some of my problems like attention deficit disorder and dyslexia and perhaps I had a few more undefined chronic emotional problems riding roughshod on my back.

Today millions of American parents are given drugs like Ridilin by their pedia-tricians to administer to their children who have been given that type of behavioral diagnosis. Uncannily, I had discovered the beneficial effects of street drugs on my problem condition at an early age and I had jumped aboard that train well in advance of the medical profession and most of my peers. I had the good sense to trust in my intuitions and follow my feelings of well being to a happier place.

As I gloomily reflected upon my developmental dilemmas, all career oppor-tunities appeared to be severely limited. Typical non-intellectual jobs like working on cars were for mechanics, and mechanics were not of my ilk. Tragically, the profession of being a milkman (which coincidentally rhymes with ilk) was disap-pearing fast in the late 1960s because that line of work appealed to me and sadly, there were almost no milk trucks left coursing around American neighborhoods by the end of the decade. Demand for the once popular milkman was waning. That was work I could have enjoyed. Get touchy-feely with a few widows now and then, picking up the empties from Mrs. Jones and not too much reading.

'Fucked up' would definitely be the proper non-medical descriptive of me as a young man at the vulnerable age of nineteen. I was unable to focus my con-centration and read books as fast as the schedules required and retain any memory of what I had read. If I liked the book, I slowed down and enjoyed it and failed the class. If I hated it, no data would adhere to the jelly between the synapses and dendrites. I was what you might call a slow eccentric avid unfocused selfish reader. My mind was always drifting away onto something else, the hair of the dog and the shape of a girl. My own language, that good ol' boy english kept tripping me up and I began to compulsively look up the meanings of words in the Oxford English Dictionary in order to better understand whatever text passed under my nose. Secretly, I overused the dictionary and probably got a little too overindulgent about it. Being either singularly compulsive or entirely unfocused and dull is another quality of mine. I spent valuable time pondering the meanings of both common and uncommon words to the detriment of my courses of study. Some words have so many meanings. Just try to use them in an ordinary conversation and see what happens. If you use a big word in an everyday conversation in America, people will most likely treat you as if you are a space alien wearing a vinyl codpiece and red latex tights.

Read three hundred pages of this scholarly fat tome by tomorrow morning and be ready for a pop quiz, the paunchy balding professor with stringy oily thin hair would say. In the back row, in the far right corner nearest the door marked EXIT, one intransigent student would be darkly thinking "That fat bald shithead with dirty black hairs growing out of his nostrils is out of his stinking mind."

You might have guessed that I was an inveterate cheater throughout high school. It was a secret that I never revealed to anyone. Cheating on tests was my technique for academic survival. I didn't see anything wrong with it. It was hard work to cheat and it took great preparation. In addition, I took psychedelic drugs to elevate my thinking and for relaxation I chased rock n roll girls who liked easy sex and because of the '60s sexual revolution I had some great successes in that field of endeavor.

Before you read any further and to clarify what we have covered up to this early point in the book, you should understand that this is an autobiographical novel written by a person who is quite possibly less intelligent than yourself, and who in the very least, has attention deficit disorder problems commonly called A-D-D in contemporary parlance. If an expert is what you are looking for or even a new William Burroughs kind of stylistic genius, you won't find that here. Apart from my own inabilities at writing, those past days when there was a Beat movement were just headier times for American social misfits. With all the medical terms and twelve step programs, recovery and rehab clinics, self help lingo, mass media disrespect, propaganda and political policies, where can a small coven of antisocial dope heads come together and create great inspired free-spirited and quite possibly self-destructive writing today? In America, the death of Allen Ginsberg and Mr. Burroughs and their compatriots has left a terrible void. We who survive here, who were moved and given courage by them are diminished and we are left to the task of constantly rolling the big rock up the hill, losing it on the steep slopes and starting anew from the slimy mud pit at the bottom again. They were the men who went over the top. Maybe one freak writer is going to pop up but a whole cogent group of wild mad geniuses with the ability to alter our consciousness and the status quo with their pens (and laptop computer keypads)? That doesn't seem likely to me in the first years of this new millennium. People are too happy living with their credit cards and digital playthings and the mass media is too overbearing and dominant to allow that kind of cultural recklessness to sustain itself anew.

The easy sex girls and the superabundance of a variety of exotic street drugs, these were the true essence of the 1960s in my kaleidoscopic corner of the world. The Haight-Ashbury phenomenon, which was in many ways the deviate spawn of the Beats of the previous generation, had engendered a monumental dynamic drug culture. LSD, methamphetamine, mescaline and peyote, hashish, seconol, psilocybin and magic mushrooms, Lebanese hashish, Mexican marijuana and opium were all my drugs of choice. Ecstacy (MDMA) was not so popular with the free love generation. Yet, no one seemed to be wanting for a greater variety of strange intoxicating substances. A hallucinogenic substance called STP (aka DOM) was a stuff of legend in the 1960s. It was feted as a much more powerful and risky psychedelic high than LSD. Many users went crazy from it at least temporarily. And DMT, (derived from South American herbs, or synthesized) also of great mythical notoriety for being a megapowerful hallucinogen, was an available substance in the '60s. A DMT high was an out of control rapid ascent often transcending hallucinations; colors and shapes could give way to full blown alien dimensions and encounters with strange enchanted critters. DMT typically only lasted ten or fifteen minutes if smoked. Ten or fifteen minutes can be a dozen lifetimes if you're completely out of your mind. It is an error to use the past tense when loosely describing these hallucinogens because STP and DMT circulate on the black market from time to time. The chemical formulas are on the internet for the contemporary risk taker bored with satellite high definition television, Hollywood films or just everyday reality. The DMT experience may cause in the user a new appreciation for the mundane and commonplace. LSD was my kick, and then speed.

Pot and hashish began to disagree with me increasingly as time progressed and I stopped using them. I never bought into heroin addiction although several of my best friends from Tremaine Junior High School in Palo Alto were already inveterate heroin users by the time we graduated high school. They tried it and they loved it. These were the nice pimply neighborhood kids who once climbed trees and rode bicycles and smoked cigarettes with me.

Two years after the Summer of Love in San Francisco, two holy preoccupations, girls and drugs, took up ninety nine percent of the floor space in The Big Play Room in my head with constantly evolving scenarios. Pop culture was my only other supermagnet. By the end of the decade my dented little teenage mind had been seriously pushed into a strange and weird universe by my overuse of therapeutic chemicals. Thank god for that I say, because rigid social conventions were attempting to drive me rapidly into a much more bleak oblivion.

A new and dangerous drug which later when it hit the streets was given the moniker "Angel Dust" or "PCP" had been circulating amongst my little in-crowd of friends. My friend Doyle Martindale knew a manufacturer of the chemical and he obtained a large vial of it in white crystalline form. That stuff really fucked us up. We ate it but most commonly it has been smoked in cigarettes. The experience was like walking on the bottom of the ocean while high on LSD for ten hours or more. It was truly weird. After about two months of group experimentation, Doyle poured it all down the toilet. Our behaviours were becoming frightfully strange under its influence.

There was a group of about twelve of us who were hanging out as a clique in the late 60's. By this time we were exiting the teenager years, almost adults, hanging out in Palo Alto, Los Altos, Los Gatos, Santa Cruz, Mill Valley and San Francisco, these being a few of the meccas of white America's drug experimentation at that time. That guy Doyle, he knew where to get da powerful shit. He had a hardwired network of connections.

Dope of all kinds had spread through the broken utopias of the suburban communities like wildfire. Through Doyle, who worked as an all-night technician at a sleep research laboratory affiliated with Stanford University, we had been obtaining various pharmaceutically pure narcotics with righteous commercial names like Sandoz on the containers. On very special occasions only, like weekends for example, he would steal uncut narcotics from the lab. Stolen narcotics and street narcotics were both illegal so we didn't discriminate against either category.

The sleep research lab was located in the middle of the grounds of a local mental institution on the border of Palo Alto and Menlo Park, reputed to have been the very one that Ken Kesey wrote into the '60s mythology. Kesey and friends of course were long gone from Palo Alto by the time we arrived on the scene. We were just a few years too young to make their party. Their behaviour was a legend and they had moved 'furthur' on down the line with their major action. We had simply inherited the jewels of their cultural psychedelic legacy considerably tarnished, commercialized and altered through time and circumstance. What a difference five years can make. My group of friends weren't endowed with the intellectual wherewithal to change American culture at that point, rather we were part of the youthful body of the culture that had been permutated by the Merry Pranksters deviance.

A small crowd of crazies on thorazine and other heavy sedatives from the mental hospital used to walk, stumble, stand perfectly rigid and languish around the green grassy expanse of lawns which surrounded the sleep science lab which was set in a quonset hut that stood apart from the other rectilinear institutional buildings. Doyle used to have nicknames for many of the patients who walked around the expansive unfenced lawns of the grounds. One of the guys he nicknamed The High Stepper, because he systematically took three or four regular steps and then he took a couple more lifting his knees high in the air. We never really discussed Ken Kesey, except that he was reputed to have worked at that hospital. Once the legend of the Merry Pranksters had been assimilated by our universal teenage cognition they were forgotten in the mad swirl of the 1960s milieu, but stolen pharmaceuticals allowed us to take our experiences to a stonier level and I felt like I had been blown to the moon all by myself by the end of 1969, independent of the NASA space program. Methamphetamine probably did me the most harm physically although I don't think that I would have survived those days at all if I didn't have the drugs to use as a safety valve. They provided an alternative world in which to live creating a kind of mobile fun room of the mind free of social constraints and stress.

After a time the street speed, white crystal meth, had begun to cause my lymph glands to swell under my arms, in my groin area, and on the sides of my throat. I didn't know what that was all about but it was not something that I wanted to endure for very long. I seriously considered quitting the substance. Ultimately, it was the nightmarish experience from the purloined pharmaceutical grade methamphetamine that left me wrecked. I took one injection in a vein on my right arm on a friday night in the summer of 1969. Eight days later I was still wide awake and my heart was racing thump thump thump; the valves were clicking so loudly that I could hear them tapping like a racing old flathead V-8 that needed a hundred thousand mile overhaul. Did you ever read that Jorge Luis Borges story about the ultimate insomniac? Every nauseating minute detail of surrounding physicality came crashing in on his mind. That was how bad I felt. By the end of the week some nasty hallucinations started, the hairy tarantula spiders that had been uneasily lurking in the shadowy corners of the room began creeping up my arms. I knew they weren't really there but still I could not take my eyes off them. Uncommon entertainment! What was I thinking? "This is fucked up. I might die today." On the ninth day I went to see the Kale family doctor at the medical clinic in downtown Palo Alto because I thought that this might be my premature end.

Dr. Leonard wore a toupee that looked like a thrift store toupee that was stuck on backwards in his haste to get out of the house in the morning. He was in his sordid '60s, an unpleasantly cold old fart.

He said to me, "You can drop the ball in life one time, son. If you are lucky you get a second chance to pick it up and run with it again. But you must not drop that ball a second time."

I didn't like football analogies and I didn't want to run with his ball. Then he sent me home. He didn't even give me one Valium. Eventually, I went to sleep and subsequently I quit the amphetamines. I'm not saying that I didn't like speed in the way that I disliked smoking pot. I just stopped taking it.

As for the military draft of 1968-69 and the war in Vietnam, I got out of that. It was easy. Demon polio blew me a flirtatious kiss on Valentines Day in '55. Only minor damage did the demon inflict on me the child, the rhomboid muscle group on my right shoulder was paralyzed. Hardly noticeable in a skinny little boy but as I grew up it was manifested by a characteristic lazy slouching posture which led to an automatic rejection from military service. I did make a special effort to inform the draftboard of my disability because shooting and killing Asian people was not something that I wanted to do. To go kill Asian people on the shifty rhetoric of politicians like Lyndon Johnson or Dick Nixon was insane and I wasn't the first person or the only person of draft age who held those visceral intuitions. Beyond the intuitions there were political and intellectual arguments by the dozens. There was a poster of Dick Nixon in that era which read: Would you buy a used car from this man?

Growing up in the 1950s and '60s, I probably had an average almost normal family for that time period. Our family life had been stained by chronic senseless vicious fighting. Mostly, my older sister and I fought. My parents and I fought. We all fought with each other and as a group. Big sis' was four years old when I was born and she resented my existence from my earliest five and a half pound post-natal appearance right up through adulthood. I was crowding in on her action and taking up space in her world. When I was eighteen my mother told me the story that when I was three years old my sister pushed me on my tricycle off of a ten foot high vertical embankment.

"We don't want you." she apparently said.

According to my mom, my tongue was nearly completely severed off from the impact. The doctors feared that it might not reattach itself in healing. That would have been nice. A boy with no tongue would be uniquely handicapped. I had no memory of the incident but I said "Thanks for the information mom." She had passed that information along to me a little bit late in the game.

Unknowingly, I lived my first scrawny awkward helpless years in the crosshairs of a child demon maniac who was playing out the lead role of Rhoda from the '50s movie 'The Bad Seed' in the real world. My sister's behavior pre-dated the movie, she was a natural, a 1950's prototype with a remarkably similar appearance. When we fought, which was daily, my aggressive big sister would enlist the aid of my mother in order to gain an even greater advantage than her age allowed her. We had violent fights in front of the TV over who could sit closest to the action during The Mickey Mouse Club.

"Mom, Ronnie is standing in front of the TV and I can't dance. Mom, Ronnie said fuck you!" I learned early some pathetic repartee.

Saying fuck you was a serious infraction for a seven year old. My mother in turn would enlist the aid of my father when he got home from the office. Then the three of them with my pop at the lead would go after me seeking punitive discipline. If he could catch me he'd whip me with his belt.

Other times, when I was no longer entertaining, my mother and sister would methodically berate my father. This was a pattern that continued right up through our teenage years. That was the domestic environment in which I grew up. We had one of those tight, intense, bickering, insular little family units. There was physical violence but mostly vociferous screaming and large overdoses of mental cruelty. My sister, whose name was Shannon, slammed my hand in a door and broke one of my fingers. As she grew into puberty she used the wily ruse of having her boy-friends beat me up away from our home. My dad whipped me with his belt or slapped my face if the occasion called for it, and I kicked several holes in the walls of the den, started a few notable fires, made gunpowder pipe bombs, sabotaged machinery, electrocuted and burned alive small animals, and broke out windows on speeding cars with brick shards.

There was also a brief period where I burglarized the homes of nearby neighbors and the local convenience stores and stole liquor. Stuff like that. This was just your basic stage one American family violence, nothing to get terribly excited over. There was rarely a need for police intervention. My mom and I had always argued vehemently even when I was a very small boy. About what, I just don't remember but we had raging wild blow-out tiffs. What kind of issues can you have at the age of four or five? After we argued I always went and broke something up. It made me feel so much better to destroy some object or property.

Early on, I began enthusiastically perpetrating petty stupid white kid crimes. Until I was 12, we lived in a small Northern California town named Rockwater Creek. Our three bedroom home was situated about a half mile from a functioning slaughterhouse, located within one of the generic stereotypical meandering 1950s ticky-tacky suburbs encroaching onto the rolling hills of shrinking western ranch land that characterized the beginning of the end of the American rural lifestyle. After summer school, accompanied by a neighbor friend on a hot June afternoon, I broke some orange clay pipes about twelve inches in diameter leading from our friendly neighborhood abattoir, a distant white stark three story building with windowless high walls except for one small window on the third floor in the back. The pipes criss-crossed a deep trickling creek bed which debouched ultimately onto our neighborhood streets. It was a major fun time smashing those pipes to bits. I hated having to go to summer school that year and playing Godzilla attacking civilization was a great release.

About an hour after I went home for dinner the neighborhood streets were flooded with fresh red animal blood. It ran for three or four blocks and puddled stagnant in the summertime heat in front of the neatly manicured lower middle-class houses. The neighbors were furious and sickened, the local meat company wanted the perps apprehended but the police investigators were unable to find the vandals. I thought it was so kool flooding the streets with blood. It was like some bizarre horror movie scene brought home to Rockwater Creek. The fire department arrived. My dad was outraged by the incident. That slaughterhouse had provided us neighborhood kids with constant adrenaline pumping entertainment. Also, we burglarized the meat house to obtain the gunpowder for homemade explosives.

Soon this little Tinytown USA was all relegated to old memories because my family packed up and moved to Palo Alto the summer when I was turning thirteen. My sister wanted to attend a junior college with cuter boys than the boys they had in Rockwater Creek. She insisted we move to Palo Alto. My mom agreed with her, they sold the house and then we did the move, pronto.

The next year in Palo Alto I was arrested by federal agents. I was the new boy in town and I soon got myself in trouble. Two friends and myself pelted with eggs some thirty or forty picketers outside a restaurant in downtown Palo Alto. We had purchased a couple of dozen eggs with malicious intent and they were sitting ducks. We didn't know in advance that they were CORE (Congress of Racial Equality) picketers. The federal agents who chased us down were reluctant to believe us. They wanted to believe that we were white supremacist youths taking out our bias on peoples of a darker skin color and those who supported them. This attack had the distinctive markings of a hate crime. The parents came down to the police station in shock. They all explained that their kids were not activist racists. These were simply stupid adolescents unaware of the real world around them maliciously throwing eggs at people for fun. The federal agents and the local police let us go. It was only a simple plain wrapped case of egg throwing for fun not hate.

Soon after the egg incident I came down with what the teenagers called the kissing disease, mononucleosis. I felt out of touch with reality and physically weak. My fun ended abruptly. The doctor insisted that I do no physical activity what-soever. After school, I was directed to go home and just sit quietly. There was no cheating on this prescription for inactivity because our Kale family doctor, the gravely serious Dr. Leonard at the Palo Alto Medical Clinic, had said that my spleen was enlarged and it might explode with physical activity. I didn't like the sound of that although the spleen remains a complete mystery to me even to this day. I don't ever want to know what it is, where it is or what it does. The mono dragged on for two years when I should have been experimenting with sex. Every month I took a blood test to measure my white blood cell count. Every month the result was bad news. This was the death of fun. Life at Tremaine Junior High School became a grey zone of monotony for me. I was sitting quietly in front of the TV sick with mono when Lee Harvey Oswald was gut shot on live TV in glorious black and white. That was exciting and it was television.

I've always had a penchant for temper tantrums around four in the afternoon, but any time will do. It's possibly caused by low blood sugar and a lack of vitamins. Once you get in the habit of fighting every day, it becomes difficult not to go there. You become an anger junkie. In the slightly bigger picture, this tight little family unit of ours was simply a volatile and mismatched combination of personalities stuck with each other for several years, no exit. Ironically, we all unquestioningly watched the common fare of family TV shows from that era, The Donna Reed Show, Bonanza and Leave It To Beaver, at night together. It was the mental stress in our family home that was so debilitating. We were cast so negatively different from the TV shows that we watched for entertainment.

By the time I reached high school my home life was simply living hell. Neither my parents nor my big sister attended my high school graduation because the three of them had all been arguing with me all afternoon. I was super pissed off upon leaving the house. I got in my father's car, one of those long heavy '60s Fords, floored it in reverse, backed it into the center post supporting the garage and dropped the garage roof onto the top of the car. It was the slapstick end to my use of the family car and I was bumfucked miserable in my cap and gown later that evening. The family boycotted the graduation ceremony in protest and I got good and drunk afterwards.

At the end of my junior year in High School my dad became ill. My father died of lung cancer and emphysema in late '68 or early '69, soon after I graduated from high school and the confusion, pain and anguish I felt from his passing gnawed at my psyche for several years. His death was not an event that I was emotionally equipped to handle. During my junior and senior years in high school I came home everyday to his lung cancer, hospitalizations, trips to intensive care, and highly stressed family dramas. Other kids didn't seem to have these problems day to day, except maybe for Beth in my homeroom whose mother threw herself in front of a speeding train one weekend. Beth appeared sullen and pale.

As I observed my dad living out his last days on earth, my thoughts and feelings were confused. I didn't know if he loved me or hated me when I was standing there in front of his bed at Stanford Hospital. He was bright yellow from liver failure and comatose there below me in the bed. I had moved out from the family at my first opportunity after high school and I hadn't seen him for six months. His color stunned me, it seemed almost inhuman. The hospital itself seemed like a nice place to die in. The walls were bright white and it wasn't so gloomy as many other hospitals. My mother had warned me to cut my hair before I went in there to see him. But I showed up with my shoulder length hair, levis, a white t-shirt, black hi-top Converse basketball shoes and no socks. It was the 1960's. I wasn't trying to make a statement, I just thought that if my father was going to die soon he really wouldn't care much how I looked. That was how I looked in those days. If I had showed up in a suit and tie he would have died sooner from shock. Then he went and did it. He croaked big time much earlier than I anticipated. I was standing there next to his bed. He couldn't speak and his eyes were open but they were unfocused and he seemed to be blind. He lifted his big hand off the blanket towards me with great effort. He had big man's hands in contrast to mine which are small and more delicate. I reached out to his hand with mine and with all his strength he shook it ever so gently. Then his hand dropped to the bed softy. In the next few seconds he died in a short jerky spasm. His eyes turned up to the heavens like they were focused suddenly on a distant star and he jerked once and was gone. His dead eyes locked in that unusual position. It was weird to see. I was aware that my friends were sitting around playing guitars and getting high less than a mile away without a care in the world.

My mother said bitterly, "He's dead. You'd better cry!" But I didn't. She acted like it was my fault. Shannon never visited my father when he was hospitalized.

My pop had been a sergeant in the U.S. Marines during WWII. The Marine Corps had been the defining experience in his life. He really loved the Marine Corps. He told me that he lied about his age to the recruiters because he was into his 30s when he enlisted. I'm sure the recruiters didn't give a damn if he was over 30 years old after Pearl Harbor was attacked. He had always seemed sort of like a duck out of water socially, as a civilian, and he worked for war veterans rights until the end of his life. He had chain-smoked Camel straights daily for forty years. Even after the doctors removed one of his lungs he continued smoking Camels. He loved Camel cigarettes, no filters. They were generously packed by Uncle Sam into his WWII K-Rations, a few samples of which he had nostalgically kept since the end of the war. After he died I smoked those K-ration Camels myself. They hadn't changed flavor a bit in 24 years. Nevertheless, we two Camel men had taken a casualty and I was the only man of the house left.

My father when he was younger was a very handsome man. He was sixty-two when he died in '69 and when I was born he was 42 years old. Some Einstein out there in Readerland is going to check my arithmetic. Its probably incorrect. On my birth certificate it said that he was an automobile salesman at Moon Motors in San Francisco. Eventually, he went to work for the Veterans Administration and stayed there for the rest of his life. When our family went dining out to fancy dinner he almost always took us to the Marines Club in San Francisco, an exclusive restaurant for Marines and veteran Marines and their families. That incredible image from WWII of several Marines heroically raising the American flag on Iwo Jima was one that I was familiar with from a very early age. His platoon had been almost completely destroyed in the fighting at Iwo Jima.

My dad had a deeply lined face that was partly due to hereditary bone structure and for the other part to real hard times. Down his cheeks were formed these deep, deep grand canyon creases extending from the cheekbones to the bottom of his jaw. These deep lines formed in his late 30s as his hairline was rapidly receding. His nose had been badly broken and was pushed to the left side of his face in the center bony part. He had a long vicious scar across his right bicep that looked as though his right arm had been nearly severed off by a metallic slash. His hands were large big boned and strong yet his physique was svelte with long lean muscles and he stood about six feet tall. He was a stylish dresser and he wore those kind of suits in the style of the guys in the film noir movies. In his closet on the far left hung the aging dress uniform of a Marine sergeant from the second World War.

He didn't have the loquacious outgoing personality one would expect of a car salesman but he believed in the American automobile until the early sixties when he bought a Chevy II and it started falling apart within the first year. He had always purchased Chevrolets but that year he traded in the Chevrolet and bought a Ford. It was a big move for him. He was a Ford man to the end after that.

My parents revealed little about themselves personally, their early lives or our family genealogy, to the two children. The well of our heritage was a shallow dry well. My dad would tell no stories about his life prior to his marriage to my mother and he told me mostly insignificant scraps about his wartime experiences. I had an intuition that he was previously married to a latina before marrying my mother. Occasionally, during the '50s and '60s he would start studying Spanish from an instructional book, as though this was some unfinished part of his life. My mother would always discourage him from pursuing Spanish. Typical of adult whities from her generation in the '50s and '60s, she had a repressed racial bias covered by a thin veneer of civility, against latinos and blacks in America. Mom believed all non-whites to be inferior but she was reluctant to admit to it overtly in conversation. Along these lines she insisted that I study French, not Spanish, as a foreign language in junior high and high school. Knowing some French in California has served no practical purpose for me living in this state overflowing with Mexicans and Central Americans. ¿Que pasa mon ami?

In 1962 my father began taking a series of courses at the University of California Berkeley campus in order that he could rise higher in the ranks of government bureaucrats. He began professionally studying doomsday nuclear bomb scenarios when the democrat John F. Kennedy was in office. It was all classified Top Secret by the government. The titles of the books he was studying read something like this, "How To Reform The United States Government After A Nuclear War." These were high security government publications of extreme paranoia targeted to professional civil service bureaucrats and he was one of them, the patriotic grey suits, being an administrator of the Veterans Administration hospitals. He read through about twelve blue jacketed hard bound volumes on these subjects to complete the course of study. When he was done with the course he appeared to be the same man but he was secretly prepared for total nuclear annihilation under his white shirt and tie. This was complete 1960s Cold War insanity and I can proudly state that my family was right there living the strange dream. He was studying these matters of national security at the same time that I was afflicted with that loathsome chronic mononucleosis.

The two women, mother and daughter, bitched and nagged at the old man and picked him apart nightly. They even criticized the way he sat at the kitchen table after dinner with his legs crossed when he was relaxing. They didn't like the way he sat. He usually didn't let any of their comments get under his skin. He loved and worshiped my mother and he never spoke one cross word to her and he never raised his voice to her throughout their entire marriage. Although, he did do one little thing that might have piqued my mother's ire for life. At some point during the Kennedy era he got hold of her private funds, then he blew a large percentage of her small nest egg inheritance overnight, fifty thousand dollars according to my uninformed estimates, playing leveraged futures, not terribly different odds than Las Vegas casinos I would guess. He was a naive investor. This information was gleaned by my eavesdropping on fragments of their arguments. They never ever discussed these matters if they thought that I was within earshot.

My mom did have a really sweet side to her but Lizzie Borden certainly had a sweet personality as well and John Wayne Gacy Jr. was Pogo The Clown, so maybe a sweet personality doesn't count for much in this world. My dad would have kicked my ass if he had ever found out that I battered my mother. Now that he was gone the two acrimonious ladies of the house would inevitably turn their archly critical eyes on me. We weren't ever a family that communicated well with each other so we couldn't work our way through these little internecine problems. My dad's daily allotment of their chronic nagging was going to fall on me. I knew that I was in big trouble if I stayed around these suburban black widows. It was a sure thing that my mother and my sister were going to rip me to shreds verbally and psychologically and I already felt like such an egregious loser after growing up under their critical gaze. This shrinking little nuclear family unit of mine was not a positive nurturing environment and it was deteriorating rapidly. My current status was that of a junior bozo-nada, something less than a young man or a human.

SUB-HOLLYWOOD — BRUCE CAEN

CHAPTER 2

The older sister, Shannon was spoiled by my two parents inasmuch as a lower middle class family can spoil a kid. I wasn't jealous of her; at least I don't think that I was feeling jealousy, but I learned to be defensive-aggressive because I was playing with a beautiful shark. Let me qualify that remark. To her little brother alone, that being me, she was a beautiful shark. To the world at large she was a pampered oversexed blond white girl riding on a fast track monorail to Bimboland.

In 1964, when Shannon was 18 years old and she was in between high school (varsity cheerleader, prom queen, the total package) and junior college, she felt that she could be made more beautiful than she already was, so the concerned parents bought her plastic surgery on her nose. The initial complaint was that she had broken her nose playing Peter Pan when I was five and she was nine. A magical leap from the box springs and mattress in my bedroom carried her into the opposing wall face first. She received a fake looking Barbie Doll nose in place of her original very pretty human nose. Actually there wasn't much difference. The following summer vacation there was another facial plastic surgery with much the same result.

She would lay in bed, her face all bruised with a bag of frozen peas over it to reduce the swelling. I said, "Hey look! It's a pea head. You look terrible. I think the doctor made a mistake."

"Get out of here you little shit!" she yelled without moving her mouth or gesturing. "Go ride your skateboard in the street. Mom! Ronnie is being an asshole!"

This was not a common practice for teenagers in the 1960s, and maybe because plastic surgery skills were still somewhat in their infancy, her nose always looked a little bit store bought, off the shelf, from that point on. Around that time all of our family photograph albums disappeared lest her new boyfriends come over to visit and see the original pretty young lady with the former genetically natural nose. New nose or old nose really made no difference because she was a natural blond bombshell with big tits and a shapely bubble booty butt that drove the guys wild. Following the surgeries my parents sent her to an expensive modeling school. Beauty after all, must be refined to achieve perfection. The James R. Pride School of Modeling in San Francisco it was called. I don't know what happened with that conceit. She never became a professional fashion model. She had her picture in the San Francisco newspapers not more than couple of times wearing JCPenney fashions.

She attended junior colleges sporadically and she probably did only a little better academically than I managed to do but she never graduated either. Watching soap operas while she studied could possibly have influenced the outcome of her college life. My parents bought her four cars in three years. I eventually was given one of her rejects, a Chevy Corvair which substantiated my fathers belief in the decline of General Motors. A nameless boyfriend, who was stoned on LSD totally wrecked a kool aqua Mercury Comet that my eager parents had purchased for her. They immediately bought her another car.

ENTER SLIMY CURLY FUZZY FURRY HARRY: Matters of love kicked into high gear in '66 when my sister acquired a fast-talking rock and roll boyfriend with big hair named Harry. She saw a man she liked and she knew what it would take for a woman like her to go get him. At a mid-sixties rock concert in an American Legion Hall she pony-danced circles around him wearing white knee-high go-go boots, a short short tight skirt and a cashmere sweater and he went for it hard. Soon he managed to marry this energetic dancing filly Vegas style and legally he became part of our family.

Strangely, the in-laws of the two families never met, except for me because I was unimportant and socially fluid. I met his folks and his brother and two sisters. You might imagine that his hairdo was blond but no, it wasn't blond at all, it was the color of black coffee and it was punctuated by white sun deprived skin. He had that curly frizzy fuzzy big and long hippie style of hair unique to that period of time. Harry knocked, rocked and hustled around the music scene in L.A. and S.F. until he eventually landed a real job as head of A&R at Selectra Records in Los Angeles at the peak of the '60s music surge, dwarfing my dad's government career and income and as well as my own status as the aspiring little man in the household. Very impressive indeed.

At the time Harry was coupling with my sister, my pop was becoming sick. My sister and my mother were completely charmed by this young, glib musical man but my ailing Daddy-o took the opposing opinion. My father's concerns about Harry's character were ignored in part because he was going to be dead soon and therefore not a player. Besides, the two ladies only valued his opinion if it suited their immediate purposes when he had been in good health.

From what I could see, Harry's main job duties at the Selectra hit factory were to sniff cocaine and drive a silver jaguar, party and talk chit-chat on the phone. He signed a few bands that went on to create hit albums. Previously, he had played bass guitar in a popular west coast rock band called "Smile", a hippie pop rock band with a typical '60s free love message. He really had little musical talent himself. His real talent resided in his gift for gab and his knack for hanging out with the right people. Harry was a consummate bullshit artist, a chatty hip, handsome smooth-talking schmoozer. He had an out-of-the-box cheshire cat grin and a sense of humor that kept you off guard. Plus, he had a mixture of street smarts and bookish knowledge that was vastly entertaining. These were not necessarily negative characteristics back in the sixties, in fact these very qualities are in-demand social skills in today's fast-paced digital business environment.

He knew the minutiae of the sounds of the era. He told me in 1967 that the drummer for bluesmaster Jimmy Reed got that unique deep resonant thud by taping a leather wallet to his snare drum. I was terrifically impressed by that information in my youth because Jimmy Reed, despite his apparent musical simplicity, had a sound that was impossible to imitate. Harry sometimes dragged me around backstage at major rock shows, occasionally introducing me to someone unimportant, and to various recording sessions where cocaine was more abundant than food or oxygen. He routinely set me aside like a wooden Indian when he pow-wowed with the big recording stars.

Harry typically carried with him a vial of coke that he cut by fifty percent with nonfat milk powder and he put that concoction up the noses of every beautiful person in the music business who crossed his path. That's probably the only calcium and protein many musicians got in their diet. Cocaine was an expensive elitist drug in those days before the crack epidemic of the '80s. I heard stories of people putting their boogers on the window sill to dry so that they could crush them and re-snort them for the cocaine content. Cocaine was equated with glamour and lavish lifestyles and erotic successes.

After their Vegas nuptials the newlywed glamorous musical media couple never let my family unit underestimate their importance. Humility was not in their character. As you can imagine, my dad disliked Harry's glib ingratiating manner and he had warned my mother that the beautiful couple would try to separate her from her money (what was left of it after his commodity debacle) when he was dead. In reality my mom was creaming in her pants over Harry's continuous name dropping. He became her pipeline to the stars. She couldn't get enough of him; she may have been more in love with him than my sister. The weaker my dad grew, the more pre-eminent my new brother-in-law became in my mother's eyes. By the time my dad was dead meat the beautiful couple had her completely starstruck, although no stars ever dropped by her house. The only stars my mom ever saw were the two of them, Shannon and Harry, when they passed through the Bay Area and via long distance on the telephone, but she lived a rich life vicariously. And she watched TV.

Harry put a great deal of work into the old lady, greasing her up courtesy of Selectra Records long distance. This was what he did best. I became increasingly aware that Schmoozerman and Shannon were working all the sucker angles on my mother to get what they could get. Moving my icon into the metaphorical trash can was part of their action. That wouldn't be too difficult. They seemingly knew more about how much money she had tucked away than I did. When they were in town they never missed an opportunity to remind me and the old lady in one thousand ways of my lack of achievements. The truth was that I couldn't even keep a job washing windows and spearing trash with a stick with a nail on the end at the junior college. I managed a grade of C in a course on food nutrition, my highest grade.

Other young hopefuls were commonly given career guidance in high school and college. For some unknown reason, no counselor ever offered to guide me towards a career. I definitely needed some guidance preferably from a lady counselor in her mid-thirties. Ronnie the bozo got nada guidance. I wouldn't have listened anyway, I guess.

Rock music was so vitally important in those days to millions and millions of Americans that it often took preeminence even over matters of family life. The aforementioned two beautiful rock and roll lovers were so completely involved with their scene that they didn't bother to fly in to the Bay Area to watch my father die and they didn't manage to make an appearance at his funeral. Croaking, even if it was a father, did not merit the time or the plane flight. I made note of it. The old man wasn't worth their shallow good-bye doodly-squat, if ever he had any worth to them. There were deep Freudian complexes at work inside of this young woman, my sister. In fact, this went well beyond my course in psychology 1A. Perhaps these troubling complexes were of a more modern post-Freudian psychological construct. What then was in reality the prime motivation of their absence? Reflecting on what I perceived to be the elder sister's true nature, I proposed a lay theory to myself. Since there wasn't any easy money in it for her yet, why should she waste her time with fake grief? Despite whatever money my dad had dropped on futures a few years before, there must be some additional little pot of gold left behind with my mother. Even though my mom wasn't rich, and even though fuzzycurly successful Hollywood Harry had a big media job, they smelled where her money was like a couple of coyotes in a henhouse.

Every nickel and dime and penny is coveted by the greedy, they want it all. It hurt me emotionally to be thinking along those lines but I believed it was totally right thinking. Intuition maybe, or was this an ugly fact slapping me in the face. No one was ever going to pull it out in the open and shine the light of day on it. This was a foggy grey zone of manipulation and greed at work. The fog of war. Part of that strategy was to paint me as a shithead (Ouch! How hard could that be?) and focus on pumping up the old lady. How was I ever going to work my way out of that one? Ignoble assholes, one of whom was my antagonistic sibling were going to get some free cash by preempting me. That was the name of the family game. I decided to fight back.

Time was moving as swiftly for me as it was for the popular culture. Mama Cass, fat and famous with a beautiful voice, had choked to death on her own vomit or maybe it was a cheese sandwich. I took the news hard with Jim Morrison, Jimi Hendrix, and Janis Joplin. There was a choking on vomit epidemic at the end of the decade. That was a sure signpost of the passing of the '60s. There was no standing still. Flunking at college (I did mention that) was bad and I knew I had to come up with a BIG PLAN to save myself. Most of my friends who were chronic druggies had their secure families with major money to fall back on when their party legs gave out. Not me. There was no money coming for Ronnie Sharkbait.

Of those several oldest best friends of mine from junior high school who had become full blown heroin addicts when they were so young, I wonder still what ever happened to them. They talked so positively about living in Hawaii and growing pot and doing heroin in the jungle mountains, living like junkie Tarzans. These hypodermically advanced friends totally bypassed what drug moralists call the gateway drugs and began their drug initiation as heroin addicts. First things first, not necessarily. This behavior even debunked our local psychedelic mind-bending heroes The Merry Pranksters, formerly of Palo Alto. They simply went furthur than LSD and turned The Pranksters' motto on its head. "Hell with this Kesey dudes swirling colors! Let's take heroin. It's the ultimate drug." Very impressive. They didn't have a care in the world except they cared about heroin. Grow pot, live in the jungle, take heroin. That wasn't my karma, in '60s lingo. I had to pass on that tropical jungle fruit picking fantasy. What was I to do?

In the total absence of professional academic counseling, I fantasized a personal career guidance counselor because I needed professional fantasy help. I toyed with the notion of becoming a pusher of narcotics. As a career move, becoming a drug dealer or a pusher was never a direction that any imagined attractive 35 year old career counselor would have recommended. I could almost lick her red Revlon lips as she leaned her ample breasts against my shoulder and spoke softly her admonitions. I could feel the expression of her firm nipples through the sheer layers of cloth when she helped me write my name. The intoxicating Chanel No. 5 rose from her breasts along with my dreams of joining the American working world, oh to be a part of team America! In the intimacy of her office, she softly murmured with warm feminine breath that I, Ronnie Kale was not a young man who was cut out for a life of crime.

"No one," she whispered with her fire engine red painted lips touching my young ear, "is going to front you a half pound of heroin with the salutation, 'Go now and make some easy cash money Ronnie dear. I trust you.'" Still, I was seeking that first pragmatic toehold in the working world and this sage advice gave me an imaginary moral foundation from which to proceed. No drug dealing.

I wanted to be an easy going relaxed sort of guy like Montgomery Clift in The Misfits, but it wasn't working for me. My father had somehow managed to instill in me an up-til-now directionless goddam Protestant work ethic. Maybe it was genetic but it was twisting me like a skewered marshmallow on a stick in a boyscout campfire. I wanted to be a good boy but have copious rolling in bountiful exuberant orgiastic sex. Work ethic hormones were definitely kicking into my bloodstream because I was increasingly concerned with being productive and keeping busy with something, even though there was nothing in the world that I could do that would keep me busy. Not one thing. No skills was my resumé. No hobbies. Hobbies: 1). Smoking Lucky Strike straight cigarettes. 2). LSD. 3). Penis satisfaction. Except for the latter (3), I wasn't a handy guy. I wasn't an intellectual but I wanted to be smart. I could break and destroy things excellently but I couldn't fix or repair any kind of contraptions or machines. I couldn't even make a decent paper airplane. I knew that I had to leave this terrible present life behind by some radical new strategy that hadn't yet been invented by me. These uneasy circumstances put me in a state of mind that could be termed confused yet determined. Fear helped get me motivated and I knew that I needed to make a positive move. The black shadow of doom was creeping up on me and I kept it a deep secret. There was no one to confide in.

My dad left me one thousand dollars on his death. I bought an inexpensive 35mm camera and a little darkroom set-up on the recommendation of a generic sort of dull guy from the junior college who had recently bought himself a 35mm camera. He told me that he had become a serious photographer with an air of self-importance and he looked by his demeanor like he might be having sex with another person for the first time in his life.

"So that's how you do it." I thought. "Just say, I am photographer. I am artist. I create. Then go do it." Not having had much experience with artists prior to this exchange, my eyes were opened to a new world.

With that revelation, I disengaged completely from my old friends, quit drugs, quit smoking ciggies (after 9 years) and went to live at my mothers apartment and set up my darkroom in her second small bathroom in the rear. This was depressing. This was my 1970.

My primeval rudimentary crawl up from the primordial slime of suburbia ensued. I had arrived or stumbled upon the strategy of ART which became the BIG PLAN which could save me from certain oblivion. That was the point at which I quit going to classes entirely and started perusing expensive fine art books in the junior college library. One exception, I did take time to fail the Photography 1A junior college course.

I especially liked artists from the early 20th century, Man Ray, Picasso, Matisse and the Surrealists. Also Expressionists. The Dada Movement was not adequately represented in the junior college library so I remained in the dark about that. I decided to do art even though I had never done it before and had never had the urge to do it. If a person must do something, art for me seemed preferable to the other options which seemed dreary or out of reach. It was possibly more by a process of elimination than an internal spark of genius that I arrived at this career choice. There has always been the sense within me that I am a fake. It was the only thing in the whole world that I could think to do at the time so I pursued it. Notwithstanding that I was possibly some kind of an artist fake, art with a capital 'A' became my arch strategy.

Had I been aware of it as an option, I may have considered going directly into the '70s porn industry in the San Fernando Valley. In hindsight, it has been such an incredible growth industry. That was an industry a young man could break into without too much education or years of working experience in the real world.

Andy Warhol had been a favorite artist of mine since high school, the repetitious images of Marilyn Monroe and Coke bottles, the unusual movie projects, the Velvet Underground album with the banana on it, the strange kool people who surrounded him. His wonderful world appeared so heavenly and deranged to me even though it was a million miles from mine. He may have been my undercover subconscious adolescent role model. Andy Warhol was OK. Yes, generally speaking I liked the look of 20th century art and it seemed to have absolutely nothing in common with junior college aspirations. It was a new world with different values. Conversely, I had absolutely no artistic talent that I could perceive although I gained a new super-empowering self-awareness by association through perusing art reproductions in expensive library books. I stole a couple of the good books. My new focus showed in the way I walked. I walked a new walk. Look at me go-go.

My scribbling was left-handed and awkward but I started, working day and night alone without training, to create a small portfolio of drawings and photography. Training takes too long and I was in a hurry. Thinking strategically, I believed that if I attempted to become the most famous artist in the world and I worked really hard at it, that I would at least end up somehow better off than I was at present. Art was definitely the ticket to ride that would take me somewhere; to hell with the drawing skills and to hell with the negative self-image. In addition, many artists like the famous Henri Matisse seemed to get better and better as they got older, so guided by his example, this gave me a great deal of time to grow and achieve my goals which were a long way off. I definitely needed time because I was an uncultivated suburban rustic, a sort of Fillmore Auditorium acid rock bumpkin. My destiny was to be a late bloomer and a crude gem in the rough travelling on a rocky road to the stars. My little bumpkin jewels were going to need a great deal of polishing and faceting and fussing over. Besides, maybe I wasn't a gem at all, maybe just a rock, a stone or a piece of clay dirt, or even an impassioned suburban dirt clod and I would have to make do with what personal qualities I had been given and mould, vacuum form and refine them. If I needed to use technology to accelerate matters, then I would use it.

This line of thinking led me to one conclusion. The best option for me, I reasoned, was to expeditiously leave the United States of America, my homeland, and study art in another country where they had never heard of me. In the USA, my PT109 was sunk and my little John John junior was hanging limp. In another country they wouldn't be accessing my unsavory academic record for the rest of my life because it wouldn't be available to them. Those bedeviling SAT scores only reminded me that there is an S-A-T in Satan. I didn't want that fucking test that I took on a Saturday after a knockdown drag out fight with the old Marine sergeant when he had lung cancer and emphysema following me around for the rest of my life. I didn't like that test any way on any day. That fucking test was a bullshit measurement of a human in my humble opinion although no one wanted my opinion. That Scholastic Aptitude Test did reveal one undeniable truth about me. I had no aptitude whatsoever for scholastics, especially in the manner they were shoveled at me, even at a second rate junior college that admitted anyone with a high school diploma. I wondered what kind of shitheads could sit around and think up concepts like an SAT. Well, they wanted to weed out characters like me. So it worked perfectly. Everybody finds a niche somewhere on down the line. The system works. My notion was that although I was permanently branded as an F-man in the USA, in a foreign country I could start with a clean slate. That was a good idea. Reasoning further, I felt that Great Britain was best choice of a foreign country for my higher education because I spoke only English, not having excelled in high school French. I imagined myself studying art in France at the college level but not understanding much of the language. It was untenable. It had to be England. Then...Pow! I found out that the English kids have their own form of SAT test to deal with. It's a universal scholastic nightmare but one that didn't affect me if I moved over there, coming from the USA. Problem solved. Good idea! Now I was a smarter mannish boy.

There was a British Consulate in San Francisco from which I was able to obtain a book entitled "Higher Education in the United Kingdom." I told my mom that I wanted to study art in England and that I was going to apply to some English art colleges.

She said, "You can't get into an art college in England! You're crazy!" She laughed at me out loud. That's where the BIG BET came in to play that I told you about in the initial pages. The BIG BET was the flipside to the BIG PLAN.

I said "I'll bet you I can. If I can get accepted into an art college in England will you pay for me to go there?"

The sucker fish went for the bait. Mom took that bet because she really didn't believe that I could ever do anything and she lost much sooner that she expected. I spent a miserable year 1970 building up a visual arts portfolio from scratch and sending versions of it off to several addresses from the UK embassy book. When I received an acceptance letter from Nordham College of Art in London in April of '71, I went nuts, rolling around on floor, screaming, doing summersaults, and dancing all night with Doogie my pet guinea pig which was all I had for a girlfriend at the time.

This blew my little mother's mind. She never in the farthest reaches of her imagination believed that I could pull off that trick. She kept to her end of the deal and it really wasn't expensive. The American dollar bought quite a lot back then. A year's tuition was only two hundred and fifty American dollars in 1971. By the end of August, I was gone. It happened fast. Gone to London! What a dream! Quite possibly, she wanted to get me out of her apartment and she was willing to send me to college if that's what it took to get rid of me. Who cares. I could have lived there with her until I was forty or fifty masturbating and getting weird. It happens all too often with young men and their mothers.

I cut off my long hair and moved to a student flat in a working class borough of London called Streatham Hill in September of 1971 and studied fine art at Nordham College until 1974. Those bright and peppy Brit citizens ride around in trains and buses over there. A car is not necessary. Those 3 years of study saved my fucking life. I had achieved that much and it couldn't be taken away from me.

My formidable guinea pig Doogie died of natural causes that summer in '71 before I left, possibly from excessive dancing. Leaving him behind would have killed me, but as it turned out, I may have overfed the little sucker and dressing him up like a girl probably was the wrong thing to do. He was one great pig and a fine temporary substitute for a girlfriend. I like to think that his little pig spirit rode with me on my shoulder on the airplane to London before it flew up the white tunnel of light to guinea pig heaven.

"Don't mourn me Ronnie!" his little spirit squeaked. "Look ahead to the future. I will always be with you looking down from Guinea Pig Heaven."

Now, at least I was making some positive moves on mom's dough before the supercouple supersucked her. Supercouple were planning to squeeze the old girl like an orange for her juice. It was me or them. My art education ruse took the stylish media pair completely by surprise.

Shannon dropped her jaw in astonishment at the news. She briefly exhibited the cold reptilian stare of a stalking rival. Then I questioned myself, was this reading of her demeanor my childish imagination? The overseas education was a fortuitously timed move on my part. In another few years whatever wealth my mom had tucked away would be taken. The married twosome fulfilled my apprehensions as time passed. Now that I was spooning honey from the family honey pot to go to college, we all tacitly knew that this was war, and that this was the only family money that I was ever going to see.

EXIT SLIMY CURLY FUZZY FURRY HARRY: For Christmas of my last year at college in England ('73-'74), I returned to California for the Holidays. This was a bad decision. That Christmas was fucked up. Very negative. That was the year my big sister Shannon, the greedy blond bombshell and her husband Harry, the likeable avaricious talkative music industry executive rode the mystery train to the end of the line, out on the spur track to the outskirts of the town without pity, to the chasm of rock and roll Splitsville. I know little about the circumstances except that Harry had been repeatedly fucking a beautiful bimbo when he said he was working. He went to Hawaii ostensibly to endeavor to scout new tropical rock music talent and surprise, the same bimbo showed up in paradise and the flashy executive and his paramour gave in to their torrid desires of the flesh. That was where my skeptical sister busted them in the full bloom of their romance. Oh yeah, love comes and love goes to hell.

I had an inkling that driving a silver Jaguar, talking on the telephone, going to rock concerts and chic parties, and sniffing gobs of cocaine was not a full enough plate for a hairy successful married record exec. Shannon divorced him immediately. In fact, she acted in haste unnecessarily. Harry was her living god and then he was shit overnight. It's tough to worship and lose one's religion at those extremes.

"He can't do that to me!" she screamed.

Before my initial departure for art college Shannon was sending him little love notes scribbled in lipstick on scented bathroom tissue.

"I love the Harry Bear." She scrawled in passionate Barbie Doll pink. Those happy bear jamboree days were abruptly over now. She dropped him flat. That may sound like the smart thing to have done except that he somehow walked away from the legal processes with their expensive house in Mill Valley, a maison that my starstruck momma had bankrolled. That was a neat trick. He got the bimbo and he could bunny-hop her ass in the little castle behind the white picket fence with impunity. Somehow that unctuous loveable record executive had walked away free and clear with the title to that expensive chic property from a California divorce.

It was located in a trendy Marin County neighborhood. The local Mill Valley bar was peopled by characters famous from the Fillmore and Avalon Ballroom era. Bill Graham, The Dead, and the whole new testament roster of hippie messianic rock prophets and musical note ticklers from the apocalyptic sixties. No judge should have awarded that house in hippie heaven to an unfaithful husband. That took some moves. Cheating husbands don't get the house in California after a divorce unless, possibly, they are excessively charming.

"I don't want that house. It reminds me of him. That fucking asshole. If he wants it he can have it." My sister declared. Smart girl.

My sister Shannon didn't know it then, but she was heading for a long career as a cocktail waitress in a Las Vegas nightclub casino; she worked in a few, but the Million Dollar Nugget became her bread and butter. Harry lost his job around '77 and soon after he was reduced to doing occasional odd freelance jobs in order to maintain his executive lifestyle. One job he took that I found out about was rather interesting. He was paid $10,000 to drive a small suitcase from the client's house in Mill Valley to a motel room with quick freeway access near Sausalito. That's $10,000 for an hours work but the stress or the client may kill you. He never moved out of that Mill Valley house. He must have really loved the maudlin old family memories or perhaps he was frozen on the same social step for life.

On that negative Christmas Eve of 1974, Harry came over to my mother's apartment about 7:30 p.m., alone, and he went directly into my mother's bedroom without giving me so much as a *hi-de-ho* Merry Christmas. He walked right by me. I was occupying the living room couch drinking liquor and watching TV. My sister was supposed to arrive the following day with her new boyfriend and Harry was scheduled in to miss her. I brooded over him as I drank. He went into the diminutive master bedroom where my mother was recumbent in bed and stayed in there the entire evening with the door closed. This was not what I wanted to be thinking about at Christmas.

Mom's apartment was tacky and depressing with that glittery flaky snow sprayed on the ceiling like they do in many cheap so-called luxury apartments, and she slept in a little matchbox master bedroom with the traffic going by continually night and day outside the window. She wasn't living on much money, not with the three of us bleeding her. There I was lying on the couch in the den watching a movie starring Lucille Ball and Henry Fonda in which they both have six kids and they get married and then they have a family with a dozen children. Perhaps you've seen it, a terrible movie. I was working hard at getting drunk on the mom's liquor. She was in bed and Harry was in there in her bedroom spooning on the sugar for at least one and a half hours. You could get good odds, if you were a betting person that he was in there mooching money by any means necessary.

My mom was a pushover for a good looking hunk of man. She loved Elvis and she was rendered weak kneed by Harry's charms. His fair sun deprived complexion was punctuated by green veins which appeared just under the flesh conjoined with the dark hair of a heavy beard which always showed through his skin even if he had just shaven. I brooded over his Italian fashion model features to the point that I lost the thread of the stupid Lucille Ball movie plot. Then the movie was over.

Please bear with me as we may have covered this before. As I sat there, the point was driven home to me that in this society, I lacked worldly clout. By comparison, Harry personally knew top entertainment people; he even hobnobbed buddy-buddy with Clyde Darian the most successful record producer of that era. Me, I was a mere art student, nevertheless a step up from my prior status. I knew that my mother was charmed to the tips of her Christmas toes to have that man in her bedroom alone at night despite the divorce from my sister. She was a woman, although well into her sixth decade. I felt that he had schmoozed enough money from my family. What the heck was he doing in there for so long? When he came out of the bedroom I called him over.

"How you doin' Harry? How's your life? You still livin' in Mill Valley?"

"Hey man, how are ya, I'm doing great. You know who you remind me of standing there? You look like Dennis Hopper. You look really good! You've really grown up since you went off to England..."

Then...Crunch! I sucker-punched him in the face hard. It wasn't premeditated. In fact, I was trying not to think about how much I would like to pound some knuckles on him. After I hit him he screamed something terrible, looked at me in the eyes holding his face in his hands and screamed again and then ran out of the back door making animal noises. I heard his tires screeching down the driveway, then again screeching down the street. He wasn't ever going to forget the Christmas Eve of 1974. My mom said he promised that he was going to give her a color TV. He was a sweetheart; she gets a token TV and he keeps the house north of San Francisco at her expense.

That was one sucker punch for the dead Marine and definitely the most satisfying big one that I have ever delivered. It broke his beautiful nose. There were several drops of blood on the kitchen floor by the back door where he scampered out. Too late to take that one back. I omitted to tell you that the deltoid muscles on my polio shoulder had grown to twice the size of those on my normal shoulder to compensate for the disability. And I was a push-up freak. Harry fled the vicious sting of the Christmas scorpion fearing a second more deadly attack.

This nose punching amounted to something of a loss to me because Harry had over the years donated a small amount of his quality time to teach me a few worthwhile things. He got me interested in William Burroughs and other Beat writers early in life when I was maybe fifteen, and he suggested that I read H.L. Menken in the place of high school textbooks. He sold me my first pot, killer-diller powerful hallucinogenic pot. I mentioned already his cheap-cut cocaine cadillac-walk big city schmooze. He taught me the value of owning a stolen handgun as opposed to a legally obtained one if, god forbid, a person should need to shoot another person and remain undetected. That valuable font of information was now dried up and gone forever.

It shouldn't go unmentioned that I fucked his foxy baby sister. I can't remember the exact chronology of that but it happened some time before the nose incident. She was the youngest daughter in his family, the one with brains and good looks. I was over at his parents house for a rare visit there and his babe-a-licious sister

Diana showed up and we went out in her car for an hour in the afternoon. She was at that age where she had just moved out of the house for the first time and we drove over to her studio apartment together. We talked and laughed. We had an alcoholic beverage, a glass of red wine. Then we got stinking drunk and to my surprise, I drunk-fucked her on her studio apartment floor. Skin on skin, rugburns, the whole deal. She was the pretty Ivy League princess of the family and I believe she was behaving a little bit out of character but then again, maybe not. We missed the family dinner that night and didn't come back to the parents house until the next morning. Upon our entrance, the whole family was overcome with a funereal pallor and grim locked jaws. My status as a *persona non gratis* for life was now carved in stone. This business of intoxicated mounting and repeatedly penetrating the sister with the erect penis, followed by the unbridled splashing of semen, was similar in form and content to what Harry had done to my sister, but his family was operating on a different value code than the Kale clan.

I tried to phone Diana when I got back home to Palo Alto but the mother lost her temper and kept answering the phone, "Diana doesn't want to talk to you! Don't ever call her again!"

One more thing, about that unpleasant Christmas of 1974. My sister had acquired a new boyfriend, another obnoxious one with *dos huevos grande* and enough stuffy attitude to match the British Royal Family, although he was just a prick from Los Angeles. They arrived on Christmas day after I punched the ex-husband, so regretfully I was on my best behavior. This one needed a good beating as well. He wanted to become a lawyer but he couldn't pass the California Bar exam. He had failed it over a dozen times. After he showed up with Shannon late on Christmas morning, we all exchanged gifts. My mother, sister and this new boyfriend and myself were all gathered in the dining area after a late breakfast. My gifts, this being my last year at college in England, were bad macaroni art sprayed with gold paint and glued to colored construction paper announcing Merry Christmas. I was broke. Then the new Mr. Hideous with great ceremony and regal bearing began giving away expensive gold jewelry to my mom and sister, only the finest gold jewelry of course, for the finest of ladies. They were very dear pieces and the elegant ladies were royally impressed. My pop never could afford that kind of gift. Clive was this new boyfriend's name. This was another one that I wanted dead. He offended my idea of Santa Claus but I couldn't punch two of 'em in the nose in two days. My mom wasn't talking about the night before but she was clearly upset by my violence. Never underestimate the power of a good sucker punch.

Then a really good thing happened. Clive was arrested in NYC a few weeks later with one million dollars worth of LSD in his possession. He was convicted of a felony and went off to prison somewhere in New York state for a few years. This was very good news. It took Clive off the streets and turned his life around and made me extremely happy as well. He obviously hadn't listened to the advice of a good career guidance counselor. After he got out of the slammer he went on to become a Beverly Hills lawyer. Perfect. My sister didn't wait around for him. She needed immediate attention.

I wrote this letter to my sister and her husband soon after I first entered Art College in London, back in the antediluvian days before email. I managed to use a big word to flaunt my new sophistication and accompany my saccharin tone of voice, saccharin being the artificial non-caloric sweetener in common use during that period of time.

December 6, 1971
Streatham Hill, London

Dear Shannon and Harry,
    Gawd! Well I'm finally writing. But I don't know where to begin. What a place London is. The days are unceasingly grey and cold. I spend most of my time at school or studying. The vacation's over if you know what I mean. Sometimes I wake up on a typically freeeeeezing morning and wonder where the hell am I? And what am I doing here? Is this still the same me? Plane flights are incredibly disorienting. I would feel much more at ease in answering those timeless questions if I had maybe rowed a boat here. Gawd! But I'm not saying I don't like it. What else can I do?
    It's odd that I've hardly drawn at all since I've gotten here. I got turned off to life drawing class. Those teachers really know how to beat a dead horse. But on the other hand I have some great teachers. They're great mainly because they don't teach, they talk. We talk about the state of the world and what we're all doing there. There? Here, I mean. We talk about the reason we're taking fine art and not commercial design or something. My sculpture teacher Martin McClaine is a conceptual artist. He sits in the corner with his finger up his nose performing new work.
    In spite of it all and because of it all, I continue avidly photo-graphically photographing. Have you ever heard of an artist named Hans Haake. He's American! I wonder why the exclamation mark, a sort of Freudian slip of the pen. I have also made a sculpture of sorts. It took me about six weeks to build. What fun though. I'll send a slide of it to you after it's assembled. This week I start work on a new sculpture of sorts. I could explain the "of sorts" but a slide would relay more information.
    I received the Christmas presents. Delightsome, really! This may sound a bit captious but (and I haven't opened anything but the vitamins yet) there are no vitamin B pills to be seen and I only have about 5 left in my old bottle and did you know that you can't get'em here. Tell mom. Also, if you ever go to City Lights Books in S.F. would you buy a book for me.

They are the only people in the world who have it. It's called 'A Coney Island of the Mind' by Lawrence Ferlinghetti. If circumstances light you on that particular flower, I'll send you the money you spent.

I never think about California. Only people. But there aren't that many people that I've known that are worth missing. I've met a lot of people here (what am I talking about maybe I should edit) but they're only people and I don't miss them because I'm still here. Roll the credits. Get the straight jacket. Play the cartoon.

I don't get any exercise here. Hopefully this week (if I buy the trunks) I'm going swimming at an indoor pool with Alex (a girl believe it or not). Maybe if she still likes me next week, we can ride horses. The bourgeois are big on horses over here you know. Alex just likes them because they're nice animals.

Love and kisses, Ronnie

CHAPTER 3

After my third final year at college, I made the mistake of coming back to California to live from Great Britain. I got educated in England, no complaints. But it never really prepared me for survival in the Golden State. It's the suck-ass state. I should have stayed over there, overseas. When I arrived back in California after graduating from Nordham College of Art, I was returned to immediate shithead status. It was like a magical transformation. Ba-Da-Bing! You're a shithead! Only now, I was the highly refined type of art educated shithead.

At the end of the last year I got married to a foxy little woman at my art college. We were married in Brixton, a multiracial South London neighborhood. I must have forgotten who I was to do that. She had graduated from a course in textile design in the fashion department at Nordham. Now, here was my mother waiting for us to get off the airplane in the USA. Mom still didn't think I was very smart. Apparently her little son hadn't yet acquired the skills to pay the bills because I didn't return with a bankroll and an immediate job plan. The new wife on the other hand was a bit too smart.

"Why are you reading that when you can't get a job?" my mom asked. I was reading Jean Jacques Rousseau's 'Confessions'. She didn't like me reading. It was impractical. Oh no, and the wife was the wrong color. I picked a bad color. She must be some kind of trash. Things weren't going right.

My mother disliked the attractive new wife, Sheena. And the new wife had a total disdain bordering on revulsion for the sharp-tongued old mother. In short, they hated each other on sight. They immediately began communicating non-verbal negative signals between them like women can do. My awareness of their mutual animosity was limited at first and besides, I was not equipped to deal with it on any level. The three of us quickly grew tight lipped and pissed off living in my mom's apartment. Sheena and I stopped having sex. It was time to buy another guinea pig and dress it in a miniskirt. There was a blatant issue of racism underlying mom's point of view. Racism is evil. My sister opted for the racist viewpoint as well. Behind Sheena's back they hit every hot button, a Kale family characteristic.

Sheena talked in that uniquely upper crust British vernacular, a manner of speech and behaviour which she termed "all jolly hockey sticks" which I interpreted to mean good breeding. No one who grew up in England seemed to have a problem with Sheena's character or mannerisms. She fluidly spoke very much like Hemingway's character Lady Brett Ashley, who spoke nicely but she was a beautiful slut.

"I say, can a chap sit down? Don't be cross, darling. Just left the count. He brought me here...Don't try and make me drunk. The count? Oh, rather. He's quite one of us...Deserves to be anyhow. Know's hell's own amount about people. Don't know where he got it all. Owns a chain of sweetshops in the States...Think he called it a chain. Something like that. Linked them all up. Told me a little about it. Damned interesting. He's one of us, though. Oh, quite. No doubt. One can always tell."

Sheena's speech patterns somewhat updated from Hemingway's 1926 literary character made my mother want to spit.

"She must have acquired that perfect British accent at a missionary school in India. She certainly wasn't educated in any of the upper class schools in Britain. She's a missionary girl, an Indian refugee. That's where she learned to talk like that." my mother admonished. Sheena, my wife, wasn't going to take that kind of shit nasty attitude for long. The ambient racism drove a divisive shattering wedge between us that didn't leave us room for communication. Neither of us had the patience or inclination to heal the malevolence of a bigoted mother. I was paralyzed and embarrassed by the whole situation.

I remember that Richard Nixon was being driven out of the White House and the women did not give a damn about the Watergate scandal. I was loving Watergate. It was so damn great to see President Nixon suffer when my life was going all to hell. Even if Sheena was just using me to get an American Green Card to gain access to the U.S. fashion market, that was fine with me. I was glad to have her use me for whatever she wanted. I wanted to fuck her and I wanted to prolong fucking her for as long as I possibly could. She was beautiful naked. This was how art students carried on. We were under no illusions of perfection. One night I dreamed that my mom chopped off her hands and sent her back to England with bandaged stubs at her wrists and a note pinned on her chest reading "Refugee Whore."

To reiterate, Sheena was of East Indian descent, dropdead pretty, smart and she wore kool fashions. At Nordham College she had learned a marketable skill designing textile fabrics. It was a skill that wasn't formally taught in the United States at the time. But more than that, she was extremely talented. She could draw beautiful designs from scratch which when applied to fabric were elegant. None of these qualities impressed momma. Sheena wasn't long for Palo Alto anyway, with its Hewlett-Packard tech industry pragmatic dress. My mom was definitely the catalyst to her leaving. More than a catalyst, my mom stuck a Vanguard rocket up her pretty Kings Road London ass and lit the fuse. My personality regressed. Loss of my manhood occurred upon returning to my mothers lair and I was completely unable to deal with the mess on any level. Only a doting protective mother could lobotomize and emasculate a young man so quickly and efficiently. Events took their own course.

Within 3 months of our arrival in California, Sheena had begun working for clothing manufacturers in the Los Angeles rag trade and taking their mean green to the bank in both hands. She made some fast money in Los Angeles. Sheena became a woman obsessed, chainsmoking Kool cigarettes, drawing and painting her designs on my mothers wooden fake antique dining room table. They were buying every design in the City of Angels. My mother watched her work and she disapproved. This kind of productivity was alien to our family environment and contradictory to our group genetic mental disease. Our family always argued and fought and scrapped rather than created. Good-bye wifey. Sheena had breathed enough Zyklon gas around our pedigreed hearth and she got the hell out of there as soon as she could make the move and of course I was left behind eating her dust and mom's fulsome dinners cooked with love.

We returned to the traditional kindred ambience of brain-death with formaldehyde for blood. I did some food throwing and screaming. The game of chess was over; you lose then throw your chess pieces on the floor, so what. By trying to please both women, I had lost the wrong one. Well ok, the wife was an opportunist. Sheena didn't do anything that I wouldn't have done. Mom made certain that the separation was accomplished with enmity. A white wife might have lasted a couple of months longer than the brown one. My mom was obsequious to my sister's hunky beau's exclusively.

My sister, who dropped in from time to time, would tolerate no other females in the household. In earlier days, I had learned to keep girlfriends a safe distance away from my family members as a general rule of thumb. There was a sickness in our household, under our skin, in our brood that was repugnant like smallpox pustules. Typically, my sister and my mother would team up in agreement that the girls I was seeing were trash bitches. My sister always had a deep basic core of animosity running through her that I never could understand and then that malevolence was all covered over with a giggling sugary personality. The pair were driving me nuts.

There are always wonderful exceptions to any rule. In the opinion of my mother and sister if the girl was excessively fat, then we were talking about a sweet girl. My second cousin Martin Schlatz had married a very fat 225 lb girl with secretarial skills, Penny, and she received that coveted maternal stamp of approval around our kitchen.

"Penny is such a sweet girl. She is perfect for Martin." Exaggerated obesity passed the mom and sister test of feminine suitability. Of course obesity was not so attractive to me although secretarial skills were a definite positive. A female with a rock and roll body with a head full of wild hair and excessive radical eye makeup was back on my wish list again but far from obtainable. I was never deeply introspective or psychoanalytical about my likes and urges. I just wanted it. I had an inkling that I may be a shallow person.

My practical daily professional progress was much more humble than Sheena's and I was a long way off from becoming the most very famous artist in the whole big wide round world. In fact, I was falling short of enacting my strategy for better or worse entirely. Consequently, I took a job as a school bus driver in Palo Alto wearing a blue uniform with official Palo Alto Unified School District bus driver patches on the shoulders. This was the fruition of the long string of events in my life. I had to go through an extensive training program to earn the privilege to drive the little monsters to and from school. I drove all grades of deranged children from kindergarten through high school. The Ohio Players 'Fire' was the number one pop song with my school bus full of adolescent black kids on my afternoon route from the junior high, reinforcing my trauma that my mother and sister were racists; and my new blond girlfriend was driving the big yellow school bus in the queue behind me during the afternoons, departing from Tremaine Junior High where I had attended with my mononucleosis disease ten years previous. This was such a strange turnaround, like a recurring psychotic dream. Tremaine Junior High School was the new hell, a distorted mirror image of the old hell.

America, it was not so good to be back home. I was undergoing some kind of reverse cultural shock process in '75, driving a 90 foot diesel bus all through the neatly blocked neighborhoods and narrow Pacific mountain two lane roads comprising the affluent Palo Alto Unified School District. It was a terrible experience but not for the reasons you might imagine. Few people outside the immediate area knew of Palo Alto's dirty little secret and probably most residents of the city itself were in the dark. This intellectually endowed small northern California city with its linear particle accelerator, research, tech companies, and big university was a rigidly racially segregated city separated along the lines of the 101 Freeway. Cross the freeway and you landed in East Palo Alto an expanse of black neighborhoods characterized by bad schools, unemployment and poverty. It was a sudden and stark contrast between lush green affluent white Palo Alto and the poor black streets of East Palo Alto. As a school bus driver, you experienced first hand the sordid scoop on the scene. Many of the black families across the 101 freeway desperately acquired a false address on the affluent side of the line and registered their kids in the better financially funded schools of Palo Alto and then they drove their children to the white kids bus stops and dropped them off in the a.m. It imparted a stink to this charming little city. In 1975, Palo Alto still needed to give all its children on both sides of the freeway equal access to the best schools. Did the city carry this tragedy into the new millennium? Well, I don't know because I couldn't get the hell out of there fast enough and I soon lost my job driving a bus. Add bus driving to my list of failures.

I wasn't popular down at the bus pool because they knew that I'd been away at school and most of the drivers were barely literate. I tried to fit in but it was a lost cause. I moved into a bland, cheap, unfurnished apartment in downtown Palo Alto. My new girlfriend Haley, the female bus driver, operated a little horse ranch in the coastal hills outside of town where she lived and stabled horses for a fee. She was a big framed woman with natural blond hair and a pretty face. She could pick up a bail of hay and toss it across the yard with ease. I liked her. We rode horses in the coastal hills. We had a lot of sex in her little ranch cabin. There was a family of skunks living under the house that had grown enormous from eating the dog's food. Haley was embarrassed by her breasts which looked and felt just fine to me. I can't explain it. Possibly, one was longer than the other. Soon, she had a couple of appointments with a gynecologist telling me that my penis was ramming her cervix when we screwed and causing her to bleed. I had never had that complaint from a lady before but it made me feel like a hung stud. I didn't know what a cervix was anyway. File that one with the spleen, mystery organs.

Haley and I were almost a couple and I had scarcely used my downtown apartment. We were cooking dinner up at her ranch one night. A heavy cast iron frying pan that I held over the flame for only a few seconds blew apart in my hands, shattering into 3 pieces with a loud bang. Haley took it to be a sign of misplaced psychic energy. She had come to believe that I had a date with destiny to go do art or whatever the hell I was supposed to do somewhere not in close proximity to her ranch. My situation really hadn't changed much from my life before I went off to school except in my mind. But what you are and what you become, comes mostly from what is in your mind. Just then, I was a bus driver who once went to school in England.

I talked about art too much so that maybe I could continue doing it. People who talk about art all the time in the wrong social context are as unpleasant to be around as people who talk about surgical procedures. That art chit-chat must have become unbearable to endure especially for a horse wrangling cowgirl sweety. I was rapidly transforming into dead neo-Dada freak meat. Maybe I didn't even like the A-word that much but it was all I had to grasp on to that could move me on ahead. Not only was it the BIG PLAN but it was the only plan that I had. I was a one plan guy with no alternates. After we fucked each others brains out in the ranch house for four or five months, I moved out by maybe sixty-five percent. I still had visitation and bone rights with her, if I called ahead, but basically I had returned to living in the empty apartment in downtown Palo Alto.

It never occurred to me to look up my old Palo Alto friends like Doyle Martindale although I had heard through the grapevine that he was back working as a technician at the sleep research lab. It was an unhappy place and I thought that his profession was hideous from an animal cruelty point of view. Doyle was only the lowly technician not the mad scientist behind the experiments. Inside the research lab they went about the nasty business of trepanning housecats and planting electrodes in their brains through a two centimeter by four centimeter hole. Each cat had an electronic data plug with twenty five prongs mounted into the top of the skull. There were maybe fifty doomed housecats living in there in wire cages at any point in time. They then gave them various drugs and measured their r.e.m. sleep patterns. They employed a wide variety drugs and some of the substances left the animals horribly crippled. One pair of cats permanently lost their equilibrium and they spent their waking hours trying to stand up and then falling down. The research scientist who was responsible for these experiments had a peculiarly appropriate name for his line of work. His name was Dr. Peter Paine. I imagine he looked longingly at those shambling mental hospital inmate patient's skulls on days when his mind wandered, feeling the need to drill human heads.

To make my self-definition more complicated, I could never settle down to one creative discipline. I never knew what the fuck I was. People would say "What are you? A painter? A sculptor?" And I would answer "Ugh! I just don't know what I am interested in today." If Haley only knew the truth of what my destiny turned out to be, not much.

I typically got a little drunk at night; mostly it was no more than a Dean Martin stumble minus the tuxedo but some of them were big drunks like alcoholics have. One sunny hangover afternoon, I was at my vacant beige cube apartment in downtown Palo Alto when I suffered a pugilistic injury. It was on a Saturday, a good day for a fight. This harm was perpetrated by myself primarily through a burst of over-enthusiasm and a zest for kung-fu action. It's not necessary to mug me on the street, I can take care of that all by myself. I was practicing Karate, one of my many dormant interests and my attack was so severe that it did a number on my third lumbar back vertebrae. That's right, by shadow boxing martial arts the protagonist of this story KO'd himself. A new sinister X variable entered into the woeful mix; crippling chronic debilitating pain. Physical injury is one of the pitfalls of a multi-discipline over-achiever. This was another setback to the master plan.

When Joe Block, the paunchy supervisor at the bus company, found out about my injury, he immediately transferred me to an old bus with a hard seat and a suspension like a bucking bronco and that did me in. It was nothing less than an attempt at murder. That's the ugly manner in which the supervisor of all the school buses in the Palo Alto Unified School District showed his appreciation of me. He would have tried to kill Oscar Wilde too, had he worked there. After a day in the hell bus, I couldn't drive anymore, or sit or walk, so I sued the school district. I was in such pain that I could hardly make it to the bathroom and then back to my sleeping blanket located on the neutral beige wall to wall carpet in my zero furniture pad. The most I could do during a day was map the passage of junk food through my intestines and try to predict the exact hour and minute of my next bathroom struggle. My world had become a smaller world now than that lived in by an average citizen of my age group. It was a world of desperation crawling, unhappiness, confusion, aspirin overdoses and whiskey. The master plan, which was not all that complicated – make a most famous artist attempt in any big city that would hold me and hope for a soft landing – had become impossible to execute. I was sidetracked in a furniture bereft crapland with an invisible injury.

The estranged wife drove up to the Bay Area from Los Angeles to visit me, her motive being basically to pick up the last of her things from my mom's digs and say goodbye to me forever. She brought along her new friend, critical Cassy from Venice Beach. Not a pretty lady was Cassy. She had acne scarred facial skin. Sheena was the classiest friend that she had ever had and Cassy was playing the part of an effete snob. There I was lying on the floor of my filthy ground floor apartment with no furniture, a quart bottle of whiskey and a bottle of aspirins spilled next to me, unbathed in a dirty crumpled P.A.U.S.D navy blue bus driver uniform; now a broken unemployed bus driver still wearing his Palo Alto Unified School District shoulder patches like an American Legion vet on memorial day. Sheena was all decked out in impeccable casual high fashion with her ultra-supportive sidekick girlfriend by her side and now we didn't have much to say to each other. Sheena was saying "Bye-bye." and I was hammered and nailed to the beige wall-to-wall carpet.

"Not much goin' on here Sheena. I hurt my back and I just gotta lay here. Lost my job driving the bus. I'm in a world of pain."

She pityingly said, "Do you want a little sex favor before I go baby?"

That surprised me a little bit. I said, "Could you suck my dick a little Sheena?" God bless her heart.

Cassy just stood there livid while Sheena gave me a blow job on the floor. We were after all, still married. Cassy could have sat down on the carpet and watched or walked out to the car, but she chose to imply that they were in a hurry by her mannerisms.

"Cassy, I've got some left for you too." I said.

She pursed her lips. "No way!" They left. At least I wasn't a bus driver any longer. That was progress.

Now I was drinking to relieve the miserable pain from the back spasms and I was drinking because I had become overnight a much weaker man. These were great reasons to be alcoholic. The American male ego is extremely delicate. It needs a few basic necessities to go out and conquer the world. Lacking these elements, it is threatened with immediate collapse. My weakened physical condition was destroying my optimistic outlook on life. A successful man swaggers around with big semen filled balls knocking side to side behind a proud ample penis; he needs money, macho, sports talk, horsepower, career and bragging rights. These props are what make the ordinary man into a big man. Start whittling away at these essential masculine elements and you will find a little guy inside full of insecurities.

I got a little money from the lawsuit settlement. It was a short term win and enough to live on for about 6 months in a shared house with roomies; so I took up with three male Stanford University students. How I linked up with those guys eludes me. Two jock jerks and a fat ninja. Basically, I just parked my torso on the floor, suffered lumbar spasms and waited for the money to run out; drank booze to alleviate the pain and feared for my future which seemed inevitable. Death by mother. I was going to have to move back in with mom. I had an apron strings problem and no one to blame but myself. My life was being lived in fear. Fear just doesn't help matters and alleviating it with hooch has its many pitfalls and some benefits.

My new abode was an Eichler style tract home on the east side of the El Camino Real, still in the white area neighborhoods. These kind of homes are open-planned inexpensive aberrations of Frank Lloyd Wright design themes knocked out with cardboard thin walls and a sense of open Western space. They're OK for mid-20th century tract homes but sometimes I felt like a strong sneeze might blow a wall out. Like everything from that era, they're ultra collectible property in today's market. I've lived in Levittown tract homes as well and I couldn't tell you which one is the better home. Does anyone care? If you drove a 1962 Lincoln Continental into an Eichler home at 25 miles an hour in a perpendicular trajectory, it would blow right through without a scratch. A Levitt home would offer more resistance and probably dent the grill.

Each roommate had a private bedroom. I was down on the West end of the house in a bedroom with no furniture and a small closet taking up my usual recumbent position on the floor. There was access to the backyard through my sliding plate glass door. The yard was large enough for a kidney shaped swimming pool but it lacked one and the earth had recently been mechanically tilled up in a rough manner which destroyed any landscaping. For the first two weeks, I heard this intermittent scratching sound in there that I couldn't place. One day in my search I pulled everything out of the closet and there I found a huge confused potato bug walking into the corner and scratching at the wall. It never occurred to it to turn around and go another direction. I picked it up and tossed it back into the soil outside. Any respectable potato bug also goes by the alias Jerusalem cricket. It is a large awkward ugly crawling earth burrowing insect and it has big fangs that can bite. It's a friendly hideous creature much in the same way that there are friendly hideous humans that will make your acquaintance. Try to avoid them. I had bonded with a spiny exoskeletoned subterranean homie.

It's strange the things that you remember clearly for many years. I felt that the big insect was just a little better looking than my three roommates. Even worse, now the life crisis of a dumb fucking bug was a big event in my life. It had no name; it was a feral creature.

My lovely roommates arrayed down the hall were considerably more domesticated than my homeboy crawler. There was Rick in the room next to me. He was generic wholesome student type and his ancestral home was in Atlanta Georgia. His amazing achievement was that he had ridden a 10-speed bicycle across the United States from west to east. He had an athletic body but he said that he had recently contracted arthritis in his spine and that he would soon be bent over and crippled. He did not use alcohol to alleviate pain and fear so we had little in common. His optimistic smile was making me sick; his area of academic study eludes me.

The second roommate, Bill, claimed he was an ex-Green Beret. He was sporting a beer and junk food engendered middle-aged spread around his waist. He had set up a waterbed in his bedroom at the opposing end of the house from my crib. Bill spent one hundred and one percent of his time with a cute little sex kitten from the junior college, fucking her on his waterbed and taking drugs. He was easily in his '40s and she couldn't have been older than nineteen. His education was being subsidized by the US Government. Goddam him.

Bill told me the story that he was a Green Beret in Vietnam prior to 1964 doing reconnaissance of the North Vietnamese troop movements. The army choppers would drop him and a few others like him in enemy territory. They lived off the land eating snakes and berries and of course, bugs while observing enemy troop movements. He said most of the guys got killed but he obviously didn't. When they got back to base after a month or two in the hostile jungle they were sent by the army to make serious whoopee in Saigon for a month and then they got sent out again. He definitely had the making whoopee part down to a fine art. Although he appeared to be out of shape, he had the ability to snatch houseflies out of the air as they buzzed by without even looking up from his beer. If one wanted a housefly dead or alive then Bill was your man. Nonetheless, that was ample proof for me that he was some kind of white Ninja.

The third roommate, Stan, wanted to take horseback-riding lessons. It was a rare stroke of luck for him that I knew the perfect local ranch for his type of sporting personality to take up a hobby such as riding. He was special. I took him up to Haley's ranch and introduced her to him. To my surprise they became engaged to be married within two weeks. She became pregnant almost the instant that they first shook hands. Love is strange. I got drunk with Stan one night down at the Eichler; all friendly friendly it was. Around midnight, we walked up to a supermarket that was closing. There was a child's coin operated bucking horse outside and I perched him up on it and dropped a few coins in. He rode it joyfully and laughed it up until the time expired. The next morning he gave me the chill. That was the end of our friendship. He behaved as if he had been forcefully sodomized against his will. He had apparently made a sober examination of our experiences and activities the night before and regretted his loss of control on the horsey.

A Stanford undergraduate, Stan was a physically awkward man and an intellectual *wannabe*. He wasn't a small man but he moved without grace and his clothes didn't seem to fit properly, like a natural born academic. Maybe he was six feet tall but he hunched forward in an awkward manner that made him appear shorter. He was already smoking a curved grandpa pipe and wearing a tweed ivy league smoking style of jacket in an attempt to appear middle-aged in his early 20s. He dreamed of academic tenure and the warm blanket of security provided by a university position. He had submitted a story about a "onion magnate" whatever that is, to The New Yorker several years prior and had it published much to his surprise. He had been surviving on that achievement alone as negotiable legal tender both socially and academically. He was studying literature of the literary kind at Stanford University primarily because he had been unable to get published since that initial success. Stan had parents who were academics in the university system in Santa Cruz, so academic tenure may have been the family business.

Stan fell in love with Haley possibly before he even met her. Credit my eloquent descriptives for that. She seemed a little too worldly to be falling in love so rapidly but she fell in turn with rapid abandon. It was a love-love equation. Even chimpanzees take a little more time than those two primates. My personal conclusion was that his folks must have had some major dollaros tucked away or I was severely underestimating his sex appeal. Haley had a baby about 8 months after they met. They were married and moved into an airstream trailer up in the coastal mountains above Palo Alto and she gave up the beautiful ranch. Stan had lost all interest in horseback riding.

Those gentle coastal mountains stretch all the way to the Pacific Ocean and they are a natural wonder with mild weather all year round. I went to see the married couple and child in the trailer one time six months after I moved to Los Angeles, when the baby was a toddler. It was unsettling and strange. It was strange for me. When I entered in the trailer, Stan was rolling to and fro on his back on the floor trying to play with the baby. The baby ignored him. The baby looked at me with his big bright green eyes, reached out his arms to me and it stepped right on Stan's face running over to me. Stan had to spit from a dirt-caked toddler foot landing in his mouth. My point is that the baby had my color of green eyes. Stan had dark coarse wavy hair and brown eyes and Holly was fair with blue eyes.

"What happened to Moose?" I asked her, not wanting to talk about the baby with the unusual eyes. Moose was this little terrier mixed breed dog that belonged to Haley. He was my favorite dog around the ranch. He went everywhere with me for several months. Moose had a deep sensitive soul; more soul than Stan. "Moose got eaten by a coyote." she said. That upset me. I loved Moose at little more than I loved Haley.

When I ran out of money, I moved into my mom's apartment some time in late '75 or early '76, when Haley was pregnant with the green-eyed baby. My mom was about 5'4" tall with a slim figure for a old gal in her '60s and she had one of these senior lady bubble hairdos on her head that were characteristic of the wrinkly grey ladies from her generation. Women who survived from the swing music hit parade generation wore tight elastic girdles to contain and shape their female figures and space bubble hairdos. I know this about girdles because my mom used to take me to pee into the women's room of Macys department store in San Francisco when I was a little boy, and I looked up in awe at women by the dozen squeezing into girdles all about the white tiled room. So then by the '70s, the beauty parlors from coast to coast were dropping those 'doos on old ladies heads by the millions. They made permanent waves with a little tasty hair coloring and then they gave them a heavy shellacking with the toxic lacquer hairspray. It was some kind of style permutation from the early 1950s and the '40s swing era. Every old lady in America who bathed regularly and drove a respectable automobile knew instinctively that this was the elegant way to fancy dress up the top of her head. I can't quite figure out how women evolved to that point from the adventurous pioneering immigrant American culture of the 19th century. The stylistic culmination of all of our American history was this spherical hair orb bubble with its strong gestalt hovering like a UFO over wrinkled porous flesh, decorated by Revlon and nurtured by the American red meat and macaroni salad diet.

I belatedly went to the medical doctor and learned a little bit about the nature of my back problem. My mom was vehemently against chiropractors, so I had taken myself to the official Kale MD., the same unkindly, cranky Dr. Leonard who had lectured me about intravenous amphetamines. My problem was a compressed disk and if I kept whining about it they were going to want to operate. I was better off trying to work my way out of it on my own if that was possible. The doctor gave me some gentle exercises which proved helpful and I began walking about 5 to 10 miles a day which was an improvement over laying around drunk. Mom really didn't seem to comprehend the back injury because it was invisible. She truly believed that I was having a mental illness over the missing wife with psychosomatic symptoms. She took every opportunity to remind me daily how rotten a wife Sheena had been. Now began the hell of obsessive repetition to a captive audience of one.

I played David Bowie records over and over, "Ziggy Stardust and The Spiders From Mars" and "The Man Who Sold The World" and "Diamond Dogs." I felt entrapped in this total cultural brain-sucking transdimensional vacuum like outer space is a vacuum; it was like the brains had been sucked out of my head through a straw and replaced with a loop recording of my mother's admonitions. I was an unknown Major Tom lost in a suburban apartment space capsule detached from the work-a-day world, the art world, the real world, the world of my peers; I was running out of breathable air. Outer space has million billion zillion stars but my stars were twinkling only in that sparkly textured plaster crap that they spray on low apartment ceilings so that they can place the word "Luxury" before the word "Apartments" on the vacancy sign out in the street. Hunter S. Thompson getting stomped and beaten by the Hell's Angels was like a vacation in Tahiti compared to my mother. Kick my ass Sonny Barger with your hell raising cycle apes but please please don't sick my mother on me.

Born to lose. My family's whole consciousness was entrapped in a mesh net of impossibilities. Other people could dream and achieve those dreams but not a member of the Kale clan. That you could not dream of doing something in the world and then go live that dream was axiomatic to my family's higher group consciousness; that notion was inculcated into us as children.

My dad's rule of thumb was simple, do good in school or he'd kick my ass. Beyond that tenet he didn't give a shit. Therefore, I waited to flunk out of junior college until after he died. Setting your sights low was the established Kale family point of view. I decided to go back to art college in a hurry. I didn't want to harm my mother but I knew I could.

My mom was now solo. The sympathetic mortician who had orchestrated my father's economical funeral had tried to date my mom immediately after he was cremated. He came over to my mom's apartment before the ashes had cooled and tried on my father's suits as if he needed to buy a dozen second hand grey business suits. Life is weird that way. Horny morticians are one of those small surprises in death that make human life worth living. TV too, can make life seem less ugly. Momma watched Mary Tyler Moore sitcoms with her '50s style fold-up TV tray holding her frozen microwaved TV dinner and hot tea every evening and then she went off to bed. There was something I found very melancholy about that tableaux.

She was nearing the end of her life and she never dated another man as a lover after my dad died. Mom bitched at the old man when he was alive and healthy but she really loved him in her own inimitable manner. My mom, the widow, went out with a Japanese man and ate sushi now and then for entertainment but he was just an Asian novelty man. He was a novelty man because she was racist, not a card carrying brownshirt, just politely so. Essentially, the old doll was a widow waiting around to die and trying to have cautious old lady fun while she awaited termination. Mom made a new friends. People liked her because she was giggly and silly in a social environment. She was mostly unable to carry on a mature conversation. That can be a good quality at times, but also it may work against a mature adult if your

acquaintances aren't completely lobotomized or besotted.

Many of her old-time friends whose prime-of-life dated back from the WWII time period were dying of alcoholism related illnesses. My mom interacted with some newer friends as now voyagers on excursions. Her more recent acquaintances weren't quite so pickled by alcohol and with these less pickled more sanitized seniors she travelled occasionally on a couple of those package tours designed for retirees. Get on the boat, float and eat, get off the boat, eat and shop, get back on the boat, float float and never get within spitting distance of a sweaty native, unless it was an Americanized native dealing retail goods. She travelled to Majorca, the tourist island in the Mediterranean with her antisemitic old lady friend Rolla. She said the excursions were fun but her expression revealed that it wasn't soul fulfilling fun. Therein, we have stumbled upon one of the mega-metaphysical game of life quiz show questions regarding the enjoyment and meaning of life. Avoid Majorca.

My mom didn't countenance adulterers and fornicators. Bill Bellflour, who visited us on Easter every year when we were children, with his wife Margy and their handsome son Denny, had been fornicating. To everyone's surprise, Bill started fucking another old lady in his old age different than Margy, whom he probably never fucked in twenty years. Margy was a relative twice removed from my mom but I'm not sure what her relation was, second cousins maybe. Ultimately, Bill Bellflour, who was at least in his 60's when he lost control of his libido, left Margy for the other woman. After that, my mom declared repeatedly that he was shit in human form. Bill Bellflour and Margy got divorced after more than thirty years of marriage. Right after the divorce, ex-husband Bellflour got a disfiguring disease where his eyes popped out of his head like two ping-pong balls, possibly a thyroid problem. He developed exaggerated cartoon eyeballs like an undersea invertebrate monster squid or a nocturnal tropical frog. My mom implied that God had punished him and that there was a lesson to be learned by his example. Well, I no longer had a wife left to cheat on so I didn't get the point of the story.

"How does his cheap girlfriend like him now?" my mom chided. The implication was that the larger his penis distended the greater his facial disfigurement became.

In order to get out into the world, I enrolled in a sculpture course at the San Francisco Art Institute with an instructor who was an ex-biker, Royce Beringer. He had a prosthetic leg and lived in a studio in an industrial neighborhood of Oakland. In his studio loft there was a tarp across an area of the ceiling that formed into a funnel shape and let out on a small upper window. He said that the tarp was there to catch the liquid human waste that spilled through the ceiling area when the father and son wino team who resided above him came home to drink. There was a young woman in the class who was removing her own blood into syringes and then making paintings using the blood as her medium. I met her again several years later in Los Angeles and she had taken employment in the film industry inking animation cells. They screen people very carefully before they hire them to work at Donald Duck Lane on the Disney Studios Lot. I guess one strange human slipped through the security checks.

At the same time I was attending Mr. Beringer's class, I attempted to enroll in the degree program there as a full-time student. The academics there didn't care to give serious consideration to what I had done in England. In my ruse to circumvent the American system, I had managed to pass through the English art college system as a local English homeboy. I wasn't affiliated with any American University's transfer program (and for good reason) and the San Francisco North Beach Art Institute Monkey Spankers didn't want to have anything to do with me. They were having a problem encapsulating both England and me in one concept. This caused them all kinds of confusion with regard to my credits and units relating to their degree programs and my now unusual permanent record. This led to an abrupt rejection from San Francisco Art Institute but I got accepted to another art institute a few months later in Los Angeles which is a much more fucked up place to live than Frisco. L.A. knew one of its own when they saw it. Boogie on down to the City of Angels with your tragic mess of a life they said. They wanted me to enroll as an undergraduate in L.A. My answer was yes. Goodbye Fisherman's Wharf and North Beach, City Lights Books and Alcatraz Island. That was all right with me. I was better off being a greater distance from mighty mom.

The Dean of the Art Institute in Los Angeles was a British expatriate and after a few discussions with him, I was able to dispense with all of the foundation courses and to follow my own direction artistically. The Dean lived to regret that decision. With art, you can have all the degrees in the world but they don't make a good artist. There are many prestigious office positions in the field of art for which a degree would be beneficial but I wasn't interested in that sort of occupation. Ultimately, I guess, there was no field in art for which I was destined but I did make some trouble along the way.

In fine art in the 1970's, everything was turned upside-down on its head. If you did traditional drawing, painting or sculpture, as a student you were considered backward and slow-minded. The art object had disappeared and what took its place must have horrified many concerned parents of students. Nonetheless, that's where the excitement was to be found. Body art, conceptual art and minimalism had hit big in London when I was there. There had been a big show of Los Angeles based artists there in 1973. Bruce Nauman's "Human Fountain" was a very influential piece of art at that time. It was a photograph of him squirting water out of his mouth. And when I moved to Los Angeles in the second half of 1976, Chris Burden was a big artist. He had his hands actually nailed through the flesh to the front fenders of a Volkswagen Beetle in the manner of a crucifixion and then a photograph of this was circulated.

Unusual crawlspaces and every conceivable permutation in between minimal shapes, gestures and body art was taken by some professional artist and written about extensively in high blown intellectual language by an art critic in an art journal or newspaper. Fine art painting wasn't seen as the cutting edge as it had once been with the fifties and sixties Expressionist and Pop art movements. Even painting got minimal. Art experts were very dogmatic in their rhetoric. Painters were considered old hat. Anything could be "an art piece." There was a German artist who was reputed to have cut off his penis and then jumped out of a high-rise window. There was an Italian artist who canned his own shit. This I had observed firsthand in a European museum.

The brilliant French artist Yves Klein was the true precursor to most of this kind of zany activity. In the early 1960s he dived skyward out of a second story window over a Parisian city street. This action was photographed when he was frozen in the air suspended over the street in the instant before he dropped to the unforgiving pavement below. That photo is a beautiful thing to see but the art isn't in the photo (although it is a good photo) it is in the flight. He also painted velvety monochrome canvases and monochrome sponges and he rolled nude women in paint and dragged their bodies across canvases to make paintings. Yves Klein died prematurely from a heart attack but he was very influential on the next generation, and that is what impacted so forcefully upon my art education. By the time I got into art school, fine art drawing and painting had been made irrelevant in the contemporary art discourse due to a great extent to the doors opened by Yves Klein's work. Of course, explain that to mom and pop from Idaho who are sending you to art college and paying the bills. In my case, my mother didn't really care what I did so long as I was out of her life. This time around, she was simply glad I was gone and she hoped I would get a job in an art supply shop when I graduated selling paints and brushes to the real artists. If I could have somehow managed to make a living out of canning my own shit in 1976, I would be living on easy street today. I always wished I had cornered that aesthetic market because that would be a steady income for life. Eat like Orson Welles and get rich.

During the first half of 1976, before I split for L.A. in the late summer of that year, my stay at my widowed mother's apartment became dangerously violent. My solicitous mother felt it necessary to remind her dysfunctional son more that a dozen times daily about the evil done to the family by my estranged wife. On rare festive occasions, my sister Shannon would visit us for dinner. During these family visits the two women would open a competition for negative adjectives describing the bird which had flown, to whom I was still married. Maintaining my sanity was no longer possible at these family soirées. Flying around my head like a swarm angry bees were these looping obsessive hateful stinging criticisms.

One dining experience with the three of us sitting around the dinner table in my mother's apartment sticks out in my memory. Proust used his tea and madeleine cookie to conjure old memories and I have spaghetti with marinara sauce to conjure familial hatred. My mother had cooked her special spaghetti recipe that reminded us children of our childhood. The ladies started vocalizing in unison with the female insults. I immediately got up and left the apartment and walked a quarter of a mile to the liquor store and bought a six-pack of Olympia 16oz cans of beer. When I returned they were still dining slowly. The food was hardly touched. They were waiting for me and the conversation was still cycling on the same topic of Sheena the Witch Hag.

They had their fishhooks in my flesh and now they wanted to tear at the wounds under the skin all evening. Two against one meant that I was never in the right. I had maybe one mouthful of that delicious spaghetti with marinara meat sauce when I lost control, smashed the plate and its contents down in the center of the table. Spaghetti and plate shards exploded all over the place. Both women were covered in spaghetti slop. It splashed all over the walls. They just sat there like perfect vandalized Grecian white marble statues with the stuff dripping off them. Silence at last. I had changed the subject temporarily. This would only cement them into their hateful opinions over the long haul. Sheena was bad, that may have been a feminine fact but spaghetti slop shut them up. I took my beers and went into the sterile little off white bedroom cubicle that was temporarily mine, with the beige shag rug and the sparkly plaster on the low ceiling, and the sound of constant traffic coming through the aluminum frame sliding window from the busy by-road nearby, on the other side of the manicured hedge plants in the narrow garden outside.

This miserable slapstick was only a teaser leading into a more terrifying episode. This was one of several times when I thought, "My life can't get any lower than this. I'm at the bottom of the pit." With age, I have learned that unless you're dead, life can always get worse. Domestic family member rage killings are the most typical kind of murders that you read about in the metro section of the newspaper.

Sons killing mothers and husbands killing wives and children, and many other familial permutations comprise the common passionate hapless tragedies of the nightly news. We like to think, "How could they have gotten to that point and let things go so far? That could never happen in my family." Then the next thing you know they're taking your sweet deranged uncle Bubba away in handcuffs, with a denim jacket thrown over his head to cover his face in shame from the prying eyes of photographers and onlookers.

My dream of rising up from the evolutionary slime of suburban pimpledom, from four scaly wet legs to two legs in designer jeans, to a culture of shaped-haircut sophistication was nearly destroyed by two acts of primal and spontaneous violence that just occurred before my eyes like a strange film noir movie scene. I felt like I was living in scenes from Stanley Kubrick's 'Killer's Kiss' with the film running away in negative and I couldn't stop it.

Once I was accepted to the art institute in Los Angeles, my mother turned up the intensity and the frequency of the repetitious bitter tirades against Sheena, just in case I didn't get the point the first one thousand times. If they had taught junior college with that kind of repetition I might have aced academia.

"I understand that concept about the Theater of the Absurd now professor. The first nine hundred and ninety nine times you said it, it made such perfect sense. Now, on the one thousandth repetition your words sound like complete utter nonsense."

Morning and night she had ranted for nearly eight months. I cracked up just when the first light of rosy fingered dawn was again shining on my future. In a month I would be living in Los Angeles if I didn't screw it up. Mom just wouldn't let loose of it even to take a breath. One evening, it went on for a few hours. Then ba-da-bing! I snapped. I hate it when that happens. It was Stanley Kubrick time. I remember seeing my mother flying through the air head first in a perfect spiral like a football being sent down field in a Hail Mary. She weighed possibly 135 lbs. How I elevated her over my head with one hand eludes me. Then I threw her long and hard.

"My back injury is much better." I thought as she sailed away. She landed on her head in the opposing corner of the room with her body stiff like an inverted mannikin, sort of like you might lean a surfboard in a convergence of two walls. It should have broken her neck or smashed her skull. Her feet were where her head should have been. Possibly, the stiffened bubble orb hairdo cushioned the fall.

My eyes were rolling around in my head like a madman. I thought, "Oh my god, I've killed my mother! I'm going to jail for life! This is the most heinous crime of matricide! I just want to go back to fucking art college."

I looked down in terror to where her feet should have been to see if her neck was broken. I was going to call for an ambulance but incredibly, she never lost a beat. Her mouth was still making the same movements, speaking the same tirade. It was absolutely surreal that she had not lost the cadence in her speech. She was undaunted. I went into my room my head swirling with adrenaline and nightmare visions. This was about as bad as it gets in family relations. To make matters worse, I did it to her again two weeks later. The exact same scenario played out in exactly the same way. The film was running in negative reverse. It was more terrifying the second time. I thought I was going to die from rage. She took it like a professional stuntperson. That just goes to show that if the cause is just, you should speak your mind without fear of reprisal. She earned the moniker. Rocket Mom! She could fly. I came to believe that she could have been shot out of a cannon and she would have come up good to go.

Now, at the very least I was a mother beater. A good fellow can't live that one down overnight. It's always there in the back of the mind somewhere haunting even the happiest of days. On another plane, the cultural and spiritual schisms of the 1960s were taking a bite out of our ability to get along peacefully, although the compulsive repetition thing was my mom's own personal invention. It was a powerful weapon to be reckoned with if you were forced to live within earshot.

The '60s was the beginning of the big meltdown of racism in America and my mom belonged in her heart to that era of the institutionalized separation of the colors; the white folks being superior in that older conception of the cosmos and the black folks and other non-white folks were the dummies who took orders from the white folks. She had become an anachronism from the era of culture which elevated Jack Benny and Rochester to mass media preeminence. She was living in a Jimi Hendrix influenced world and James Brown was entirely off her roadmap. Jack Benny was a comedian from her generation whom I had watched on early television in the 1950s; he had a loyal comical Negro manservant named Rochester. "Yessir Mr. Benny. Yes boss." he would say. Rochester was the kind of mass media Negro who was stereotyped as being afraid of ghosts, so that at the mere mention of a few spooks he would open his eyes wide in fear and run.

Somewhat predictably, over the years I had changed my philosophy to parallel the popular culture; from that of an eight year old Nazi to an eighteen year old hippie believing in a one world one people view of life. Reverend King not-withstanding, for me and I'm sure many others of my age, Jimi Hendrix just tore apart the old Bing Crosby-Bob Hope white dance party on a completely essential level. When I first heard a Jimi Hendrix Experience record I knew that there was no going back to a white Christmas. The song 'Purple Haze' was so far removed from my parent's generation's frame of reference that they could never hope to understand it. Just the guitar chorus alone is revolutionary in its strange dissonance. Of equal importance was the small detail that Purple Haze was the name of a batch of Stanley Owsley manufactured LSD that was sold illegally around the world. I worked my way up to the stage at Hendrix concerts and stood within inches of him. He was the embodiment of a vast generational rift.

I saw the Black Panthers appear in the audience at one particular Jimi Hendrix Experience concert at Winterland in San Francisco; a group of Panthers came in, maybe 10 or 12 of them and stood in a block in the rear on the floor at stage level. I watched their reactions really closely. They looked like they were seeing a new strange exotic animal for the first time. Even they seemed to be nonplussed. There was three guys, guitar bass and drums, two wafer thin white guys and Jimi, and it sounded so powerful, complex, primitive and erotic.

In the 60's, his music was a jam far ahead in the universal mind of race and the human family of what is to become the America of the future; Sly Stone was delivering the same message over in funky Oakland. I wondered that night, did the white kids ever really reference Hendrix as an American Negro, already an outdated term? I concluded that no, those race considerations didn't enter in to "The Experience". They loved him, Jimi, race was invisible. Later on in his post Experience group he adopted a more African-American bias to his sound but I don't think that most people perceived black or white when he performed. Jimi Hendrix was one of many new performers in that era who walked that line. Janis Joplin, Richie Havens, Paul Butterfield, Love (Arthur Lee). Their music kicked the hell out of the race divide. This is all common pop culture history now and I was having to deal with these issues most awkwardly in my own family.

With mom, bigotry was latent, tucked away under the surface waiting for an opportunity to show itself. I found out the hard way that scratching the surface led to trouble. My mom was even prejudiced against her own mother and therefore herself. I didn't put two and two together until my later teen years but I suspected that my mom tried to hide the truth from my sister and I, that my grandma, her mother, was Jewish. This suspicion is based upon two pieces of childhood evidence. My mom never ever would admit to this even when she was near death. We were raised as suburban Presbyterians, carrying lambs in Christmas plays to the baby Jesus, drinking Welches Grape Juice for Holy Communion, believing that we were similar to the families in those '50s and '60s sitcoms; they were our artificial family role models and our positive reflections in the mirror.

My maternal grandma died when I was six years old but I remember that one time she spoke a few words of Yiddish in the backyard of our suburban home in the year before she died, 1955. Grandma died in the bedroom across the hall from my bedroom in Rockwater Creek, California around the year 1956. My parents had built on an additional master bedroom onto the house probably in anticipation of accommodating my Grandma after Grandpa died in 1954.

The way I piece the story together is that my Grandpa was a Aryan German who had married a Jewish lady and they moved to America, arriving through Ellis Island at the turn of the century. They settled in San Francisco and lived through the 1906 earthquake camping out in Golden Gate Park. After Grandma died, I moved into her bedroom and when I was about 9 years old, I found artifacts that probably belonged to the old woman hidden way back in the upper reaches of the closet. Tucked deeply away at the bottom of a box was a book written in Hebrew. It appeared to me to be a Bible.

We children were told almost nothing about any of our grandparents heritage and what little I know was picked up by snooping and constant questioning of my mom in later years. I resorted to off-the-cuff trick questions to catch her in a contradiction. She was wily and never admitted openly that her mother was Jewish or to much of anything else for that matter. There is a chance that I'm wrong. Grandma could have been speaking German and the Bible could have been a Russian Bible but my memories from when I was five and nine years old seem to me to be clear.

When my mother was on her deathbed in the Stanford Hospital in Palo Alto, I sadly absent-mindedly thumbed through her desk drawer in her bedroom at her apartment. The fifty or so letters I had written her from England when I was studying there were carefully sorted in one compartment. In the front tray of the top drawer there was the little 6-inch ruler that I had taken to grammar school every day in second and third grades. I had carved swastikas all over it by scribbling hard with a ballpoint pen and then I had written the slogan "I like Hitler" in bold letters. With me at the age of eight, bad was good so I admired Adolf Hitler. I was shocked when I came across the Nazi swastika ruler at the age of twenty nine. Why had she kept it so long? Why had she never discussed it with me?

It would have been in the least considerate to inform the eight year old neo-Nazi youth, "Ronnie, you probably won't have a very successful career as a neo-Nazi, a Hell's Angel or a Klan member because your maternal Grandmother was a Jew."

I never started worshipping in a Jewish temple simply because I suspected that my grandmother might be a Jew. The Mexican version of Catholicism, the Virgin of Guadalupe and the other Mexican saints suited me. For me, Mexican culture has many enjoyable aspects to it. So although I rarely go to church anyway, unless someone dies, I prefer to go to a Mexican Catholic Church. God doesn't care. Not only did my mom put the lid on our family heritage but similarly, her brother Guy Sherman, raised his four children as Roman Catholics. That's America for you, we've got freedom of religion. These family issues were all screwed up. There is a crazy racial genetic hook with Judaism which is what my mother apparently was trying to bury in time. It's a religion but it's also considered a race by those who are looking for race.

My maternal grandparents were buried in San Jose in the mid 1950s and in the late 1980s I drove past an old cemetery in downtown San Jose and realized by its odd characteristic physical shape and age that my grandparents were buried in there. That shut down the whole day's activities. I spent several hours searching for their graves which I hadn't visited since 1959 with the entire family unit of four when I was turning ten. We drove there in the '58 Chevrolet Impala with the big fins from Rockwater Creek. I remembered the location where their adjacent headstones were located but the headstones made of a rose-colored granite were now missing. In short, an entire generation of expired Asians had been buried over the top of my grandparents some time in the 1970s. It's not an uncommon practice for cemeteries in California to do that sort of illegal stacking when they run out of land. When they get caught they face prosecution. I didn't sue the cemetery or inform authorities. On the contrary, I felt that maybe my grandparents could learn how to cook some rice dishes while they are down there.

Grammatical note — Political correctness may be an issue to some. I spell Latino with a capital 'L' and a lower case 'l' and I call white people 'whities' and people of African lineage on American soil 'negroes' or 'Negroes' if the time period is mid-sixties or earlier, blacks or Black people if it's in the 1970s era and at some undefined point in time they arrive at the term African-American in my lexicon. Italians, I don't think are mentioned in this narrative. Jews get a cap 'J' and so do Catholics and Protestants. Croatians and Latvians and Polish and Japanese people would all probably get an initial capitalized letter. Cap Asians. Basically, it all depends on who is holding the gun and that we all try to respect small incongruities of culture. I once had a friend from Borneo who told me that some people in his society shrunk heads, not through psychiatry but actually cut them off and reduced their size.

I said, "Is that why you left? Can you get me one?"

CHAPTER 4

Mom and I drove down to Los Angeles together to look for an inexpensive apartment in the neighborhood of the art institute. I was always a little bit of a sicky mamas boy underneath the skin. She wanted to make sure that I was safe and to rubberneck eyeball the crummy neighborhood surrounding the school. She was as anxious to get me out of her apartment as I was to leave there, but we were still trying to find the love between mother and son. The college was located near to downtown Los Angeles at the west end of MacArthur Park nearby the intersection of Alvarado and Wilshire Blvd. I was familiar with this neighborhood from my hitchhiking travels through Los Angeles in the 1960s. This area was characterized by swarming masses of poor Latinos coursing up and down the streets in a human river, mostly illegal immigrants from south of the border places like El Salvador. It was an intense experience to walk those streets in 1969 around 7th and Alvarado especially for a white suburban kid. Graffiti taggers had marked up with spray paint every square foot of available wall space for miles in all directions. The school itself was isolated on the side of a small hill next to the enormous multi-storied Elks Lodge building.

My mom was horrified by the darker complexioned Spanish speaking people and we tried to find an apartment on a block with no spray paint markings. Everywhere was tagged. There were unusual little landmark places in Los Angeles that you didn't see the likes of in the sanitized neighborhoods up north. The Church of the Superet Light was a favorite place of mine. A small Christian denomination church structure painted white had an accompanying courtyard garden containing a life sized sculptured icon of Jesus enshrined under glass. It was very precious and there was a conspicuous absence of public vandalism. No one messed with it. And there was kitsch L.A. street sculpture like the giant Chicken Boy standing on the rooftop of a restaurant in downtown L.A. on funky Broadway.

Once the original fashionable cinema theater district around the turn of the century, this downtown area too had become a concourse for an endless stream of poor latino immigrants and other disenfranchised peoples. Between 3rd Street and 9th Street on Broadway there remains today the weathered dirty decorative facades of a dozen cinema movie houses from the first decades of the 20th century;

Orpheum, Rialto, United Artists, Tower, Globe, Loew's State, Million Dollar, Los Angeles, Palace, Arcade, Roxie and Cameo cinema theaters. It must have been a glamorous stretch of urban beauty in its heyday, when the sun dipped below the horizon and the lights of the many theaters lured the people with their charm and entertainment. These streets like many other neighborhoods in Los Angeles became more bloodied mean streets by the mid-'80s with the advent of the rock cocaine drug gangs. During the sixties and seventies they weren't so dangerous from streetgang driven gun crimes.

The first time that I came to this neighborhood was almost ten years previous in '68 or '69, so I was already completely familiar with the intense street life. In fact, I had lived and worked there for several months. There were three brothers from Texas that I was hanging out with back then around the small city of Cupertino, California. My mother had an apartment there for a while. These brothers were probably somewhat atypical triplets. Two were identical and one named Sigmund was different looking and he had a skewed posture from polio. Sigmund's polio damage was much worse than mine. More than a slouch, he had some kind of pretzel effect with a bony lean to his upper torso. Sean and Theo were the identical ones and they were normal physically. All three of them were kind of stupid and they were taller than me by several inches. It was one of them who first introduced me to the risky thrills of intravenous methamphetamine. I was kind of stupid myself and that's probably the best reason to explain why I spent time with them. They were unchallenging to be around and one was more or less like the other one. They were searching for something metaphysical in that eery way that identical siblings have, in unison, and they believed that they had found it in a new religion called Schemetology.

When Schemetology was officially thrown out of its place of origin, Australia, in the mid-60s, a big piece of it landed in Los Angeles and other parts of California had developed satellite Churches. One and another of the triplets would tell me fantastic stories about Schemetology practitioners. They told me that the high up mucky-mucks called Transparent Spirits could leave their bodies and fly out into outer space, fly around earth's moon sort of as tourists, and fly back to earth and find their bodies and re-enter them with no detrimental effects.

I said, "Wow, man! They can do that? No wonder you're interested in Schemetology."

Myself and Theo had hitched-hiked to Los Angeles a few times from the San Francisco Bay Area and we had visited the main Schemetology Organization Church located in a renovated three story Victorian house in the Alvarado and

Wilshire neighborhood. This was one of the older neighborhoods of Los Angeles near to downtown, many large beautiful old Victorian houses still remained intact here and there; by the '60s the property value was inexpensive because this turf had been engulfed by the Latin barrio. That was the first place in the USA where the central organizational beehive of the church had been setup. On our longest inner city religious sojourn we had taken my '56 Volkswagen Beetle down to L.A. and arranged to work full-time for the Church of Schemetology for free religious and mental processing and a less than scrimpy weekly paycheck. This meant we were now insiders of the secret temple! Processing meant that the neophyte held these two chromed metallic joy stick handles which were attached to what they called a Dynalectronometer, a 5' electronic game screen gadget with an interactive green wavy line and a moving dot like a pong ball and the high priest, observing the screen, asked you unusual seemingly ridiculous questions. The Brainwave-Dynalectrometer was a device that measured electric impulses through your skin contact and movements with left and right metallic joystick handles. Logically, disabled Schemetologists missing a hand or arm were problematic.

There were white plaster busts, in the style of Roman marble busts exalting the ancient emperors, of the fearless Church mainman D. Don Durrell all over the place. He was their founder and leader and a former mercenary soldier turned UFO and Extraterrestrial Being encounter enthusiast cum advocate writer on the controversial topic, focusing primarily on the theme of ancient civilizations and their symbiosis with extraterrestrial and multidimensional aliens sharing our earthly sphere. He also conjectured arguments for an extraterrestrial co-habitation with earthlings in the present day and explained the abundance of apparent global UFO joyriding incidents photographed. Durrell was imprisoned in Africa for a short stint for dealing arms in Rhodesia. So, although he was a worldly romantic sort of adventurous character, D. Don Durrell wasn't especially charismatic to me as a plaster bust and he either never set foot on dry land, only moved around in public while incognito, or avoided making appearances in his own church like the plague. The contemporary prophet ran his church like the reclusive Howard Hughes ran his business empire. No one ever saw him. He continually recorded and sent in taped messages in the old reel to reel format which played to packed auditoriums of Schematologists eager to hear his words. I tried my best not to entertain forbidden thoughts like imagining the D. Don head as an inflatable sex toy or D. Don as a small nude full figure marionette performing the lecture onstage next to the tape recorder, like a naked Howdy Doody, the 1950s TV puppet. The D. Don person represented in the marble bust had an old puffy puss as if 30 years of nightly martini cocktails were etched into the stony flesh. I could appreciate the value of those lines. There was also one classically posed photo of a vibrant D. Don smiling with his arm around his beloved dog Boy-o, a Rhodesian Ridgeback, which hung in the main entranceway to every church, even the smaller satellite churches.

It was said that he lived on the official Church Ship which was a big seagoing yacht within global reach of any port. D. Don was the Skipper, afloat with the most elite group of marine Schemetologists. A group of these religious sailors landed or docked periodically in the Los Angeles marina and came into town as an organized group. I was working at the original old Victorian Church house when a phalanx of 20 of the maritime elite marched up the dirty urban street in unison in front of the old ornate three story home of Schemetology. They wore special uniforms that uncannily resembled Star Trek gear, except that they more brightly reflected daylight due to the purest white color of the zip-up full-length jump suits appointed with black patent leather three inch deep belts, polished black ten inch lace up military style boots for street marching, and shiny special white hard hats worn even in the summer heat, although they weren't involved in any type of building trade, construction or combat. They were unique in the world of religion.

Because the Church Organization was located in this neighborhood, Theo and I moved into a tiny apartment nearby, south of 7th Street, with about ten other eager neophytes. The apartment living was squalid and overcrowded. This was a one bathroom studio with a kitchenette. Cockroaches swam in the toilet for recreational relief in the summer heat. Cucarachas crawled, swarmed, partied and mated and hatched with abandon in every corner of the apartment. They should have paid a share of the rent. The place always smelled of fried eggs and stale greasy air. Eggs and cooking grease were cheap. As I mentioned, we were paid almost no money for working full time jobs but we were taken through the expensive mental and religious processing of great financial and spiritual value at no cost. I kept comparing the progressive steps of my religious enlightenment to my previous extensive LSD experiences and LSD always proved more enlightening, less time consuming and a negligible drain on a tight budget. Then again, my cult affiliation was predictably short-lived.

My job was to deliver the internal mail throughout the organization and occasionally to handle the PBX telephone system which was the original ancient old fashioned technology with the wires that plugged into a vertical panel with holes in a grid to connect or transfer a call. During my PBX shift, I sent almost every incoming call to the wrong person. Soon people called into the Schemetology switchboard just to scream at me.

"You fucking idiot! I'm calling from London and you've disconnected me twice. If you do it again I'm going to fly into Los Angeles just to strangle you to death." Then I'd disconnect them again. I regularly performed an unintentional Jerry Lewis routine getting myself all tangled up in cords and jacks yelling "Hello! Hello! Who? Who?" into the phone receiver.

The Church used the white three story Victorian house for recruitment and day-to-day business and another adjacent structure, which was newer, held the big hoodoo voodoo mucky-muck high priest sci-fi tekno transcendent superheads called Transparent Spirits and even higher up above them were the way-out Free Haruspex. This is the best I can describe what they were because I was never allowed into the inner circle, although I was curious to become one. I imagined that they held all the secrets of the pharaohs of ancient Egypt.

The old Victorian and its adjacent annex was a very busy place with all the little intrigues that go on in office situations. I couldn't tell who was fucking whom but I knew for certain that there was a lot of it going on all around me. I was at that age when you can smell it like a bloodhound although I had only the status in the church hierarchy of a pee-dog. They continually asked us for money as a downpayment on future religious processing. In my case that was a futile request. My family was lower middle class; my mom and sister thought that I had been brainwashed by a cult. They were very concerned and not inclined to send money.

I got to see everybody in the organization at that location everyday for about six months because of my very important mail delivery job. The most interesting guys and ladies were over there in the big voodoo building. They wore the futuristic white uniforms over there. I looped around there near the end of my mail deliveries every day. It was a long white wood structured building with old fashioned siding, no stucco. Inside the first set of double doors sat one of those people who wore the white jumpsuits and hard hats. The uniformed Schemetologists all smiled intensely and looked at you with glassy unblinking eyes. They had definitely achieved a happier state of mind than their mail delivery guy. They were all getting something wonderful out of this religion that I was not getting. Behind the desk, where this uniformed person sat was an enormous cyan blue tapestry hanging on the wall which had an embroidered globe representing the earth with gold olive wreaths sewn around it and a slogan above which read Trans-Galactic Central Control.

When I first saw that I said, "Wow, man! You people are livin' in a spacy space." The girl in the jumpsuit behind the desk smiled at me and said, "Yes we are!"

Spacy. Jetsons. Flash Gordon. Lost In Space. You almost never, if ever, saw people proudly flying Trans-Galactic Central Control colors in the day-to-day real world. These advanced Schemetologists were completely serious beneath their Free Haruspex smiles. Now I truly believed that they were flying around the moon but I never saw one do it. Then down the outside corridor to the rear, up the stairs and turn left, there were two big able-bodied men. One big guy was tall, lean, athletic and mean looking. The other one, was shorter and stocky and heavyset with thick muscle development and he was unfriendly. They were similar in appearance to professional tough guys that you see in the movies. They had a international ham radio in there and it seemed to be the focus of their attention frequently. They were in the habit of pacing in front of it and appearing agitated.

Once, just before I decided to give my two week notice that I was quitting, I found the door closed when I arrived at the top of the stairs. It was just slightly ajar and I pushed it open and walked in with the mail. They were pacing uneasily and wearing big handguns in shoulder holsters. I surprised them. They gave me a stern warning about pushing my way in the door unannounced in a manner which mimicked Hollywood tough guys of the film noir genre. Of course, I had never met a real life gangster hood or enforcer. I was instructed to walk up to the tall wiry guy and hand him the mail packet. I kept trying to look away from the guns while they were berating me. I didn't want to die so soon. Then I made for the door hurriedly yet slowly in abject terror. They probably had a big laugh.

Then there was a problem with my religious-mental processing. It wasn't working on me with the Dynabrainometer machine. They began asking new sets of questions of me on stranger subjects. I got in trouble for swallowing two aspirins with a sip of wine when I had a headache. They didn't allow any drugs. They had all managed to grow that crazy without the use of any drugs. I violated their drug ban with the wine and aspirin. I was punished. They replaced my interlocutor three times with someone higher up the ladder because my processing was failing. It wasn't working on me. They suspected that I wasn't one of them. Finally, they had recourse to open a secret vault containing a set of high security risk questions.

"Are you an enemy of Schemetology?" the man asked dourly.

"No. I am not an enemy." I said firmly.

The Dynabrainometer revealed the truth. I was not an enemy. They believed me because I was wired up to the Dynalectrobrainometer pong ball machine. I felt some indifference to them at this point. If the Church had paid me for working, I would have believed in anything they fucking wanted. If I had gotten paid and laid it could have been my religion for life.

On weekend evenings they sent us up to Groman's Chinese Theater in Hollywood to hand out religious pamphlets to the tourists. That was my first taste of the real Hollywood and I was thrilled to be at the Chinese Theater, a landmark. Nevertheless, when I gave my two week notice to quit my job, they sent me up the street to meet with four authoritative suits in an office building. Herein, I learned a lesson about life. Never give a two week quitting notice to a religious cult. The quartet of suits told me that I couldn't leave the Church. The four of them stood over me, as I sat on a cheap metal frame waiting-room chair, with their balls at about my eye level. That would add up to eight testicles at two testicles per suit, boxers, jockey shorts or free swinging. I had to look up to see their faces. It took all four of them wearing four matching neatly pressed white shirts and four dapper ties to tell me that I couldn't quit the Church organization.

I listened to them attentively and said "OK sirs, I will stay with the Church. I am definitely in. I'm a keeper. I've changed my mind about leaving."

One evening, about a week after my meeting with the four suits, this hippie guy with a big grocery bag, another of the endless numbers of spiritually lost souls from the 1960s seeking metaphysical truth, came into our overcrowded apartment and a group of us talked to him about the Church of Schemetology for the entire evening. He was hanging on every word. As the hour got late the conversation was paired down to Theo the triplet, myself, and the guy with the grocery bag. Everyone else had wandered off, but I was on a roll preaching and testifying like a sidewalk evangelist. I proselytized him. I had no idea what I was talking about but I said it with the impassioned energy of a zealot and this young man saw the light of truth.

Suddenly, he jumped up to his feet and held up the grocery bag and he said, "You have convinced me to join the Church of Schemetology and to give up drugs and to change my life for the better. I'm going to leave this bag of marijuana here on the table and never take drugs again!"

With that said, he shook our hands excitedly and turned and walked out of the apartment. We had no idea that the bag was full of marijuana. It easily contained more than a pound of the stuff. Theo and I looked at each other speechless. We both tacitly understood. After a few minutes of silence, I said, "Lets take this bag of pot and leave for San Francisco before he comes back and changes his mind." Within five minutes we were on the Hollywood freeway in my '56 Volkswagen heading north out of Los Angeles and away from the Church of Schemetology and the neighborhood of MacArthur Park. I immediately got stoned out of my mind and couldn't drive. Theo drove and I yattered on into the night up past Oxnard then Santa Barbara, and San Luis Obispo.

Each of the triplets inherited $5000 when their father was murdered by a shotgun blast to the stomach in Texas the following year. One of them, Sean, immediately paid that money to the Church of Schemetology for mental and religious processing. Soon after he was done with the chrome handle rigmarole they threw him out of the Church. He'd run out of money. Five grand didn't take a person far in Schemetology. Having no money would get you tossed and being classified a bad person would get you banished as well. There was a certain percentage of people who were considered just plain bad people and they were enemies of the Church. If they found a bad person in the group, they banished them. In defense of the church, my friend was basically an idiot. At the time, the church was busy courting movie stars and rock musicians. The last I heard of Sean, he was hired to crawl under houses working for an exterminator. The other identical one, Theo, went off to UC Davis to study animal husbandry and the odd one Sigmund was making candles for the Renaissance Faire.

With this in mind, I never anticipated that I would ever return to that MacArthur Park neighborhood at Wilshire and Alvarado. Now in 1976, I was moving back to that exact same hood. My Mom soon tired of looking for a safe apartment and she settled for a cheap apartment; she left me to do whatever it was that I did at college and she got the hell out of L.A., a city which she seemed to hate. Los Angeles was either too expensive, like fancy dining at Chasens in Beverly Hills where a minimum $100 cash would purchase only a meager dinner for one and she was embarrassed by the prices, or it was teeming with dark-skinned masses that caused her primeval fear. And I remember now that I began driving a recent model of Volkswagen Beetle soon after my arrival in L.A. Mom bought me that car to go to college. That was nice. Now I was living in Los Angeles and I was mobile with a dependable car. Mom had set me up.

I had the singular ability to choose the wrong worst apartment to live in. Consequently, I bounced around four apartments in my first year in L.A. I owned no furniture so moving wasn't exactly a big problem. I bought a Patti Smith and an Iggy Pop Stooges album and played them in every one of my dirty little apartments through headphones with the volume up. I was in rock and roll headphone heaven. I drank beer and played their music over and over. Stooge power. My first apartment was located across the street from Paramount Studios off of Melrose Avenue in Hollywood on a street named Plymouth Avenue. I used to jump rope in the back parking lot for an hour a day to strengthen my back. An old gay man used to come downstairs habitually and sit on the brick wall and watch me every day. He told me as I was jumping up and down that he wrote pornography novels for a living. I was already attracting influential Hollywood literati and I was still the new boy in town.

When it rained, the roof leaked and water poured into my kitchen in torrents. The building manager would say that he had fixed the leak and then the next time it rained water would pour in just the same as it did before. The building manager was a frail geezer named Bill and he was in his late 60s or older and he had a girlfriend who was a black girl with only about five misshapen green teeth in her mouth. She couldn't have been over 21 and she was all fucked up physically, rickety, herpes, bloodshot eyes, speech problems, poor and unclean and she was obviously completely illiterate. She looked like she might have had several more coexistent diseases which mutually shared her as their host. Her speech was terrible because she wasn't educated and because her mouth had only a few teeth in it. She didn't seem to have exceeded an 8th grade education or even a 3rd grade education. Possibly, she was mentally retarded. She had southern speech patterns like maybe she was from Mississippi, I thought. She had a serious crush on me and she used to come over in the afternoon and sit on my filthy couch and ask questions about sex and other things. I had put down a huge blue plastic tarp on the floor to cover the white shag carpet that was brown with filth. She wanted to fuck me but she was so messed up that I thought I might die if I fucked her. She was so sweet a person, I thought that if I was a millionaire, I would like to fix her up like a princess. Well, maybe get her a whole mouthful of new white teeth and a sparkling rhinestone tiara. I felt bad for her. She must have really had her ass kicked around in just a few years of living. I understood maybe thirty percent of the words she spoke. I soon moved out of there to an apartment where the roof didn't leak.

I moved into a Latino apartment building just off of the corner of Kenmore and 3rd Street on the ground floor in the rear. It had brick wall panoramas from every window. Most of the tenants were illegal immigrants from Central American countries. They probably weren't from Mexico but they were from farther south. There were so many cockroaches in that little ground floor apartment that I almost killed myself from spraying aerosol poison all over the place. There were thousands crawling everywhere riding piggyback in roach rodeos.

The apartment upstairs from me had a party one Saturday afternoon. It was a big party. I was in my kitchen washing some dishes listening to the oompa oompa thump thump squeezebox melodies of ethnic pop music coming to me through the ceiling and staring at the brick wall when two urine streams appeared spilling down from a fire escape balcony above in front of my window. Soon the two became three urine streams. As the party gathered strength so did the number and intensity of the urine streams. After a couple of hours during which I couldn't stop staring at the variety of streams of urine, my mind snapped and I called the cops. After about three angry phone calls they finally came. There were two of them standing there when I opened the door. They were two white cops. They both had that cynical pissed off facial expression that L.A. cops get. I told them the problem. They gave me some traditional stink-eye bad guy attitude and held the moment a little too long for my comfort. They would have liked to bust me for possession of pot but I didn't smoke pot and so I gave them a reciprocal I ain't got no drugs in here look. Soon after they went upstairs the urine streams which had grown to a gushing five and six at a time were discontinued for about a half an hour. After that, you would have thought that Hoover Dam had collapsed. So I went for the easy fix and stayed in the back room for the duration.

From there, I moved into a one room place behind a house on a hill near the 101 freeway on a street called Benton Way which was near to the Rampart Division Police Station which serviced the MacArthur Park neighborhood. This is where I was living at the end of my first year of college in Los Angeles. At night after midnight, the night air would frequently carry the sound of a police bullhorn braying, "Step out of the vehicle. Get down on your knees. Put your hands behind your back." It wasn't difficult to imagine the cops with their guns drawn moving up from behind to handcuff people on their knees. It was the same routine night after night like a little one-act street play. Some nights the little dramas lasted longer than others. I wondered exactly where this was coming from. It sounded like they had set up some kind of trap for motorists on a nearby street. Was it near the freeway offramp? On that hill the sounds carried strangely in the night.

Coming back from our official college party at the end of the first school year in May of '77, I was driving home solo up to Benton Way and a little tipsy at about 2am when I picked up a LAPD black and white cruiser from the Rampart station on my tail. They pulled me in an unlit sidestreet about 3 blocks from my place. There was a pair of them and they were physically small for policemen, not big burly guys like you would expect.

"Toy cops." I thought as I looked them over, "How weird is L.A.?"

I was wearing these light beige sort of English rock star shoes and they were a little effeminate and my t-shirt was a nearly flesh colored earth hue, with blue jeans. It was my attempt to achieve that fancy funky chic affectation of dressing that had been perennially popular since the New York Dolls broke loose. I soon learned not to dress that way because it just wasn't working out to be fun for me. So I was literally looking down at these two policemen on this dark sidestreet and they seemed to be reading my mind.

"Turn around and walk down that straight line in the sidewalk." One of them ordered, casually shifting his weight. The other one smiled at me.

"Uh oh!" I thought. "A difficult test."

I turned around and walked very carefully. That was when they kicked my ass. I hit the pavement hard face first with both of them on my back. A heavy knee hammered the middle of my back once, twice; then a baton was pressed hard across the back of my neck crushing it into the concrete and hand reached around and jerked my head up against the baton. That was painful because necks don't usually bend at extreme angles. Then another hand reached around and pressed my windpipe cutting off my oxygen. I couldn't get any air through the pain; then I began to float away like I was asleep dreaming; then I was gone, blissfully happy. As I floated away, I felt the urine spill out of my bladder in a warm rush. When I was dreaming, I was in a happy place; then I woke up handcuffed behind the back and face down on the cement. There was laughter. I was tossed onto the rear seat of the police cruiser on my belly. The cops were laughing at me for being covered in piss. The cuffs were definitely clamped on painfully tight. Off we went into the night. They drove us around L.A. for what seemed like forever. The smallest toy cop on the passenger side was the one who played the nympho slut girl and the driver who was also small but a bit larger than the female boy played the straight man setting up the jokes. Slut girl wanted to fuck me. She started erotic dancing on the front seat as we rode around downtown Los Angeles.

"Do you want to fuck me Ronnie? Do you think I dance sexy?" said the slut cop. This went on for what felt like a long time, extended real time and extended subjective time in miserable congruence.

I thought, "These are homicidal sex pervert toy cops and they have me handcuffed in their back seat at 3am." They also had some entertainment value. They were unique to my experience.

At some point of no return I said, "You guys have been a lot of fun but tonight's probably not a good night for me to go out on a date. I'm covered in piss. Maybe we could do this again next Saturday."

They liked that idea. Big laughs. These were not your average methodical, boring policemen. We all laughed. Then to my surprise they didn't kill me and dump me on the side of the freeway. We eventually arrived at the men's jail downtown. I walked in handcuffed and my faded blue Levis were soaked in piss down to my knees. Pee chic. Perfectly normal here, no one blinked an eye. Covered in piss with a clotted bloody knot on my head above the hairline and a split lip, this was just a routine DUI. I failed the breath test and according to the two arresting officer's scientific calculations, I was proven to be drunk. I spent 48 hours in the slammer

SUB-HOLLYWOOD — BRUCE CAEN

and arrived in front of a judge on Monday morning.

My voice had dropped a full octave. I sounded like the bass singer in a Doo-Wop group. My theory about it was that my neck had been stretched. There was the additional crime of resisting arrest being read to me. Great. I was being charged with fighting the two policemen. I wasn't sure if it was a felony charge or a misdemeanor but it didn't smell like a dozen carnations. They assigned me a public defender. I said to the judge, "I didn't punch any police. I'm not guilty." Then I was allowed to go home on my O.R. I guess the judge figured that I wasn't a flight risk. The first thing I did was pack up my clothes and move to beautiful So Pass. I completely totally moved out of that Rampart neighborhood within two days. Up, up and away to South Pasadena, where I moved into my fourth apartment for the year since I started college in September. This one was completely unfurnished except for a stove in the kitchen so I was back to living on the floor but it was such a pretty neighborhood.

My joy toy cops had sternly admonished me as I was entering the jail, "Plead guilty to all the charges sweetheart. Remember, we know where you live."

I spent the summer going in to see the public defender and sitting in court trying to project an aura of angelic innocence and intellectuality. As a defense, my court appointed attorney tried to subpoena the records of the two cops. There were legal feathers flying off the city attorney and consequently the city attorney bumped it up to the district attorney to prosecute. The attorneys on both sides were getting too excited over this small matter and elevating their blood pressure, costing the city money and wasting time when they should be prosecuting criminals. I worried. It turned out in the end that my two toy cops had no records at all of their activities as policemen. The police department had shredded their records for the previous five years in error. This is not unusual behavior for the L.A.P.D. They have a group problem concerning authority and violence and other matters which is beyond the scope of this narrative. They changed their mind about me. They asked me if I would make a trade off with them. They were willing to drop all charges against me if I would sign a piece of paper that said that I would not sue the police department.

I said, "O.K." and signed away a million dollar lawsuit.

I had another trivial legal matter during that first year in L.A. With the aid of a book entitled, "Do Your Own Divorce Without An Attorney" I was terminating the yoke of the joke marriage. It seemed fairly easy so I initiated the process on my own by filing papers down at the courthouse and going through the necessary steps. I remember that year as being hot and sunny right into the month of February. Summer never seemed to end during my first year in Los Angeles. Gary Gilmore's unusual execution in Utah by firing squad was in the news and the African dictator Idi Amin was running amok. Art students seem to have a fascination with the morbid and unusual events that occur in the world.

CHAPTER 4.0 LEVEL UPGRADED TO CHAPTER 4.5.1—THIS SECTION RECOMMENDED FOR ADVANCED READERS: I made a friend at school named Ty Eason who was a dedicated fan of Iggy Pop and The Stooges and near the end of the year, he began dragging me off to punk rock shows on the Sunset Strip. We would go to an art opening that was typically boring and then stop at a night spot to see a punk band like The Avengers from San Francisco at The Whisky. Sexy blond singer, tight black leather pants, a torn up tight white t-shirt, butch haircut, crazy eye make-up, wild looking kids, loud raw punk rock, goodbye boredom. Slash Magazine, a local well written punk rock fanzine and Search & Destroy from San Francisco were circulating around the college. Wham! Punk rock steamrolled me. Let's not underestimate its effect. I was gone. Smoke was billowing out of my ears. I loved everything about it...the look of it, the sound of it. Punk girls. They were perfect. All their pain was externalized in their appearance. When I talked with them they behaved like real people who weren't repressing the bad shit that they grew up with.

There was a writer for Slash Magazine whom I idolized as the paragon of koolness and rabid intellect named Kick Boy. He was from France but an L.A. punk. He was musically punk obsessed and his enthusiasm just exploded from his vitriolic writing. He was a very romantic character who was at the forefront of the L.A. punk music scene as much as anybody was. Recording industry affiliations with him were non-existent; he was all about the music. The idea that a group of people could publish such a radical and cool magazine fascinated me.

I kept my distance from rock music since the end of the '60s due to the death of many of the great ones, my drug addiction problems and the negative asshole factor of my ex-brother-in-law, the slimy big shot A&R exec producer, who got his unholy nose punched. Pop culture was always an obsession, and I was sucked back in now because here was this new music pulling at me like a strong rip tide. Punk rock and the other kind of rock had absolutely nothing in common in '76 and '77, so I felt pretty good about my attraction. The minimal art of the era just couldn't deliver for me enough bang for the buck and it was accompanied by such overbearing inflated pompous critical writing, kind of phony.

When I was a teenager I took myself alone up to a porno theater in San Francisco to see the Warhol/Morrissey film 'Lonesome Cowboys.' It was being shown in a filthy porn theater full of masturbators with newspapers on their laps. It shared a double bill with an X-rated porn flick. I loved that movie. It seemed to have no audience on the west coast so they just marketed it as pornography. That's what I mean by delivering the pizza hot, bang for the buck.

This is directly opposed to a white wedge filling a gallery space which has all this highblown criticism to substantiate why it is an amazing exhibition of genius and artistic wonder. If you read all that verbiage, then it is not a boring wedge anymore it becomes an art wedge, a wonder of genius. There is your P.T Barnum factor at work in the art world and Warhol used it. Nevertheless, the wedge still sucks and you've been conned. The Velvet Underground came out of an art environment but they soiled you inside and out and Warhol wasn't devoid of content, he was more than Pop if you care to delve into his oeuvre. It's the basic good/bad equation in which bad is good. Go with the wedge or get dirty with the banana.

During that first school year I had gone down to USC dental school and begun poking around to see if I could find some human teeth. I asked a student there if he could get me any old teeth which had been pulled out of people's mouths by student dentists. He looked around and came back holding quart sized glass object filled with dirty things in a brown liquid. It was a jar of about 150 teeth all with greenish meat hanging off them in hideous decay and rottenness. I took them home and cleaned them up carefully, one at a time as an act of love and obsession. It was a beautiful collection. My jar of teeth had an Ed Gein–Texas Chainsaw Massacre beauty to it and the strangeness of it had a strong appeal to me. I cast in bronze my used tooth paste tube when it was all squished up and my old toothbrush; and also collected a dozen very small clear glass vials of toothpaste samples and put it all on display in a customized wooden fetish box which I had made for the little collection. It was beautiful to me; a used bronzed toothpaste tube and brush, colorful vials of product and a small clear glass jar of decayed human teeth all neatly displayed in a small handmade wooden box. That's what I made that year in college. It was fairly conservative by comparison to many other students.

This was a strange time we lived in. As a group of students, we used to all sit around the common room talking and laughing. We all really laughed as a group. Some of the guys used to bring in inhalants that they had purchased from the sex shops in West Hollywood. We would pass them around the room and sniff the fumes from the opened bottles. These were industrial liquid substances marketed in small one inch vial bottles with names like Locker Room. They were legal chemicals, industrial solvents of some sort re-packaged primarily for the West Hollywood gay disco bar culture and marketed as erotic stimulants. It was toxic stuff that had an effect like amyl nitrates when inhaled. Amyl nitrates were popular on the disco dance floors as a 30 second high. Poppers they were called because they came in a glass tube that was wrapped in a fabric to be broken by snapping in the hands, then inhaled. Medically, amyl nitrates are meant for individuals having a heart attack, so I was told. The '70s overindulgences were hideous like that in so many ways. Shake shake shake, shake shake shake, shake your booty, shake your booty. KC and the Sunshine Band. That was the thing they were doing in the '70s. Add the industrial solvents...it was a formula for a par-tay! Even at college.

There were a kazillion bondage parlours back then tucked away around Hollywood. Professional bondage and discipline in Hollywood was a lucrative endeavor and much of it was out in the open. There was a bondage and discipline wonderland at the top of La Cienega Boulevard where it meets the Sunset Strip that was located in a circular building and it was called The Circus. Sometimes, I think that I am just fantasizing all this because almost none of the architectural structures are the same anymore. I didn't go into that one in particular but I went into a few others. There were attractive women in the B&D places who were employed to beat and humiliate men for money. This wasn't a military style of discipline but more the kind that involved clothes pins on the nipples, diaper humiliation, and the ubiquitous leather whips. The dominatrix ladies told me that many men in positions of authority like judges came in to be disciplined and degraded. These were the heady days of John Holmes foot long schlong pornography and promiscuous sex without fear of death by disease.

A few of the girls in art school were inserting different cuts of meat and also specifically a big fish into their vaginas and making videos of that as art projects. Also anal fist-fucking videos and dildo videos as art were popular with the students. One male student made a video of himself inserting a 24 inch double dick dildo up his ass until it disappeared entirely inside his body. That last half inch was seemingly insurmountable. It just wouldn't go in out of sight; the videotape ran on and on.

A male student had a lawn party at a lovely house in the Hollywood hills where he had his blood removed by a girl in a nurses uniform while he screamed with his head inside a metal bucket. The students and art instructors stood around drinking beer and talking. They smoked pot and danced to rock music while casually observing his periodic controlled bloodletting and yelping. The students and faculty were comfortable with this performance which most certainly felt was on the cutting edge. Blood being sucked into glass tubes subdued the more festive mood of a beer drunk for me and the hideous screaming from inside the bucket reminded me unpleasantly of myself when my mother was giving me too much personality. At the end of the evening, one of the faculty members had to be carried out, taken to emergency and later get a knee operation after falling off the poolside patio and rolling down an embankment while dancing drunk.

All of these videotaped body abuse projects were torturing the senior tenured conservative elements of the faculty whose passion was to give instruction in drawing and painting. Several students had nothing to show at the end of the year for the final critique in painting. 'Painting is dead' was the catch phrase. One girl for example, when asked to show her work produced an automobile sales catalogue from a Ford Motor Company dealership. On each page containing a photo of a car, she had painted in all the windows of the cars with a metallic silver felt tip marker pen. The painting instructor, an elderly frail Japanese man with silvery grey hair was livid. Painting was no longer a popular discipline with the students and he was at that moment angry at her for the whole darn mess. She was mocking him. He pulled out of his pocket a twenty five cent coin and he said that making good art was about focusing one's energy through a medium to produce a result. It wasn't so easy, he said, as just coloring in shapes with a felt tip pen. Then he held up the coin and bent it in half over his thumb.

"Focus the attention!" he admonished.

She looked him in the eye and said confidently, "I just don't give a shit about painting. It's an outdated form of communication." That was Lisa. She was intellectual looking, svelte and blond and she smiled infrequently. She moved to New York City within six months of that day and started a successful punk band. Lisa never put stuff in her vagina as an art project.

She was one of many of my friends I made who left L.A. But I never left. I burrowed in to the low dirty end of Hollywood like a pajahuello tick on a feral dogs ass. I had many friends who moved away from Hollywood in the next few years, but I could never get out. Maybe I never wanted to leave. Many of them started rock bands in garages and went on to tour the world or did any number of other successful ventures away from L.A. For me it was like an unusual life sentence, not the Hollywood of TV and the movies but the black leather punked out all night Hollywood which existed deep beneath the world of media glamour.

One night, I saw Bette Midler show up outside a Cramps performance at Baces Hall in the late '70s. Well, this was a person who looked and talked like Bette Midler from a few feet distance but in Hollywood looks can be deceiving; it could have been a guy named Henry dressed up like a woman who looked like Bette

Midler. I was imbibing a quick drink outside and I saw her enter the show for about 30 seconds. She came back outside hurriedly. She was disgusted.

"Oh my god they're awful!" she shouted, and headed for her expensive car dragging her male escort in tow. To me, the Cramps were the greatest and I hurried back inside.

My life began to be centered entirely on the seedy fey raucous night clubs that popped up in the alleyways, slum lofts and bars of the side streets from Hollywood to downtown and into East L.A. My haunts became increasingly estranged from the art galleries and that kind of art; art gallery art or artart. I rarely went west out to the beach cities. That sun and fun type of hedonism that is postcard Southern California didn't suit me. I became an increasingly unsavoury, unkempt and miserable wretch. I was intrinsically a happy person who had been twisted into a painful distortion of a mature adult; a million dollars would have helped cure my misery but I was keeping thoroughly busy heading in the other direction. Also, I lacked self-confidence about what I was undertaking so I drank alcohol to compensate and numb my apprehensions. Life was an unpredictable process of rolling and tumbling from one night into the next through a seemingly endless spiked and studded black leather daisy chain of live punk rock shows.

Beach fashions didn't suit me. I didn't like to go barefoot and wear shorts. The boots the punks wore, steel-toed black engineer boots suited me fine in any weather. I was spending a lot of time on the streets late at night hanging out. Bombed. With a tape recorder and a 35mm camera.

•••  •••

CHAPTER 5

My second and final year at the art institute is a raging blur. Everything seemed to accelerate to light speed. The city was trying to sell the art institution into private ownership. Consequently, the conservative and staid faction of the faculty that had survived on some sort of tenure and the notion of the return to the lessons of Renaissance space were on the run.

The beauty of the past and the extremely different conceptions of the present seemed to blend together more easily in people's minds over in England. While it seems the reverse should be true, the present was abrading on the past a bit more abruptly here in L. A., although there was not much of an apparent past to deal with in Los Angeles. Father Junipero Serra's Missions. Possibly Americans, Angelinos in particular are more obtuse. The L.A. present is always busy tearing yesterday down. What was the past in L.A. anyway? A photo of Clark Gable riding in a Duesenberg or Hearst castle up the coast, the crypt of a deceased movie star? A 75 year old apartment building? There wasn't much history, so why be conservative about the present? Nothing much has a chance to age in Los Angeles because they're always flattening architecture only to put up something even more ostentatious and ugly.

The animation film industry was represented mainly in the drawing classes at the art institute. The Walt Disney Art Movement and the Max Fleisher Popeye-Betty Boop Movement could certainly stand up and be counted but more sophisticated or contemporary ideas were swept under the rug by the conservative faction of the college art faculty. Most damning for the college was that on the conservative side, they provided no pragmatic follow through to real world employment in commercial art and design.

I took some drawing classes just to keep a point of reference because everything else there was spinning off out of control. It felt like the students were running the school. The drawing teacher had a Disney animation background and he didn't like my approach to the sheet of paper in front of me. He said that I had a perceptual problem. "Duh! I've got that problem and some more to go with it sir! Are you going to forbid me to draw with charcoal?" We had a problem from the get-go and I enjoyed drawing.

That instructor was a moron by my definition. Cezanne couldn't draw or it would be more accurate to say the Cezanne drew awkwardly. He could never have been a Disney animator nor would he have wanted to be. The drawing instructor didn't like anything about me. But I knew that was going to happen and I just ignored him and stuck it out. I wasn't cut out for the magical kingdom and we both knew it. I signed up for his drawing class for a second semester out of some perversion. That particular drawing instructor was professionally involved with some Winnie The Pooh cartoons. I noticed his name roll by in the credits as I was laying in bed with the joneses one afternoon watching children's shows a few years later.

One day after life-drawing class a movie star came in. I was in there alone smoking a cigarette and enjoying the atmosphere without the instructor. It was about five in the afternoon on a typically warm day with all that great ambient light that a life figure drawing studio has about it. I turned around and Peter Falk was down on his hands and knees on the cement floor staring closely at a drawing that someone had thrown away and left on the floor. I knew him from that Cassavetes movie 'A Woman Under The Influence'. That was a great film but I never expected to see him down here at the edge of MacArthur Park crawling around on the floor. He was blind in one eye so he had to look at the drawing a little askew. I said, "Hi man, what's going on?" He looked up at me from a crouching position and he pointed at the drawing on the floor and said, "This is really a great drawing. This is really great!" It looked like every other drawing that was laying around on the floor done by every other student. In fact, they all looked pretty much the same.

I said, "I think so too. It's really great." Someone told me later that he had recently divorced his wife. That seemed to explain it. He was just unhappy.

During this second and final year in art college, I had started smoking again. I had gone through hell to quit in 1970 after smoking for 9 years. I started in 1961 when I was eleven. I would run down to the Greyhound Bus station in downtown Rockwood Creek, California after grade school and buy a pack out of the machine for a quarter. I was smoking about a pack every two days at the age of eleven. After my dad had the lung removed and he was still unable to quit and he died (whether he quit or not he was at the end of his rope), I got it in my head that I'd better quit. They sliced him up with very little finesse at the VA Hospital. I was starting to feel the stress about what I was going to do with myself after that last year in college. Smoking cigarettes is great for absorbing stress.

And Elvis Presley died that year. That indicated to me that time was racing like a wildfire. Elvis was a big deal in the nuclear family of my childhood. My mother loved him. She bought me an electric guitar and set me up with guitar lessons by the age of nine. She wanted me to be an Elvis. My sister of course, loved Elvis until he went into the army and then I think she moved on and loved somebody else. Personally, I loved Ricky Nelson, Duane Eddy, The Everly Brothers and Annette Funicello from The Mickey Mouse Club on TV. I used to hold my circumcised little dick and dream dreams of love about Annette Funicello when I was six years old. One reason that I never played music with a rock band after I grew into adulthood was that probably I was rebelling against my mothers efforts to mold me into Elvis. Also, I played like shit.

On that fateful day, I was up at my mother's apartment in Northern California and I was washing her car, a red 1970 Dodge Demon with a slant 6-cylinder engine and an automatic tranny. I was with her when she bought it and I helped her pick it out. Those old Mopar engines would run until the body rusted off the chassis. I had a transistor radio playing a black music station out of Oakland, KSOL, and the Afro deejay broke into the programming and said that he had an announcement to make, "The King of Rock and Roll is dead. Elvis Presley has died in his home of an appar-ent heart attack." Then he said that in tribute to Elvis Presley he was going to play one of his hit records. Following that announcement, he played 'Blue Suede Shoes' but it was Carl Perkins singing. I wondered if any other listeners but me noticed.

My mom took the 'Heartbreak Hotel' bad news pretty hard. It was one of those changes in life like the death of John Wayne (The Duke) and having to pump her own gas at the gas station that just made her life not worth living anymore. I think that's the point in time when she first began to die slowly. Now it was time for her to begin to give in to the shadow of death. She was getting old and the stability of her era, the things she loved about life were leaving the earth one by one. And of course her dear friends were dying. Many of them were serious drinkers and they were succumbing to liver disease. My mom never had a problem with vice.

Downtown Los Angeles was beginning to develop an art community in 1977. Artists were moving into industrial buildings and creating lofts. The city eased up on zoning restrictions in downtown to allow for this. There were galleries popping up here and there and restaurants for the artists. Some of the lofts were in hardcore skidrow neighborhoods and others that the more well-to-do bourgeois types had opened up and renovated were in areas with less street people, just old industrial neighborhoods. The prevailing attitude was one of separation from the Venice Beach artists who weren't really considered effete, just commercially successful. New artists felt that the doors were closed to them in Venice.

In downtown L.A., the common thinking allowed that this was an opportunity to create something akin to a New York City style loft scene. From downtown a new magazine arrived promoting the kind of performance art that Yves Kline had initiated in the early 1960's. A performance could be done in front of an audience but it didn't necessarily need an audience to be complete. It was enough to have a photographic record of the activity and an intellectual explanation and rationalization of the activity. That was a performance as well. Here was an opportunity for young artists who were not involved in traditional media to get some publicity and show their stuff. This was possibly viable territory for us students (soon to be graduated) to explore and a counterpoint to the punk rock music scene which was rapidly coming on. But let there be no mistake, the two were completely incompatible bed partners here in Los Angeles.

Punks did not like art performance. Art performance was not punk because it wrapped itself in a mantle of aesthetic rationalization and overrefined intellectualization. Iggy Pop was punk and he was known to have cut himself intentionally onstage. Chris Burden, probably the most engaging of the performance genre artists, may have cut himself intentionally but he was not punk. If you were going to go in one of those directions as an artist it was going to exclude the other direction. The two groups rarely mixed socially in Los Angeles. In San Francisco, the two were a little more homogenous in people's minds. But I didn't live in San Francisco and if I went back up there to live it would be over my dead body.

There was one exception of a performance in L.A. around this time by an Austrian artist who worked with the entrails of cattle. Hermann Nitsch's 'Orgy Mystery Theater' involved hundreds of pounds of raw guts from disemboweled cattle being poured and spread over nude "performers" who were hung and posed in positions resembling disaster scenarios and inverted crucifixions. Nitsch had managed to assemble a random group of Los Angeles' punk musicians for his event. He wore all black clothing with an oversized black latex glove on one hand and he moved in a stiff jerky robotic manner almost as if he was trying to be farcical and when he raised the rubber-gloved hand the action began and the musicians played a crescendo of noise. When he lowered his hand abruptly the action stopped. This went on for hours of repetition.

The guts had arrived late in the afternoon at a rented studio space in Santa Monica in large clear plastic bags, delivered from a meat packing company. They were sort of the real star of the show with no name on the marquee. Orgy Mystery Theater starring "Guts" with Hermann Nitsch directing! But of course there was no real marquee, it was just taking place in raw studio space. During the performance, the spectators stood and sat around the periphery and watched and hoped they didn't get splashed biological matter on their stylish clothing.

Ty Eason became a sort of partner in crime with whom I worked during that last year in college. He was a sort of Germanic looking young man who was from one of the beach communities, possibly Huntington Beach. He wore sandals or flip-flops frequently and he had shoulder length blond hair. We went along in the same direction for a short time doing art projects together. The first serious activity that we did together was a performance in the student gallery at the art institute. It caused a great deal of excitement. Well for me, someone who had been invisible for his whole life, it seemed like there was a stir about. In fifth grade, I had been photographed holding a snake that I had captured on a class field trip and my picture was published in the local Rockwood Creek newspaper. They mistakenly substituted the name of somebody else in my class in the caption. That was the extent of my fame in life so far.

For this two-man performance we each did separate things which blended together to make a single event. I photographed myself wearing blue jeans and a t-shirt performing dog tricks and lifting my leg and fake peeing. Dog things. Then for the performance I made a human size cage and I sat in there naked and wore a rubber dog mask. The photographs of my dog tricks were hung in inexpensive frames on the sides of the cage. I just sat in there like I was a dog. I watched the people and they watched me. Ty was set up several feet away and he was wearing only a diaper. He built a structure that he sat on and inserted his head into a square channel tube that contained a TV running a video loop of two actual diaper commercials. He repeated the dialogue of the video outloud as it ran. We kept the gallery open and did this from 9am to 6pm without a break for a week. We drew large crowds and I saw locally well-known artists and gallery people cruising the show sometimes repeatedly. One matronly old gal who looked to be very rich came in more than twice and she stood outside the dog cage and stared at my penis for what seemed like long periods of time. The dean of the school slipped a note under the door asking us if we would close the show down a day early because he had some potential private investors coming to tour the campus. That was amusing. We were completely exhausted and we were glad to comply with his request even though we knew he was trying to censor us.

I bought some large rats at a pet store and I was going to try to develop another art performance using two rats. I was being allowed to take the video tape equipment home and play with 'live' video outside of the campus. Unfortunately for me and the rats, the rats became insanely vicious when I got them home. I poked a pencil in the cage and one bit it in half in a split second. They were nasty characters, tough and bloodthirsty. Consequently, I tried to drown them by submerging their cage in the bathtub and they both managed to get out of the cage and they started jumping up at my face. These were killer pitbulls in little rat bodies. I had to beat them with a toilet scrubber brush to keep them off of me. I decided not to videotape the rat murders.

I decided to kill them another way, with poison, traditionally considered a feminine technique for committing murder. I started feeding them rat poison mixed with their food and they still didn't die. Finally, I fed them exclusively rat poison and it took them two full weeks to die. I was afraid to pick up their dead bodies in fear that they might return to life. Those two little bastards scared the hell out of me. When they were dead I tossed them in the garbage can out back and gave up on the rat idea. They were harmless soft little fur balls once life had departed them.

I began having ESP occurrences. Two to be exact. Living in this inexpensive apartment near the arroyo in South Pasadena during my last year in college, I experienced extrasensory perception type of events. First there was the fleshy white worm incident. That was strange but could be explained away as accidental. I was translating a poem by Rimbaud from French into English, just for my own interest. I thought that the English translation that I was reading might have been done poorly. So, having taken some French in high school and because I had travelled there a few times, I felt empowered to do so.

At this point, it should be noted that I was drinking a little whiskey at night and reading into the wee hours. Also, I was exercising fanatically. During this period, I was doing 800 push-ups on my knuckles a day, bicycle riding in the hills along the arroyo and jumping rope for an hour a day.

It started with a scratching sound at night that I couldn't place. It was much the same as my incident with the unattractive Jerusalem cricket a few years previous. I looked high and low in my apartment which contained not one piece of furniture, except an art drafting desk and chair. In addition, I owned the proverbial stolen plastic milk crates that students used for shelving. There was no place for a rambling bug to hide.

In my translation of this poem there was a line that read 'the white worms (or maggots) will run through your veins'. I had typed out a total of about 12 double spaced pages of English translation that were my own. One afternoon, when I picked up the translation which was paper clipped together to reread it, I noticed that two of the pages were stuck together. Upon closer inspection, holding the paper up to the daylight in the window, I saw through its translucence that there was a fat fleshy worm the size of my little finger living in between the two pages in a sort of cocoon. It made a noise when it wriggled employing the paper almost like drum skins to amplify the sounds. I got a chill on the back of my neck and quickly took the two pages out to the garden and ripped them apart, dropping this fat fleshy creature into the soil. It was similar in color to my pallid skin color. That was no pretty caterpillar that plopped out. The odd thing was that it had made its home right over the typed lines about the wriggling white worms, like it was a giant Rimbaudian maggot.

I used a set of springs with handles on the ends for exercising the upper back. Having had polio as a child with the paralysis of a muscle group in one shoulder, I was continually trying to build my shoulder up in the area where the paralysis occurred. Of course, it remained atrophied. This exercise caused me to pinch a nerve in the bottom of my neck and over a period of about two weeks it was growing more painful and affecting my breathing. It hurt like hell to take a deep breath. My mom had instilled her own fear of chiropractors in me but I knew that this time I really had to see one.

In pain, I picked up the yellow pages of the phonebook and opened it to Chiropractors. I began running my fingers over the listings and over one name, I received a picture of a little lady in a white doctors smock in my mind's eye. The picture was very strong and clear. She wore black framed eyeglasses and had short cut blond hair. I dialed that number and made an appointment fully expecting to see the person that I imagined in my mind. The next day I went in there and a woman with dark hair came out to the reception area.

I thought to myself, "This is not the right woman!" The lady asked me to write down my information on a form and then five minutes later led me into the back office and there was my vision in the flesh, perfect in every respect. Eyeglasses, hair, white smock, facial features, height all matched. I told the chiropractor about the ESP experience and she cured the terrible pain over a series of five visits. She then told me an unusual story about herself.

She told me that she was born into the Nazi aristocracy during World War II. All high born Nazi babies were marked with a special scar at birth she said. She of course had that marking. When the Third Reich was destroyed, she was orphaned and fell into the hands of the Americans, whereupon she was adopted by an American family and raised to adulthood in North Carolina. She said that she was still a Nazi in her blood and her deepest hearts desire was to fly a warplane and bomb a city. She said that her husband was Irish and an IRA supporter and on Memorial Day they put a Nazi flag side by side with an IRA flag outside their house on public display. I told her that I found her story to be very interesting. When I felt better, I stopped visiting her. She had a marvelous healing touch.

Curiously, on the topic of Nazis, my neighbor upstairs in the duplex apartment at that time in S. Pasadena revealed to me that he was a flag waving Nazi. He was a blond jock type of sports fan college guy. He was studying to become a professional embalmer of dead bodies, a mortician. He didn't really look to be the type of guy to be attracted to that morbid profession, but he was. I was working on some little sculpture project out by the garages in the back and he came back there to talk to me carrying a little red flag with a swastika. He said, "Hey Ronnie, I'm a Nazi. I've joined a club with a group of other Nazis." He waved his flag a little in front of me.

I said sarcastically, "Oh Allen, that's a won-n-nderful hobby!" He was bubbling over with happiness about it. He loved waving the little flag. Those flags were nicely designed. Great for marching. I was reminded of Albert Speer and Leni Riefenstahl but I didn't guess Allen was aware of them. Somehow though I didn't think Nazi parades were going get too popular in this community. When the marching brown shirts and swastikas replace the Rose Parade in Pasadena, then its time to start worrying about America. And happy new year to all. It must have been my new punky haircut that excited him. I was wearing it short and with stuff in it to make it stand up in spikes, a Nazi magnet perhaps. That was more than I cared to know about either the embalming student or the chiropractor. Punk was so new in the culture at the time that it was easily misinterpreted.

At that time in L.A., the punks were isolated to a small community in Hollywood located near to their often frequented nightspots the Masque, a filthy basement off an alley near Hollywood Blvd. and Cherokee Ave. and the Whisky, the famous rock venue on the Sunset Strip.

After the Christmas holidays and approaching the final months of our time in art college, when we were going out at night frequently to art events or punk rock shows, Ty Eason had become extremely competitive with me. His behaviour was often mean-spirited but it was well crafted so that I would take the brunt of the rudeness while no one else appeared to notice that I was being slammed in some manner. He had dyed his hair day-glo blond and cropped it and as I directly observed, a new ego was being born unto our earthly sphere. We were both suffering strange art student growing pains.

In addition, he was especially critical of my relationship with my mother. For one thing, I was still mooching money from her as best I could and that was a point of ridicule to which I was sensitive. Also, deep down I loved her I guess. I could have said to Ty, "Don't go there!" but he went there. He was seeking areas of vulnerability in me and there he found one with momma. I never asked Ty if he had a mother. Odds are that he had one at some point in time or he was hatched.

In the early spring, I came up with an idea that stirred things up quite a bit. It also gave me an instant moniker which I never managed to shed. I had been reading about a feminist performance artist, Adrian Piper, who did actions in public that bordered on the psychotic except that they were done as art projects. For example, she filled up her purse with tomato ketchup and then when she went to purchase something in a department store, there was a messy situation. Keeping this in mind, I had the intention of satirizing the punk rock haircuts and styles, and never being able to hit something straight on, I invented my own style of haircut.

My hair was already short so it was an easy step to shave a bald stripe right up the middle about two inches wide going from front to back like an inverted mohawk. In this bald strip I placed a long thin piece of raw beef liver which was secured with three strips of surgical tape going across at the perpendicular. 'Liverhead' was born. Liverhead was me. I and I became a natty Liverhead dread all over town. I published full page ads in the most popular West Coast punk rock magazines. It read 'The Liver Haircut' and then it gave in logical order the several steps needed to produce the style, purchasing the proper strip of beef liver, the placement on the top of the head and securing the liver with the surgical tape. Lastly there was a three quarter page deadpan close-up photo of myself wearing my creation.

These underground publications were very popular worldwide and I got a lot of bang for the buck especially in Great Britain, Europe, Japan and the USA. Letters of inquiry flooded in to me from all over the world. In addition, I wore my fashion statement out in public two or three nights a week for a couple of months, going to art gatherings and punk rock shows. Sometimes I went out alone and sometimes with Ty. It wasn't exactly getting me female dates. I wore it to The Whisky to see The Screamers perform and some pretty punkettes dragged me into the girls bathroom and signed my head with a felt tip pen. That was fun.

On another evening, I went up to a closeted gay art professor from the ceramics department at an opening at the art institute and said, "Hi Tom! How are you tonight?" The liver had dried on the surface because it was a hot evening and it looked like a giant scab on top of my head. He looked at me in complete terror and his mouth fell open and he ran away. He never spoke to me again. As you might expect, Liverhead found a safe harbor with punk audiences at shows by the inflammatory punk band The Germs or with other local punk players like The Plugz.

Larry Benton, a student artist in my class got a line on an entire building available for development as studio lofts in the downtown area and he wanted to bring me in on it. Larry, who had an air about him of moral rectitude, was in the very least endowed with an unimpeachable clean cut wholesome American appearance. The

Arcade Theater Building on Broadway which opened its doors in 1910 was vacant and unused on the seven floors above the movie house. It was one of those buildings I mentioned, that were slated to become historical landmarks as many were in that neighborhood, comprising the original highbrow theater district of Los Angeles, including vaudeville and cinema. The owner was anxious to make a profit from the new downtown art boom. This was raw dilapidated office space that had been vacated for many years, even decades, although the theater itself at street level was fully active.

The foot traffic at street level was intense and required that you be alert to danger at all times. There were occasional knife fights and countless destroyed crippled humans out front on the Broadway sidewalk. They were joined by the inevitable street hustlers trying to sell stolen jewelry and other exquisite merchandise which could be concealed in a pocket or up a sleeve. The heroin street dealers were around the corner by 3rd Street and Spring. The street skank dealers kept the heroin balloons hidden in their mouths usually tucked between their gums and cheeks beneath their back molars. If the cops came down on them they could swallow the balloons and if a customer wished to purchase a balloon they pulled it out on the tip of their tongue and exchanged it for the buyers money. Mostly, the great masses of people coursing along the streets in the daytime were indigent Third World families trying to gain a legal foothold in the good ol' USA.

We went off to West Hollywood, the group of us interested in the upper floors, and talked to the owner, he was a slick suit. He was willing to set the rent at $250 per month per floor. Each floor was 2000 square feet. He was hoping we would renovate the building in the manner that artists do, drywall, lighting, plumbing, refurbished floors, security. The floor I was to take was two stories above street level. On the scale at which the structure was constructed, it was fairly high up there, high enough to be secure from the street plus it had the added attraction of having gargoyles along the architectural moulding outside the windows. We took the deal with a short term lease of two years. I started doing temp work to generate some income and I told my mom about it via telephone and she was unsupportive. I only owned a tubular art design desk with matching chair and a typewriter, a Volkswagen Beetle, blue jeans, t-shirt, leather jacket and some records, in particular Iggy, The Buzzcocks, Wire, Ramones and The Fugs first album. Moving was a breeze.

Ty and I, after much discussion, had decided to attempt to launch a punk rock magazine of our own. We hoped to be more negative and nihilistic in our approach to culture than the current independently published periodicals supporting the new scene. There was Slash out of Hollywood, Flipside from Los Angeles, Search and Destroy from San Francisco, New York Rocker and many more. With the exception of Flipside, all were short-lived. We were not fond of the big business recording industry and we didn't want to adopt the format of the major publications supported by them. There were to be no record reviews with star ratings in our magazine. Just interesting people and a new approach to journalism which we had never attempted. In fact, we didn't know what the hell we were doing. We didn't know anything about printing processes and we had never written anything for publication. We didn't have any money and we didn't have any investors and we had no business plan. We named the new publication, P*NK Magazine. We went about the business of scraping up money and creating articles with photography simultaneously. This was all going on while we were still in our final Bachelor of Arts quarter of college. So, it began as a kind of school project. Ty Eason borrowed money from other students, thousands of dollars.

Liz Taylor's daughter was enrolled there at the Art Institute those last two semesters that I was there. I was deeply in love with her but she didn't have eyes for me. She was pretty and fun-loving and she fit right in with the rest of us up to the point of creating extremely poor taste and genital insertions, something at which my graduating class of '78 excelled. I considered cutting off her head and putting it in a jar of formaldehyde as a kind of pop art project but the negative aspects of that outweighed the positive by too high a margin. Then there was one other inaccessible beauty at the Art Institute with whom I was enamored, the Dean's private secretary named Darcy. She was fresh from Nebraska. She had a beautiful full round ass and a tiny waist and large perfect breasts, a gap between her two front teeth and cascading blond hair. She wore secretarial style clothes exclusively. When she walked by me in the hallway, I would almost fall over on my face. This poor art student was definitely smitten.

I would have asked her out to dinner if I had any fucking money. I would have asked her to go for a cup of coffee if I had a quarter of a dollar to spare. She was not a bohemian type who could appreciate the impecunious lifestyle of a twenty eight year old insecure nihilistic art student. I did have one idea that would at least get me talking to her or maybe better. Unfortunately, I either didn't see or was unwilling to admit the folly of my plan. There were several obvious problems but it was my best shot.

Having had some success with raw beef liver in the recent past, I felt that it might be opportune for me to give it a go again and try to wring out every drop of hard earned success that I could from the organ. I made up a story about a secretary (whom I imagined to be much like Darcy) and storyboarded it in nine panels.

This imagined secretary was disgruntled with her boss who was making her work long hours and weekends on a fixed salary with no additional remuneration. She became so angry over time that she staged a silent protest one day on the job. On the day of protest she got up out of bed and showered, then ate a light breakfast wearing her beige terry cloth bathrobe. She put on her make-up at her bedroom mirror. Then, before putting on her undergarments she broke with her usual routine and returned to the kitchen. She picked up a strip of raw beef liver which she had placed on the cutting board by the kitchen sink at breakfast and with great aplomb inserted it fully up into her rectum until it disappeared within her body. This being done she washed her hands and wiped off her private parts with a moist towel and then proceeded to put on her underwear and then her outer garments.

She had lost almost no time at all and she left her apartment for the office at 8:30 a.m., plenty of time to spare. She worked the whole day with a pleasant professional demeanor, with an occasional wry little smile on her face. She told no one about her secret protest or the manner in which it was staged. After working one hour and a half past the end of the regular work day, she drove home, whereupon she removed the liver from her internal cavity and discarded it. She then prepared a frozen dinner in the microwave, watched TV, talked on the telephone for two hours, and went to bed.

I talked to Darcy in the hall about playing the protagonist in this story. This meant that I would photograph her in a series of stills, getting out of bed in the morning, running around in her bathrobe, eating breakfast, inserting the beef liver into her anus, driving off to work, then sitting at her desk in the deans office in character, and finally possibly a closing shot of her watching TV. The deans office which was the location of her real world job was also to double as my set for the story. Darcy said after thinking about it overnight, that she would be happy to do the project with the exception of the photo of the beef liver being held up against her naked butt. After a few days consideration, she told me that it was all right with her if we used a body double to photograph the hand ready to insert a piece of raw liver up into a bare ladies butt. I told her that we were starting a new magazine and that this was going to be published and that many people would read it and they might possibly think not only that it was her butt, but also that the story was true. She was OK with it if we used a double for the ass shot.

I went over to her apartment one morning and photographed her getting ready for work that morning. Needless to say, I was in heaven on earth just to have gotten that far. She skillfully didn't leave me a window of opportunity to throw her down on the bed and pull open her robe revealing her beautiful naked body still damp from the shower. I did get some great shots of her in her bathrobe, eating breakfast, and driving off to work in her economy vehicle, while I stood behind on the sidewalk with my camera. The photos I took of her in the dean's office also came out splendid and she was smiling warmly.

That same week there was a benefit for The Masque, which was the original punk venue in Hollywood that belonged solely to the rockers themselves. It was staged next door to the art institute at the Elks Lodge Building, which was a monumentally huge building with multiple auditoriums, a gymnasium with a professional boxing ring in it, and a grand foyer with cascading stairs which could hold an entire lavish MGM musical replete with Fred Astaire and Ginger Rogers dancing the night away. Ty and myself booked the video equipment for the weekend and arranged permission from the people putting on the show to shoot videos.

Punks loved to be photographed. That much was easy. It was an exciting event and many of the bands were just absolutely great. There were newspaper reporters there from the major Los Angeles newspapers. They were standing in the crowd taking notes in exactly the same manner as the reporters in the film noir movies do when they've got a scoop. This was prior to his cutting and bleaching his hair and Ty got ridiculed for having long hair by the punk girls. They hated that long hippie hair and they hated hippie music and they hated hippie clothes. Ty changed his persona, he was never the same after that night.

Punk was an attempt at a clean break with the culture of the 1960s. We took probably the first videos of the original L.A. punk bands that night. It was black and white reel to reel videotape. It was definitely of some historical significance. At the end of the night, up on the stage unfortunately, Ty spilled his beer directly into the tape machine so everything was lost. He took me aside and said, "I'm sorry man, I spilled my beer into the tape machine by accident." He was totally shaken by those girls making fun of his hair and he'd knocked down too much beer to compensate. Being up on the stage, he was the object of a hundred insults. We knew the tape was destroyed because it was soaked but we didn't know if the machine itself was broken from the liquid. On Monday, after we had cleaned it up on the outside, we just turned it in as if nothing had happened to it.

The big surprise on Monday was that Ty had not only gotten a short haircut but that he had dyed it bright white and made it stand up vertically in punky spikes. He had become an Insta-Punk. That was the way it happened to everybody who turned out a punk. They transformed. He stopped wearing beach flip-flops on his feet and started wearing black boots. His personality was transformed quite possibly not for the better I might add. Ty was already a handful and now like science fiction he was super-energized by his electric hair and big boots; there was a high voltage electric

SUB-HOLLYWOOD — BRUCE CAEN

plug coming straight out of his asshole and Sex Pistols had just plugged him into the wall socket for the first time. The young man lit up like Las Vegas neon.

We set about the business of publishing the first issue of P*NK Magazine, a rabid underground publication. We had begun living the lifestyle and walking the walk and the outside world in turn had its opinions. The temporary agency sent me on a job to Wells Fargo Bank. At the end of the day my supervisor asked me to soften my haircut a little so it wasn't so spiky when I came back to work the next day. I didn't do it and they fired me on day two.

At the time when Melrose was becoming chic, we began going to the trendy Melrose Avenue stores to solicit advertising for our new magazine which didn't exist yet. It was hard going but we got some ads. Simultaneously, Ty started a nihilistic type of band in which he was the singer-songwriter. It initially had a nonsensical Dadaist name of 'Seeing Eye Dog'. The name of the band changed daily and they began practicing downstairs at the art institute. I was so consumed by the magazine that I forgot about the dean's secretary. Her spoof about the beef liver up the butt was entitled "Linda Modern." After the first issue of P*NK was published with her piece in it, the dean summarily fired her. I didn't find out about that until years later.

We published that first issue of P*NK out of the loft I had rented on Broadway. Because of the scatological nature of much of the material we had a problem finding a printer that would print it. That first issue was printed on an offset web press in tabloid format on newsprint in black and white only. We found a Mexican printer in San Francisco named Arturo, a former zoot suit so he claimed, who would print it for cash in advance only. He said that he was one of the original L.A. zoot suits and he was missing a finger on his right hand which counted for something. Arturo had a huge printing operation but he was glad to take our cash, which was three thousand dollars. He did a great job considering that we had the paste-up skills of a pair of elephants. My mom saw the magazines because we were up in the San Francisco Bay Area for the printing and she was unimpressed to say the least. The punk band 'X' was on the cover. Ty Eason met my mom and he didn't like her.

Back in L.A., life in the loft was a little bit rough. There was no shower but there was a great firehose. When Ty was downtown I'd have him hose me off with the firehose while I stood nude out on the fire escape over the alley between buildings. Other times I would drag the firehose out there myself. There would rise up from the abyss below a moaning hue and cry coming from the street bums living in the lee of the building. Other times, I would shower at the art institute although I had now graduated (with little pomp and ceremony).

We improvised for toilets; one sink on the floor was designated for peeing in. I had a professional plumber come in and he quoted me an astronomical sum to install a functioning toilet on my floor. He said that it had to be vented up on the roof and he would have to run some bullshit up the outside of the building that would have to meet the special city codes and the bill for that would give him enough money for the down payment on a small mansion once owned by Jane Mansfield in Belair Estates. Either that or I could shit on the floor.

In this problem was bundled the essential hustle by the landlord. He expected us to pay for those improvements in return for cheap rent. He never expected any of us to be so primitive as to work around the toilet problem. I don't know what the other residents chose as their option but I chose the latter one, shit on the floor. There was a large public restroom on the fifth floor with several toilets. They were a vision of hell on earth. Those five toilets looked like they had been stopped up since the First World War and they had been growing a new mutant species of multicolored goo-fungus for the past fifty years. Imagine if you can, a fifty year old floating turd in a clogged toilet multiplied by five toilets. Fixing five of those would have bought the plumber another mansion and besides the fifth floor wasn't my floor. My floor number was three and even if those five upper bogs were flushing, it was a long lonely walk up to floor five to do business. I could afford to purchase a man-sized bucket from the hardware store, plastic garbage bags, and a set of brown paper lunch sacks. So that was how I did it. Put the plastic bag in the bucket, then sit on that in the middle of the floor. When finished, I would put that whole package in a brown paper lunch sack and casually drop it off in the public trash can on the street in the morning. Pity the poor indigent looking for a bite to eat. That was my solution to city codes.

I never watched a movie in the theater on the ground floor of the Broadway Arcade building because there was a good chance that more than one of the patrons would murder me. Wilson Pickett's '60s soul song title 'Funky Funky Broadway' surely applied to that historic section of Broadway in downtown Los Angeles in 1977. The dialogue of the films playing in the Arcade Theater was always in English, while many of the other theaters on Broadway were running Spanish dialogue exclusively. The snack concession in the theater had one of those rotating carousels for hot dogs where the happy wieners ride around on display like they are on a small Ferris Wheel while glistening with twinkling beads of sweat as they are lit up from lights inside the display. It made the hot dogs appear to be plump easy riders enjoying their evening.

One evening a party of us new denizens of the Arcade Theater building, including my friend Larry Benton, went down into the basement under the building to explore. Just the alley alone, outside the entrance to the upper floors of the building was a poignant experience. There were some big super-sized rats scampering around, rivaling some smaller breeds of dogs in size and personality. Protecting our entrance from the crowded street traffic on foot was a heavy duty steel door about fifteen feet high which required a key on the west sidewalk side and then the walkway blind alley terminated on the east side by a contiguous structure or another part of the same structure, it was hard to tell. It smelled so bad there from stale trash and raw sewage that it was too unsavory to stand around and contemplate the turn-of-the-century architecture.

The group of us Arcade residents, five or six, descended under the building. This was an entirely new terrain from the alley, a subterranean labyrinth beneath Los Angeles which was seemingly endless. We had one flashlight for the group. We walked around down there for a long time and feared we might get lost. It was not unlike the endless descending labyrinths H.P. Lovecraft imagined as gateways to the underworld of primeval gods and damned creatures except that what we found down there was considerably more dark, dirty and boring, no ancient deities to supplicate and fear. When we doubled back through the dirt and rubble, we returned unintentionally by a different route than we had departed and when we came upon a dusty brick room directly under the theater lobby with an uneven rough dirt floor, we perceived a flickering eerie blue flame. We moved up on it as a group with our single flashlight and there revealed was a large five gallon, used, dirty tar bucket with a propane campers torch under it. Inside the tar bucket was boiling water churning with a dozen soiled brackish weenies, bubbling and tumbling, destined soon no doubt for the display carousel up above, and ultimately for the mouths of theater goers positioned at the bottom of the American economic ladder. We went back upstairs.

A few Saturday nights later into summertime, about one a.m., there was a serious breach in security. You would have thought that no one could get through the fifteen foot high steel door interfacing with the Broadway sidewalk, and then to open the automatic deadbolt lock allowing access to the interior of the upper floors was another impossibility. Once inside, each floor was locked from access via the stairwell. We were safe from the turmoil of the streets.

I was laying around in just a pair of blue jeans on my bed which consisted of a box springs on four plastic milk containers with the windows wide open when this deliciously pretty teenage girl wearing a sparkly short silver dress and high heels climbed in the open window from the narrow stone ledge entablature over Broadway. She had red lipstick on her beautiful lips.

She jumped in the window and said "Hi! How are you doing Ronnie?" Talk about a sex fantasy come true.

I said, "Leda, my god how did you get in here?" It was Leda Lacy who was the girlfriend of one of the guitar players in one of the really big punk groups. Lucky me! When I had met her she was taking a bath with the door wide open and I had just arrived to interview her boyfriend at his apartment on Melrose Avenue in Hollywood. She was all giggles splashing around with indescribably pretty white skin covered with pale freckles and firm little teacup tits and completely unembarrassed by her nudity. She introduced herself to me while sitting in the bathtub and we exchanged laughs.

Somehow, I managed to arrange to interview her on another day all about the weather. I didn't care what I interviewed her about. The boyfriend was a bit chagrined but it was harmless up until tonight. She had a slight southern accent. She was sixteen and he was thirty. I never thought I would get her in bed. Her flimsy sparkly little dress came off so easily. Her breasts didn't need a bra. We talked just a few minutes there on the box springs. She had a tampon inside of her and she pulled it out and I grabbed it and tossed it out the window where it dropped down on the sidewalk in front of the ticket window of the theater. We laughed about it and then we fucked up there in the night over funky L.A. Broadway.

That Rolling Stones song 'Miss You' with the repetitive harmonica riff seemed to be continually blowing in from the street below through the open window past the gargoyle on the breeze. The music from a boom box on the sidewalk was rolling in the open windows with the languid summer evening air. In the morning, she climbed back out on the ledge with her high heels in one hand and left the same way she came in. The goddam security in that building really wasn't working. I asked her how she got up there. She just said, "It's easy!"

Some friends of mine from art school, Trey and Wanda, moved into an old wino flophouse located on skid row at 5th and Wall Streets. They were an intimate couple. Was it love? Who knows. They wanted to live together in the new L.A. art frontier that was downtown of the late '70s. That location made my Broadway studio look like an address on the Yellow Brick Road. The streets smelled of human waste and it was common to see men with open sores filled with maggots living on the unyielding pavement.

Trey and Wanda had to throw out about 60 bedframes, each with a million sad stories of sleeping broken men imbued in every rusted squeaky spring. Gradually, they fashioned that unhappy firetrap hotel into a functioning art studio space and lived in there for nearly ten years. Outside, Skid Row misery happened day in and day out and all through the night. The corners at 5th and Wall streets was the locus of Los Angeles' skid row in 1977-8. Life at the bottom of society gets under your skin if you experience it with regularity. Not everyone has the divine inspiration of Mother Theresa. It breaks you down, the wasted irretrievable human misery. Initially, the artists installed a hidden video camera at street level with a 24 hour live monitor in the main room upstairs. They watched the hideous parade on TV as if this could somehow ameliorate and nullify the reality and put it on the level of conceptual art. As a stratagem for mental health it didn't work. When Trey and Wanda moved away from there several years on, they had really become products of that environment. Hard core drug addiction with the needle and spoon, going uptown sometimes and downtown other times. Gradually, the art impulses subsided and the numbing narcotics and disease took their toll.

The original Los Angeles Hard Rock Cafe was a skid row bar located downstairs and one door over on 5th Street. It is no longer there and the name itself was sold to an upscale restaurant chain. Where these troubled buildings were once standing, the ones that housed my artist friends and the bar on that block and a few others, there is a police station today that looks like an fortified military bunker. The surrounding neighborhood has become known as the Los Angeles Toy District and it has been flooded with cheap Asian toys being marketed in countless hole-in-the-wall toy shops.

Inside the original downtown Hard Rock Café there was a circular bar with stools around it standing in the center of a bare shabby room with time-worn linoleum floors, peeling faded white paint on the walls, and malodorous bathrooms in the rear. The bartender stood in the center of the bar with yellow-toothed wizened drinkers perched all around him. I had a few beers in there. It was mostly full of besotted old lonely geezers, the wealthier ones of the neighborhood who could afford a draft beer instead of the dirt cheap bottled port or muscatel. Night Train. They were better company than Night of the Living Dead zombies and they certainly had some stories to tell if the bad breath didn't kill you. There was no big-assed woman strutting around for anyone to fight over, it was a geezer shindig. I'm sure the ladies showed up later but I was only drinking in there in the daytime.

The hardcore skid row denizens of the first years of the new millennium have been pushed amongst the steel-ribbed warehouses and grim shopfronts several blocks south. The All-Night Mission nearby has a sign outside on the sidewalk that warns individuals that they must sleep within the white lines similar to parking spaces in a supermarket lot, bringing some silly order to the chaos of being homeless, destitute, jobless, alcoholic, mentally ill, living without a net in America.

My friends Trey and Wanda produced great paintings in their studio next door to the Hard Rock Café in the first few years they resided at 5th and Wall. Then, a few years later on, I saw them at Al's Bar, the skanky trashy downtown Punk rock venue, and they were strung out on heroin. They produced less art. That night they were nonchalantly vomiting on the sidewalk during our conversation outside of Al's Bar. No big deal that, a retch, hurl and gush was no reason to interrupt any conversation. Heroin addicts have a casual relationship with the act of vomiting that's very unlike the vomiting that an inexperienced drinker does. A heroin addict will just casually turn his or her head and toss off a sizeable splash of puke almost with the ease of blowing out a puff of cigarette smoke. When Trey and Wanda performed their keck, spritz and chat, I knew that one of life's little problems had become their problem.

Addicts talk occasionally about an exotic disease called Cotton Fever. Mostly, I heard addicts from San Francisco speak of it. I always found it curious. A person may get the fever when they use the needle frequently. It was explained to me by a friend of mine who took a lot of 'H' that a little fiber of cotton gets into the solution that is injected intravenously and the fiber irritates the brain as it passes through it in such a way that it causes a fever. This fever lasts about 24 hours and the sufferer feels like toasted pigshit for that time and then recovers. The narcotic in solution is strained through a small wad of cotton as it is pulled into the syringe and that's where the fever is generated. I believed that these heroin addicts were crazy with this Cotton Fever talk and that they were just worn out from shooting up all the time. But, I looked it up in the dictionary one day and it actually is listed as a real disease. There is a virus that occasionally attaches itself to a cotton fiber and if a person uses that cotton to strain a drug into a syringe and injects it, Cotton Fever occurs. Only intravenous addicts talk about Cotton Fever. Never heard of it, hmm?

One of the characters who became a permanent fixture downtown at the skid row studio was a diabetic fellow with the moniker Black Dick, and he had a steady supply of legal insulin needles that he carried around in a natty little kit. His kit was a little black briefcase about six inches wide by two inches deep with typical latches and a carrying handle. It was a source of pride and he would flip it open and show off his array of needles and narcotics with little or no provocation. Initially the drug of choice at the Skid Row studio was methamphetamine. Black Dick (he was all white meat) was charismatic to some scenemakers and others found him repulsive. I fell firmly into the latter category. His influence over my school chum, Trey, became a dominant factor in his life to his detriment. BD was also a talented performer during the early days of the L.A. punk rock scene. In addition, he was part owner of an early prototype indie label Badwater Records, which germinated many grass roots seeds of musical creativity and independence establishing a precedent for a zillion other indie labels to follow. In fact, he was one of the most entertaining and amusing performers associated with early punk around L.A. His shows were always full of biting satire and a burlesque kind of comedy centered around the theme of the well-known mass media musical heroes. Black Dick didn't truly play punk rock music. He satirized other popular hip and trendy commercial recording stars and he could be an outrageously funny performer on a good night.

Within the initial small subculture, the punk hoi polloi hated him personally and they had their own private reasons stemming from insane and vicious things he had done to them or said about them. For bread and butter (so to speak) commonly known as money, BD was a fast talking telephone solicitor pushing some kind of office supplies to people working in Nebraska and Oklahoma etc., middle America. After shooting speed, he could apparently sell anything and his skills as a salesman of cheap office supplies achieved a legendary status around Hollywood. He could sell a bunch of junk over the telephone to an unsuspecting secretary in the midwest better than Ronald Reagan could sell the right wing to the working class.

I enjoyed the Black Dick's musical act but the man gave me the creeps. It was a sort of visceral animal fear I experienced when he came into the room. He enjoyed being malicious. Although he was chubby, he also had a romantic attraction about him for the many people who saw him as a rock star and punk record company power broker and they were flattered to be hanging out in his company.

That is what Hollywood is all about. There are a million crazy bastards around L.A. with Hollywood Star Attractions Vibe Magnets taking advantage of a million other lost and bedazzled souls looking for star power to attract them. Microcosmic rock stars, producers, club owners and management in small cultish style movements are abundant. Star pow-pow-power. People want to get next to it. Punk Rock in Hollywood was once just such a micro-movement. Initially sales of only several thousand indie records were considered an L.A. punk rock success, although the influence of the early Los Angeles punk recordings has been massive.

During the period we're talking about now '77-'80 there was no AIDS and there was a lot of narcotic needle use on the West Coast. In spite of the negatives, American punk music has lived on as a viable outlet for youthful expression. Drugs and punk are two separate entities. Punk music doesn't need or equate to drug abuse. Does the music have the same meaning after so many years? That is a complex question and the answer should be yes it does and no it doesn't. Playing in punk bands is far better than sticking up mini-markets and a million other things that can entertain a young person. Consider the communication skills that are honed and sharpened while playing with electronics and vociferously voicing caustic lyrics.

In 1978, there was the predictable rumor circulating around about Black Dick and the size and color of his close friend Mr. Johnson. Basically, it was rumored that his Johnson, which was of notable size according to gossip, was of a dark brown color from the base at the torso to its uncut tippy tip due to a painful and expensive tattoo job. He encouraged this rumor no doubt. It would be more accurate, according to my second hand but reliable sources to state that it was only temporarily colored dark brown on various festive occasions due to a variety of different topical treatments. All accounts of its large size remain constant coming up just short of movie star cowboy Roy Roger's horse Trigger which is stuffed and on display in a museum in Victorville California, although to be accurate, I read that they're moving the museum to Branson Missouri. Good idea. There is also a strong possibility that there may have been some legerdemain, the switching of a dark prosthetic for the real deal when Mr. Johnson came into public view at a party. Black Dick loved a good joke.

AT THE FROLIC ROOM ON HOLLYWOOD BLVD: "Joe, have you met Tony Freep? He produced Artificial Flowers new record. Tony, this is Joe, he plays toy piano in Melted Rocky Road Ice Cream."

"Sounds like bum trip to the bathroom. I've never heard of them. Have they been together long?"

"We opened for Three-Legged Pope on the Southern California leg of their world tour."

"Three-Legged Pope, they used to be really cool but they've run out of good material. Their last album 'Pray for Duh!' was really dull, don't you think?"

"I thought so too. Well, they completely sold out. We stayed in our own dressing room and didn't party with them for almost the entire time. We really dig your work with Artificial Flowers. We're looking for a hot producer to work on our demo."

"Well Joe, would you mind sticking your nose way far up my ass so that it picks up some earth colors. Where are you guys from?"

"We're from Carpenteria. That's north of L.A. about a hundred miles. But we all live in Hollywood now, except for Eric the bass player, he has a girlfriend who wants to have a baby and she doesn't want to live in L.A. so he commutes."

"The way life works in Hollywood Joe is that if you crawl far enough up the right asshole you can build a lovely condo up there and maybe so much more. The Artificial Flowers have been very happy with our arrangement. Why don't you talk to Brian and he can call me or he has my office number and he can give it to you

99

and we can set up a meeting and get something going. I see Joy Velvet over there and I want to say hi. Nice meeting you."

"Joe, he wanted you to stick your nose way up his ass, show some initiative. What is wrong with you?"

"Brian, I had it so far up your ass that I couldn't pull it out fast enough. I must have looked stupid. I shouldn't have mentioned Three-Legged Pope."

"Joe, Tony Freep created Three-Legged Pope and then they left him to go with Media Shark. It was a big mess and now Three-Legged Pope is huge and Tony is suing them for twenty five million dollars. I though you knew that. It's all right. You didn't say anything really stupid. Put your nose back up my ass where I like it and let's go have a drink at the bar. Let me buy you a drink. What'll you have?"

"I'd like a martini very dry, extremely dry, just go extra light on the vermouth."

"You are ordering straight gin big guy. Is that really what you want?"

"Oh. Well then, I'll have just a regular martini with two olives without pimentos."

"You want a beer?"

"A Heiniken."

"Jimmy...two Budweisers over here."

Late in 1977, Ty Eason and myself started working on the second issue of P*NK Magazine in the Arcade Theater building. L.A.'s original high-class theater district was beat to hell by '77 all right, but not in the sense of '50s hip culture. Over time, Broadway had its fancy ass kicked. It was as if the beautifully ornate architecture of the district had been sent down to the stinking well of Hades dipped in destructo garbage sauce and then returned to the surface complete with a tainted population of extremely poor tragic people. We came to live in there with them, above them actually. The new issue of P*NK magazine was characterized by lurid pictorial features, presenting a male cadaver having its throat cut open on the front cover. An artist that I had known at the art college gave me a stack of these sicko pictures cut out of university library books surreptitiously with a razor blade. We were a small enough publication at the time that we could steal and reprint photos with impunity. We were flying like bats under the radar with regard to copyright infringement.

The huge yellow landmark record store, Power Records, up on the Sunset Strip was terrorized by this content when it was published. The cover photo was rendered in a stark black and white graphic style in the manner of Andy Warhols' 'Race Riot' silkscreen image of the '60s. This for them was going too far beyond punk music and its compartmentalization as a definable music style. The store manager who was responsible for buying and merchandising periodicals there came out to talk to me and he was pouring with sweat from nervousness. His thinning hair was combed at the part and matted and he wore a white shirt and black tie loosely done; black rimmed eyeglasses were perched precariously on his nose.

He behaved as though he suspected that we were actually killing people and quite possibly eating the tasty parts of some of them in savory sauces at dinner parties. This was definitely a step up the ladder of civilization from consuming uncooked victims but not far enough along the evolutionary chain for lunch and a beer and talk of a distribution deal. The record store wanted to appear to be 'hip' and they wanted to increase their cachet with the public by following the current trends but cadavers in a rock magazine, realistic photo stories about trendy parties with human cannibalism in Hollywood, further augmented by illustrated tales of female circumcision in Africa were all beyond the line of propriety. For the record, female circumcision was a very real problem for tribal women in Africa and may still be. Maybe 18 months later, the chain store initiated its own in-house magazine and to my surprise, they wanted to interview me and write an exploratory article. To some, I was already becoming normalized.

Advertising for Pasolini's 'Salo: The 120 Days of Sodom' found its way into our pages at that time as well, after the film was banned from mention in the Los Angeles Times and other affluent publications which were taking care to prevent a crisis of morality in America. It was censorship then and they still do that sort of thing routinely at present. We had crossed that proverbial line in the sand which is occasionally drawn by some authoritative persons with a metaphorical disciplinary stick and proprietorship of some dominion, moral and property. It's so hard to shock people with art but just shaking up the contextual use of the content a little bit really did the job. This to me, was a petite morsel of artistic success and very satisfying although not at all lucrative. By those who didn't get the black Bunuelian humor, P*NK magazine was feared and loathed.

Along these lines, San Francisco was to become a sales headache with its increasing emphasis over time on political correctness. The era of John Waters 'Pink Flamingos' outrageous laughter was giving way to a rigid stylistic correctness. The English fell victim to the intransigent dictates of political correctness as the '80s developed and to them, we were anathema. P*NK Magazine pushed the boundaries of a genre music publication in completely irrational directions and it was up against a set of new taboos in the new politically correct chic, a philosophy rife in Great Britain and an intrinsically humorless mindset. If this was a boxing match and the bell was rung, then blammo, P*NK Magazine was down and out in the second minute of round one. Saved by the bell, uh oh, it's down again!

Several problems developed downtown. Ty and I started cat fighting about the second issue. We definitely weren't in agreement about the way things should be presented. The fights got progressively worse. In addition, a nerdish artist tenant downstairs, Nelson, began to toss his noodles and I became the object of his anger. I was in his studio one time only and I saw that he had some sort of intense packrat maze situation going on down there. A human packrat. Endless filthy junk that created a quirky sickening labyrinth of narrow paths from floor to ceiling with no purpose, this was his odd world of Nelson. He looked a little psychotic. We were definitely in much better mental health upstairs with punk rock and autopsy photos and beer.

I figured Nelson wasn't some sort of environmental design artist or primitive back to the basics type but rather he was a freeform trash spelunker who delighted in tunneling through mounds of stale carpet remnants and acquired bric-a-brac. That was how my deceased pet rats behaved after I started feeding them rat poison. They tunneled in the saw dust and cloth scraps. Nelson never directly expressed his problems with me. Other tenants in the building told me repeatedly that he was angry and then the landlord began phoning me and endlessly reiterating Nelson's grievances. Nelson was disturbed by the typing from my Olivetti typewriter and the occasional sound of a chair moving away from a table at night. He was ultra-sound sensitive. This was in a building with windows facing Broadway, fifteen foot high ceilings, nine inch thick concrete floors, and two thousand square feet of raw floor space per studio in which to roam.

Initially, my electric razor was stolen and it was found broken in the stairwell by Larry Benton, who was occupying the grungy seventh floor penthouse. Then even stranger, someone came into my studio when I was away and smashed and stomped my pristine first edition recording, "The Fugs First Album" a pop trash relic from the 1960s that was irreplaceable. Who would do such a terrible crime? Destroy The Fugs? These were two small violations. Larry told me that Nelson had been running up and down the stairs with a loaded handgun and he intended to shoot me. Right about then, I took another trip up to Arturo the printer in San Francisco to get the second issue out. Ty Eason, in my absence, staged a gala magazine party at his studio in Pasadena in celebration of the new issue but he forgot to invite me. In fact, he never told me about it. Then when I returned the next week, my studio had been flooded by someone as a nasty joke.

A daft person with bad sprinkling intentions had got serious with the firehose and let it run for a long period of time. There was four inches of water under my bed and

I came back with the flu and just went to sleep over the water for three days. That water just wouldn't evaporate. It must not have leaked onto Nelson's head down below or he would have surely shot me dead. I moved out.

Ty Eason quit the publication. After playing a few tentative shows with his L.A. musical group 'Seeing Eye Dog' and other names, wearing his new white spiky hair, he moved to New York City on the heels of Lisa from my painting class. In L.A., the other musicians in his band leaked some gossip that they hated him because he insisted on complete domination over them. Like other performers he had a deep need to stand up in front of crowds of people and be their sole focus of attention and admiration. Unlike other performers, he had an extremely morbid aesthetic. Eventually his sound developed into a repetitive drone death knell kind of industrial music with darkly visceral lyrics. It was an intellectually tormented good bad sound. Ty Eason did many recordings which were artistically successful and he gained an international audience. They liked him in Germany. He attracted the same sort of audience as Einsturzende Neubauten and Throbbing Gristle. He rarely returned to L.A.

I moved to an office space on the corner of Hollywood Boulevard and Las Palmas Ave., into what was called "The Pioneer Spirit Building". There were many offices in the building occupied by businessmen such as myself who couldn't afford a proper apartment but who needed the professionalism that an office environment provided. The Hollywood Boulevard address gave us professionals living there that extra razmatazz.

The manager of the building was the man who ran the shoe shine stand down on the sidewalk at the Hollywood Boulevard entrance. His name was Cowboy Brown and he was an African American man, a gentleman in his late '60s, who wore a Stetson cowboy hat. He also had a nephew who was not yet of drinking age who went by the moniker of Young CB, and he studied at college law school. Unlike his uncle, Young CB never wore a cowboy hat. Down the hall from me was the modern dance instructor Bill, who was also a black man, and he was very handsome with a completely bald head. His space was a nicely turned out dance studio with a polished wooden floor which faced the rear of the building and overlooked the vast commercial parking lot that stretched the length of the block behind all the build-ings along the north side of Hollywood Blvd. There was no parking structure back there just an amorphous lot with hundreds of parking spaces drawn out on the rough tarmacadam surface. There was a uniformed attendant who stood at each end of the lot in a little concession structure not much larger that a phone booth.

Next door to me was another African American man who wore a derby hat and the sign on his office door stated that he was a theatrical talent agent. We said "Hi" but never talked too much. My windows overlooked Hollywood Boulevard and on the Las Palmas side, an Indian Tandoori Restaurant and a Hollywood poster and memorabilia shop. The Indian restaurant always reeked of insecticide and marsala spices and The Hollywood Collectors Poster Shop which was next to it was just bursting at the seams with memorabilia. My office was a pair of corner rooms divided in two by a glass door in a partition wall with high ceilings and two skylights with no toilet or running water. The public bathroom which was down the hall about four doors had no showers. Only the public that could get past Cowboy Brown at the shine stand was allowed upstairs. He watched everyone. One block up at the north end of Las Palmas was the liquor store and beneath me on Hollywood Boulevard was a pizza parlor. I could get along with that arrangement.

We weren't supposed to live in there but Cowboy Brown turned a blind eye to it if we were kool and didn't get rowdy. Life on Hollywood Boulevard had a million ways of becoming rapidly unruly and lawless that a person could never anticipate. There always was some kind of crazy infectious energy coming up off of the street. And there were unsavoury goings on, that were in the habit of going on most all the time. That street corner was a strange hoochie-coochie magnet.

In the month of May, a small army of white trash guys would arrive like clock-work, by hitchhiking or grey dog bus and stay through to the end of summer. They looked like hardcore bikers but they didn't have one bike between them. These guys didn't have the class of one half a Hell's Angel. The white trashers lived on the streets all summer and they never worked and they didn't have money. They came to Hollywood for a good time. These scum-bummers managed to stay drunk or stoned and slept in alleyways and crawl spaces or abandoned buildings. A number of these guys made the Las Palmas sidewalks their home; the ones whom I observed on a daily basis, would hang out in shadowy groups under this big tree that was behind the liquor store up on Las Palmas Ave at Yucca.

A knowledgeable person wanted to steer clear of that tree at night because a few of them might jump out suddenly to greet you. They all carried lockback buck knives and held a primitive philosophy of life. The white trashers also slept and partied in back alleyways, stairwells and trash bin alcoves in the rear of fashion and souvenir shops that faced Hollywood Boulevard on the south side where there were no parking lot kiosks. Basically, they were straggling all over the place and they weren't as adaptive and intelligent as the runaway teens along the boulevard. These transient guys were older than teenagers and they seemed to be solely in pursuit of earthly delights. They came for sexgirls and drugs and parties on that theme. They were a unique class of macho summer street thug migrating tourists.

By the fourth week of summer after they found no California girls were interested in them for obvious reasons, they started dating the black transgender or transvestite streetwalkers who were in abundance in the neighborhood. By the month of August, the trash tourists were noticeably more unwashed and filthy. These men now seemed extremely happy with what they found for party sex in Hollywood, which was typically a hard black penis in a colorful dress. Down at the Las Palmas end of the building on the second floor there were french doors at the termination of the hallway which overlooked the rear parking lot. They were kept open all summer for fresh air. There was a straight twenty five foot drop with a balustrade for safety. Late in the evening from the hall overlooking the parking lot it wasn't unusual to see the macho badboys giving blowjobs to black guys in dresses inbetween parked cars on the tarmac, or vice versa, while tourists were coming and going to their cars from restaurants and movie houses. I felt privileged to have this bird's eye view of Hollywood at night. All of the ubiquitous tourists that were wandering around were so preoccupied with the embedded stars on Hollywood Boulevard, they never noticed the side show.

There was so much going on along the sidewalks down there on the street. The Vietnam Veterans had a Harley-Davidson motorcycle club that parked in front of the pizza parlor on Hollywood Boulevard every night of the week but their numbers grew especially large on weekends. Some nights there were fifty Harley-Davidsons parked in a row. Those guys were semi-friendly and you always saw the same faces. Vets had a permanent sadness to them and a moral rectitude. You learn to appreciate semi-friendly people on the streets because friendly means you're in for some kind of trouble. The biker vets anchored that corner every night until midnight and I imagine kept it safe from crime just by their presence.

Black Flag formed around this time and their flyers were being pasted up all over Hollywood promoting their shows and recordings. Keith, their singer at the time and his crew of South Bay homies did constant legwork at night with the paste bucket slapping up illegal wild posting. Pettibon's unusual poignant cartoon style drawings on these flyers gave an added dimension to Los Angeles street life. These wild postings punctuated by Pettibon's wry intelligence augmented the band's hardcore image with unusual depth. Pettibon drawings appeared on the first Black Flag record sleeves revealing an uncommonly perverse sophistication. They were the first L.A. punk rock band outside of Hollywood to really kick up some action and they represented not just a stylistic change to an even harder sound but the spread of punk to the vast sprawl of communities beyond the Hollywood purlieus. Black Flag's Greg Ginn was my favorite guitarist. He was inventive and intense. There was plenty of genius spread about in these local Punk Rock groups, X, The Germs, The Weirdos, The Deadbeats, The Alleycats, The Plugz, The Screamers, Fear, and Black Flag, Wall of Voodoo. Then The Gun Club, Circle Jerks and Social Distortion appeared.

A huge scene was developing and there was no recording industry support for Los Angeles punk bands and that fact in itself kept P*NK Magazine afloat. Moreover, that lack of industry support helped to make the scene really fun. I knew also that when the recording industry did manage to move in and put the wraps on punk that it was the end of my publication. The recording industry would only tolerate total control. I could have done an A&R job. I had the chops. I'd lived with it in my family through my teen years. Then I punched the record industry in the face and it ran out of the house screaming. If I had stuck my nose up in the right place and kissed a pair of dirty sleazeballs hanging below a fat ass after my sister divorced it, I could have been nurtured as a little junior exec, a ball licker at first but soon I would have acquired that magic coveted corporate power.

Black Flag from the South Bay pioneered their own record company and many other Indie record labels popped up along with new avenues of distribution. P*NK Magazine was able to get these new Indie label product distributors to carry the magazines and market them everywhere that the non-industry records were sold. A typical pressing of a Los Angeles punk rock indie record in those early days was 10,000 copies or less. The Germs early single 'Lexicon Devil' initially sold for $1.50 by mail order. In spite of their small numbers the influence of the records from these early days was enormous. Some of the best bands, like The Screamers never left a legacy of recording.

This small independent group of musicians and artists was what kept me interested and once the whole scene went upscale to the big time I knew that I wasn't going to make the leap. Times would eventually change and when they did I would have to go do something else. Darby Crash, the Germs singer said to me one day as we were talking on the sidewalk on Hollywood Boulevard, downstairs from my office in front of the pizza parlor, that the only way that punk could keep its essence and continue to make a vital statement was to keep changing and negating itself before the greedy fat cats could package it up into another media product. He was thinking dialectically and I thought that with guys like him up front the whole movement was in pretty good shape. Darby moved like a wild leopard onstage stalking wild-eyed shirtless back and forth before his audience. He soon killed himself.

CHAPTER 6

HOLLYWOOD IS TALKING ABOUT GEZA X: Geza X was born in a quonset hut in Warsaw, Peru, in 1909. Memories of famine, early morning migraines, and petticoats that his parent had soiled unfold in the manic recollections of his first days on earth. Prompted by electronic gadgetry as an infant, the result of telecommunications with an off-balance washing machine left by G.I.'s during the Indo-Crustacean War, he learned to differentiate between the ancient music of the spheres and the music of worn nylon bearings expressing their (albeit mechano-dysfunctional) tormented polyrhythms, graced by their groanings of mechanical tragedy. The next step was chaos!

The son of a crashed spaced alien UFO 'Queen' that escaped Area 51 disguised as a female Chupacabra who ran a bondage parlour using medical instruments as a means of torture to American soldiers, Geza X glimpsed his own destiny as one far from any socially sanctioned profession. Experimenting on his own with his father's medical instruments, Geza X enacted a post-WWII scene of frenzied self-experiment creating a self-defined womb-laboratory that nurtured the infant creative genius. Personal investigation led him to believe that something odd was going on in life — he began to suspect that his father had impregnated himself by the use of his own non-human surgical contrivances. Geza X who had been prodding and poking at his own body, being one of the first precursors of the post-war fad in body art, soon realized that his self-mutilation was a dead end.

Perplexed, he unhesitatingly quizzed his cheerful father whom he affectionately called 'mommy man' about what might be the nature of his future, since he apparently wasn't cut out to scale the heights of medical science. His mommy also played the ukulele to hula tunes. This could be his first musical influence albeit confused by the over-abundance of medical toys with which he and 'mommy' wrangled. Geza X remembered the abundant storehouse of musi-medical information he had absorbed in the womb when his obsessive-compulsive 'mommy-man' had placed a 'music-box' next to his-her inflated womb and played Xavier Cugat's 'Music From Death Space' in his pre-natal state. These sounds proved to be the seeds of his almost Freudian preoccupations with music as analogy to masturbation and self-inflicted scar-tattoos. His needs for social annihilation met, he began his quest for anthropological vibe-clues to the nature of human civilization and social torture-taboos which influence negative behavior in seven tenths of individuals without their consent, and learned to falsify information magnificently much to his credit (this may be the only explanation for his otherwise questionable survival in an era of witch-brackets and feed-hand-tampons generated by shame greed motivation).

Even as a mature adult of his species, he constantly tests his penis theories by placing a nylon stocking around his turgid(!) member and experimenting with blood pressure deprivation scenarios; hoping to devise a no-contest thinktank solution to the injustices from which he feels all civilization suffers. "These are no idle whims." states Geza. "Systems analysis proves that civilization is a foreign entity, introduced into our society by false ad campaigns and over-suggestions of warmth and safety in an otherwise disconsolate society. Bad breath, vaginal odor, and underarm reek are all reflections on a reflective or reflexive mania generated by our mentors 'The Doom Crystals' in their natural state. Some dispute the existence of these highly trained logic puzzles, but the evidence is overwhelmingly in their favor. Men masturbate for much the same reason as they bleed: defiance of all natural laws while manifesting them nevertheless. Human consciousness is stuck in a malarial rut."

These feverish preoccupations became convulsive obsessions driving the precocious young rebel Geza X as his pulse throbbed to delirious tribal nightmares drifting frantic on the airwaves into Antsohimbondrona, Madagascar, a dropzone and landing point for disk shaped space vehicles fueling up on methane from planet Uranus, from the American black ghettos via the sole all night rock station in Madagascar, WMAD radio. Playing negro blues as a transient musician, Geza X soon found himself on a passenger ship to New York, entertaining nightly to the formally dressed passengers around the swimming pool on the great luxury liner Queen Mary XIX.

A new era of social unrest at hand, Geza X penetrated our shores in what was at that time a one man crusade, crossing and recrossing our proud land, singing songs of protest and social awareness, social injustice and utopia, aesthetic awareness and religious revelation to a confused sports-crazed public in a style that was soon to catch on with the more avant-garde musicians of the decade, influencing them in their formative stages during the late 1950s and early '60s. The broad appeal of Geza X's viewpoint, a consequence of his experiences in post-war Europe, was immediately appreciated and soon to be further emulated.

A freak meeting with a young Jewish homosexual in a gay bar in Des Moines proved fruitful to the music of the 1960s, although not to the unselfish and rabid genius Geza. "I was really quite bored with all that liberal mush.", says Geza X, "It was just a childish phase of the general populace but never something that I entertained with any seriousness." After long hours of intellectual discourse, smoking reefers and acting generally hip, Geza X persuaded this transient musician, a traveller similar to himself only in lightness of his gear, to broaden the scope of his songs. "One song in particular remains conspicuous in my mind." asserts Geza. "I convinced him to broaden the thematic scope of the song...'Blowin' in the Wind'...from one of gay liberation to a theme of broader social import, one which would involve the greater consciousness of the whole populace."

Although such freak encounters were rare, young Geza X felt that his electro-mechanical yearnings would be surfeit if he did not unify his difficult and oftentimes disturbing anthro-dynamic concept into one bold tableau — a tapestry of social physics so socially defiant yet so self-defined, that it could become the overriding and far reaching principle of an era, much as a sperm subtly influences the climate within the womb to cancerously replicate its own genetic structure endlessly until a new form is established. This was the beginning of 'social seeding' as we know it. Locked in the hold of a cargo carrier, Geza was struggling to redefine reality. It was on one of these nauseating seafaring voyages that his legendary encounter with the aborigines began. Many speculate that this nine year period provided the groundwork for Geza's unique viewpoint on civilization.

Iceland has few deserts but such as they are, they are impenetrable. When the Icelandic gypsy aborigines attempted to steal the cargo of dogskins that the 'Nikon Traveller' had been carrying, naturally they were speared on sight, but trade routes being what they are, when the dogskins reached the market they landed in the hands of aborigine prince Chee-Whip along with their unexpected stowaway passenger Geza X. Chee-Whip proved to be Geza's mentor, training him in Iclandic mastur-bation rituals until he felt bold enough to invoke the 'Glue-Eyed God' himself. With Chee-Whip's blessing Geza X began his study of electronics and science, hoping to unite the ancient frenzy of ritual exposure with modern technology. The electro-musical counterpoint to primitive emotion was being established, along with hints of a new telepathy; not simple mindreading, but an entire emotion sensing appa-ratus ground from the wheels of apathy and misfortune by a dedicated and gullible pack of followers known to the public as 'Geza's Few'. As Geza X once stated back in the early days, "Some people don't know shit from shoeshine."

It was then, in the early 1970s that the great negro purges began. Geza X, fearless and unshakable, elected to singlehandedly preserve the memory of Negro music along with his new found dream of White Urban Voodoo. Through these troubled times, life was not easy. A squad of superpolicemen known as The Logic Squad was attempting to erase every trace of negro music, pseudo-science, koo-koo pop, masturbation, and telepathy from public memory, and thus from the entire planet Earth.

This bleak period in history was further compounded by the suppression of the electro-acoustic muscular phenomenon commonly termed 'dancing'. According to Doctor X "This involves a subtle interplay of neural impulses and theta brainwave patterns which create muscular disruptions in the large majority of participants." Geza vowed to document the history of dancing through this dark age. He sat for untold hours in his metal-studded black leather hut by the Caspian Sea, translating musical documents from the original Negro dialects and including his observations on schizophrenia and masturbation. This huge body of literature stands alone in history as the definitive commentary on racial memory, group ritual, and the leanings of the impending fissures of doom. However, these violent paroxysms of thought did not go unnoticed for long by The Logic Squad. They soon made it their sacred duty to persecute 'Geza's Few' and to permanently abolish this last trace of Negro rhythm. 'Geza's Few' were relentlessly tortured but, idiot savants that they were, these first followers of the faith offered no apology, and no clue to their master's whereabouts.

The Nobel Prize for Peace within his reach, Geza X beat a path for Hollywood in 1977. It began as a bleak year, riddled with cheap cons, backyard champagne picnic politics and illegal tax dodges. Secret negotiations were underway between The White House and the recording industry. Master tapes were being blessed at a Satanist Temple in Beverly Hills, pressed in plastic explosive and sent by the billions to Communist bloc countries around the world; hypnotizing the Red Communists with their insipid mutation of mariachi known to the entire world as 'disco' music. As one overexcited record executive put it, "Gold? Platinum? Hell, we're shipping Plutonium! They'll never send these records back!"

Stomach wrenched into monkey knots with disgust, the ever-zealous and justice crazed Geza X swore revenge for the political faux-pas that had cost him his nose. It is a little known secret that Geza X had his nose shot off in a firearms mishap in Dallas, Texas, on November 22, 1963, and now maintains in place a well-concealed plastic prosthesis due to the miracle of cosmetic surgery. Thus he began his descent into the sordid bowels of the big money recording industry armed only with Sucrets lozenges and the truth. His three year one man campaign of terrorism is so often roundly retold generation after generation at family gatherings that there is no further need to elaborate on it here, save to mention that the closing years of the decade were marked by open civil war on the streets of Hollywood with Geza X leading the Revolutionary Protest Movement (RPM) to bloody victory single-handedly crushing the cigar-belching cancerous fatcats spines.

The Suffering-Artists-Of-The-Fourth-World-Post-Negro-Musical-Militia waited patiently in the wings, knowing that their time had come. And what became of these murderous phonograph records? Every freedom-loving man, woman and child was put to work pressing counter-anti-record-records. These were subsequently broadcast on every radio station in the world not controlled by the Arab petroleum cartels, warning the public of the dangers of the ultra-low-computer generated frequencies present on the bogus 'disco' records. "These demon frequencies," began Geza X in his famous impassioned speech of 1980, "will be certain to cause incurable brainwave disruptions, and the friction of the needle will create enough heat to set off the plastic explosive, instantly killing your loved ones. I beg you!" he concluded, "Don't let this hellish mockery of Negro music *burn your booty!*" The epic drama and unbearable emotion of that moment caused Geza to become prematurely insane, and he was hospitalized a broken man. From that day on, he spoke only pidgin English (an admixture of porpoise mating chirps and Oxford accents). Unfortunately, there were only four radio stations in the whole world not owned by oil cartel Arabs (they had a vested interest in vinyl, a petroleum derivative) so the 'disco boom' continued.

Geza X laughed himself into a coma the next year when he discovered he couldn't understand himself talk. His pidgin dialect-accent had grown so thick you could not have cut through it with a helicopter eggbeater.

CHAPTER 7

PERSONAL LIVE-IN SLAVE WANTED! Time to be adjusted. Only requirement, must have own car and gas. Domestic chores, daily beatings, and live-in slave accommodations. Must be a man over 40 years old. "I'm a mean hateful bitch! I don't let no man touch me. I beat'em or I shit on 'em. They know if they touch me, I'll kill 'em. I'll break their bones. Which whip do you like for the photos?"

Mistress Tina billed herself as 'The 300lb Love Goddess' and she was known to be the toughest dominatrix in the city. She lived up toward the hills, off of Franklin Avenue just across Highland, about a quarter mile to the west of my office in a three story '60s style apartment building, stucco, horizontal slab roof, sliding plate glass doors opening onto a tiny functionless veranda large enough to store a bicycle. Two people who were Hollywood Boulevard veterans, a skinny hippie with stringy long hair and a corpulent woman who wore granny glasses and old fashioned bodices, introduced her to me. This curious duo were publishers of one of the several porn tabloids that were sold out of coin stands on the street corners around Los Angeles. They used to hang around punk rock shows occasionally, and they were fellow office neighbors of mine on Hollywood Boulevard. One afternoon, when I was visiting their offices they suggested to me that the massive Mistress might be a good subject for P*NK Magazine to explore. As soon as Mistress Tina got my telephone number, she began calling me.

When I picked up the phone and she would say, "Come over here slave and do my laundry! I'm too big and fat to go up and down the stairs to the laundry room. Don't say no to me! If you want to take pictures of me you have to do what I tell you! Get over here right now slave!"

Myself and Danté, who had become my main photographer and new official co-publisher for the next two years, kept procrastinating. Her reputation as a bone breaker was daunting. As a photographer, Danté Rossetti could handle most situations. He would get right in the middle of a seething punk audience and start shooting pictures of the band playing, right from the floor. He always got great shots. He also got knocked all over the place.

I don't know if his parents named him after the Pre-Raphaelite painter of the same name or if they just plain gave him the name Danté because it rolled off the tongue pleasantly. He was a working class Italian-American guy who had done a little time at a more respectable L.A. art college than the one I attended. Also, he drove a mighty-mighty leadsled, a silver grey '51 Merc with a purring flathead V8, just about the coolest car on the planet as far as I was concerned.

We were a little bit afraid to bop over there across Highland from the P*NK Magazine offices to see the terrible Love Goddess and it took us several weeks to build up the nerve. Finally, we spontaneously decided to surprise her and just knock on her door one friday evening about 7:30. We did some deep breathing to calm down in the parking lot below her apartment and then we walked up the stairs to the third floor and tapped on her door. She opened the door wearing a skimpy petite see-thru black negligee and she said aggressively "What do you want?"

Danté said with a big smile, "We're here from P*NK Magazine and we were hoping to take some pictures of you right now. We want to feature you in an article for the next issue!" We were now all jacked up mentally for this surprise photoshoot and Danté and I pushed through the door hurriedly and with great alacrity like we were going in for a glamour shoot with an international runway model.

The place was extremely cramped and this quality was exaggerated even more by her enormity. She gave us a small tour of her torture devices which consisted primarily of a large selection of serious whips and other bondage accoutrements such as paddles, clubs, cuffs, leather dog collars with spikes on the inside and outside surfaces, ropes and leather belts and lanyards for tying and restraining a person. Her massive form dominated the restricted space of the third floor studio apartment. There was a small kitchen with an adjoining dining area and a doorless entry from the dining area near the plate glass sliding balcony door; this led to the bedroom which had inadequate wiggle room with the double bed, two chests of drawers, a floor to ceiling mirror, and a TV on a table. When the mistress turned around she displaced half the air in any room.

Business hadn't been so good lately and she was hoping that the free publicity would give her a boost. The porn newspaper folks had told me that she didn't have many returning clients because her bonebreaking was a deterrent to repeat business. Her coup de grace torture device was a portable wooden framed toilet apparatus that she kept in the hall closet. She proudly pulled it out into the hallway for us to see. It was painted glossy white on top with a white toilet seat anchored to a sturdy custom made wooden box also painted pristine white. It was about the same size, height and overall dimension as a regular toilet when it was set in place on the floor. It had a swinging trap door in the front.

I stupidly asked, "What's that door for under the seat?"

She said, "That's where he sticks in his head honey, when I crap on him on his face!" I could tell from the distorted grimace that Danté exhibited on his demeanor, that P*NK Magazine's co-publisher was impressed by this last remark.

Being a professional, Danté wasted no time. He started shooting photos of her and she pulled off the panties of her skimpy negligee and bent forward to reveal her corpulent mountain of an ass spreading the cheeks open. Now I was awestruck, frozen with my jaw hanging open. Danté was given a privileged view of her giant clam which challenged the capacities of his wide angle lens. She grabbed a black whip and started whipping her ass as she did the R&B shake and shimmy for the camera lens. Somehow she managed to turn her head back one hundred and eighty degrees to look directly into the camera lens as she lashed her giant ass cheeks.

She passionately screamed "Wesley! Wesley! Wesley!" over and over as she whipped herself with a black leather cat-o-nine-tails.

"Who is Wesley?" I asked.

"Wesley is that no good man who left me who I loved." she said. All in all, the Mistress was very accommodating although she served no refreshments and we asked for none. She was only about thirty years old with dark hair and very fair skin, and she had enormous breasts, as massive as my thighs, that were not artificially enhanced. I would speculate that her breasts were about as big as human breasts ever get in the natural world. It's possible that Mistress Tina had a Guinness World Record pair of breasts going on there but she wasn't interested in that sort of speculation. She was a big angry woman with a broken heart. The Mistress told me that she had been raped as a teenager. This was partly her reason for being a dominatrix. If we stayed a minute too long she was going to beat us. There was no role playing or creation of a campy persona to attract clients with her. Her fantasy was reality. The 300lb Love Goddess was a 20th century Venus of Willendorf and she wanted to beat us severely for admiring her beauty and then there was the matter of her laundry and other chores.

Danté and I said our goodbyes politely and scurried off to safety across Highland Avenue to my office and then we went and had a stiff drink over at Boardners Bar on Cherokee. Danté had always wanted to do high fashion photography and I was typically dragging him into these unsavoury situations. He was usually a great sport, 'a brick' was the English term. We laughed wild and hard in those days.

The truth is that there were a lot of weird people living in Hollywood in 1978-9. That was the city I lived in. It became my aesthetic goal to mix up all this crazy content from around Hollywood and then drop it into the pages of P*NK music magazine and see what the sum of it produced. The result was that P*NK Magazine became a patchwork of genres but it remained essentially a punk rock music magazine.

To me, this eccentricity was the real Hollywood not the fictitious glitz that the entertainment industry manufactured. I admit, P*NK Magazine went overboard with autopsies, cannibalism, and several other manufactured horrors of our own. Nevertheless, from reality we had the real General Hersheybar standing on the corner of Sunset and Vine in a full dress military uniform with a rack of plastic intercontinental ballistic missiles glued to the visor of his general's hat and a General Hersheybar Jr., in training, standing next to him in full top brass regalia but not quite filling out the shoulders of his generals uniform, with a slightly smaller rack of ICBMs adorning his visor. Zsa Zsa LeMay the seven foot transgender Ginger Rogers dancer. The Radiohead Robot Man who walked the streets daily with a strange boombox electronic apparatus fused to his head. The Stick-Mud-Cottage Cheese Man who climbed to the top of telephone poles. At some point, P*NK Magazine became an experiment in black humor, graphic arts, weird people and punk rock music, with a little bit of pop science thrown in. Those weird fucked up people were real sweethearts when it all came right down to it. They were people that I truly liked. The lesson learned may have been that you can't beat the big cheeses with indigenous cannibalism and cadavers. A more intelligent person would have chosen a different path. But my lack of intelligence isn't an issue, it should be clear.

My life had become a miserable Hollywood Tropic of Cancer and I was not a Henry Miller. I wasn't hardened, gritty, intellectual or streetsmart enough of a character to pull it off. On the other hand, being any kind of somebody in Hollywood, even if it was an unsavoury punky publisher type of somebody was definitely light years ahead of being absolutely nobody as an art student. And P*NK Magazine did in fact terrorize a certain sector of the population. Goddam that was fun. This was probably my greatest talent and success. The delightfully sinister combo of cadavers and deformities, dominatrixes and other fringe personas combined with American punk rock put the fear of social chaos into the right thinking citizens and industry professionals who encountered it. The effect on their minds was possibly like scenes from Artaud's "Theater and the Plague" being envisioned on the streets of Los Angeles.

I stayed drunk mostly to get through the harsh realities of living. In addition my office, as I have mentioned, didn't have any running water in it and it was necessary for me to carry in liquids. I kept several cases of beer and malt liquor stashed under the bed and at that time, I was still running over to the art institute to shower. I never drank water. If I ever did take the time to indulge myself in mental depression that was going to be the end of me. On the day that I took a hard sober account of my life, I was washed up. So a large serving of delusion and self deception was necessary for my keeping on. Things rolled along best if I was a little drunk and carefree and in a major denial about my situation but not so drunk that the fear of failure and being tossed out on the street was completely diminished. This worked well for a while until I started having the kind of accidents that happen to alcoholics. These accidents weren't to happen for a while yet.

More than one girlfriend appointed my social schedule. One small accident occurred when my new girlfriend Dana, pushed me playfully into the wired safety glass of my office front door. It broke outward in a torso shaped bulge into the main hallway. There was no time to fix it as we were leaving for San Francisco that night. We spent four intoxicated nights there running wild and bar-hopping. Dana got up onstage at Mabuhay Gardens and sang "Cease To Exist" a song that Charles Manson had written and recorded as a demo in the 1960s before the Tate-LaBianca killings. When I returned to L.A., Cowboy Brown had alerted his nephew Young CB to the infraction of the broken window glass and YCB was on me like a Highway Patrol car with its cherries flashing.

And then there was my girlfriend Valerie. All she had to do was walk into the building off of Hollywood Boulevard and pass the shine stand and I was in trouble. Out of the corner of his eye, Cowboy Brown saw her battered youthful visage. She was having a tough time of it. She came over several times beat up real bad. Sometimes Valerie looked like she had done fifteen rounds with Smokin' Joe Frazier. She had more bumps and lumps and purple contusions than she had space on her head to hold them. Occasionally, in the daytime, we two walked together on Hollywood Boulevard up to Johnnys Steakhouse for lunch; she was a light eater. Even I was surprised at the bizarre shadowy homicidal cretins who would crawl out of dark doorways and crevices when she walked by on the street in the bright Los Angeles sunlight. In spite of her acquaintances, I liked her very much.

There were countless low down, petty criminal sacks of scum living around Hollywood Boulevard that rarely showed their faces out of the shadows. They preyed primarily on the drug addicted strung out social fringes. When I walked up the boulevard with Valerie she would draw out a long trail of 'Night of the Living Dead' style creeps. The effect was similar to sunlight striking shithead vampires. It was their kind that was always beating her up over some little drug deal and another forty dollars. She was bashed up and she had a bright smile behind the contusions. Black eyes, lumps, cuts and bruises were all part of her daily make-up. Cowboy

Brown would say to me that she shouldn't be allowed in the building because she looked so messed up and it was asking for trouble. She upset the tenants. He always let her come on through and upstairs to my office. I took her in when she came over. She had a strong spirit and she had beautiful tits. When the swelling went down on her face, she was a pretty girl. Her mother was apparently some kind of major psycho nightmare with a slowly advancing cancer who had a large inheritance waiting for Valerie when she croaked. Mothers have a tough time of it in this novel. Valerie was the granddaughter of a newspaper magnate from the 1920s, who had gone after the Chicago gangsters.

Valerie came into the office one night and she said that she had just gotten this Valium prescription in a heavy dosage, 20s they're called. She opened the bottle and suddenly tilted it up and started pouring the entire contents into her mouth, fifty or a hundred pills. Some got in there but I smacked the bottle and the rest flew all over the floor in a million places and we spent the next hour picking them up one by one. She wasn't mad, she thought it was funny.

"You're tits are no good to me dead sweetheart." I did my best Bogart.

And on Thanksgiving holiday of 1979, Valerie and myself went up the street to see some friends of hers who were rock musicians and dedicated heroin addicts. These weren't the scumbags who beat her up. The rockers had a holiday party in an old deco style apartment building that just wreaked and oozed of the old Hollywood yesteryears. It had the air of being lavishly decadent coming from an era before we were born, when people could get stoned and party madly in a less densely populated unpolluted city. It was actually located right on Hollywood Boulevard but set back on its grounds from the street some distance. The structure was torn down a few years later to make room for a newer more ugly structure, as is the custom in L.A.

Her friends had made this extravagantly beautiful spread with turkey and stuffing and pumpkin pies and all the trimmings but no one ate a single bite of it because they were junkies. It all just sat there impeccably perfect on the table as if it was a movie prop made of wax. I ate some pumpkin pie. Well, actually I ate quite a bit of it. I will stuff pumpkin pie in my face even if the planet earth itself is exploding. Heroin was a drug I avoided and couldn't afford to buy anyway. I needed speed. I was always trying to cut back on sleep and keep busy. Her friends were as a group all clad in black with hair either bleached out or dyed jet black. They were exceedingly stylish and some kind of fashion precursors to the Gothic death rockers of the next decade. And that was my Thanksgiving in 1979. That pumpkin pie was all mine!

Danté and I photographed an early configuration of Black Flag members at night on Hollywood Boulevard with some sexy punk girls. And while I was adept at organizing this kind of a happening, there were many practicalities of daily life that I was putting aside while I pursued the details of publishing. My intellectual pursuits never developed with an overview of the big picture, schemes of high finance and corporate investors; and I was finding that being an office rat publisher on an underground magazine wasn't terrifically glamorous as a day-to-day grind. Each issue was a strange stew cooked up of social misfits, musicians and local contemporary George Groszs putting pen and ink to paper.

It was a Saturday night on Hollywood Boulevard in the heat of Indian summer and the crowd walking around on the star bedecked sidewalks was very dense. This was what the chamber of commerce had so dishonestly misnamed the Hollywood Walk of Fame, a continuous stream of theater goers, street cruisers, walk-around dates, American tourists, dull locals and movie obsessed eccentrics wearing strange headgear, native Americans, beat cops, bar-hoppers, sidewalk evangelists, runaway street kids, pseudo-neo-glitter pussies, people waiting for the bus, foreign tourists, whiteskinned black patent leather punk girls, skateboarders, fancydress diners, Harley-Davidson bikers forty deep, wannabe rock musicians, magicians, mimes, studded punk rockers, heavy metal headbangers, gangbangers, skinheads, the mentally insane and homeless, break dancers, transvestites, muggers, bad actors, foxy ladies, boom box dance steppers, steroid pimpleback machomen, spandex-wrapped asses, one seven foot tall promenading black man wearing maternity clothes and showing a large-sized bun in his oven with a sign stencilled on his back reading The Pregnant Man, an amphetamine jacked thalidomide deformed dancing dwarf, and just ordinary families. General Hersheybar, the five star general with the ICBM rockets arrayed along the visor of his military hat typically paraded only in the daytime. Military men need to be early risers.

We set up for the photo shoot in front of Fredericks of Hollywood, the crotchless panties and erotic lingerie superstore which was about two and a half blocks east of my office. With the camera flashing on the rock group posing with the pretty girls all painted up like Kings Road punk angels, a crowd of spectators gathered and paused to observe the glam photoshoot. Only the band wasn't a glam band. They were punks. The Power Rat Pack Elvis Presleys Black Flag! One of the guys in the band pushed another band member through the plate glass display window behind which were six to eight mannikens modeling sexy underwear. There was a huge crash of breaking glass and the strident burglar alarm sounded immediately. It was a lucky accident that one of the guys wasn't viciously sliced by a heavy falling razor-sharp shard as he tumbled through the shattering pane onto the display. The random movement of the entire sidewalk froze in stop motion for about ten seconds as all the people within earshot took in the event. We perpetrators of the broken glass ran in six different directions as fast as our feet would carry us. We all landed back up in my office about an hour later. No one had been hurt or arrested. Danté got the shot. We all walked over to Boardners bar on Cherokee and had a few martini cocktails.

Danté and myself organized a fashion shoot unlike any other to be created downtown after midnight beneath the causeways that traverse the L.A. River which has a completely cemented over riverbed, as if nature was wrong and the river needed the hand of man to cosmetically make it look industrial and lifeless. Models wore clothing creations made of various sharp-edged industrial materials, shiny metals and mud, sticks and stems, second hand altered affectations and many tattoos. One of the Go-Gos had a real black eye. These idiosyncrasies were worn by punk girls and guys and a couple of high fashion models and all pieced together as improvisations on the spot. Everything but the kitchen sink was being modeled and the mudman from Venice Beach carefully prepared his sticks and mud and soiled fabrics and then covered himself with cottage cheese over the layers of mud and he disgusted the Go-Gos girl group.

That year plummeted along for me like a vintage Continental black Lincoln accelerating downhill with no brakes. My new girlfriend became my ex-girlfriend, as my lovemaking with Dana came to an end. We had mixed our sexual juices on beds, car seats, floors and sleeping bags, cheap motels, staining fancy plushy loveseats and couches and bedspreads that weren't our own all over Los Angeles and San Francisco. She was ten years younger than me, still a teenager. When she became pregnant after the Thanksgiving holiday, she decided to get an abortion. That red flagged to me that Dana was decisively at the end of her tenure as underground magazine exec girlfriend semen passionflower. For her, the physical pain of it was probably much less than her emotional pain. You must realize by now that I don't really know much about women. I can tell you that for Dana, my opinion was never a consideration. She chose not to give birth to a Hollywood office rat baby.

She invited me down to her parents house in Laguna Beach for Christmas dinner. It was supposed to be an overnighter, maybe for four or five days. Our relations and personal interplay had been strained since she had aborted the baby and I was debating with myself whether to go to Laguna or stay in the office alone. Also, Dana had told me that her dad was a redneck tough guy and she revealed a recent story about him beating up another driver on the freeway after they got in an argument over a lane change or some trifling traffic related incident. The two cars pulled over to the side of the freeway and her daddy got out of the car and started arguing with the driver of the other vehicle. Then her senior citizen daddy beat the stuffings out of the other big man on the side of the road. She said the other driver was less than half her Dad's age and very big and muscular like a football player.

I seriously reasoned with myself whether or not I wanted to meet this ass-kicking paterfamilias of hers. My conclusion was no, that I didn't want to meet the pugilist papa who might beat me to a pulp with a turkey drumstick or worse, but I went with Dana anyway. To place matters in more of a decline, I had come down with a case of crablice, creatures which frequently inhabited the men's room down the hall, and I brought along the A200 Lotion with the intention of killing them off when I got an opportunity to shower down there in her family castle by the sea. All the portents were not in my favor. The chicken gizzards and the tea leaves I was reading were telling me to stay in Hollywood. I could foresee that an unpleasant trip was in my future and I went to meet my fate.

There was a warm fuzzy family dinner awaiting the night we arrived. Dana's immediate family consisted of a little brother in awkward adolescence, an older sister Cathy with whom I had attended art college for two years, and her mom and silver-haired pop. Pop was every bit the nasty prick that Dana had described. What I wasn't prepared for was the germanic paternal nuclear family structure combined with their obvious abundant wealth. I was just a tumbling tumble weed blowing across his golf course out at the country club, an empty dented Budweiser beer can his new white El Dorado Cadillac crushed under its tires, a piece of whitetrash punk his errant daughter dragged in. I came from a destroyed fucked up nuclear family of the lower middle class kind and now what was left of me was sliding down to the lower lower class. By definition, I made bad art in a bad publication and I was dirty and poor and by his standards a failure and a slimeball loser to be tossed out with the evenings trash.

If I had shot that tough old grey-haired stud fuck between the eyes with a Saturday night special with his Christmas turkey between us and his wife and children sitting nearby and then been condemned to death in the California gas chamber, I would have had no regrets and no one in the family who witnessed the crime would have been terribly surprised. After a miserable tense dinner, I told Dana that I thought it would be better if I went back to the office. I would have got down on my knees and kissed Hollywood Boulevard if only I could have been magically transported back. The only reason that I was still there at her poppas was because he was reluctant to beat me up on the front lawn and kick me out bloodied to the curb on a religious holiday. I understood why his daughter became a punk rocker but in truth, they were probably one-and-all a family of Reagan Republicans at heart, just going through some growing pains. She convinced me to stay on through the weekend. Mistake.

I slept on the couch in my clothes in the living room. They gave me a skimpy, short, thin blanket and a pillow. My leather jacket was a lifesaver. You could always count on your punky black leather jacket to keep you warm in a pinch. In the morning, there was family breakfast. It was the same theme continued. Poppa was the petulant king at the end of the table. I guess I was getting a little angry. After breakfast, I was allowed into the bathroom to shower and I deployed the A200, the bane of all crab lice, cleansing and de-lousing my body and then casually leaving the empty A200 bottle on the bathroom counter for the elder lady of the family to discover. That really caused a repressed explosion within the family unit. There apparently isn't a great deal of verbal fighting and screaming in an authoritarian dictatorship type of family. This was my neutron bomb, the buildings were left standing but the people were obliterated.

When we had dinner that evening the entire family all just stared at me wide-eyed and their complete silence was palpable and perilous. I almost spoke aloud the forbidden words.

"Please pass the live crawly A200 lice sauce." I chose life and didn't even fart.

At the end of the evening, a few hours after the endless silent dinner, Dana's dad came out into the den and announced that I had to sleep on the open floor between the dining table and the couch. The couch was off limits. This was not a warm and fuzzy Christmas but a mini-war in Laguna Beach. I was at least filling in some of the lonely empty holes in my heart caused by the Christmas Holidays and possibly it was more entertaining to be an object of loathing by Dana's family than to be alone dining on Fritos Corn Chips and beer. Dana was going to do just fine, and run off with a guitar player or a drummer and fall in love all over again. I was going back to being a curmudgeon punk publisher living in my office.

I had spent a few years sleeping on hardwood floors because it helped with my back problem and also, I often occupied apartments with no furniture because I didn't own any furniture. After I injured my lower back, the 3rd lumbar vertebrae to be precise a few years before, it had taken a short period to get used to the hardness of floors but I had become inured against it. I even grew to like sleeping on a hard floor. It was the creepy crawlies on the floors of the Broadway building and the office in Hollywood that kept me motivated to elevate into the air when I slept. There were no bugs in this Laguna Beach house except for the ones that I brought in, so I slept really well down there with the central heating and when I woke up in the morning the whole family was already sitting at the table eating breakfast. They were all staring at me. I felt like an unwanted tramp dog that was about to be sent to the pound for euthanasia. I raised up from the floor and had some uneasy breakfast hospitality, difficult to swallow under the circumstances, but this morning I left immediately for my offices at Hollywood and Las Palmas. Dana stayed behind with her clan and we were completely entirely finished. It wasn't a charming story book finish but it had to end in some manner if it was going to end. The old man had the decency not to throttle me. Short affairs shouldn't have been so painful by this time because I was having so many of them.

There was an earlier punk magazine called 'Search and Destroy' published out of San Francisco and the publisher of that magazine told me that they planned to run it for a dozen issues and then stop. He had his organization together more than me, but I was determined to see the aesthetic of my publication run through at least a dozen issues. Let it run its course. Quitting no matter how hard the road, was not an option. I was scared as hell in addition to having a great fun time and suffering with melancholy all at once. And Dana, she had a thing for older guys and within a week she was attached to a rockabilly guitar player who was slightly older than me. He made more money and he probably wasn't as big a drinker as I had become. With her dyed black cropped hair and exaggerated eye make-up, foxy girl youth and tough kid clothes, she was a real doll. A year later, she had covered her body with exotic tattoos.

When I got back into the office there was a message on the answering machine, "Hey Ronnie! Are you there? Pick up the phone! Quick turn on the TV if you can hear this! Jimmy Swaggert the evangelist is doing a TV show and he's holding up your magazines. He's calling them immoral trash. He's got your magazines on television. Ronnie pick up the phone! OK this is Larry Benton. Call me back." I think that message came in a couple of days before Christmas eve.

Borracho!...Springtime, in the shadows of Mount Hollywood lie the dirty L.A. streets where I wandered about intoxicated by night; Selma and Yucca, two streets which ran parallel to Hollywood and Sunset Boulevards like infected whores with tracks on their legs. Losing my grip incrementally, a small fragment at a time or by giant leaps on a big day, running out to punky nightclubs with the dedication of a religious zealot, immersing myself in the exploding music scene. I remained dutifully circumspect of the big tree by the liquor store up on Yucca with the bad buck knife guys hiding in it, purchased an afternoon libation, and stopped nearly every lazy sundown at Big Dog Taco down on La Brea between Franklin Avenue and Sunset Boulevard; there I met with our leather clad group of inveterate party goers who gathered regularly for an early, warm-up social howling with the pack.

The host of these evening warm-up parties was a southerner, a large framed jovial young man, who everybody called Big Billy. He had one of those prodigious outgoing southern personalities that spilled out of him like the Chattahoochee River, just flowin' and drawlin' and chatterin' and hostin' the after-seven off-the-clock specialty patrons of the Big Dog Taco stand. Beautiful Dana was a regular there until she broke up with me, but now she wasn't coming around. After the stand closed for the day which was about seven pm, Big Billy would quickly clean up and then he would fill the orange slush machine with a quart of cheap vodka added to some powdered orange slush mix and water, then bingo, you had a Big Billy Dog Taco Southern style Hollywood sidewalk party. There was no indoor seating at the stand. It was one of those L.A. kind of establishments where you sit outside on benches and stools and the cooking kitchen of the restaurant is about eight feet deep; so then during business hours the rear entrance is usually open and a person could sit at the formica dining counter and easily spit out the open back door onto a gravel back lot strewn with struggling weeds and flattened beer cans, no harm done. Meaty Meat Burgers, Jay's Jay Burger, Mike's Double Mini-Burger and Grandma's Kitchen down on Selma Avenue were similarly configured dining establishments.

Danté and I cruised by the Big Dog in the silver leadsled on every evening that we were able. We were really having a huge barrel of fun and the stress of publishing was just being shuffled from one empty pocket to another; the solution was to drink a couple vodka slushes and forget it, because it didn't make matters improve by worrying about them. Most of the punks in L.A. had money problems, it wasn't an artistic or social movement that was able to generate too many economic opportunities at this stage. There was no war to protest or civil rights issues outstanding in American society and consequently there was little organization along those lines. Sidewalk vodka slush parties were a good motivation. The people who were involved with them were dressed for rebellion and loved it to death but they weren't rebelling against any one specific issue like a bad war or a military-industrial complex. For the most part, they were just rebelling for the fun and excitement of the new music. There was a restless social ennui going around like an epidemic rash that needed scratching. Teenagers caught it quickly.

Big Billy was not just a drunk, he was a blues singer par excellence who was rambling down that well-travelled Lost Highway that Hank Williams immortalized on New Year's Day of 1953, when he became the archetype of death for so many musicians, country, rock, jazz and blues. Big Billy lived east of Santa Monica Boulevard at La Brea Avenue in a cheap flophouse style one room apartment at that time. Santa Monica Boulevard in that neighborhood was lined with male homosexual street hustlers day and night, many of them just teenagers, but Billy was absolutely a ladies man.

I remember Billy so vividly on one afternoon. He was a purist when it came to living the alcoholic lifestyle. Reclining on his bed on the fourth floor at four in the afternoon on a weekday, his window opening onto a blind sunless bricked up alleyway, with a nearly empty bottle of Jack Daniels whiskey in his hand, he was complaining about the alcoholic upstairs fighting all night with his old lady. He finished off the bottle straight up and with a chuckle tossed it out the open window, then he listened for the delayed crash on the cement below.

He said, "Whoops! I'll go down and pick it up later." then he chuckled. "Everybody else tosses their empty bottles down there. I hear their goddam glass bottles breaking all night long." If he was given a Beverly Hills mansion to live in, I think he would have stayed in that filthy dump one room apartment day to day for the love of it, and nothing much in his lifestyle would change.

Then again, he was just as likely to show up onstage at the Whisky in a top hat and tuxedo and belt out some sweet blues sounds. There was quite a traffic jam that year on the Lost Highway coming out of Los Angeles, and in our crowd, the spiritual travellers were to be found hanging out at the Big Dog Taco stand every evening when the weather was warm and the red sun dipped into the warm pacific ocean somewhere out beyond the Santa Monica pier. In actual fact, we paid little attention to the California sun. Its glorious beautiful light increasingly made me feel ill and shaky. We were night people; we regularly tried to use up the whole of the darkness, the opposite of light.

Many of the L.A. musicians of that period were doomed to another kind of oblivion and that was their inability to record their music. This was to a great extent due to their being tyrannically shut out by the major record companies but also as in the case of Big Billy and many others, there was a personal resistance to completing a project due partly to fighting between band members and substance abuse. Billy and his band members were known to have violent vicious physical fights amongst themselves causing black eyes, contusions and broken bones.

Punk rock in L.A. was very anti just about everything, especially commercialism. The commercial recording industry was not going to touch them no matter what. Except for the live performances and the live scene, other pursuits were under suspicion. The audience and the performers were unified and of one kind. The performers mixed seamlessly with their audience and this made the live shows stupendous total immersion events. The official starmaking vehicle was missing its wheels partly because the musicians and audience rejected it and also because the recording industry flat-out hated the early Angelino Punk Rockers. Still some groups like Social Distortion managed to make good recordings on their own backs. The only radio airplay for the indie recordings came by way of the DJ Rodney Bingenheimer whose esteemed show was on one night a week for a couple of hours, and the college radio station KXLU which had a limited broadcast range.

The basic sound of Big Billy was indebted to Muddy Waters. Billy's voice was deep and fully nuanced without frilly fake emotion, the blues music just rolled out of him easy. There was a beauty to the early punk rock music scene in Los Angeles, in that it was in reality a roots rock movement encompassing several genres and contemporary idioms all of which had the same ultimate goal of finding a rough and rowdy essence and purity that was intrinsic to early rock and blues like Link Wray's guitar music, Big Joe Turner's R&B, but especially the more recently influential Iggy and the Stooges and the Ramones. After '77 every punky idiom was filtered to some degree through The Stooges and the mighty Ramones. All the bands were pushing their sound in an opposite direction from the over produced, over played, over indulgent, ubiquitous sugary recording industry product of the era. On any night, two seemingly incongruous bands which were punk influenced could share the same bill at a club, even share equipment on the same stage.

There were bands around L.A. that were pure rockabilly and deviant rockabilly, and shockabilly, garage bands, speed punks with fast short songs, angry brat bands that embraced a snot-nosed brash sound enhanced by cheap equipment, X was a punk band with a rockabilly guitar player, East L.A. and Latino rockers, art bands, electronic industrial bands, noisemetalpunk bands, hardcore punks, surf punks, cowpunks and powerpoppunks, death goth punks, speed glam, folk acoustic punk.

... ...

BANDS: Of the West Coast bands associated with punk music between '77 and '82, most all had great impudent names: The Zeros. Weirdos. Germs. The Dils. X. Screamers. Deadbeats. Skulls. Avengers. Alleycats. The Cramps (NY) played frequently in L.A. The Dead Kennedys. Rhino 39. Negative Trend. Flipper. Plugz. The Flesheaters. B-People. Human Hands. Leaving Trains. Meat Puppets (AZ). Black Flag. Circle Jerks. The Bags. Stains. Minutemen. The Blasters. F–Word. Speed Queens. Fear. The Controllers. Redd Kross (aka Red Cross). The Mentors. Suburban Lawns. Wasted Youth. DOA. Descendents. The Crowd. Go-Gos. Levi & The Rockats. Social Distortion. Monitor. Middle Class. Dickies. UXA. The Kingbees. Black Randy and The Metro Squad. Jody Foster's Army (AZ). The Eyes. Top Jimmy and The Rhythm Pigs. The Last. Saccharine Trust. Nuns.

Twisted Roots. Agent Orange. Nervous Gender. Tex and the Horseheads. Devo. The Gun Club. The Extremes. Shattered Faith. Mau-Maus. Brat. The Vandals. Gary Panter. The Adolescents. D.I. China White. The Disposals. The Sleepers. Factrix. Tuxedo Moon. Pink Section. 45 Grave. Christian Death. T.S.O.L. Wall of Voodoo. Minimal Man. Odd Squad. Arthur J and the Gold Cups. Johanna Went. Plimsouls. The Mutants. D.I.s. Angry Samoans. Bad Religion. Suicidal Tendencies. Savage Republic. Legal Weapon. Offs. Phranc. Geza X. Non. Runaways. Salvation Army. Zippers. The Gears. Urinals. The Cheifs. Castration Squad. Berlin Brats. Fibonaccis. The Detours. Rik L. Rik. The Blades. Hal Negro and the Satin Tones. Vicious Circle. The Earwigs. Vox Pop. SWA. The Hated. DeDetroit. Firehose. Ozzi Hares. Overkill. Circle One. Toxic Shock. Mood of Defiance. The Detours. Youth Brigade. Abandoned. The Atoms. Aggression. The Klan. The Slashers. The Outsiders. The Skrews. Spitting Teeth. The Vidiots. Stingers. Holly and the Italians. The Silencers. Green On Red. Eddie and the Subtitles. Channel 3. Child Molesters. The Flyboys. Simpletones. The Dogs. Saigon. Reactionaries. Dead Hippie. Strong Silent Types. Snakefinger. Super Heroines. Screamin Sirens. 100 Flowers. Secret Hate. Choir Invisible. The Residents. Dream Syndicate. Joan Jett. Hangmen. Pandoras. Bangles. Randoms. Funeral. Mad Society. Millions of Dead Cops. Kommunity FK. Youth Gone Mad. Modern Warfare. The Knitters. The Runns. Jeffrey Lee Pearce. Blood On The Saddle. Catholic Discipline. Hesitations. Fat and Fucked Up. Swinging Madisons. Stepmothers. Battalion of Saints. Crewd. Units. Josie Cotton. Hollywood Hillbillies. Henry Kaiser. Los Lobos. Sheiks of Shake. Screws. Venus and the Razorblades. Nerves. Red Scare. Phast Phreddie. Toiling Midgets. Wipers. Z'EV. Hard as Nails Cheap as Dirt. In 1981-2, even L.A.'s metal glam upstarts Motley Crue put out their initial efforts as a self-financed record album.

THE A&R EXEC FAT-CLAM RECORDS: Over-confident and conspicuously posed at the bar like a skinny cosmopolitan mega-media dude hired gun, gazing emptily left then right, then left then right (to make sure he's being stared at), an unctuous erotic grin like a warped crescent moon hangs over his mod tailored plaid jacket uplifted by wedge-shaped shoulder pads, stuck to his lapel a PIL button, on his neck an impression of Jane Mansfield lips in red lipstick, a powder blue turquoise and silver American Indian necklace, slightly torn, neck cut low 'Sid Vicious Is Dead' T-shirt underneath, revealing his Pop Art perfect cosmetically retouched right nipple as the jacket falls open, trendy but slightly thinning hair like the universal rock star cut mirroring '70s style Rod Stewart nattily trimmed mullet, a little bit of NYDolls and Johnny Rotten, new Mods and Kings Road understated overstyled fetishistically casual tailoring, pierced ear and tasteful diamond disco unisex earing, a vague odor of amyl nitrate and hair spray emanating from somewhere, and white crusty crystalline snot stuck to the nose hairs hovering over his smiling clean shaven upper lip, a conspicuous rice pudding splash stain decorating a semi-erect bulge distorting the symmetrical cut of the crotch of his ultra-skin hugging super tight Euro-designer disco jeans tailored Brit punk narrow at the ankles, terminated at the feet by white suede brothel creepers, a pseudo-tough mod style snake leather unimaginably expensive belt around his slender waist, oozing plastic money and three digit green from every cuff and pocket, sipping a Perrier, Mr. Starmaker, the man who can lift your act to the top overnight simply for giving twelve rounds of heavy duty head, Mr. Starbreaker, or leave you to rot in the gutter outside of the white stretched Lincoln Continental limo back seat with full bar and entertainment center, just like the gutter outside of the inner city hospital you were born in or will die in, because he has a more important job to do; he is the now Hollywood company man, a vital part of the powerful hitmaker machine, and now, you are a career slum rebel, laid out prostrate in the gutter next to his parked limo like a discarded flat tire, your eye makeup smeared and your crooked smile bloodied and penetrated.

Danté, who had logged a few years past thirty, was obsessing on this pretty little blond scenemaker from the midwest with an endearing drawl in her speech. Her name was Mandy Lane and she was maybe pushing twenty years old. She had moved to Los Angeles wanting to be a starlet or perhaps just to meet a rock star boyfriend and have excessive fun Hollywood style. Young, beautiful and fresh, they come to Los Angeles only for those reasons, like they come to no other place. She showed up frequently to the early evening Taco stand parties mingling with the roadies and band members and other characters from the music scene. Buck and Lana, a tough looking biker-styled professional roadie and his love squeeze showed up frequently and were favored subjects of Dantés camera as was Big Billy himself. In fact, Billy The Big had a couple of freelance photographers who followed him around night and day, vying for his attention, continuously photographing his every move. A new photograph of Big Billy appeared in at least one local newspaper's music section every week. The general consensus was that he was going to be a major star one day and these lens heads wanted to get in early on a good thing.

Danté's dream self-image was that he would live the life of the trendy 1960s London ultra-hip photographer from Michelangelo Antonioni's film 'Blowup' but a generation later, in a radically punked out Los Angeles and Mandy's pretty ass was to be this year's prize. In his mind, his working class background weighed him down and even though he was a dark handsome man with a uniquely Italian charm, he couldn't shake the fact that he had been a plumber by trade and he carried this as a burden of some kind of class inferiority. His past profession didn't mean much to me or anyone else but it made Danté see himself as less legitimate in his own eyes than some rich son of a millionaire who put on airs, was better educated, and whose dad set him up in business; and in addition Danté was troubled that his older brother was an ex-con. Whether his dad was a Pre-Raphaelite loving plumber or what he was, I don't know and I never asked, simple deduction indicated a standard working class upbringing. Maybe it was these little mental self image demons that turned Mandy away from Danté when she started dating Big Billy on nights when she wasn't seen with Danté. Billy was onstage frequently and that gave him an overwhelming edge with the ladies in the punk milieu. There was one more problem with Mandy.

"Mandy likes heroin." Danté told me as we were cruising around Hollywood behind the purr of his flathead engine. That meant that she was building a second secret life around the drug, a life that Danté couldn't hope to penetrate unless he became an addict.

Danté had moved to a large live-in studio in North Hollywood and he had adopted a roommate who was a complete opposite personality to the crazy scene that we were frequenting. This roommate, who never spoke to me much was a voice of rationality and sanity that Danté kept apart from the punk world. He was a neutral gay or he was just seemingly a genderless preppy man, passive aggressive, boring and efficient and he ran the photo studio they shared in NOHO. He was probably once a fellow student with Danté, a pillar of stability and staunchness, from the art college that Danté had attended and his artistic profession was that of a small product photographer. Inanimate objects and products for catalogues were his stock and trade. Don was his name but he could have been a generic Rob or a normal Larry or a shallow Bob. He was the polar opposite of a punk rocker; he wore no black boots, no boots at all, no black clothes, no leather jacket, no funny haircut, no black eye-makeup, no studs and he displayed no personality problems, no anti-social rebellious characteristics or even mild affectations of negativity.

Punks talked to you right in your face and looked you in the eye. What you saw is what you got. Don didn't manifest those ingenuous qualities around me. He became the voice of reason and sanity whispering in one ear of Danté while in both ears, I was baiting him into eccentric projects with real humans. Danté had ambitions to do album jackets for the punk bands as the new music scene rose to levels of professional success and P*NK Magazine was a vehicle to get his name out there and show his stuff. He was frustrated that I was only putting contributing credits in the masthead of the magazine instead of tagging every photo and art image although he was listed as the co-publisher-editor. So there were some problems not far under the surface. In addition, I was drinking heavily and punctilious puritanical Don Normal was more sober than the Chief of Police.

DREAM DEATH AT THE PLAYBOY MANSION: Heff, founder, publisher, media empire builder, erotic visionary, pajama clad with pipe swishes casually towards his bedroom suite in the rear eastern wing third floor of his Beverly Hills mansion looking down on the rose garden and a broad expanse of neatly cut grass and grand eucalyptus trees. A perfect full breasted nude blond in red high heels on his right hand and an equally perfect red headed vixen in puss print high heels on the other hand accompany him as he attempts to turn the doorknob leading into his world famous Temple of Eros. He shouts, "This door is locked! Goddammit! Whatsuckass chunkypukegarbage sackofshitscum has locked my bedroom door?! Heads are going to roll in the fetish dungeon when I find out who is responsible! Somebody has locked me out of my own bedroom. Miss January! Run to daddy's office and get my Glock .45 caliber semi-automatic handgun out of the gun cabinet, will you sweet cheeks? And be very very careful because its loaded."

He shakes the doorknob again to no avail. "Who the fuck is in there? Nobody parties in daddy's bed but daddy and his bunnies. We've gotta double the security around here. Take a note Miss February to get a fly-over helicopter patrol, put armed men in the tree house, get more electronic surveillance, get more patrol K-9's roaming the grounds."

Miss January returns hurriedly holding her high heels in one hand and the .45 awkwardly in the other. Heffy takes it and blows the door handle out of this world with one shot. He kicks the door open with his bedroom slipper and enters the room with Miss J taking up the rear and Miss F holding on tightly to his trailing robe. Upon entering his lavish Temple of Eros, the Rococo flying cherubs painted in the domed ceiling sky part hurriedly in fear as the sky turns green and a menacing tornado touches down. Heffy falls back on his heels and Miss J is pushed back out the door and it slams shut leaving Heffy tumbled back on Miss F like an unbalanced top. In the distance behind the swirling winds there is a heavy ominous mass forming, the floor creaking under the force of its weight, a fully corporal dark colossal rhinoceros with blood red eyes, a two ton sexcrazed jungle superbull paws the floor aggressively and impatiently stampedes a metallic blitzkrieg bearing an ominous horn down on the incredulous Heffy with Miss February scrambling for the door handle in the rear. Semi-dazed Heffy wonders how did this impossible zoo attraction find him in his bedroom and go unnoticed by his security? Like a juggernaut locomotive in a dizzying Max Beckman perspective the primal horn explodes into Heffy's knotted lower intestinal guts, the rhino bears down then lifts up on splintering impact ripping apart the once nicely attired sternum. Heffy explodes apart at his torso and dies sloppy face up on the floor and Miss February is blown backwards through the wooden door and halfway down the long hallway at the feet of the frightened Miss January. The primitive horn of the rhinoceros has created a huge vagina shaped wound in the lifeless body of the famous publisher suggesting the need for a giant tampon to absorb the blood.

The police investigation turns up no hideous murder weapon large enough that could have caused a deadly wound of that size. Heffy is buried with great ceremony in Arlington National Cemetery in Virginia with full military honors for his uplifting contributions to lonely soldiers; his much bereaved hollowed out purple cadaver now at peace, wearing the same bathrobe and slippers that adorned him in life; another gouged out American success story meeting with a violent, unexplained fate, exalted in death. Miss January and Miss February form Bunnies Against Violence, an organization to aid unwanted, unemployed, clothed and unclothed, aging and distressed non-violent bunnies worldwide. The Playboy mansion and its archives are donated to the Smithsonian Museum as cherished examples of 20th century American hedonism and breast obsession. Heffy's unharmed genitalia are preserved in a clear Lucite block for eternity and displayed behind four inch deep bullet proof glass. America appreciates its heroes and charges $15 a ticket for individuals meeting the height requirement (of four foot two inches) to tour the mansion in the Hollywood Hills after declaring it a National Monument.

Danté and I had major big fun but it is the jagged fragments and shards of memories, mostly painful, that return to me from those past days and they are tied to no particular time line, except that I know they happened during that period when I was an office rat on Las Palmas and Hollywood. The threads of my life began unraveling. My mom was showing the first signs of becoming seriously ill, symptoms of which she related to me over the telephone and my sister, to whom I rarely spoke, was becoming more verbally vicious than usual for reasons which I couldn't understand at the time. I absorbed it all with a tablespoon of guilt, berating myself that I was not a better son and that my chosen profession was not much more honorable than that of an armed robber. Probably, I would have gotten more respect if I had robbed banks during those years than I did peddling punk rock tabloids. There was certainly more money to be had in the bank robbery business. I did feel like a kind of criminal. I was certainly living life beyond the pale of your average American.

Other residents in my building were having their troubles as well. Most notably Bill, the dance instructor, had been quietly purchasing heroin from a drug gang that resided up on Wilcox. They had a big little serious operation going on in an old run down deco apartment building between Hollywood and Sunset and sometimes, in the afternoon is when I noticed it, they would post sentries, African-American gang guys, at points around the building and on the street. This was going on right there in Hollywood only two blocks from the police station. It was obvious to me that some tough business was running through that location. Bill slowly got indebted to them over his head. Time passed. He couldn't pay them back and he was strung out on the stuff and they killed him. That was the talk around the Pioneer Spirit Building. If only he could have traded them dance lessons to pay his debt the whole neighborhood would have been better off, but it doesn't work that way.

I got so broke that I sold my blood plasma several times for ten dollars a pop. Some of the musicians were doing it regularly and they invited me to come on down for the ceremonies. This is a career step that I have professionally moved away from for greener pastures, but I seem to think that they don't purchase plasma that way any more since the AIDS epidemic. Some medical company had set up these twenty bed clinics around Los Angeles in cheap office spaces and they would buy human blood plasma from the indigents for profit. The two offices that I was cognizant of were located in downtown Los Angeles near to skid row and then another was located on Sunset Boulevard in Hollywood. The skid row guys would work both locations. There was even a third beach location if you rode along the main bus routes into Santa Monica. The chronic alcoholic bums would sell their blood plasma downtown and then catch a bus ride into Hollywood and do it all over again. Then they'd use the money to buy Night Train back downtown on skid row.

The professional bloodsucking company hired individuals who dressed up as nurses and they would remove a pint of your blood into a plastic blood bag and then centrifuge it separating out the corpuscles from the plasma. This involved placing you on a gurney, then sticking a thick needle and tube into your arm at the inside of the elbow. Plus, each donor was given in addition to a gurney, a white sheet and then allowed to rest in a recumbent position during the process. In Hollywood, the stark room itself was filled with twenty of these gurney beds and each bed supported a donor in a different stage of bloodletting. There was no shortage of donors. There was usually a wait of at least a half an hour after the signing in process.

The nurses would remove the plasma and keep it for the company to sell at a big profit and they would replace the plasma in the plastic bag with a saline solution. So this saline solution was added back into your own personal plastic blood bag, wherein they would return intravenously to the donor their original corpuscles. Having the watered down blood returned was just as unpleasant as having it removed. It gave you a little chill because the saline solution was refrigerated. It was a hideous process and it took about two hours after you walked in the door to complete. They asked you if you had ever had hepatitis and that was about it for the screening. If you said no, you were in the blood club baby!

They pricked your finger with a needle at the outset to get a drop of your red stuff for some little test. There was this one dark handsome young man who had a heavy metal haircut and rocker clothes and he looked like he was possibly a Latino and he had the ability to squirt the blood out of the tip of his little finger to a distance of up to five or even six feet. He did this by pinching his finger behind where it was pricked and pointing the blood jet. He freely decorated the white walls of the waiting room with swirling loops of blood. That was mildly entertaining. I tried his technique on my finger but it wouldn't squirt.

The medical company caught on to the skid row guys scam of selling their fluids multiple times in a day in different locations and they disapproved not out of concern for the health of the poor hobos but because they were buying their own saline solution back. They began marking guys thumbs with dayglow indelible ink so they couldn't move around to the various clinics undetected on the same day. There's always a way to work around something if you really want to do it. That extra ten dollars bought them more Night Train when they got back downtown. Losing blood was making me sick. After my pint was sucked out into the bag, I usually got nauseous, dizzy and my lips went numb. They were in reality sucking me for a little extra bit more than the pint they said they were obtaining. Who was to know or complain? Bums? It gave the company a little bigger profit margin. One evening I let it slip over the telephone to my seasoned ol' mother and she flipped.

She said to me, "Our family doesn't usually die of heart attacks. Nearly every member of our family dies of a blood disease. So don't mess with your blood Ronnie. You're playing with fire." That was really all I needed, and I retired from the blood business.

My mom came down to Los Angeles for Thanksgiving and she stayed at my sister's apartment in Studio City. I was inside her apartment briefly at one time and it was an expensive apartment and I wondered how my sister could pay for it without a job. That's a question that will never be answered. On the holiday, I drove up over the hill to Studio City to meet them for dinner, a warm and cheery holiday dinner with my aging mother. The fun was short-lived. My sister began her unique style of hysterical shrill screaming tirade via the intercom before I even penetrated the outside gate of the residential units. It was like encountering a verbal wall of hate. My mom was sitting in there next to her. She only managed to get a word or two in. I left and returned back over the hill to my little office overlooking Las Palmas Avenue and Hollywood Boulevard. That was the year I had Thanksgiving with the heroin addicts who didn't eat and I was glad to be with them.

The Hollywood Christmas Parade came the Sunday after Thanksgiving and some friends came by my office and we had a few drinks and then we all watched the parade celebrations through my scenic windows. Unlike most adults, I still believed in Santa Claus. Black Dick, Wanda and Trey from 5th and Wall showed up. They wanted to go up on the roof of the building and watch from the catbird's seat. Cowboy Brown and Young CB had that action covered. Every year there were always wise asses from the street trying to get on the roof for the parade and the Pioneer Spirit Building owners didn't want that. Black D and Trey started running up and down the hallway looking for a window or fire escape that could lead to the top of the building. I was following behind them saying, "Hey you guys they don't want you to go up on the roof." Young CB saw what they were up to and he told them that they weren't allowed up there and he said that they would have to leave if he caught them trying to climb up onto the roof again. Young CB was very polite to them but he ran them the rules in no uncertain terms. Black Dick got pissed. I saw the anger flush red across his face. I went to talk to some of my other guests. A couple of minutes later Young CB, who by the way was studying law so that he could represent indigent black people in the legal system, came running up to me very upset.

"You can't deface this property like that! What is wrong with you man? You can't stay in this building doing things like that!" said he to me.

"What are you talkin' about CB? I didn't do anything."

Pointing he says "Over on that wall, what is that?"

It was the wall of the hallway where my office was located down toward the dance studio. I walked over there and in big blue letters from a super fat indelible marker pen, the letters were over a foot high and ran the length of the wall, was scrawled, "FUCK YOU NIGGER!". Black Dick had the marker pen with him. He even played with it in front of me to make sure that I had seen it, but now he and Trey and Wanda had run out the Las Palmas door and into the crowd of a million people.

I said, "I didn't do that! It was Black Dick. Black Dick did it that asshole! He's the guy you wouldn't let up on the roof."

Young CB didn't understand what I was talking about with this Black Dick jive talk. I was just digging a bigger hole for myself. He didn't know that Black Dick was the name of a person. He thought that I might be insulting him and he just got hotter under the collar. I tried to back peddle.

"Black Dick is that guys name that was trying to get up on the roof. He did it. I'm really sorry. I never would have let him up here if I had known that he was capable of doing that."

That last part was a lie because I knew that he was capable of doing that and many other things but I didn't anticipate his actions and I had other guests. The Black Dick had struck. Young CB never looked at me the same again. He was always suspicious of me after that. It was the goddam American race problem that always seems to recur like a chronic disease. To make matters worse, the next week I purchased some matching paint which didn't quite match, the wall was a little soiled and the color had altered with time, and the FUCK YOU NIGGER kept leaching through the paint and coming to the surface again. It wouldn't go away. It took several coats of sealer and overpainting to get rid of it and the letters were still there ghosted back three weeks later. It was a sharp pain in the ass that lasted on and on. The other African American residents in the building who had to walk by it every day were politely reticent about it. I was thankful for that courtesy. When the Black Dick died of AIDS a couple of years on, I was one of those happy mourners who was pleased to see him go. It's lowbrow to speak poorly of the dead but he's in another place which is not among the living. That's just the place where I want him. I was so anxious for Black Dick to die, I informed you prematurely in the narrative.

Prior to his early death, Black McDick still had plenty of time and desire for making mischief. Trey and Black Dick spent a few years collecting dated neon fixtures off of L.A.'s old downtown buildings, taking a treasure trove of unwanted fixtures from derelict buildings and stealing others as well when they could. Trey often had entertaining social events at his skid row studio, such as spaghetti dinners for large groups. His girlfriend Wanda became successful behind the scenes in the entertainment industry, she won major awards and eventually she left him. In time, after Black Dick had croaked ugly, diseased and drugged out, Trey quietly moved back home to live with his mother in the burbs of Stockton. Shortly thereafter, Trey burned down the family home in a drug and alcohol related accident. They were probably insured. He grew so fat that he looked unrecognizable as the Trey I had known. Probably there was more to the equation than mamma's cooking that accounted for his obesity. Donuts and mental illness. Lack of cardiovascular exercise. TV.

Let me get to the point here. On a weekday before the Black Dick graffiti incident and all the AIDS epidemic tragedy began in the 1980s, Wanda dropped in over to my Hollywood office where she encountered Danté. Within a very short time she gave him a rousing and sloppy blow job leaving semen splashes all over his blue jeans. Need to read some details? There were a few other friends over that day coming and going. Danté and her were fooling around together, laughing and they came up with some reason to go out to his car which was parked on the street below. After a half an hour Danté came back alone and he said that he had given Wanda a ride up to Hollywood and Vine and dropped her off. He was sort of standing funny and a person couldn't help but notice that he had splashed wet semen stains all over the crotch area of his bluejeans, nearly down to his knees. It was a Jackson Pollock style semen splash and drip. I imagine Wanda swallowed her limit.

I said, "What the hell is that stuff all over your jeans Danté?" and he started blushing and grinning.

Danté replied, "That was Wanda's way of saying thanks for the ride."

There were some bands playing in the late afternoon at the Masque, across Hollywood Boulevard and east up the street a block. The Masque was downstairs below street level and it was about three thousand square feet of raw cement basement space with a few filthy reeking toilets. It was genuine squalid freedom in the city and it was run by one of us, a displaced Scottish guy named Brendon who imparted a genuine bit of class to the scene. He was sort of like having Brian Epstein, the manager of The Beatles, organizing the Hollywood punk scene.

I arrived after sunset, a little bit late for the party but ran into Bad Dog (not any family relation to Big Dog taco), a young, African-American girl drummer. She was hanging out in the alley with a small group of rockers that was gradually splintering off down to Hollywood Boulevard in many directions. After saying my hellos I started talking to another black lady who was a stunning beauty and she was wildly attracted to me. I was pleased. She was stoned on one drug or maybe two drugs. After getting sort of lost in her beauty and chit-chat, I looked around and everyone had peeled away from the group slowly leaving we two at the end of the alley. The sun had long gone down now and there were large evening crowds moving up and down the boulevard carrying the excitement of the potential of a new night-on-the-town in Hollywood. My lady was becoming very erotic up against the wall as we whispered back and forth there on Cherokee and she began unzipping her designer jeans and pulling them down to her knees. I felt a sudden mixture of joy and fear but mostly joy. She was probably going to get us popped by the two uniformed beat cops who walked Hollywood Blvd. in the late afternoon and evenings. They had a nasty habit of showing up at very inopportune times, just like this one. There she was with her jeans and panties coming down and we were barely in the shadows on the side street. I pulled her down around the corner into The Masque stairwell just below street level, kissed her bountifully, unzipped my pants and slipped my cock inbetween her beautiful red painted lips as she sat on the steps. I begged "Please, please, please."

She let me hold her head gently and slide my rigid cock deep to the back of her throat. I pushed it between her lips slowly until the shank disappeared completely once, and then slowly again, and her watery eyes were following its movement. One of those times when it slipped in so deep, I moved it back and forth sideways gently rubbing the wet soft flesh at the back of her throat, pumping my warm semen there until it was completely spent. I forgot where I was.

"C'mon, let's go up to my place. It's just across the street upstairs." We gathered ourselves together then moved up to street level in each others arms.

"Wait here a second!" I said, then ran the ten yards or so up to Hollywood Boulevard and looked both ways up and down the street to see where the two beat cops were strolling. I'd lived on that corner long enough to have a intuition for their presence. The only cops who walked a beat in all of Los Angeles were in my neighborhood. They were a block away from us eastward towards Vine Street on the south side, our side of the street. They were talking to some heavy metal runaway types. This brown skinned girl was extremely stoned. I zipped her up a little and took her furtively down the alley to Las Palmas and then across the street with the green light and up to my office where we were safe from the street, and we drank some warm Colt 45s from under the bed and I got her naked and fucked her on my wooden packing crate bed with an old mattress on it. She wasn't a punk girl. I was willing to overlook that small detail and I considered myself an extremely lucky guy. What a doll. I took her home very late at night into the early morning up into the Hollywood hills, to an expensive but not ostentatious house tucked away in lush Nichols Canyon.

I learned the next day from someone who was familiar with her, that she was the daughter of the '60s comedian Red Greene, who did stand-up in the Negro comedy circuit and then in the 1970's parlayed that into a modest B-movie career. As a teenager, I had heard a few of his records, but his movies, I had never seen even one, although he was a popular entertainer. His daughter's name was Cilia, a beautiful name I thought, and she had forgotten some trivial items in my studio and I didn't think much of it. Two days later, Bad Dog told me that Cilia had been hospitalized the following night after a car ride up the Sunset Strip. She was the passenger in a convertible Mustang with the top down and she made some kind of wisecrack to a group of hookers standing on the sidewalk while the car was stopped at a red light. Down in the neighborhood of Hollywood High School where the cheap hotels are, there were always hookers at night. The small gang of women pulled her right up out of the car and beat her face and torso with hard brutal intentions on the sidewalk. Cilia had to be taken to the hospital emergency.

I went up to her home to see her the next afternoon and brought the stuff she had left in my office. Her face was all puffed up and she was constrained in a neck brace. She looked miserable and medicated. Cilia said thanks but she wasn't happy to see me. Of course, I never saw her again, except in a couple of B-movies a few years later. I no longer had any doubts about whether it was me or the mystery drugs that made her behave so erotically. Besides, relationships had never been my strong suit. If my strong suit ever showed up I must have missed it.

And then, there was this girl's mother who I fucked. Whom I fucked would be more correct language in readerdom, but I could never fuck a whom. I went over to the art institute one evening for an art opening and a shower in the ceramics department. When I arrived at the opening, I realized that I no longer had the look and demeanor of a fine artist as I did during my days in art college. The punk rock shows five nights a week, the alcoholism and the stress of publishing had remolded me. Also, after my Liverhead haircut, I had dyed my fair hair blueblack and slicked it back. One of several bad hair styles that followed in a tasteless sequence but hair styles aren't for dining. This was a more typical and pragmatic punky look which lacked the world famous impact of the Liver Haircut. People I knew from my previous existence as an art student appeared so very clean and sparkly shiny and healthy, and complacent; the perfect bourgeoisie of Marxist dialectical materialism. Maybe I was being a little arrogant but they were now alien to me. I was a strange new revolutionary like Woody Allen with a Fidel Castro beard.

"Hello earthling, I am Ronnie from planet Plunko. We have unsightly brain implants which enable our survival in your atmosphere and we are considering using your species as a food source. May I take your mother home with me for some experimentation. She will be returned safely in the morning." I began talking to this female student I had known from my college days and she was with her mom who was maybe 45 or 50. We chatted for a short time and then I took mom back to my office for some alien sexual experimentations which lasted overnight. After that, her daughter began showing up at nightclubs. She would point at me in a crowded club and shout repeatedly, "He fucked my mother!"

One night, Danté and I took off for Club 88 down in the seedy visually polluted sprawling southwest side of West L.A. We rode out on his ex-con brother's cammed and carbed 1200 Harley Sportser, a fast bike. X, The Plugz and Black Flag had been playing jam-packed shows there frequently. We scooted between lanes through the heavy traffic along the Santa Monica Freeway on a warm L.A. evening melting into the infinite ribbon of lights that was both futuristic and beautiful. Once inside the nightclub, I ran into one of my instructors from the art institute hanging out in the audience, a cool worldly guy in his '60s from NYC named Giles.

He, being one who had been around the block and then some, pulled me aside, looked me squarely in the eyes and said, "Be careful now Ronnie, you're running with a pretty fast crowd!"

ß/R𝒯H

Why does God let me suffer? Sick sex and soul starvation?
Break through to the birth of regurgitation, complex
mutilation, radical new designs, death of man, woman and
child, stagnation. What's it like to find a skeleton of
unknown species? Ghosts in the city of glass? True portraits
of Heaven and Hell? Celebration. Nerve cells firing ice
cubes. Power to pull life from the womb, interacting from
cover to cover, fallen not from but into grace. Power to laugh
like dogs, to cry past the walls of asylums, prisons, streets.
One mother dedicates her life, kills her child to help end the
world, the medical childbirth establishment fighting to end
your death. Pressing teeth against teeth, I want to know you.
I want to bite through your infant skin, and we will drown in
glory. Now, who will come to the water?

—penned by ROZZ WILLIAMS (Christian Death) & RON ATHEY
First published in print ©1982†. Rozz Williams (1963-1998)

CHAPTER 8

DEATHNURSE: "MY PATIENTS ALL DIE SCREAMING!"

AN INTRODUCTORY LESSON FOR BEGINNING HATCHET PSYCHOS: First let me admonish any of you Second Amendment gun advocates who may have mistakenly stumbled upon this course with your bang-bang shoot'em up cowboy ethics that this field of study is not for you. This lesson does not support gun violence and long distance killing. A hatchet murder is an intimate, up close and personal encounter involving a razor sharp heavy steel wedge balanced on the end of a fine piece of hardwood, swung with high velocity to impact upon a human victim within arms reach, leading to a death blow and then a complete dismemberment and ritual blood bath. A hatchet murder provides all encompassing intimate sensual experiences for the perpetrator and victim that are not possible for the common gun hoodlum. Yes, I did say sexual experiences. These pure and powerful experiences are the raison d'etre of the axe fiend. Use your imagination!

For today's topic, we will cover one of the most important aspects of the deadly operation of the axe psychopath, getting away with the murder to be free to kill again on another day. Other topics we will discuss in future dates will be the advantages of a thorough knowledge of medical anatomy, disguising your crimes as copycat crimes, where to find the best victims to suit your lifestyle, society's misconceptions about psychopathic killings, the advantage of wearing costumes and disguises, working in convalescent homes, cutting down on your grocery bills by eliminating beef, recipes for cordon bleu cannibals, how to make your neighbors thigh taste like venison, taking advantage of the mock morbidity of Halloween parties, road kill and aiding stranded motorists, the perfect cutting techniques of Jack The Ripper, how many victims is too many victims, the poetry of the axe and of course the pros and cons of digital video, and finally keeping drug abuse out of the death ritual. And I cannot emphasize this last item enough, drugs have no place in a hatchet murder. Please only kill when you are stone cold sober. If you have to be intoxicated to decapitate the Mr. or Mrs., or Little Johnny or baby Daphne, or the neighbor next door or whomever you have selected as your victim, you are not

SUB-HOLLYWOOD — BRUCE CAEN

a true psychopath and you need to hang up your axe and reconsider the motives for your actions. Now, as they say in the poultry business, parts is parts, so happy chopping!

Let's face the facts, nearly all hatchet jobs are carried out in a delirious frenzied blood-splattered maelstrom of sadistic erotic violence. Now, once you have committed a violent psychopathic axe crime, how do you proceed from there to avoid detection? First of all, do not try to clean up the crime scene. The cops hire professionals to do this type of work so you don't have to worry about it. These are your tax dollars at work. This is simply not your job. If the scene is indoors and it's magnificently messy, pour in a gallon or two of gasoline and torch the place on your way out the door. The hotter the better. Goodbye evidence.

Disposing of the recently deceased is another matter. Don't give the cops a break. This takes some preparation and care. Wear protective gloves and a safe breathing apparatus. Always dissolve amputated anatomy with a strong neat acid like sulfuric or hydrochloric, for example. Typically, carelessness after the victim's demise will result in the perpetrator's apprehension by over-zealous law enforcement sleuths seeking to make a name for themselves through local and national TV exposure. Always bring a small steel sledgehammer in your toolkit and use it to smash up a dead idiots head. Carry a selection of charged up cordless power tools and a variety of manual hand saws and remember, chainsaws are beautiful. Black plastic heavy duty 45 gallon trash bags are a necessity. Bring along two large military style heavy duty buckets, the kind with a self-closing lid because you'll be creating psychopath noodle soup in there. Just toss those chopped up victim parts in that acid bath and they're ready for transport in the trunk of your car. Toss in a few carrots and a celery if you are in a humorous mindset. Most weekend axe butchers who inevitably end up in the arms of police have improperly discarded the butchered victims body parts. Do you have a meatgrinder and a freezer at your rural home? Grind the victims up before they stiffen and freeze them in plastic wrap. Dead humans make excellent dogfood for pitbulls. The most notorious case of unprofessional blundering by novice idiots at the scene of the crime was of course, Charlie Manson's Sharon Tate-LaBianca Comedy Show. Please keep the clumsiness of the Manson-Tate death scene in mind as you cleanup your own carnage...and never, never scrawl trendy slogans on the walls. That is just crazy!

Don't get caught in awkward situations. For example, what can you say to a Highway Patrol Officer when he asks you why there is an amputated hand lying on your back seat? You certainly can't tell him that you are saving it for lunch, you use it for masturbation, or that you forgot to toss it over the cliff with the rest of the chopped up corpse. Don't expect the cops to have a sense of humor! Preferably, all body parts once soaked in a strong neat acid should then be transported to an obscure disposal area in your heavy duty buckets. That acid should dissolve your corpse into something that resembles canned Chicken Noodle Soup in about an hour. It's perfectly legal to transport soup. Use industrial rubber gloves so that you don't dissolve yourself along with your victim. Any larger identifiable body parts that are left out in the woods should disappear in a day or two. Coyotes love that kind of ready-to-eat dining. Be sure to break up those large bony parts with your sledgehammer. This will insure their rapid breakdown and assimilation into the landscape. Your victim's fat sightless meathead will be the most troublesome, being typically all bones and teeth and no brains. Bash that head into a soft mushy pancake so that the skull parts are unrecognizable. The teeth which are delightfully collectible mementos are also hard evidence that is traceable through dental records as we see so often on TV detective shows. To be safe, scatter them randomly along a stretch of rural or deserted freeway by tossing one or two of them at a time casually out the window at high speed.

Be sure to send for my inexpensive brochures 'Acids and Anatomy', and 'Death Nurse's Military Surplus'. All correspondence is confidential and orders are wrapped brown paper to protect your parcel from prying eyes. Your first assignment to do over the weekend is to go out and kill with your hatchet or axe, and then escape! And make sure they all die screaming!

Next weeks lesson will be 'The Advantages of Working in a Nursing Home for the Aged' followed by 'Inserting Needles in the Eyes of the Comatose'. For those of you concerned with keeping in balance with nature, remember to begin a life after you have taken one. As a hobby, I raise nests and colonies of black widow spiders (*Latrodectus mactans*.) Their venom is 15 times more toxic than a rattlesnake.

"You can get up onstage and play good or bad, in or out of tune and it really doesn't matter. What matters is that you have an attitude, that is something to express and therefore a real reason for being there."

—KIM FOWLEY, emceeing at
the Whisky a Go Go nightclub in the 1970s *

CHAPTER 9

Buck, Dantés motorcycle riding friend, party animal homosapien erectus and an early co-founding member of the taco stand slush parties got fired from his job as a roadie for the punk band L.A. Subs. I thought that was a job for life. They were a tightly knit family of punkers. Danté told me that Bucky needed a place to stay for a while and I said that he could stay in the extra space in my office for a few weeks. The L.A. Subs were one of the biggest punk bands in Los Angeles and they were one of the first original sounding punk groups that L.A. was able to export as sophisticated Los Angeles nuanced music back at New York City and the English as early as 1978. Before Black Flag launched hardcore and its influence spread like a gasoline fire, much of the style in L.A. punk music was dissipated in a search for identity. Being a professional roadie for L.A.S. was a good gig, especially suitable for a guy who appeared to be just a tough biker to the marrow of his bones. Bucky always had an elusive special charming devilish twinkle in his eyes. We had partied more than a few times from sundown into the middle of the night up at the ruins of the Errol Flynn mansion in Runyon Canyon with the whole gang, at Big Billys Taco Parties, and at Club 88 shows and numerous other after-hours party locations. I wondered for a time why he had been fired from the group but it didn't take me long to figure out the probable reason.

The first night he stayed over at the office, Lana his girlfriend came with him on the back of his 750 Triumph Bonneville. I always felt she was a studied case of white trash because she had a layer of refinement hidden deeply under the poor speech, street mannerisms and impeccably accurate white trash clothing. They were both perfectly styled white trash. Lana would string together concatenations of colloquialisms like a truly illiterate person so that everything that she said was spoken all melted together like one long word.

In her parlance people were always talking shit. "Johnny said this and that and the other and he was just talking shit. So I said 'Johnny, quit talking shit all the time because you're gonna make me puke. You're such a liar!'" Lana was very pretty but she played it down in favor of the tough look. By 1979, those British bikes like the one Buck and his lady raced around Hollywood were already becoming rarities.

They were popular hot and fast rides in the '60s and then they got blown out of the market by the Honda and Kawasaki products in the 1970s. The group L.A. Subs, and many of the other L.A. punk bands who shared a spin-off retro American sound were simply not sympathetic to Japanese motorcycles and automobiles. Big Billy called the Jap bikes 'rice burners'. In the morning, after the night Buck and Lana arrived at my magazine offices, I was dogged by my proverbial American malt liquor hangover when Bucky came out of the back room with an insulin syringe loaded with meth-amphetamine. With my headache, I had forgotten that they had slept over.

He said, "Do you want some?" with that fetching sparkle in his eyes.

He took me by surprise completely. I said, "What is it?"

He said, "It's methedrine."

I had forced myself to forget all about that chemical. It was definitely the solution to any hangover and I was generally feeling extremely run down from too much cheap drinking.

I said, "Yeah, OK."

He was lightning fast with his outfit and that surprised me as well. He had that needle in and out the vein in my forearm before I could say 'jackrabbit'. There were no formalities of tying my arm off. Bucky shot me up with a wham-bam-thank-you-maam-and-goodbye motion. I wasn't going to race my dogs anymore and there I had gone and set them running after the jackrabbit. It had been ten years that I had been almost entirely clean from all drugs. I had even quit smoking entirely until my publishing career was jump started in '77. There was the red flag of the blood under pressure squirting back in the narcotic filled syringe. The strange sensation of ether in the back of the throat when the methamphetamine hits the heart and gets pumped through the lungs; this was the beginning of a chemical rush that I had left behind in the '60s. The ponies were out of the gate and the mad dogs were chasing the running rabbits.

This penchant for the spike just may have been one salient reason why Buck was fired from his roadie job. This was the first that I had seen of it. L.A.S. were on the way up and their modicum of genuine success was too precarious to risk failure from the perils of the needle and spoon. To a healthy mind the needle is a macabre and hideous practice. The band members, their counterculture personas notwithstanding, were talented creative souls but they weren't sick or suicidal. May-be once or twice a year, they would have overlooked it, but chronic intravenous drug use definitely would have gotten a roadie fired. You had to respect the band for giving Bucky the boot. Then again, Johnny Thunders was a glam guitar legend and he was a junkie from NYC. Wrong coast, blame it all on Lou Reed and Nico, drug songs, a messy topic. Joseph Bayer, the guy who invented aspirin invented heroin. He's dead. Around the late 1970s, it seemed to me that the whole West Coast became needle and spoon obsessed. People that I would never have imagined doing that bad thing, did it. My personal advice would be to take up Zen Buddhism as a way of life.

This was just a couple of years before AIDS arrived on the world scene and I remember that little space in time as a wild and Bacchanalian period across varied cultural groups in Los Angeles. It all recalled to me a song lyric that used to haunt me in the sixties by a boogie blues band named Savoy Brown, "I sleep with the sun, I rise with the moon, I feel all right with my needle and spoon." People in the gay bars also were excessively stoned, in the discos and the rock nightclubs too it was the same. I wasn't gone immediately but this was a sign that my rowboat was beginning to leak in the bathtub and I might get wet in my black leather jacket punk uniform.

I definitely knew better than to be sharing needles like I had just done with Bucky. Selling my blood to the plasma center had effectively desensitized me to needle prodding. The needle that they had used to remove and return fluids at that bloodsucking clinic was gauged for a quarterhorse. It left a huge hole in the arm that inevitably bruised badly. The so-called technicians (in white lab coats) were so fiendishly clumsy that it was always a more miserable experience than a joyous simple bloodletting for little cash.

I saw first hand plenty of hepatitis disease in the late '60s due to intravenous drug use. I had shot up maybe twenty five times back then but as a rule I popped, dropped or snorted whatever drug I could get my hands on. The needle was a fast way lose your youth to a wasting deadly chronic disease if the drug didn't kill you first; but it was exciting. Some people want to die and the spike is simply the way they choose to pursue that end. They bring other people down with them under the adage that misery loves company. People who shoot downers and heroin will frequently show off abscesses the size of golfballs in their arms and hands where they missed the vein and the shit grew infected. Valerie, with the beautiful tits, had two or three abscesses, located on her right hand and forearm.

There is also that other small concern about the purity of chemicals brewed by criminals in illegal fly-by-night labs in a fast cash environment. Speed is made from volatile deadly carcinogenic chemicals usually concocted by amateur chemists in homemade labs under conditions of poor hygiene; bathtub speed and biker speed are common terms among amphetamine users. Biker speed is the polar toxic opposite of a multivitamin. Nevertheless, professional biker gangs are more organized, scientific and methodical than first time tweekers brewing chemicals in a Mojave desert shack. One rumor about speed is that it was developed by the Nazis

SUB-HOLLYWOOD —— BRUCE CAEN

for use by their troops and the other rumor is that it has been produced in the USA by the big well-organized biker gangs as a cash crop. Adolf Hitler supposedly used it. Bucky and I used it. This is the common lore of the drug that circulates at the consumer street level but users don't tend to do any genuine historical research on the subject, they're too wired to think.

Buck was a biker but he didn't belong to any gang. He stayed in the office with me for a few weeks, maybe a month, and I guess he felt that keeping me high on meth was a kind of rental payment. Hello needle. There is one other detail that I have forgotten to mention. Buck had flown off his motorcycle a few years before and he had rocketed headfirst into a freeway overpass pylon. He didn't have any obvious brain damage, in fact, he probably didn't have any more brain damage after the accident than before, but his head and facial features were slightly asymmetrical due to some surgical reconstruction. There were no mandatory helmet laws for motorcycles in 1979, so you know that Buck wouldn't be caught dead wearing one; he came very near to death in the accident. Maybe his brains getting squashed cushioned his neck vertebrae from the impact and prevented him from becoming paralyzed. He didn't seem to worry much about life and death issues. He was what he wanted to be and teasing death was part of the package. Danté told me that story about the accident. It cleared up several questions I had partially formed in my mind about Buck.

Following on the heels of Buck came Danté's brother Jolly. For reasons that escape me Danté was lining up the houseguests at my office space. He and Don Normal had three thousand square feet of open studio space devoted to an occasional photo shoot of a line of vitamin pill bottles or kitchenware. Apparently that was not enough space to put up Buck and Lana and now his brother and his brother's old lady were guesting with me for a week. 'Old Lady' was the 1960s vernacular used by biker outlaws, hippies and white trash types during that time period meaning a fairly permanent girlfriend or even a wife. It was not derogatory to be an *old lady* even if you were young and beautiful. Bucky carried knives and syringes, and wore the chains hanging from his belt, and denim and leather and rode a Triumph 750 motorcycle but he was in reality just a big, miscreant teddy bear disaster, especially if you stacked him next to Danté's elder sibling Jolly, who was the real deal replete with penitentiary time and a dark ominous aura that seemed to follow him around like a cloud of lethal nerve gas. His lady, whose name was Olga, had the looks that you might expect of a lone wolf biker's *old lady*. She sported a beautifully displayed full rack up top of quality genuine Vargas Girl breasts. Any panhead riding macho man would have been proud to parade her up and down the boulevard leaning back on the sissy bar of his softail rear seat. Then she squeezed a fully endowed bottom half into a pair of skin tight denims which drew attention to her generous shapely labia. In contrast to these feminine qualities, she appeared emotionally drawn and pale. Her eyes had that look of being cried out of tears. They stayed with me for an uneventful week occupying the same room Buck and Lana had used. They didn't drink or take any drugs that I could see and I avoided them like the plague.

During this Hollywood Boulevard office period of my publishing life we (the editorial we) held three benefit concerts to help finance our voracious publishing needs. Many potential advertisers were reluctant to make that vital final commitment of money to this local magazine that appeared to sponsor random acts of cannibalism, presented rabid deranged drawings, anarchistic punks and other insalubrious behaviors. The community of citizens who supported those activities was as yet small and not self-sufficient.

Punk really had no intellectual or obvious socio-political focus for its rebelliousness comparable to those issues which were catalysts to the 1960s, such as an unpopular war, the Civil Rights Movement, police brutality and LSD consciousness. In the late '70s, there was developing a very tangible agonizing social ennui and dissatisfaction with the status quo that rose to the surface and broke out in young people like a bad case of the smallpox and punk for a short period in time in the span of human growth offered them a conduit to express that anxiety. If the punks didn't rebel against whatever was available in society, it seemed like the whole world would die sleepwalking. Daily routine life was a greyed out ho-hum droning to meaningless nowhere from 9 to 5 and musical entertainment was solid gold disco dancing and overproduced sugar pop. Punks were the obverse side of the coin to the Reagan revolution. They wanted no part of it and they were never invited to participate. The punks rebelled just to do it and they attempted to take back rock and roll music and make it raw, real and essential. As it ran its course, those involved looked around desperately for a contemporary Neal Cassady or a Jim Morrison to act as a catalyst and fertilize the scene and take it to a higher level. The west coast punks never really found that ubiquitous ruler of the culture. Even the venerable Ramones were still denied airplay. Then in the '80s music television sent most of that early generation down the garbage disposal of history as best they could.

In the visual arts, Raymond Pettibon and Gary Panter contributed enormously to the look and identity of West Coast punk culture in a similar manner to efforts made a generation earlier by Stanley Mouse and Alton Kelley, Robert Williams, Rick

Griffin, R. Crumb, and S. Clay Wilson who radically rearranged and tuned in visual data for psychedelia and the heads of the 1960s. They explored and defined areas of strange consciousness which were unique to their time and their audiences, expressing their sense of unease, fractured mental health, disenfranchisement, individuality, perversity, social alienation and distorted perceptions. At the magazine we tried to work with the artists Pettibon and Panter, Georganne Deen, the Piz, Shawn Kerri, Richard Duardo, Carol Lay, Minimal Man, quadriplegic dwarf Mark Gash and others with graphic art skills who rigorously contributed to the gestalt of the L.A. punk scene, believing they were the wunderkind of our social morass.

The Los Angeles musicians were always ready to help pull us through our publishing crises and when the occasional well-meaning person would come along and offer a free venue for a live show, P*NK Magazine would capitalize on that opportunity. This kind of entrepreneurship, combining publishing and entertainment which required skills that could have made me a rich man, was truly too much for the frayed nerves of my already shattered and fragile psyche. There was any number of musical groups that I was working with at any time period who went on to become major acts. Let me qualify that by saying that they weren't major acts just yet and the higher percentage of the groups bottomed out, burned out or just went to the dead musician graveyard. Nevertheless, I had a vast pool of talent at my disposal and a truly unique opportunity to sponsor some great shows. There was just one problem and it was always the same problem in a new and different configuration. Something always went terribly wrong the night of the show.

The first benefactor was Ricky Lynne. He was a professional interior designer who went to art openings and he was a lover of the new music scene who went out frequently to see the live punk shows. He offered me the use of his large art studio in Venice Beach for one night to put on a benefit show for P*NK Magazine with any three or four live acts of my choice. This opportunity really was my only chance to get the mean green cash to hand to my nine fingered Latino printer in the Bay Area. I believed that I was a desperate man staring at publishing extinction in the face. The list of account executives in Los Angeles, Hollywood, and Beverly Hills who were willing to work for free was extremely short.

Ricky Lynne was an articulate and successful businessman with a big friendly smile and he had a penchant for wearing white three piece suits, just the opposite of the punk styles. A Saturday Night Fever John Travolta clone, he was not. His white suits were not coming from the world of disco fever, they were another kind of white suit. Ricky's suits had a kind of Great Gatsby casual air of affluence about them. In fact, he looked sharp and natty except his dry cleaning bills must have been orbiting the moon. He was in his early forties and balding with a smidgen of grey in his thinning hair. The studio was finished entirely in white in the manner that artists do with loft space. There were no plastic milk cartons for tables. Everything was high design keyed in white leather and wood grain and brushed metal.

To my surprise, it required only two mischievous punk girls to make short work of Ricky's place the night of the benefit show. Because of their efforts, no one in attendance could complain about a lack of excitement. After his studio filled up with an audience and the second band was playing their first song there was a kind of small disaster. Helen Killer, one of L.A.'s original punk girls and her girlfriend Lizzie broke a few things that were breakable; then they uprooted Ricky's thirty foot tall exotic indoor plant that grew up into an elegantly designed vertical skylight and they killed it dead. They broke its stem. Then came the sudden noxious explosion. The girls set off a large chemical fire extinguisher that they found which in one instant blast filled the entire studio, over 3000 square feet, with a thick yellow cloud that was a harsh irritant to the mucous membranes, throat and eyes. Everything in the place, on the ground floor and up in the loft, including the cat and the crowd of humans, was covered with a thick yellow powder. Ricky Lynne's white suit was now chemically yellowed, as was his designer furniture. Myself and three other P*NK Magazine representatives, concerned about the survival of the publication escaped to a park across the street with the cashbox. From our seat on a grassy knoll in the dark we could see in the distance that the interior of Ricky's studio was a chaos of people running around in this bright yellow gaseous vapor. At that point in time, we had no idea what was the cause of that chemical haze explosion.

I said to Dante, "If we go back in there he's going to want all this money to pay for damages to his place. Let's all split up. Dante, we'd better take the money now and ride out of here. I'll phone Ricky tomorrow."

So we ran with the money to the leadsled Merc, leaving the bands, the entire audience and Ricky behind choking in the yellow gas.

The second benefit show was put in motion when a well-meaning and sophisticated lady with a German accent whom I had become acquainted with through various art openings offered me the use of her art studio in the old Bank District of downtown Los Angeles to put on a show with three or four live punk rock groups as entertainment. Her name was Elisa. I supplied her with a gently couched warning although I was not wanting to scare her off the whole deal.

"Elisa," I said, "these bands play at an extremely loud volume and the place will be packed as tight as a sardine can with rockers, punk rockers."

"Oh, the noise doesn't matter at all," she said, "and there is really nothing to break or destroy in there. The studio is six floors above the street so there shouldn't be any problems. We can even set up a bar if you like."

Without a doubt, Elisa's loft was a great place to put on a show. At street level, there was a brightly lit extremely narrow Chinese restaurant greasy dive that skewed off to the right and shared part of the entranceway to the building although this location wasn't in L.A.'s Chinatown. The old Bank District was tucked away down below Broadway a few blocks. Chinatown was nestled about a mile to the west. The Chinese diners adjacent to Elisa's loft building all stared with wide-eyed curiosity as we entered and exited the building. Inside there was a freight elevator with wooden slats so that a person standing outside the elevator could look in and see a rider in the elevator even when the door was closed and vice versa. Then to the right of the elevator was a stairwell going up. There was an abundance of red brick and cement and raunchy downtown L.A. atmosphere. The sidewalks outside smelled fusty sweet from stale urine. Elisa's studio itself was an enormous airy loft about four thousand square feet with twenty-four foot high ceilings and beautiful expanses of old warehouse windows which gave it great light during the daytime. There wasn't an abundance of things in there to wreck and there was even an elevated area with ample power outlets that would work well as a stage. We set the date, booked four bands, did the advertising and promotions, and word-of-mouthed the hell out of the event. This project was an A-OK GO just like a space mission and the countdown was on. This one smelled of success and punk rocket fuel.

On the night of the show Danté and I took turns handling the cash box and working the door. We had hired no security. The punks didn't fight with each other as a rule. There was a great comraderie amongst them; mosh pits hadn't yet at that period in time been spontaneously invented by audiences. The place filled up with people, just like magic. Money, money, money, slurp, slurp, slurp. A new band named No Warning played first. The sound system worked great. In the middle of their set three guys who looked like boot camp soldier recruits on leave or maybe the B-string guards from the UCLA Bruins football team started heckling the singer Rick. We must have got the word out too far. Rick was a skinny guy about 5'11" who had a face like a grinning skull with bleached out wild hair and he always wore black funereal type of clothes, lace sleeved shirts, black trousers and black well-heeled boots with decorative silver toe points. He was singing... "Dead are alive! Dead are alive! I wanna know why the dead are alive." The audience was jumping and dancing madly and the three frat jock buddies started heckling him...he left the stage like a buzzsaw, teeth biting, fists flying, kicking, he was all over those three beefy non-punks. You wouldn't imagine that it was remotely possible, but he tore the stuffings out of all three of them while the song went to a bridge, and then popped back up onstage in time for the next set of lyrics. Scrappy and vicious.

In its own way, it was a beautiful thing to behold and I made a note to myself, 'Next show, I should hire some kind of floor security. I'll find a tough guy who is a part of the punk rock scene.'

Then another nearly unpleasant circumstance almost happened. A friend of mine, Kenneth McLean, showed up on my invitation. He was an artist, crippled, confined to a wheelchair. He was severely handicapped from a disease. I should know what he had but I realize now that I don't know exactly even though I had put him to bed and bathed him from time to time. I think he was afflicted with an advanced case of Lou Gehrig's disease. He had a tracheotomy and he required mechanical breathing assistance nearly all of the time and he had lost all use of his arms and legs. At home, he turned the pages of a book, he loved reading, with an unsharpened pencil turned eraser forward and clenched between his teeth. While he was watching this same punk band later in the set, a pimply punk kid came running out of the rear of the audience, grabbed Kenneth by the neck and shoulders and swung him and his chair around in a couple of loop de loops, and then he ran back and disappeared into the crowd. Kenneth was wide-eyed and gasping for air. Seeing this from a little distance, I raced over to aid him.

"He choked me!" he heaved in terror.

Kenneth's caretaker, who was a college art student trying to earn a few dollars wasn't around to be seen. He was off chasing girls and drinking alcohol. That was how Kenneth got by. He paid minimum wage to college students to care for him. He needed expensive professional medical care twenty-four seven. But this is America where the rich get quality medical care, so Kenneth hired whatever college kids he could find to do the job, cheap and cheaper. He needed to be bathed and clothed and fed and pooped. He had art assistants and he sold his art through NYC high end dealers. He was a very brave guy to keep going on with his life like he did. One night his caretaker went out for a few beers after Kenneth was put into bed. His respirator failed. The respirator failure alarm was on the mattress next to him. He hit the alarm lever with his head, and it rang loudly but no one heard. When the caretaker returned, Kenneth was dead.

After the 'No Warning' played, 'Boozoo Hogs' set up onstage and began playing their loud erotic bad music. Danté was out in the audience somewhere having fun while I took care of the duties at the door.

Suddenly Danté came rushing up to me and he said excitedly, "Kickface just came up from downstairs. He says there are a dozen cops down there and they're coming up right now in the elevator!"

I said, "Are you kidding me? I don't believe it! How could they have a complaint about us up here on the sixth floor?"

He said, "There's a whole mess of them down there and police cars are lined up in rows in the street."

"When they come up here, they're gonna confiscate our cashbox. L.A. cops are assholes. If they're coming up the elevator, we can boogie on down the stairs. Grab the cash from the bar. We've gotta escape Danté!"

I closed up the cashbox and without looking back, Danté and myself surreptitiously sped down the six flights of stairs leaving the audience and bands and the party behind to their fate. When we hit the ground floor running; we popped out of the stairwell into the freight elevator lobby a bit too quickly. There was the see-thru elevator stuffed full of L.A.P.D. The whole darn dozen of them had fit inside there at once. They were all in such a hurry to get upstairs that no one wanted to be left behind. The noise of the elevator motor kicking in coincided with our sudden appearance in the lobby, and the lift jerked upward. Danté and I looked guilty as hell standing there just six feet away from all of them with the metal cashbox. They didn't see us because they were all looking straight up at the source of the guitar music and noise. The sound of that raucous music up there was not to their liking. We walked calmly past the group of wide-eyed Chinese diners and smiled; then we passed the string of empty police cruisers that lined the red curb with their flashing lights. We walked calmly and deliberately in a beeline to the commercial parking lot where Danté's silver ledsled was waiting and drove back to the Hollywood office. Once there, we counted the money.

"I'll call Elisa in the morning." I said.

"I bet she'll be glad to hear from you." laughed Danté.

The third benefit show came off a bit differently. It was held at the venerable Whisky nightclub up on the Sunset Strip. The Whisky offered me the use of the club for a show and a percentage of the door. We proceeded with the usual wind up and countdown preparations. The day of the show arrived. The bands did soundchecks in the late afternoon, all went smoothly, the club filled up, packed with punk styled people after the doors opened in the evening. The Whisky supplied their own typical security, a couple of three hundred pound six foot five walls of beef with the three foot flashlights which doubled as nightsticks. Security was that one detail which I had made a special note to follow up on from the previous P*NK Magazine benefit shows. The consequences of tight professional security became clear to me early in the evening. I spent the greater part of the evening outside on the Sunset

Strip sidewalk in front of the club because I got eighty-sixed during the first thirty minutes. One of the bouncers found me objectionable. I made several attempts to re-enter the club and regain my position as the gracious and inebriated host for the evening.

"You can't throw me out! This is my fucking show." I insisted.

"It's not your show." Another bouncer said looking down at me. Then out to the street I again was roughly bounced. I waited a while and built up momentum for the next attempt and then ended up right back out on the street. The band Redd Kross pulled up to the curb in a long early seventies four door American gas guzzler about a half block down the street and I sauntered down to their car to hang out for an hour or so. This teenaged girl named Kathy who I knew from the scene told me that she had climbed up on the roof of the Whisky one night just for fun and she had found a small apartment up there that was not being used by anyone. Kathy told me she had been secretly living in it and that no one ever came up there. She said that for six months she had been squatting up there. I went across the street and bought a few beers and Kathy and me climbed up the hill behind The Whisky and got into the back seat of Dantés ledsled and we fucked. Kathy had black hair and fair skin and she wasn't too skinny and bony like some rock and roll girls get. I always preferred the softer curvy serpentine ones. That was how I spent my P*NK Magazine benefit night on the Sunset Strip. When I returned later to the interior of the world famous Whisky nightclub as the show finished, I was able to penetrate the massive wall of bouncers. I attempted to collect my share of the money.

Now, according to the hands on the official Whisky clock it was shuck-and-jive time on the beautiful famous and glamorous Sunset Strip. They paid me, but they used that funny math that seems to crop up in fast cash situations when one side has the predominance of muscle. There was the ticket doll in the glass booth, three three hundred pound red neck gorillas, a wan bean counter in the back office, the stage manager, the sound guy, the janitor, the three cocktail waitresses, the club owner and the property taxes on a high rent corner lot building on the Sunset Strip, all of which needed to be paid for in full for the evening before I could take my percentage. P*NK Magazine (represented solely by myself) then received fifty percent of the remaining ten percent of the door. I could accept this lean and mean deal for the cash that they offered or get beat up right now and thrown out on the street again, and get nothing but extra lumps, more professionally administered contusions. Danté was off duty having a good time, partying backstage, not concerned with the cashbox. It was always fun partying backstage at The Whisky.

The Orpheum, The Masque, Baces Hall, The Whisky a Go Go, Hong Kong Café, King's Palace (later became Raji's), Cathey De Grande, Godzillas, Zero One, Blackies, Alpine Gardens, The Starwood, Anti-Club, L.A. Elks Lodge, Cuckoos Nest, The Fleetwood, Club 88, The Stardust Ballroom, The Vex, Al's Bar, Vern and the Vanguard Gallery.

Hanging out at night in punk rock nightclubs and unlicensed venues, on the sidewalk, in parking lots and illegal after hours clubs was where the scene came together and coalesced. Initially hanging out had made me feel uneasy. It was time consuming. Not that I had anything better to be doing with my talents. There were feelings about the inadequate use of my time that I had to reckon with, considering the creeping work ethic which had saturated my genes. I tape recorded conversations with punk bands and talkative people. The insignificant off-the-wall conversation snippets were what intrigued me the most. Formal interviews with star people just killed me with boredom except that I wanted to fuck the pretty ones. People get self-important, self-conscious, and cautious in front of a microphone. They are reluctant to reveal their unguarded true nature in a formal interview situation, so I would try to break that barrier down completely with anyone I talked to by appearing to be completely incompetent, not much of a problem for me.

"I was listening to the music and minding my own business when 'boom', somebody hits me in the back of the head," a very hot looking punkette with long red hair revealed to me. "I turned to see who or what it was and there was this distorted, anger, shit frozen all over face. I thought 'Great, just great! Another neurotic edging her way towards disaster is trying to drag me with her into the abyss of a grand mal fantasy.' Well what I really did was just like, hit her back, you know. Upon my audacious attempt at defense, more fists come flying. There were so many people crowded near the stage and I'm so short that all the attacker could get at was my head. It felt like golf balls were dropping on me from the rafters. A-ha! It's a set up. And whatever for? Jeez. Is my hair too long? Too long for what? Excuse me. I'll run right out and cut it. Then, I grabbed some purple-headed girl's hair, tucked my head and just sort of held on, riding her like a bronco. I didn't even know if the girl whose hair I had attached myself to was my attacker. She asked me afterwards why I had pulled her hair. I had thought that it was obvious. So anyway, they're all screaming for me to let go of her hair. All the while it's still raining rocks, right? Then I heard a r-r-rip! Since I had on a dress and things didn't seem to be progressing any, I let go of her head. Never do that! Get a hold of someone and hang on because it makes it hard for them to move you around and do stuff to you. After I let go they flung me around like a piece of shit, or more vividly, like dogs fighting over a piece of meat, from one end of the floor to the other."

"I don't remember what it was like after that 'cause I split. My body was out there but the rest of me was up in the sound booth just watching and shaking my imaginary head and thinking, 'Wow, when this is over, she's not going to have any clothes on. I bet she's glad she joined the spa. Look at that, she should have worked on her butt more.'"

"Then it was over and I went back to my poor abandoned body and sort of just shook my head. Whew! It was just like stepping off a motherfucker roller coaster ride that just got jammed. As suddenly as it began it had ended and I was just standing there. I tilted my head down and winced. There they were, bare tits, pubes and somewhere behind me, I hoped, optimistically, was my ass. The bouncer just kept saying, 'Are you OK?' and I just kept saying, 'Give me your coat! Give me your coat!'

"For me, the intrigue lies not in why it happened. It happened because my hair is too fucking long or I think I'm hot shit or something else. Who cares? It happened because they were battered children, or had never had an orgasm, or were malnutritioned before the age of five and left with irreversible brain damage. Who cares? What intrigues me is the feeling that I was left with. Elation? No, too strong. Stoked. Refreshed. Maybe that's it. Refreshed. Purged. Maybe I should start a new self-help program where you pay money and then let people beat you."

Club 88 was on Pico Boulevard near Culver City. I rode down there with Danté on his brother's Harley-Davidson. We left off the story thread with Danté and myself riding up the freeway at night a few pages back if you remember. It was the night of an X show. It was a fun show. The club was super-packed and everybody was sweaty and drunk by the end of the evening. After the usual talky–talk with friends, Danté and I rode the iron pony up to a party at an fancy expansive maison in the Hollywood hills; following us was a large contingent of the audience from the nightclub including my senior citizen friend, the art instructor Giles. Once there, I partook of a party item which was on my extremely short list of banned substances, marijuana. I hadn't smoked that popular weed in over ten years. People who smoke it get uneasy around people who say, "No thanks." They immediately decide that you're not a bro. Try to find a heroin addict who wants to share with you. It's that paranoia state of mind that the cannabis engenders, a false brotherhood of the roach. Marijuana knocked my little mind too far off balance and I knew that but I was drinking free champagne at the party and got a little too drunk and then I smoked. Also, champagne isn't a good thing to be drinking if you are a chronic juicer. What I did is called casual and social drug taking, but I was never casual or social about drugs and drinking. I was already drunk when we left Hollywood on the motorcycle for Club 88.

Later, I got a ride to another party at the L.A. Subs apartment on a hilly sidestreet off of Sunset Boulevard across the street from the Chateau Marmont and in some proximity to a lifesize statue of Bullwinkle the Moose (eat your heart out Paris France) and left Danté and Giles behind at the canyon party with the address on a torn piece of paper. Eamonn, the skinny wise-ass red-haired Irish singer of the band (and part time cross-dresser) was still up at the party in the hills and several people were loitering on the street waiting for his arrival. The party-goers on the street were stranded outside even though the party seemed to be raging four floors up, judging by the movement behind the windows. This was due to the locked security doors and a faulty intercom. So everyone was waiting for Eamonn to arrive. Life in Los Angeles before cell phones is hard to imagine today. How did people survive in 1979?

They survived at a disadvantage compared to modern man. After about five minutes on the sidewalk I felt it necessary to verify that the door was indeed locked. This door was in fact a pair of metal framed plate glass doors with thick glass for security, and which was was set to automatically lock for the safety of the residents. So I shook the handle. It didn't open. Then I knocked on the door and when I looked down my arm had punched a hole all the way through the heavy plate glass. I got a good look at the slice and it was terrible, running bone deep down and across the inside of my wrist for five inches, a harsh lesson in human anatomy. Blood quickly covered the sidewalk and was flowing in a broad swath down the sloping cement. People were silent for an indefinite period after it happened and then things got strange. I grabbed the wound and applied pressure tightly with my opposing hand. I may have walked around in circles for a bit.

Soon, I leaned up against a parked car and said, "Could somebody call an ambulance."

There was no pay phone nearby, but up on Sunset Boulevard somewhere there would have been one if someone had wanted to run up there and look for one. In Los Angeles, when you try to find a pay phone in a hurry and you're on foot and it's an emergency, suddenly the exaggerated distances of the city blocks become real and nightmarish stretched perspectives. You may run around the sidewalks for twenty minutes trying to find a pay phone and when you do, someone will have stuck their chewing gum in the coin slot. I doubt if anyone went to seek a pay phone for my benefit. Several punk kids began water ski sliding down the sloping sidewalk on the sheet of blood which slickened the surface. Punk kids had a way of making fun out of pain.

An art gallery owner with whom I was acquainted came up to me with white beach towel and he said, "Ronnie, take this and wrap your arm in it."

"I don't want a to wrap it in a towel Tony. I'll bleed to death. It'll suck all of the blood out of me."

"Take it Ronnie!" He admonished me.

"No thanks!"

"Fuck you then. I hope you die. I hope you fucking die!" He shouted in my face. He was furious.

"I feel your love but I don't want the towel." I said. I was so calm that I was just going to stay there leaning on that car and bleed, unable to help myself. In reality, I was in no shape to go to look for a phone and it was getting harder and harder for me to form any kind of speech at all. I must have looked a sight, covered in blood, dripping down my shirt and blue jeans, bloody shoes, hands and forearms. I heard a person making a commotion down the street and I looked up and Giles was there about ten yards away in the crowd pushing people aside, rushing up to me. He appeared like an ugly old angel from heaven. If he had a pair of white wings attached to his back I wouldn't have been surprised. That wrinkly old sage beatnik face looked me straight in the eyes through the mental fog.

He said, "Get in my car now. I'm taking you to the hospital."

I said, "Thanks Giles, I was waiting for an ambulance."

"I don't think one is coming Ronnie." he said.

I made some small talk with him but he wasn't laughing at my jokes. He drove me to Cedars-Sinai Emergency and they booked me into a room immediately. That's all I remember of that night.

In the morning, when I awoke, I was surprised to be in a hospital. They announced that I wasn't going to be released today or the following day. My mom still carried me on her health insurance policy. The wrist was so bad it needed a specialist surgeon to perform an operation. I was in there a couple of days, three days. Next to my bed were the blood soaked shoes that I was wearing the night before. I was shocked at the mess of it. They were the same beige European chic steppers that I was wearing the night that the police beat me up. Those were the only two times that I had ever worn them. I had to wear all those bloody clothes out of the hospital when I was released. When I got home, back to Hollywood Boulevard, I threw my bloody shoes in the trash bin.

"Bad luck shoes! Get out of my life." I said.

Eamonn called me up when I was in the hospital and said he was in dutch with his landlord because I broke the door glass. I told him that I didn't try to break it. The glass just gave way. My mom was beginning to suspect that I was crazy. I couldn't deal with that concern. I was crazy and I had a magazine to publish unless I decided to do something else with my life.

Four or five months later, Danté and I were cruising around Hollywood in his '51 Merc in the early part of a cool clear evening. It was a friday night and I was little bit drunk on malt liquor and we were enjoying ourselves, laughing, driving east to west on Melrose Avenue. The shops were closing and the twinkling lights were coming on. One light began twinkling a bit too conspicuously and Danté said,

"Uh oh, Ronnie. We've got a cop behind us. Don't worry about it. I can handle this. You don't have any open beer do you?"

"No beer anywhere, open or unopen Mr D."

One cop came over to the driver's window with the flashlight while his partner stood back four paces with his hand on his 9mm. The LAPD used to pull their pistols during routine traffic stops but they passed a law to restrain them because the LAPD had a record of being notoriously aggressive. It all happened really fast while I sat cozy in the passenger seat. They gave Danté a physical drunk test on the side of the road. Touch your nose with your index finger. Very good. Hard to miss that formidable nose. Walk the line like Johnny Cash. He was stone cold sober. Meanwhile, the other one had run Danté's name for outstanding warrants. He was the one who cuffed Danté. I jumped out of the passenger seat.

"Hey, what's going on? Why is he handcuffed?"

"There's a warrant issued for his arrest."

"Wait a second. Where are you taking him?"

"To jail. Na na na. That's where you can find him."

He was pushed into the back seat of the patrol car and they were gone. They wouldn't speak to me. He could have said to jail in Mozambique. They do that on purpose. They don't want to make it easy to find a person under arrest so they mumble the information and look the other way when they speak. They never check-ed to see if I was in any condition to drive. I wasn't. The keys were in the car and so I drove it down a residential street and parked it. My adrenaline was pumping and I thought it would be a prudent idea to just walk up Highland Avenue to Hollywood Boulevard, get some fresh air, think about what I was going to do next. My car was parked at the office. It was thirty minutes by foot at the most. Jail and bail seemed to be the unexpected themes for this evening. Danté was probably arrested for missing a date in court for a speeding violation. That was about as bad a miscreant as he ever was. They arrested the sober driver and left the drunk guy with the car.

At the intersection of Highland Avenue and Sunset Boulevard, just across from Hollywood High School I stopped and pushed the little annoying Wait/Walk button and then I waited. This intersection is one of those long Los Angeles crosswalks that seem to stretch out like a bad dream when you are on foot in the middle of the intersection, with cars swirling around you performing left turns and right turns at high speed, detesting pedestrians especially the elderly and women with baby strollers, running their tires inches from any pedestrian's toes; and that is how it works at best when the light instructs you to walk. Good luck. Everyone in any car in Los Angeles, hates the pedestrian. Then after dark, because there are so many cars in so many lanes, with flashing lights, stop and go, smelly exhaust, neon advertising, blasting stereo systems, glaring headlights, those pissed off drivers have a difficult time separating a sole pedestrian from the visual pollution. I was halfway into the intersection when this guy people called Benny The Rat sticks his head out of a car stopped in the left turn lane three cars back going east on Sunset Boulevard, waiting to turn up Highland toward Hollywood Boulevard.

"Hey Ronnie! How are you doing?" shouts BTR.

Benny The Rat was a small time dealer of party drugs in the nightclubs. Those were the only kind of dealers that peopled my world. I wasn't acquainted with any dealers with the status of Scarface. A little idea went off in my head and it said that maybe if I was persuasive, Benny The Rat would loan me a hundred dollars in cash to help bail out Danté. Everybody loved Danté. So I ran out of the crosswalk and up to the window of the car which was full of punk kids on the way to a club.

"Hey, Danté just got arrested on a warrant. I'm just walking up to my office to try to fix his bail." I said.

I wanted to draw his interest in the circumstances so I could get him to pull over to the side of the road up on Highland and then filch some cash. He was one of the more likely scenemakers to be carrying a pocket full of Jacksons. Who is Jackson? Andrew Jackson, Stonewall Jackson, Jesse Jackson? And what denomination is he on anyway? Then the light changed, their car jerked forward into the intersection leaving me exposed and I turned around to greet the hard rectangular bumper of a powder blue Cadillac Seville moving westward on the green light in opposing traffic. Looking down at my knee, I saw it hyperextend backwards at a forty five degree angle as the chromed bumper struck it, the wrong direction for a knee to bend. Next, I'm lying flat out on the double yellow line on Sunset Boulevard in front of Hollywood High School. I never could have imagined that occurring when I first moved to Los Angeles. Traffic, always extremely heavy on a friday evening, ground to a standstill, total gridlock. There was a body in the middle of the road, my body. Cars stopped in both directions all around me, honking, yelling, gawking, harsh headlights, taillights, brake lights, streetlights. Excruciating pain.

"This is great. I'm having fun now." I said out loud to myself.

Now I saw there were some friends of mine standing at the bus stop in front of the high school over across the multiple lanes of opposing traffic waving to me. I waved back. It all seemed too surreal.

"Hi! How are you doing? Nice to see you?" I said wryly. They probably saw my lips move but didn't hear me.

"Hi, Ronnie!" I could hear them shouting.

Then a siren approached. An ambulance, thank god get me out of here. Two uniformed attendants walked up to me. They stood over me. Looked at me down on the pavement. They had seen worse. They were unimpressed.

"Get up!" shouted one.

"Get up!" shouted the other one. Comedy night.

"He was running around in the middle of the goddam traffic!" shouted the driver of the Cadillac, a black middle-aged man in a blue dress shirt with a dark tie. He was indignant.

"If I could get up, I wouldn't be layin' here in the street would I?" I barked back at the attendants.

"Stand up!" the first one shouted again. This was apparently as good as the dialogue was going to get under these circumstances.

"I can't stand up. He hit my leg with his fucking car. So you're just going to have to pick me up yourselves. Isn't that your fucking job?" I shouted, eyeing the rectilinear angles of the Cadillac. I was thinking that any Cadillac Seville from the 1950s would have been much more sympathetic to the human form that these contemporary angular models. A Volkswagen Beetle would have made a heavenly soft impact by comparison. My life was becoming an unglamorous J.G. Ballard simulation. The uniforms all did their paperwork as prescribed by law, then they placed me on a gurney and transported me to Hollywood Presbyterian Hospital because it was their job and duty. This was not so attractive a hospital as Cedars-Sinai. In fact it was dismal.

"No movie stars come to this hospital to die." I thought. Nobody was going to appreciate my humor this night. Two cops came in to the emergency room after about an hour and threw some papers on my chest.

"You're lucky you didn't dent the car." said the one beefy cop who looked exactly like the other one, carnivores. They kind of sneered in disdain and walked out.

They took all night to x-ray the knee and get the results back. About 5 a.m. a technician, male nurse or a doctor, (they all looked the same), came in and said to me that nothing was broken but I probably had some cartilage damage and that I should see an orthopedic specialist. By this hour, my leg was swollen and enlarged, like an elephantiasis victim in a photo from an old National Geographic Magazine. Another male attendant put me in a wheelchair and wheeled me out into an anteroom at about 6 a.m. There I sat blindly signing any paperwork that was pushed in front of me. Then, the male attendant briskly wheeled me out to the curb on Vermont Avenue. It was a beautiful sunshine bathed Saturday morning in Los Angeles, and upon arriving at Vermont Avenue he tilted the wheelchair forward and tried to shake me into the gutter at a No Parking zone where the curb was marked in red.

I said, "What do you think you are doing asshole?"

"You've been discharged. Get out of the chair." he said.

"You must be out of your fucking mind. You're not going to dump me out of this chair." My dad made me wear an itchy wool suit to Presbyterian Sunday School every week as a child.

He started shaking the chair from left to right and tilting it forward again. It must have been my clothes and the haircut. My appearance had a bad effect on the ambulance attendants and the two policemen as well, all were guys in uniform.

"You're one crazy motherfucker aren't you? I'm not going anywhere. You're going to wheel me back in the hospital. Then you're going to call me a taxicab and then wheel me out to the cab when it arrives. So now let's go! C'mon! Turn it around big boy." It did not go unnoticed by me that there were no cheering friends from the Sunset Boulevard busstop awaiting my release.

The attendant went silent and wheeled me back into the hospital. Then he disappeared down a hallway, called for a taxi and when it arrived he wheeled me back out to the street with a sullen demeanor. If this was the rude handling that Presbyterians gave people in pain then I was ashamed for them. My father had always taken our family to a Presbyterian Church and now I suffered this indignity by their hands. This was barbaric and uncivilized behavior, definitely not the red carpet executive treatment that I received at the Cedars-Sinai Hospital for the wrist injury. Crap hospital. It follows from grape juice for Holy Communion. Serve Pepsi Cola and corn chips as the body and blood of Christ and see what happens to the world.

Based upon my experience as a victim, I would say that it is a better medical holiday to be hospitalized on the west side of town where the movie stars and sexy starlets patronize. A five dollar taxi ride took me to Hollywood and Las Palmas. I unlocked the door on the street and hopped up the twenty-eight steeply inclined back steps leading into the Pioneer Spirit Building from Las Palmas Avenue on one leg and rested for an hour. Then I got on the telephone. I called a different former art instructor other than Giles for this disaster, seeking help in getting Danté freed from jail. I was running out of former art instructors to ask for favors. I pulled down my blue jeans for a looksee and the left leg was already turning completely blue from the mid-thigh down to the calf and the knee had swelled painfully and become rigid. Alan picked up the phone on the second ring and listened to my sad tale. Fortunately for me and for Danté he was an early riser.

"C'mon over and we'll see what we can do for you." he said. "Can you drive? I'll make some coffee."

"I'll be right over. I think I can drive." Hopping up from my recumbent position, I felt a bit exhausted from the night before but those sensations were cast aside by my excitement at having found a helpmate to get me through the dismal process at the County Jail while bunny hopping on one leg. That was where citizens and non-citizens under arrest ended up if they were detained all night. Downtown L.A. Off I went, with a severe limp-hop to Alans studio on the east side of Hollywood, in the rundown section of Melrose Avenue east of Western at about 8:00 am.

Ka-da-bump—ka-da-bump—ka-da-bump—ka-da-bump—ka-da-bump—ka-da-bumpbump—ka-da-bump—ka-da-bump—ka-da-bump—ka-da-bump—ka-da-bump—ka-da-bumpthump!

"Shit! Fuck!...Anything new broken?" I asked aloud with a forced calmness to my voice.

I looked at my arms and shook them. I was sitting upright, my head turned to the left and to the right, nose wasn't broken, the toes wiggled, ribs were pain free. There were a few painful knots on my head, but that was to be expected. I looked up at the stairs behind me. Twenty-eight stairs head over heels at eight a.m., not a bad accomplishment...for a Hollywood stuntman maybe. Putting some weight on that injured leg at the top of the stairs was my downfall. No time for a play on words, once I went over and gravity took control there was no option left but to roll up into a ball and shoot the whole flight. Stopped abruptly by the concrete slab at ground level, it was a thriller but at least I had landed in a sitting position because at the speed I had attained by the time I reached the bottom, I could have rolled through the plate glass door just two feet in front of me.

"Steep wooden stairs, outside edges are worn down by the years, lucky they aren't concrete." I thought. "No harm done, better get going. Pretend it didn't happen. Just add the lumps to the limp. No need to tell anybody about this one."

There was another kind of damage that occurred which didn't escape me, in fact it raced across my mind even as I was in the throes of noisily tumbling down and picking up speed at every rotation. There was a negative metaphor therein which was going to settle into my cheery mindset and be recalcitrant to erasure by positive thinking, a way of self-description about which I felt some malaise. A subsurface man diving and spiralling down down never to return to the surface again. A man spinning downward into oblivion, not unconscious but in a bad dream state of awakeness, in an out-of-control descent into destruction.

Picking myself up almost immediately and shaking it off, I hopped out to the parking lot where my Volkswagon was residing in the early morning sunshine. Getting into the car was a problem but not insurmountable, driving it was nearly impossible. The new elephant leg which I had acquired was too intractable to allow the foot to meet the clutch pedal. The leg was as stiff as a fire hydrant and it extended beyond the pedal to floor. This was not a time to panic although it was extremely painful. I was looking at a basic work around situation. The new bumps on my head actually alleviated some of the pain from the knee injury and the adrenaline from the fall had cleared the sleep from my mind. I managed to drive by clutching with the right leg, accelerating with the same, and braking primarily with the handbrake. In this manner I made it down to Melrose Ave. from Hollywood Boulevard avoiding the Wilcox Police station by going down Van Ness which is several blocks to the East. People in Volkswagon Beetles always were driving like they were from a strange planet so I doubted that I would raise suspicions. I was sober anyway, and there's nothing illegal about driving a standard four speed transmission with one foot if you have the skills. Nevertheless, I didn't want to talk to anymore cops in one day than was absolutely necessary and jail was going to be a meaty cop mecca. That hot coffee that was waiting for me at Alan's was drawing me like a battered puppy to a dog biscuit. That morning I decided to sell the VW Beetle and get a larger car.

Alan had family problems to reckon with of the maternal kind. He had some kind of crazy mother who tormented him. His hair was cut short and it had the same textural characteristics as a wire-haired fox terrier. It was colored a neutral dark brown and it capped a freckly pale skinned baby-face with a happy-sad demeanor. His face seemed to say, "I am a happy person but I am saddened by life's problems." He taught drawing at the art institute and I had never even taken any of his classes. For reasons that I don't understand, I only enrolled in drawing classes with the asshole dictatorial old school anachronistic pompous bag of Renaissance art and Winnie the Pooh intestinal wind, the kind of instructor that was completely unsuited to my disposition. I had been punishing myself with my choice of drawing instructors. Alan would have been the perfect drawing instructor for a student like myself, so I never took his classes. There was an inverted logic in it. The Renaissance was not bad in itself but it needed to be imbued with an understanding of racing technology as described by Marshall McLuhan, at the very least, after the 1960s media explosion evolved and changed our culture or the instructor was just an irrelevant dinosaur. The media explosion was/is this ongoing explosion of human data perpetuating itself through technology like the nuclear fires of the sun that alters and contorts human culture and global species inter-communication. It's all part of our homosapien genetic rush to super-evolution or super-destruction through technology. It would be more exciting if we made less garbage and shit.

Nevertheless, outside of class, Alan and I had become friends. And he had a crazy bent to him. His girlfriend Dahlia, an art student when I attended college, had shown me the wall outside her second story guest house apartment in Mount Washington, the somewhat trendy hills which rise above the poorer latino lowland neighborhoods of Highland Park.

"Do you see this wall? Look how far up it is to that window. After I locked him out of the front door, he climbed up that wall somehow just holding on to the stucco with his fingertips and cowboy boots and he opened my window. He defied gravity. It seems impossible." she laughed. "He was so angry at me that he punched me in the stomach. That's why I won't see him anymore."

The male art instructors, even the grey-haired ones, and administrative faculty at the art institute fucked as many of the female students as they could bed. Alan was just in his early thirties but he was keeping up his sexual quota with that of the randy greys. Alan's mom was a hypochondriac sadist from what I could tell by his brief and miserable descriptions. She had caused him to bear the burden of a deep anxiety and sadness beyond adolescence and far into adulthood. I had to live with my own ugly familial animosities which caused me to bear paralyzing anxieties and consequently I found Alan's pain and suffering somewhat amusing. That another man suffered from his mother's behavior, made me feel secretly stronger. I suppose my lack of sympathy was a cold personality flaw on my part. We were so similar. Moreover, he talked freely about his mother and his problems relating to her but I kept my mouth shut tight about my family. So, we talked about our lives for a half hour or so in his art studio on that morning of my injury and then we got on the phone and began calling the L.A.P.D. to find out the why, the where and how much about posting bail for Danté.

"I can help you until four o'clock. Then I have to drive up to Carpenteria to see mother. She isn't feeling well." he said with his typical facial expression. There were wrinkles forming in the myriad of freckles that marked his complexion. Creeping age revealed in a moment of soft reflected sunlight on flesh.

"We are all travelers on the road to death." I thought.

"Maybe we can stop at a Salvation Army or Goodwill Store and pick up some cheap crutches on the way down to the jail? I'm not going to be able to hop around on one leg for too long." I said, making an ingratiating statement in the form of a question.

So we did just that. We took Alan's car, a rusting economy deathtrap oil burning sardine can on bald tires, stopping at a thrift store by a hospital on the east end of Sunset Boulevard just before it turns sharply toward the Silverlake District and downtown L.A. I picked out a pair of used wooden crutches with brand new rubber pads on the street ends for five dollars. There were no rubber buffer pads for the armpit cradles but it is down below where the rubber meets the road that tread depth is critical for grip and this pair had all new rubber down below colored in beige which complemented the brown wood. The aluminum tube crutches on display were just not to my taste. They were too Helmut Newton in character and I didn't have the svelte scantily clothed female fashion model body to show off that kind of hardware favorably. It would have been just plain bad fashion for me to be caught wearing aluminum tube crutches. Although, spray-painted multicolor day-glo aluminum crutches would have been a sight. Then we went down to the County Jail. We sprung Danté in no time at all which is good because L.A. County Jail is depressing as hell. Alan put the entire bill on his credit card. We promised Alan we would pay him back. Danté was all smiles when he came out of his holding cell. I was thinking that I should have just taken his car, gone to a nightclub, and left him in there to party until his court date if he was so goddam happy in incarceration.

The next evening I put Danté to work carrying me up and down the stairs to the balcony bar inside The Starwood. There was a series of punk shows taking place there often featuring some of the new bands from the South Bay. The Adolescents were a huge draw and they were packing in sold out audiences. They had a skinny little singer named Tony who drove the audience into a frenzy. This new hybrid audience was comprised of a large percentage of punkers up from Orange County and the beach communities and it was the beginning of the end of the insular Hollywood clique of punk rockers. Black Flag was the first big influential punk rock group from the South Bay, with Social Distortion and the Circle Jerks riding hard on their tail. The local newsprint press had labeled the audiences and musical groups from the South Bay surf punks and much of this faster harder punk music was labeled hardcore. Those were journalistic tags that stuck. Social Distortion didn't look like surfers to me so I didn't entertain that simplified limiting terminology. Music critics get paid to chatter and slap labels on bands but you can be certain that the Sex Pistols, the Clash, and Siouxsie and the Banshees never surfed at Brighton.

On the other hand, if I travelled ten miles to the south of Hollywood I became completely lost. All of those communities to me were a complete blur of small incorporated city and town vagueness that was more or less the same, a contemporary suburban conurbation admixture with generic mini-malls, bad signage and chain stores, more or less expensive. Manhattan Beach and Orange County, Huntington Beach and West Covina were all just like a bowl of oatmeal spilled out and smeared on the table in my mind. Driven mad by suburbia, possibly by the rapid oversaturation of minimalls, the audiences from the many various So Cal burb and beach communities were growing more raucous and that testosterone driven phenomenon known as a mosh pit up front near the stage was forming nightly in a swirling violent vortex at punk shows all over Southern California.

Stage diving was spontaneously initiated at around this time. Typically, a punk kid or two would hop up on stage when the band was playing to the chagrin of the bouncers and insurance carriers, maybe dance around a little, and before they could get grabbed by a heavily muscled meatball security man and ejected from the club, they would dive off the stage and somersault in flight, landing (sometimes) softly on the audience below where they immediately blended into the energized crowd, their own kind. These new audience expressions of thrashing, moshing and diving were sometimes the cause of dislocated shoulders, punches in the solar plexus, black eyes, and other injuries. Stage diving became so ubiquitous that even Big Billy tried it one night at The Whisky while performing a blues song with his R&B band. His great 250 lb. body rotated in the air as he performed an open 360 degree somersault above the audience, but instead of closing together under him, the people split apart fearing the walloping impact from his burly mass. He landed hard on the concrete floor injuring his back and that evening he was carried out on a stretcher.

Into this maelstrom, P*NK Magazine sent redoubtable Danté armed with his

35mm Nikon to photograph the interaction of the audiences with the band perform-ing onstage. After the first couple of nights of hanging at The Starwood, I gained the necessary skills to climb with crutches up to the balcony bar without assistance. It was there that I resided nightly ensconced in a plushy chair with a mixed drink. It was a great place to watch punk shows. The Starwood had previously been the hot venue for metal bands on the way up including Van Halen. If you approached the stage and went through a sort of door-tunnel opening you magically appeared inside a disco bar behind the stage that was completely soundproofed from the live performances, and there you would find on a good night Rodney Bingenheimer, the hip and influential Los Angeles radio DJ spinning 45s.

These years capping off the seventies and launching the eighties were an era of wild promiscuity in L.A., as I saw them play out. People of all sexual orientations were having a ball. Many people had acquired a variety of sexual orientations that quite possibly weren't directed by nature so much as fad and fashion. It was hot to explore the weird and wild even if you were square as a packing box.

The West Hollywood gay bars were just up the street from the Starwood, creating a clash of cultures. Gay punks weren't seen running back and forth between the West Hollywood gay bars and the Starwood in a dizzy race of gender identity confusion. Gay punks stayed with punks. Now and then an angry group of gay men would single out a few punks on the street to fight them outside the Starwood. They felt that punks were bringing down the quality of life in the neighborhood (and probably lowering property values). This reverse gay bashing was short-lived in West Hollywood because the Starwood closed up and ultimately got bulldozed. The Starwood was a piece of the Hole-In-The-Wall-Gang club network owned by Eddie Nash, a drug gangster involved with the porn industry. Eddie Nash owned primarily stripper nightclubs and he was a major player cocaine drug dealer. That's what the cops wanted to prove anyway, drug dealing and then murder. The implication of his involvement in the gruesome Wonderland murders (also known as Four on the Floor Laurel Canyon murders) with an accomplice, the strung out porn star John Holmes, played out in the TV evening news. This public attention to Nash marked the approach of the end of the punk shows at the Starwood and then its demise as a venue; this all occurred around 1980-81. Holmes died of AIDS later in the decade and Nash was too slippery for a conviction.

The Black Dick played a wonderfully offensively entertaining show at the Starwood to a packed house, wearing a scanty glittering sheer jock strap, a purple cowboy hat with rhinestones, a white feather boa, black patent leather S&M heels and a rubber medical device with tubes; he was no Liza Minnelli from Cabaret, he was layered with fat in spite of amphetamine abuse, his skin was so sun deprived that it was translucent white revealing greenish veins networking around the jellied dancing flesh. He was a laugh riot because he was such a nasty sarcastic son-of-a-bitch backed by a great eclectic punky new wave band that absorbed current styles and spit them back out in satire. Goodbye Starwood. And goodbye Black Dick. As I mentioned carelessly ahead of time, a small annoyance for those obsessed with sequence, Black Dick and his girlfriend (she was not introduced earlier in this narrative and now zip, she's gone) died young as a result of intravenous drug use. Some people don't care much if they die young and they don't care a damn who they take along with them. I would assume that the couple suffered appropriately in death but I can't tell you that for certain. This book is, if I may remind you, fiction but it is set against a historical background. You get the best of both worlds in one package. Some of the crudest of literary critics may call that wordplay plain bullshit. After dying the same death more than one time, Black Dick is now hopefully out of the narrative.

CHAPTER 10

LOTUS LAME: "Are we making any money? Do I support myself with this musical group? Only spiritually. I work everyday at a bank. I'm the assistant vice president. Who is the drummer? We only dance and sing. We sing to tapes. We don't play any instruments. Well now, I do play the bongos but I am not what you would call a practicing bongo player. I have to tell you this. When we play for straight audiences, the guys like die for us, for our outfits and stuff, and gay men just love us too. We're the women they want to be. I mean they all want to be up there in those outfits and just be as campy as they can be. You know, the butcher the better. But the thing is that we played two nights at a dyke bar and let me tell you, that next to Catholics, lesbians have absolutely no sense of humor in the whole world. None. They expected Patty LaBelle & The Bluebells and I started singing 'The butcher, the baker, the candlestickmaker, long, short, fat, tall, I've had them all.'...and these women hated us. They didn't do anything. They were totally apathetic. They didn't get it because they have no sense of humor. They thought we were going to be like Aretha Franklin and get up there and sing some tortured love song. You know how lesbians are all tortured. They thought we were going to get up there and sing,

'Ohhh..ohhh...ode..to muff diving.'

"We are really bad. But the point is that we're really bad because we really want to be bad. We practice very hard to be bad. We used to wear jock straps. Our original costumes were red studded jock straps, black fishnet stockings...I used to stuff my jock strap so it looked like I had Dick and Harry down there, sometimes I can, it depends on how drunk I get them, but anyway we would wear jockstraps and these little tight t-shirts that said Lotus Lame & The Crotch Monsters with our names on the back, Lotus, Luana, Lolita, L'Angostino, and Tour of Vulgaria. That was our tour t-shirt and we'd only done a tour of the 'One-Way' bar. So we had jockstraps, t-shirts and I wore high black boots and they wore boots and masks. We wore masks. And then there was this designer who was a friend of ours who said 'I'm going to make you these wonderful costumes so you really look like showgirls, sleazy showgirls.' However, I often wear a nightgown. I found it better after I do my shows to have a nightgown on because you never know when you'll just be getting right in bed with someone. You don't have to even change the costume. You just get off stage and say 'I'm ready! I've got my nightgown on. You've got the missile, I've go the launching pad.'

"Dick, Harry, Joe and Ted. I had them all last night. I'm very inspired by Armenians. Armenians I believe are sexually repressed people and they come to this country and they flip out because they think that American women are up for anything. So you say,

'Hi. Can I have $5 worth of gas?'

...'You mee-raid?'

"This really did happen when I used to live over in Silverlake, on Griffith Park Blvd. There is an Arco station there and this guy who worked there loved me so much. I would lead him on. I would tell him all sorts of stories. I'd say,

'I only have $4.'

And he'd say 'Oh, you take 5 dolla worth of gas. That's OK. I own the place.'

"Then he finally wanted my phone number. I think that's one reason I finally went to signals. I have a certain signal, and then I'll answer my phone. Sometimes I get completely bombed and give my number to the wrong person. There's a lot of flipped out foreigners in this country you know, particularly Armenian and Mexican men, and you can really manipulate them and do anything that you want to them if you show them a little tit and you act nice to them. And then you give them your phone number but what you have to do is devise a code so that you never answer your phone, because you know if you change your phone number there are people from like 4 years ago that you know you would like to have one day to call you, however, since now that you have this new system anyway, a code, you never get to talk to them anyway, so you might as well just change your phone number.

"What happens is that it got to where for a while I would like someone, because you see I go on crushes, like I can have a heavy crush for 2 days, so I will be compelled to tell the person the signal and then all of a sudden after about the 3rd day, I realize I hate this persons guts or maybe it was like, you know, I made a mistake and fucked a lesbian or something, and so like it was a mistake. So I made a mistake!...but I gave them the signal and so what happens is that the signal would increase, and it finally got to 15 rings, hang up, call back, 12 rings, hang up, call back, 5 rings, hang up, call back. It became so confusing I needed a calculator to answer my phone. 15 rings, 20 rings, 18 rings, that's gotta be Ann. And then after a while, these people, you would give them these signals, and you'd say,

'What week am I on? What signal? Where is that person?'...and I'd give these persons these signals and finally they'd say 'Forget it. You call me!'

"The whole point about sex is that none of us takes sex seriously. I mean we do. Well I don't. I can't speak for them. I don't take it seriously. That's why I end up with 14 rings, call back, 12 rings, call back, 8 rings, call back. You know it's like whatever I was into is OK. So I made a mistake. So I went home with a girl. So what. Just don't call me. People just take it too seriously. To me the people who really take sex seriously are like your basic sex murderer rapist, kill you, cut the genitals out and throw them out the window. These people are seriously into sex. They have a serious outlook on life and sex. Now us, we're just fun-loving gals. We'd never commit a sexual crime. I mean maybe, maybe I gave a bad blowjob but I mean I wouldn't go to jail for that.

"We're cheap dates and usually we're buying anyway, so we're really cheap. But the thing is that there is so much to be made fun of about sex. We used to be called Lotus Lame and the Crotch Monsters. That was as funny as we could get because we really are crotch monsters. But the L.A. Times dictated that we could not have such a name because we were starting to be reviewed in the Times, and we were starting to have ads and then we were interviewed on television and stuff like that, and we couldn't use Crotch Monsters and so we had to change it to The Lame Flames when actually we still are crotch monsters at heart and always will be. But you see, people take it so seriously that when they heard Lotus Lame and the Crotch Monsters they said,

'You're not going to go very far with that name.'

"The real premise of the group is to really poke fun at what everyone takes so seriously.

"The original phone signal is an interesting story. I used to live in Silverlake in a house that I shared with someone. We used to have insane wild parties all the time and there was these oriental people that used to live across the street from us and they were too horrified by me to ever say anything. We would have these wild parties all night and throw bottles in the streets and just carry on, and they would like be in there, I think they were like Hiroshima refugees or something. They would always prefer to stay in their house and just come out to pull bananas off the trees. They never complained about anything, and there were no other neighbors. Well, finally they died or moved out or something. They were gone. I never saw them anymore. The bananas were growing and I knew they were gone. That's the only way I knew they came out, is bananas would be missing off the tree, otherwise I would never see them.

"One day we had this huge party for these friends of ours. It was a party that went on for three days, and it just kept going and going, and I was in the middle of breaking up with a boyfriend who was extremely insane. He would kill you as fast as he would look at you. He had no considerations about killing people. None. None at all. And he really believed that he had the right to do it because certain people just were not worthy of living. They just weren't. They had no significance. If he loved you he would kill for you. I mean that's a small step for mankind but it's a big step for Lotus Lame. If I wanted you done in, you know. I decided that I didn't want to date this guy anymore because he was a little too intense.

"I had a car accident and I almost died. This is very funny. I had about 80 stitches in my body. I had just come home from the hospital and I was laying in bed and he wanted to fuck. Ha, ha, ha and I wouldn't. I said,

'Are you kidding?'...

"He said 'I just want to make you feel better!'...

I said, 'I feel great. I'm on Demerol. What are you talking about? Leave me alone!'...

"So he said, 'I'll fuck you anyway.'...

"He takes his dick out. So I thought that I really have to break up with this guy because he's really nuts. Not to mention that I had 20 stitches in my mouth and he wanted to stick his tongue in there. He was really a weird guy, and with the blue thread sticking out, and crusty blood and stuff. So when I was breaking up with him, he used to stand outside and watch the house when we had parties, and at other times too. So we were having this wild party go on and I was entertaining that night, someone had slept over, not to mention that there was about 100 people strewn all over the place, and everyone knew about this mental case who would kill for me, and that meant anyone else in the house who was with me at that time.

"So the next morning we were sleeping and there is this knock. I tell you it was like this (pound pound pound) on the door. It was loud loud pounding. Everyone jumped up and said the guys name. They went,

'It's him!' and everyone hid.

"They hid in the bathroom, in the closet, and the person I was entertaining ran behind the dishwasher. I mean people were just horrified and there was this pounding, pounding, pounding at the door, and I thought,

'I'm going to have to answer it. I'm going to be dead! This guy is going to kill me!'

"I'm expecting an AK-47 bullet between the eyes and lo and behold there is this vision of loveliness, a person I had never seen before dressed in full leather regalia at 12 noon on a Sunday. He had on those police motorcycle boots, black leather pants, black leather jacket, black leather hat, gloves shoved through the epaulets of the jacket, leather sunglasses, and a big moustache. This guy was all in leather except that he had on a leopard puss print t-shirt. It was very attractive attire. He was like this killer leather queen with a Fred Segal t-shirt on, and he had this red hair and this big red moustache. I said,

'Yeah?'...I mean who is this guy? The party's over you know and this thing is standing there, my gawd. He said with a French accent,

'No-o-o! I want to tell you that I leev across the street over there. My name is Jacques Desiree, Jacques Desiree, my name is Jacques Desiree.'...

"And I say to myself, 'Oh well.'

...'I hear zee par-tee last week and I say hey hey hey! This is zee par-tee girl. Well what can I do? Ho ho ho...but I tell you when the following weekend you have another par-tee, I say this is too much with this party girl. Hey hey hey. I am going to call the police on you.'

"So there was this leather thing standing there, going on and on with this ridiculous accent. I thought he was a joke. I thought it was like a Dial-A-Joke or Send-A-Joke, you know. I thought it was a joke because I was expecting my old boyfriend to be standing there with an AK-47 ready to get me between the eyes, and everyone is still hiding and he's got a similar accent to my old boyfriend. My guests heard his screaming and you know they were all shaking. With this guy, what I decided that I would do is befriend him rather than have this antagonistic leather queen living across the street from me. I would just befriend him and invite him to my parties.

"Wrong. Really wrong move, because the guy started to come to the parties in his full leather regalia, and let me tell you I could never get rid of him, and suddenly a stream of boys would be going from my house to his house. He was like this stud but he was such a gross pig. These little young fags that would come to my parties would be so intrigued with him and run off to his house and you would hear yelling and screaming...

'Ahhh-h-h-h-h! Ahhh-h-h-h-h!'...because this guy was heavy duty into S&M.

"You'd walk into his closet, he had variety of enormous dildoes hanging in there. A woman could have had a litter of children and not fit one of those up her cunt. I touched one once, I mean I just couldn't imagine it. I mean I probably got gay cancer from touching it. It was disgusting. He had other S&M accoutrements in there that you never even dreamed of. He had a little rabbit that he loved. He used to give it lettuce, but to make a very long and tormenting story short, I could not get rid of him. As time went by I started getting really mean with him and he liked it. I should have known right? It got to where I would say to him,

'You are a fucking asshole! Fuck off you pig!'...and he would start to cry, this big leather queen.

"He would stand there in front of my door and go...'Booo oooh oooh oooh!'...and he would love it and come back for more, like...

'Yell at me more! Yell at me more'...because this guy was heavy into S&M, and he would make me so mad and I have such a violent temper, and I would say,

'Leave me the fuck alone! You're an asshole!'...and he would go...

'Booo oooh oooh oooh!'...and he would cry.

"The killer boyfriend is probably I would say like a mercenary now somewhere because he was into it, probably in El Salvador or somewhere like that because he was into it. He would read those magazines like Soldier Of Fortune because he just believed that people should die. I'll tell you something, if he ever reads this and Lotus Lame is missing...Did you hear about the woman that walked home from the fishmarket and was followed by two cats and three dykes?

"I met this person and I will not say his name but he is very famous. He is extremely famous. I met him at a bar one night. He was acting very much like...don't I know you?...And we ended up where he wanted me to have a 3-way with him and this other famous person. They were two men, and I told him I wasn't into it, and he really admired that.

"So we go home, and we're snorting cocaine in the car and taking quaaludes. He had a 450SL with the top down, so while we were trying to catch blows of cocaine with the top down I said to him,

'Mr. X, don't you think it would be easier to snort it if you put the top up?'...

'But everyone couldn't see me then. I'm famous!'...So we get to my house and I say,

'Thank you very much for dropping me off.'

"And he goes, 'Dropping you off! I want you all for myself. You didn't want to fuck so-and-so. I want you all for myself anyway!'

"I said, 'All right c'mon in.'

"So we get in the house and he says to me, 'Won't you dress up?'...

"To make a long story short I put on a little 'Fredericks of Hollywood' here, a little of this here, and la-la-la, you know, the works. I come out in one of these kind of outfits and he's like,

'Oh baby! Oh baby! Oh baby!'...and I said,

'OK now, you want to get down, I'll get down. I get down with the best of 'em Mr. Famous!'...

"And he says, 'Well, what do you have for me to wear?'...And I thought well what do you want to be, like a Nazi, do you want to be the mailman? I mean, I've got limited costumes over here.

"I said, 'What do you want to be? Gawd, take your fucking pants off and lets do it already. It's 4 in the morning. I've had enough!'

"This guy wants to dress up. He says, 'I'd like to wear what you're wearing.'

"I said, 'Oh...but I'm wearing it. Only one of us can fit in this bra, do you know what I mean?'...

'Yes I know. Don't you have anymore of that kind of stuff?'

"I said, 'Yeah I do. Do you want it?'...

"And he said, 'Yeah.'

"I could just have seen me and him and his friend. It would have been pretty scary because you know the third guy would have been the dominatrix for sure. So I go into my bedroom and sort of like dig around the drawer thinking, 'This is this person? I can't believe this.'...pulling out the black push-up bra, do you know what I mean, and the panties from Fredericks and everything, and I come out and I say, 'Here you go.' Now dig this. He goes in the bathroom, he's got all his clothes and all that, he comes out of the bathroom with a towel on, we're talking like a Greta Garbo grand entrance, and I'm sitting on the couch going, 'Am I tripping or what? Am I having a reoccurrence from an old acid trip from the '60s?'

"I want to describe it physically. He comes out, drops the towel, and has on the black push-up bra that is 12 times too small for him so he actually looks like he has tits, and he has on the bikini bottoms and we are talkin' bikini, the garters and the stockings, and I took one look at him and I went, 'Oh my gawd!'...

"Honey, I knew I was into the lamest lay I was ever going to have in my life. I said, 'Who's going to be the boy? Are we going to shoot for it or what?' He decided that I should be the boy. So I said, 'That's great. How are you going to be the girl? You know, it's a little awkward for me.'

"I had to be the boy and since I don't have a dick, it was not much fun for me, and he wanted to keep the clothes on the whole time while I was being the boy, and we went around like this for a while and he managed somehow to have an orgasm, and then I really decided that that was enough, and that I had enough of being the boy, and I didn't know how I was going to have any more fun being the boy because what was he going to do, what the hell was he going to do?

"So I said, 'Well I guess that's it then isn't it?'

"And you know what? He kept some of my lingerie. He wouldn't give it back to me. So besides being a lame lay and me having to figure out how to be the boy with what little accoutrements I had, he took my best panties from Fredericks of Hollywood. We're talking nine dollars and this guy is a millionaire, and you know he's driving around in his 450SL with my Fredericks crotchless underwear on. That's why we sing the songs we sing. We're talking bad sex."

CHAPTER 11

The '60's underground film director Paul Roman was living in Los Angeles and a friend put me in touch with him. This was exciting to me because people who knew me were aware that I admired 1960s New York pop art, Warhol, The Velvet Underground and the peripherals. An easy phone call was all it took and I arranged to go over and see him. Judging solely from my appearance, one could see that I was in obvious bad shape. It wasn't the three-piece tailored suit, or a clean dress shirt and trousers that I was lacking; and it wasn't even the freshly washed pair of blue jeans and the clean white t-shirt that I was not wearing upon arrival; it was that the dirty blue jeans and a filthy greasy suede leather vest, scuffed and worn black engineer boots, blue-black dyed uncombed unkempt teased unwashed hair and my faithful wooden crutches were the wardrobe of choice of the day, every day and night. On top of everything else I was still being ravaged periodically by crab lice from the shared bathroom toilets down the hall from my office. Of course, I had my suspicions about my neighbors but no proof. One and two inch long waterbugs had the unpleasant habit of appearing like prehistoric invertebrate predators from the floor drain of the urinal and running for the cuff of my pant leg. It was impossible to determine their exact length while jumping and hopping in terror.

Danté came along with me to the interview and he took care to dress a bit upscale to offset my poor appearance. Certainly his balls were 100% clean, not a micro-tenement housing project for unemployed parasitic critters with no notions of birth control. I could have been in worse shape. Life can always get worse. I interviewed Paul Roman and Danté took pleasant personality photos. To my mind pleasant typical photos of a strong personality were dull but I was excited just to be doing this at all.

In the wake of Dana's departure, I went through quick a succession of girlfriends, which can be more accurately termed abrupt encounters. Probably the most painful was the terrifying ear-biting incident which occurred in the freewheeling period spent between accidents when I was recovering from the wrist mishap and prior to the damaged knee. This event occurred when I was still sleeping at the Hollywood and Las Palmas P*NK Magazine offices. I say 'still sleeping' because I was soon to begin sleeping elsewhere. The lovely vicious toothsome biter was an attractive (nearly everybody in L.A. believes that they're attractive and fashionable) French fashion designer named Giselle. The victim, the recipient of the bite was me, on the right ear. Giselle and I had been seeing quite a lot of each other for several weeks and much of that recreational time was spent in bed joining up sex organs which was among other things inexpensive and fun. We spent most of our time in her penthouse apartment. Giselle had money. She lived near the top of one of those monumental Deco condo-apartment buildings that stack about 20 stories high and sit just below Sunset Boulevard off the strip. Lovely views. Privacy. Thick masonry soundproof walls, ceilings and floors.

She was located just a few blocks west of the L.A. Subs crib. One evening Eamonn and a couple of musicians and their friends dropped by. It didn't take twenty minutes before Giselle lost her dignity. She was wearing a pair of long johns style underwear like men and women wear in cold climates under their clothing and she had unbuttoned the top half so her perfect little teacup shaped french tits were supplicating for attention. Crawling on her knees in front of Eamonn she began begging.

"Please Eamonn! Stay here and fuck me. Please don't go Eamonn."

"We want to go to a club. Why don't you get dressed and come with?"

"Please fuck me Eamonn. I want you so much."

"Some other time Giselle. We have things to do tonight."

Giselle was entertaining. I was standing right there watching with the small party. Eamonn was laughing. She was on her knees hugging him around the waist and crying. He was immaculately dressed in all black with the exception of a clean pressed white fancy dress shirt with lace cuffs and black western bow tie. After several minutes Eamonn managed to separate from Giselle and he came into the kitchen where I had moved to talk with a guitar player.

"There are six bottles of expensive French champagne in the fridge." I said. I kicked the fridge door open with my boot revealing the six bottles on chill. "Why don't you heist those bottles and split." I suggested.

"Do you think that's a good idea Ronnie? I think it's a great idea." Immediately, Eamonn grabs three bottles then hands them to the guitar player who finds places in his long black overcoat to make them disappear. Eamonn's eyes are twinkling with joy behind black mascara. He calls the other musicians into the hallway and hands them each a bottle. The bottles disappear from sight and then Eamonn and his gang disappear through the hallway door in complete silence and are gone from the apartment. Giselle and I are alone.

Giselle comes into the kitchen. "Where are they? Where have they gone?"

"They left." I said. "I don't know where they went."

"Why did they leave?" she says with a slight tremor in her voice.

She opens the refrigerator door. "Where is my champagne? You gave them my champagne? And you told them to leave? That is what you did. My champagne is gone!" She opens the freezer compartment door and peers in. She opens and slams the cupboards hopelessly, agitated.

"I was jealous. You were crawling around on your knees chasing after Eamonn. It was pathetic."

"You fucking leetle bastard. Do you know how much that champagne cost?"

"You can't put a price on love." I said as a barb.

That was when the fireworks began. Bastille Day. Giselle went berserk, running around the apartment hysterically, screaming in French and English. I sat down. She ran up to me. At a loss for something to do in revenge, she pulled off my boots in rapid jerks and then she ran holding them high over her head in the air across the living room to the open window and threw them out into the black night. They flew down into the black abyss from twenty floors up. Shoe death. She found my leather jacket hanging on a dining room chair and threw that out the window. Cuir mort. She had my attention now and I stood up. Then she ran at me swearing in French and English and punched at my face rabidly. When I blocked the punches she became more enraged; she lunged at me snarling and bit onto my right ear and hung on to it with her Euro-teeth and began ripping and dragging at the flesh using the weight of her body to fulcrum the pain. We ran around her apartment in this position for what seemed like several minutes which was a limited but seemingly endless eternity. Blood flowed.

"Get off my ear! Get off my ear! Get off my fucking ear Giselle!" I screamed. "Ow! Ow! Ow! Get off my ear!" We ran around and around the apartment with her teeth clenched in my ear until we were both physically exhausted. I wished I had film of that evening. I might have sent it off to Roman Polanski. And then it stopped abruptly. She had decided against biting it completely off. The ear, in one piece still attached to my head at any rate, was a bloodied, ravaged brave trooper.

Then we two sat in silence for a long time. "I'm sorry about the champagne. I just wanted to get rid of them."

"It's irreplaceable."

"So is my ear. Thanks for not biting it completely off."

"I could have. I was so fucking mad. I am still mad. How could you be so stupid?"

"You threw all my shit out the window. My boots. My jacket. What's down below there on the ground?"

"I don't know. A patio. A garden. I will go down and find your things."

"Why don't you call Eamonn. Get the champagne back. He's probably just around the corner at his place. He can't have drank it all yet. Tell him it cost a lot of money. It was a mistake."

"No. It's gone. I don't want to call him."

A tall beautiful blond with charms to rival the runway babes and supermodels of haute couture rode up on a motorcycle. Rio. Born to strut the catwalk. Her name sounds south of the border but she was an aryan blond. It's fun to say, Rio. She arrived at a smallish party at an apartment in Hollywood on a cherried out Norton 750 Commando. What a girl. South of Wilshire and east of Crenshaw, the party wasn't quite in Hollywood. I was standing outside with Kickface. "I want to fuck her." He said as she sashayed by.

"And she comes with a kool British bike. Wild in the streets." I remarked.

Later inside, I managed to talk to her for a short while. Down the line, now and then when I bumped into Rio in nightclubs and I put in a few words with her. Then a couple of months later I saw her again at another party. It was a wild night at Dukes Tropicana, a motel in West Hollywood, a rock and roll layover, popular with travelling bands on the nightclub circuit. Duke's is no longer standing. Two floors of rooms encircled a central swimming pool which was painted black for a strange effect which made the water look like liquid tar at night. It was a party-swim-fuck-eat-sleep-a-little-go-nightclubbing setting in no particular sequential order. This night I came there for the party. This party was a real party that happened outside the world of fiction. Call it the Dee Dee Ramone Party or perhaps call it the anti-Dee-Dee Ramone Party. There were so many parties that they blur together in the haze of the past but this one was unique. The Dee Dee Party will satisfy the needs of this story and it's probably the same party I went to where I encountered Rio. People still talk about that party in part because the revelers inside the party wouldn't allow Dee Dee Ramone to enter inside. Define fun, is that fun? Not only is Duke's demolished but Dee Dee is dead since June 5, 2002. Joey Ramone, dead.

Johnny Ramone, dead. This clearly elucidates the problem of entering the real factual world of non-fiction and then returning to fiction. The party took place in a small Duke's Tropicana motel room on the second floor; crammed from the floor to the ceiling with intoxicated writhing punks wearing their full spiky torn black skintight gear and extreme make-up. The only punks on the outside were Dee Dee Ramone and his girlfriend standing on the walkway in front of the door. Someone kept slamming the door shut. They wouldn't let him inside. That was where I arrived.

"Let me in. I'm Dee Dee Ramone!" he shouted and pounded on the door. "Go away!" a voice shouted from inside over the din of a hundred people.

Dee Dee walked over to his girlfriend. "Gimme the bottle." He gulped down a clear neat distilled liquor, gin or vodka. "They won't open the goddam door." He looked at me. I was looking at him and then the door. He was wearing a t-shirt with white and black horizontal stripes with the sleeves cut off and the neck scissor cut low, tight black Levis, and black Converse hi-tops. He was smaller man than me physically but he was athletically lean and street tough.

"What's their problem?" I said. I tried the door handle. It was locked. I pounded on the door.

"Open up it's the Sheriff! This is the Los Angeles County Sheriff! You are under arrest!" I shouted. Dee Dee handed the bottle back to his girlfriend then he rushed the door and began pounding it with both fists up around his head.

"Open the door, I'm Dee Dee Ramone! I'm Dee Dee Ramone! Open the door!" He turned to walk back to the girl left holding the bottle and the door flew open wide for an instant. It was like a teaser. This party was raging inside the tiny motel room; at least thirty people were carousing, romping and rolling on the double bed and then there was not a square inch of floor space open; extreme facial makeup, bizarre hair, black leather and metal studs were superanimated everywhere like this was a Hollywood studio film scene of an dionysiac punk rock hotel party and the director had just admonished the actors, "Be animated everybody. This is a punk rocker party in a hotel room in Hollywood and you're all supposed to be having a wild drunken raging good fun time. Now on action, I want to see everybody acting. Go crazy! Go apeshit! OK. Ready. Action!" Dee Dee turned and ran for the open door and someone slammed it shut, locked again.

"Let me in. I'm Dee Dee Ramone! Open the door!" He pounded with futility on the door with his clenched hands. Dee Dee was the original punk rocker. Without Dee Dee they would all have been some kind of rock and roll formless vague non-entities. This was equivalent to preventing Gene Vincent and the Blue Caps from entering a Rockabilly hep cat dance hop.

"Maybe this is a stupid Los Angeles-New York City problemo." I am thinking. Just then Rio walks up to me and here we return to the fictional narrative.

"What's going on?" she says. "Why won't they open the door?"

"I don't know. It's a mystery to me." Dee Dee was back drinking from the bottle. "You wanna walk around a little bit. Maybe they'll open up in a while. We can sit by the pool or something."

"OK," she said. We walked together and about ten doors down we found an empty room with the curtains open. I tried the door handle and it opened.

"Let's go in here." I said. We went in and laid down on the bed and made small talk. Maybe an hour went by, Rio and I were laughing and telling stories about mutual people we knew in San Francisco. Punked out members of Hunde Prutter (dog farts) and their friends walked by and laughed at us, looking in the window. By this time I had learned that Rio was a transgender sex change. We didn't fuck that night and before midnight we vacated the Tropicana room and went on our separate ways. I completely forgot to go back to the party.

A few weeks later I ran into Rio at a bar, Al's Bar downtown. Packed in there tightly were the regular tattooed punkettes and extensively inked guys in black leather, bootchains and studs. My eyes followed her through the thick cigarette smoke from the audience to the bar. I watched her move to the music. The whole place stomped and rocked to the crude beat. Rio stood and talked with a group of people in-between bands. She looked sophisticated, beautiful. I went outside for a smoke and some fresh air. At Al's bar everyone chainsmoked and drank beer; every corner and alcove had a group of dressed-up and dressed-down scenesters. Trashy, tough, erotic and harsh in appearance, they were universally making a big party characterized by waves of laughter and shouting from one group and then another. Every square inch of wall space was scribbled and marked with graffiti.

Outside of Al's bar, the dry Santa Ana winds were blowing violently. The full moon was hung in the black starless sky, transmitting an eerie white light. From a safe distance the orb scowled with its barren sorrowful visage at the ongoing drama of life and death on earth. The front of Al's Bar was in the lee of the wind, sheltered by a warehouse building across the street which now contained several neatly upscale artist's lofts. Any sparse urban vegetation, mostly stunted trees and large ugly weeds that could be seen from the sidewalk, was bent and thrashing wildly in the wind. A battered galvanized metal garbage can rolled rapidly up the middle of second street seemingly self propelled...clonk, clonk, clonk. D.O.A. was scheduled to go onstage in an hour. They were a punk band from Canada and their singer Joey

Shithead was a total punk rock riot act. Catherine Smalley, the film director was leaning on a car talking to some youths twenty five years younger than her, among them the guitar player, singer and bass player from the south bay punk band Hunde Prutter. They were arguing and joking with a curious repartee.

"I only got one cigarette left."

"Gimme one anyways. I don't care!"

"Give him a cigarette. Give him a cigarette."

"If you don't give me a fucking cigarette, I'm going to stab you because you're a fag."

"Stab me Charlie and I'll cum on your face."

"Gimme something now! Gimme something I can fucking smoke!"

"That's all you want out of life Charlie, somebody else's cigarette."

"And a nice gutter in my mouth. Ronald Reagan that's his name. I am anarchy, one two three four go! One two three four fuck you! I've fagged off with lots of hardcores. Gimme another hit man. It's like being stuck on an island with these pricks because I've got to do fucking everything they want me to do. Oh yeah...we got suggestions about this and that. You're suggestions don't mean shit. I am everything. I'm the leader. I'm connubial bliss. You are all my concubines. I'm a piece. So what? I've got a small dick so I stretch it a little bit. Stretch your imagination. I've got a blue mohawk, Ronald Reagan sucks my cock."

"What do you think of Black Flag?"

"I think they suck but I'd like to play with them. I like Dez. I think Dez and Greg are bad."

"I think Henry is a babe."

"They're full on babes. Listen to this, I got my clothes from this girl and she stole my fucking tube top. It's a fag."

"So who's your sex idol?"

"Jimmy Page. Tom Selleck and that black homosexual dude who drives an airplane. I think he's got a big cock."

"I like Mr. T."

"Who's your favorite cuddle fantasy?"

"I imagine I'm tied up between four construction workers and they're all sweating on me and I'm reading 'Mandate' magazine, and they're beating me off while I'm fucking totally getting lubed out, and I'm like so lubed that I can't get anymore. I met Richard Simmons at The Probe. Or maybe it was The Manhole. Or it could've been The Spike? I play in a band so I can fag off with more boys than in Palos Verdes."

"I was hoping to be a star."

"Not anymore."

"Charlie, what would you do if you were in a room with Lux Interior and Iggy Pop at the same time?"

"I would beat Iggy off with one hand and fuckin' give Lux a rad hand job and a mouth job with the other. What other alternative is there? Lux and Iggy are two fucking hot males to get next to."

"Where did you get that blister on your lip?"

"Uh oh. Charlie's got herpes."

"I got hit. I got hit man, and it made me real social."

"Do you think that scar makes you feel more sexy that ever?"

"I feel more secure going to a gig and I think that punk rock should be a real viable alternative to everything. All punks should be real punk."

"You're cum white."

"You're eggshell white when you give me a pearl necklace."

"I put this band together because I called him up and him up, because someone called me up about doing a video. So I said hey let's jam and do a few songs."

"You lied. I wrote all the music you fag. I started it. I'm a fag."

"I know. Charlie wrote all the music but I got the band together. Then we got Briana somehow. She plays the bass."

"It's all bad. Avoid stupidity. Avoid flying objects that people throw at you. I could fag off forty two times in the next hour."

"Hello Ronnie." Rio had come up behind me and spoken into my ear so that I could smell her perfume. She was wearing a short skirt and a black vest, a crucifix around her neck on a silver chain and green Dr. Martens lace up boots.

"Hey Rio! You have to come outside for a breath of air now and then if you want to survive the night here. Did you ride your Norton Commando down here tonight in this wind?"

"No I didn't ride it. If fact I think my ride left. Do you know Trina Trip? She used to go out with a guy from Pure Hell. Have you heard of them? They're from Philadelphia. But then they broke up and she moved out here because her stepbrother lives in Studio City and she has a place to stay for free."

"Sure I heard of them. You need a ride home. I just got my '52 Ford running. It's a fun ride."

The VW Beetle was sold after the leg incident. Danté and I had gone to look at a light green '52 Ford V-8 with 3-speed on the column with overdrive that we saw advertised in the Recycler Automotive section. It was a beautiful 1950s color of mint green; a shade they don't use anymore on current automobiles. I kicked the tires and bought it for $800 cash from a pale introverted man in his late twenties who lived with his mother in a small house near Pico and Highland, a serious masturbator by the look of him. The engine blew up about a mile from the point of purchase. It was a keeper.

I towed it to Danté's North Hollywood studio and in a relatively short time we managed to drop in a rebuilt flathead V-8 which I picked up at Moons Speed Shop in Santa Fe Springs. It was a duplicate engine to the one that was in Danté's Mercury. We found a master mechanic, a greasy grey-bearded geezer who loved those old flatheads. I had it all fixed up, cherry. They used to drive those Fords in the film noir movies. I was so anxious to drive it that I was running it without pipes. It had headers but no pipes and logically no mufflers. Those old flatheads made a beautiful noise. I told Rio the story of the car as we walked up 2nd Street to admire the beautiful green beast. We climbed into the car to get out of the wind.

"Let's drive up to The Frolic Room and get a cocktail up there." I couldn't wait to drive the '52 Ford again. So we forgot about D.O.A. and drove up to Hollywood Boulevard. I managed to get plastered in the Frolic Room. The long wall along the east side of the room was made up of Herschfield's character illustrations of the classic movie stars. When they start dancing around, you're due to leave. Martinis have an olive. Gibsons are a martini endowed with an small onion instead of an olive. We had a couple of each. I have no memory of our conversation and I learned nothing personal about Rio. I'm not a good listener. People hate that. How did she earn a living? Was she an artist? Had she gone to college? By the time we left the bar I was preoccupied with alcoholic erotic urges and we drove to her studio loft down on Sixth Street. It was a beautiful loft (by punk rock era standards) in a large building with an ornately carved stone facade.

We entered from the rear, no pun intended, of the building on the ground floor. Inside, the loft area was uncluttered studio space with a few artists artifacts laying about. Resting underneath a black leather cushioned wooden table, curiously adorned with several restraining straps on all the sides was a pretty girl with blond hair wearing only a white tank top and panties torn in the crotch which revealed pink dayglo pubic hair. She was smoking and reading a book on top of a sleeping bag with the aid of a large pillow and a clip-on reading light attached to the table leg.

"Who is that?" I asked, indicating the blond girl who completely ignored us.

"That's Kitten. She rents the space under the table from me."

"Hi Kitten!" I said.

"Back at ya spermbank. I'm tellin' your mom." she said. She had a velvety voice like Marilyn Monroe in 'Some Like It Hot'.

Rio led me up some stairs to an intimate but open space in the manner that artist's lofts are often configured, elevated but with an open wall overlooking the larger room below. She put on a rock record. My head was swimming from the gin and vermouth. She seemed to have an orderly technique or method of doing this and that. Her moves were rather deft and systematic. The martinis had a slow motion effect on my behavior and perceptions although we certainly seemed to be progressing in the right direction. Soon I found myself laying flat on my back on the hardwood floor with my pants pulled down below my knees. I had a big hard on. That was all good so far. As Rio was gaining some momentum, I felt a bit removed like a passive observer but it's always great to see lil Ronnie standing up at attention. Next, Rio was sitting over me wearing only a bra and panties. She was on her knees sitting back on her ankles with my legs under her. She was playing with my penis with both hands. Then with a flourish of her wrist, she made appear out of nowhere with the legerdemain of a Las Vegas stage magician, a squirt bottle of Johnson's Baby Oil. She must have had it waiting at a special place somewhere out of sight which meant that I was on her predetermined sex action spot. Swaying back and forth and holding the bottle high she began squirting my genitals with the oil. She appeared from my recumbent position to be mimicking Jimi Hendrix in the Monterey Pop film squirting lighter fluid onto his flaming guitar. That was not a comforting image. I entertained a flaming surrealist genital terror fantasy in my mind. Barbeque dick.

Aided by the sweet odor of the baby oil, I snapped out of my dizziness just a little. She had spurted out the entire contents of the plastic bottle. I was feeling too passive in my position and my white ass and all my clothing were completely steeped in the spreading puddle of sweetly fragranced baby oil. Rio had super-lubricated me on her special penis oiling spot. It was an oil and lube job. It couldn't have been done on an actual bed for obvious reasons. I fleetingly imagined the suaveness of the Brat Pack, Frank, Deano, Joey, Sammy in sticky situations for an urbane way out because they were the true kings of the martini sleaze. I asked myself what would Sammy D Junior or Frank do on an evening that ended like this. This was an exit situation. Maybe I could pretend that I was someone else and scoot out with some grace and greasy pants around my ankles. Then again this was too late for style and grace because I mostly lacked those qualities and I was covered in oil like a perfumed sardine. The sweet smell of it mixed with the martinis in my bloodstream. It was time to wash my underpants, no more excuses.

Since my verifiable ESP look-see into the near future involving the pretty blond

Nazi chiropractor, I was never certain if a vision in my mind was an imaginary phantasmagoria or a real picture of reality imprinted from the preternatural realm. This young man was not an Edgar Cayce going forth with a message to the world. Unencumbered by the demands of reality, my mind routinely played short unsavoury garbage movies which I mostly perceived and then sent out with the trash. Also, I felt that I was in the business of conjuring images because I believed myself to be an artist, so these visions weren't perceived by me as a mental problem. It's so darn hard to be truly creative with post-Cubist, post-Surrealist, post-Dada, post-Expressionist, post-Op, post-Pop, post-Conceptual, post-Body, post-Performance, post-Environment post-Industrial modern art; an artist would have to be crazy to shut off the tap or filter the flow of images. That was my thinking at the time.

As Rio was Monterey Pop lap dancing over lil Ronnie, I saw clearly in my mind the image of a doctor cutting off Rio's penis while she was laying on a surgical table in a small shabby outpatient office operating room. Indifferently, he cut it off with a scalpel and then tossed it with a casual underhand movement into a bucket lined with a plastic trash liner, the amputated penis of less value now than a common Ball Park Frank. Then in a sweeping slash of the blade the flaccid scrotum was sliced and lastly the unwanted testicles were removed and dropped with a bloody splat into the plastic lined bucket. These images appeared vividly in front of my eyes in cheap B-movie bright colors like my imagination was directed by Herschel Gordon Lewis with two exaggerated ghoulish waxen character actors (although Rio was unconscious from a general anesthetic).

One instant I realized that all my clothing was completely imbued with baby oil; the next instant I was confronted with Rio's sexual pain and the routine procedural amputation gestures of an imagined middle-aged sex doctor; rather short he was, paunchy, balding, complete with a greasy comb-over on his shiny pate; tossing Rio's bloody testicles into the bucket, over and over as my brain looped. This was a Sergio Eisenstein cinematic technique, slow motion repetition, which invaded my genital slash fantasy, too much art college. Was Dr. Dick Remover thinking about eating pizza for lunch? Or a cheeseburger? Next he had to cut the vaginal opening and tamper with the nerve endings. Did he only work on an outpatient basis from this cramped low rent office? Not a bad business, altering the sex of men. He was just the plumber. Would a penis transplant be possible in which the penis of an accidental death victim was transported in ice and then attached to the end of another man's penis making for an exceptional length? Could a doctor of this specialty create a secret penis collection storing quantities of the amputated specimens in jars of formaldehyde or possibly freeze-drying them. Freeze-dried and mounted on purple velvet, a black specimen and a white one, foreskin and not, arrayed under glass. Yes he could. Imagination, clairvoyance or bullshit, I sat upright suddenly in the middle of the greasy puddle; this was the wrong mindset.

"Rio. I drank too much. I think I'm gonna be sick. I'm sorry. I better go." I pulled myself together quickly and apologetically pushed off on the slippery floor for the rear exit door below. Kitten was gone. I wanted another peek at her perky breasts under the tank top and the pink pubic delight showing through her torn panties, pink on pink. I jerked the security door open, felt the fresh cold air on my face and ran into the eery brisk dry Santa Ana night winds with the dazzling bright full moon. The moon was even brighter now, higher in the sky and more distant, pure and white, a small frigid orb. I read that the moon is moving an inch further away from the earth each year. Don't believe everything that you read. The winds whipped the sweet odor of baby oil under my nostrils as I ambled, now more slowly, for the '52 Ford. I drove up Wilshire Boulevard for a while watching the tall palms bending and waving in the winds. I listened to the beautiful rumble of my engine. I loved my car more than any human. If an L.A.P.D. black and white had stopped me, I could never have explained in a million years why I was so drunk and marinated with the unmistakable scent of Johnson's Baby Oil.

"I should have gone for a blow job from Rio. Then run out. That's what Sammy would have done. That's what any sane man would have done. A mouthful of greasy cock and splashy cum can perform wonders."

"Suck on this lollipop for the *Candyman* baby." Sammy would have crooned.

I spoke out loud to myself over the roar of the engine. A year or so later I heard from Kitten that Rio's new boyfriend was an FBI agent. They were living together and she was a happy woman; just another couple of satisfied Johnson Baby Oil customers living the J. Edgar Hoover lifestyle.

I continued showering at the art college in part because I had discovered Naoko. I liked to watch her walking around. My eyes were riveted to her ass or her tits or basically all of her at once. Naoko had style, she was a trashy pretty Japanese sex bomb. Japanese girls can do that stylish trashy chic sex kitten look with great aplomb. It works for me. She was from Japan (as opposed to being born in America of Japanese descent), maybe twenty one years old. She dressed like a British rocker girl. She spoke entertainingly broken English. Her eye make-up was typically extreme, even early in the morning. Call me superficial but I love that crazy shit in a girl. And wild Japanese girls are even better. I managed to talk to her a few times around campus. Then when I started the P*NK Magazine project with Ty Eason, I was immediately pulled into the greater outside world and away from the campus, that was about when Naoko had first started in the painting studio and classes.

One day, nearly two years since my departure from college, I dropped in to the campus for my periodic shower which was located in the rear of the ceramics building. After I was freshened up, I went outside and the lunch truck (a greasy spoon on wheels, common to Los Angeles with a full kitchen) was parked nearby with a crowd gathered around it. I saw Naoko and maneuvered myself next to her. By the time I left campus that afternoon I had her phone number in my pocket. Shazaam! It only took me two years and she was almost ready to graduate. I wanted her under me naked with her ankles wrapped back around her ears. We were the children of the brave WWII warriors from both sides who fought the terrible war in the Pacific, the inheritors of the legacy of world history, Pearl Harbor, Tarawa, Bataan Death March, Iwo Jima, Fat Man and Little Boy. The soldiers fought and died so their forebears could fuck and prosper in peace.

I gave her a tinkle in a few days. "Come over tonight if you want. I'm going to be at home." she said. Because I was a small art star whose name was familiar around the art college and I was nudging thirty and a little bit debauched looking, which carries a certain charm if it is perceived to be grouped with youthful verve, success and great intelligence, the god Eros was aiding my sexual wants to a near perfection. This intellectual stature was augmented by black leather, blue jeans and a pointy style haircut. Metaphorically surfing this new wave of some small successes, meeting people of importance through this new culture of punk, now I was even getting laid by my Japanese sex fantasy. Ba-da-bing. Ba-da-boom! The metamorphosis initiated by raw liver taped to my reverse mohawk shaved head into a publisher of the new culture was evolving with a post-Darwin nuclear genetic acceleration characteristic of comic book mutations. Oh Hollywood! What a land of uncommon opportunity. Dorothy was no longer in Kansas and Ronnie wasn't in Palo Alto anymore. And Naoko shrieked "Oh baby! Oh baby!" as we fell out of her bed and continued fucking on the floor.

Naoko and myself hung out now and then when we could arrange it. Naoko made an oil painting of me. She worked from a photo and I sat for it in her studio three or four times.

I was feeling trapped, restless, and trouble was seeking me out. A pretty young lady's displeased husband visited me one evening with a nasty looking switchblade and offered to puncture some of my arteries. He took me by surprise. I told him I didn't fuck his wife. He didn't believe me, of course. I almost fucked her but how do you explain that to a knife. She kept visiting me, I didn't encourage her much.

"Every morning when I get up to piss there is a hot cup of coffee and a fresh donut waiting outside my door. Gwendolyn has been doing that every day for two weeks. Keep her at home and apologize for whatever the hell it is that you did to her. Look around you, there's no where for her to bathe here, no running water. She would not be happy here Hector. Do you have crabs, genital lice, *Phthirius pubis?*"

"No."

"I recently almost lost a large piece of my ear to another woman's angry bite, so I'm not looking for love right now Hector." Hector looked at me without blinking. His hair was prematurely thinning, he was mad at the world like a shallow American existentialist and he worked at a boring career as a graphic designer. Silence was dangerous. I continued talking.

"Well the odds are that Gwendolyn kept her pants on over here because if you spend any time in this building you get crabs in the pubic area. Everybody's got'em. I've had'em so many times I know their scientific names. There are various kinds that live on humans. They own these damn bathrooms and all the tenants have 'em in multiple species. If I were you I wouldn't sit on that bed. Those blankets haven't been washed in months. You should wash your clothes in boiling hot water as soon as you get home and get some A200 at a drug store."

"I can't forgive you for interfering in my marriage. You son-of-a-bitch!"

"Well, if you're bug free that's proof that I'm an innocent man, at least with regard to hanky-panky which is a killing offense. Did you get that switchblade in Tijuana? That has a ferocious looking blade on it. The lice from Tijuana can survive just on your leg and ankle hairs and they're completely resistant to A200. They bite hard and hold on tight and permanent as a barnacle. They're nearly impossible to get rid of and they're quite large. They're big. You can easily see them except they're translucent so they're camouflaged."

"I'm leaving. I'm already starting to itch. Stay away from Gwendolyn or I'll be back and next time I'll use the blade on you."

"Watch out yourself for these *Pediculus humanus* and their cousins *Phthirius pubis.* And thanks for not killing me tonight!"

Ultimately, I kept the offices at Hollywood and Las Palmas, they felt like home. I moved my sleeping quarters to a lilliputian squalid place just north of Sunset and south of Hollywood Boulevard and a couple of blocks east of Western Avenue. My driving approach was always from the Sunset Boulevard direction so that the actual true proximity to Hollywood Boulevard was not taken into my reckoning. This way I felt further removed from Hollywood Boulevard. This uniquely placed habitat wasn't even an actual apartment. It was a matchbox-sized dump in the air, located on a kind of pseudo-bridge that traversed a driveway with cottage bungalows on either side. The bridge crib had a room in it with a sink and toilet. Although it was a small useless bridge in the scale of humans to the Los Angeles cockroach community it was a superhighway in the sky. The party was all over me and my belongings. The idea that one might crawl into my ear hadn't occurred to me because if it had I would have drunkenly taped my ears up before I went to sleep on my filthy bedding. Cars drove under my penthouse along the driveway and roaches traversed it avoiding the cars by crossing the bridge.

Down below my window overlooking the driveway, I watched the daily activities of a brachycephalic family with stunted legs and thick rotund torsos, as muscular as they were obese. During the day the swaggering husband loitered up at the street end of the driveway with six to eight other men, all with heavy brushy moustaches. Clouds of cigarette smoke would continually rise from the gesturing men. They would disappear together about mid-morning and then reappear at four thirty in the afternoon and smoke more cigarettes. The bridge crib was a new place for me to sleep. It was unarguably a piece of shit but it was necessary for me to keep my balancing act in motion, I reasoned. In the morning, the busy mother below would kick her two urchins around the front room like soccer balls as she performed her chores. Late in the morning, she would routinely sit outside her front door on an aluminum tube folding beach chair eating sunflower seeds and spitting the shells on the ground in front of her. She was my Hollywood movie starlet fantasy from Farmer Joe's Bacon and Sausage Products factory with a slaughterhouse in the City of Industry and a preservative stuffed meat product in every Los Angeles market. I was reluctant to stare directly at her but by glancing at angles I noticed that she had a female moustache. I held her in revulsion. There was a pile of sunflower seed shells six inches deep in front of her aluminum tube beach chair. She too had a jealous husband.

My mom was going to die soon. I was drinking twenty four seven; beer in the early morning, bourbon whiskey by noon and gin, cold duck or nouveau beaujolais after dark. I had become the man trapped in the bottle, a drunken man coiffed with artificially colored blue black hair. The bottle now owned me. This was my only means of coping with the sickness and approaching death of my mother. She hadn't been diagnosed with a particular disease, she reported to me over the telephone. Her body was systematically shutting down on a determined downhill course. She was still working her secretarial job at this point but it was becoming impossible to continue. One day her hearing went out in one ear. A month later she began to have trouble with her jaw. The bones of her face began to change shape and contort. Her flesh was being remolded like pliant putty by the hideous hand of death. Her facial bones were rapidly altering from month to month. She began to limp. The dentist gave her a plastic form to insert into her mouth when she slept. Capillaries near the surface of the skin on her arms were breaking daily and this caused unusual looking blue marks that resembled contusions. Her face grew into a distorted version of itself. The Kale family doctor, that very same Dr. Leonard with the bad toupee whom I went to see more than ten years prior for my amphetamine overdose, refused to treat her. He didn't want to work with a gravely sick person. Sure, I went into therapy in order to cope with my loss, it was called 'Black Flag'.

CHAPTER 12

I felt that a part-time job might possibly put some order in my mess although I was a completely unemployable specimen. With a breakfast and lunch diet of four sixteen ounce brewskies before 10 a.m. and then a half pint of bourbon or vodka at 11 a.m., I was a tough interview. I had no job resumé or portfolio with the exception of the publication of bizarre punk magazines preoccupied with horrible gratuitous images. And I unabashedly loved those magazines. Publish or die! On the plus side for me, was a small sympathy angle. I was a punkrocker using crutches to get around and punk music was now exploding in Los Angeles.

I came across a classified advertisement for a clerk needed to assist in the accounting department of the popular weekly tabloid GO L.A., which featured entertainment guides and calendars admixed with ambitious liberal journalism, over-intellectualized film reviews and pompous wordy pop music criticism. These local tabloid writers and critics were highly esteemed and admired by many including myself. Readers like myself understood that if a writer isn't an overly bombastic intellectualizing critic of the arts, there is not much in terms of content to explore. A critic has got to impress people and nobody is impressed with plain talk. In addition, GO L.A. paid writers by the word; a weighty ten cents per was the usual fee. Logorrhea is the common disease among dime a word boffo critics. With all this on my mind, I pointed my crutches for the hallowed offices of GO L.A.

GO L.A. was a successful entrepreneurial small newspaper with a staff of about forty people. The bridge-over-the-driveway apartment was only several blocks away from the mighty metropolitan offices from which GO L.A. was published. I could walk down there drunk on crutches and not risk the drunk driving charges. This was convenient. It was just a beeline buzz southward down to Santa Monica Boulevard with my neighborhood liquor store unavoidably on the route. The GO L.A. media center was sandwiched in an unattractively stuccoed mustard colored two story house located in a dense multi-ethnic, low rent neighborhood comprised of Armenians, Latinos, Blacks, Filipinos, miscellaneous Asians, disenfranchised whites, a few Russians and unsavoury street hookers of all possible genders and permutations.

Compared to my operation this was a vertical upscale climb but neither the GO L.A. offices nor location was going to appear on any Hollywood landmark postcard. The inside of the house was designless and filled room to room with used worn office furniture.the staff wore hip office clothes and appeared to be freshly showered and cynical. My garb was a bit out of place, black steel-toe engineer boots with blue jeans tucked in, a dirty suede leather vest over a sleeveless t-shirt with the crew neck cut out, a relatively new tattoo of a coiled snake with fangs, blue black unkempt hair, wooden crutches. With the exception of the tattoo, these clothing items should be familiar to the attentive reader. In addition, I was drunk at ten in the morning. I could have tumbled out of the pages of Hunter S. Thompson's 'Hell's Angels' except I was a bookish geek who worked all night on P*NK magazine layouts. I was sending out to the world mixed messages. And I wore corrected sunglasses day and night, even for reading. It was the only pair of eyeglasses that I owned and I was unable to recognize Santa Claus from five feet away without them.

Upon arriving, the diminutive balding male receptionist who was also an aspiring actor sent me to the rear of the house and upstairs. I entered the accounting office expecting the worst. Behind a large wooden desk facing into the room seated with her back to the wall in the executive manner sat a pleasant looking woman who had the appearance of a dyke lesbian. She was wearing mens casual dress clothes. This was possibly my first encounter, real encounter with one, mano a mano, but I didn't have time to give it much consideration.

"Hi. Are you Tracy?"

"Yes."

"My name is Ronnie Kale. I talked to you on the phone about the part time job you have advertised in your classified section."

"Oh yes. Come on in. Have a seat. What happened to your leg?"

"I was hit by a car crossing Sunset Boulevard."

"Oh you poor dear. If you don't mind waiting just a minute while I finish what I'm doing here. Some of these sales people keep very sloppy records of their sales if you know what I mean. They drive me crazy."

So I sat down and propped up my crutches against the wall. I sensed that she liked me which is outrageous because except for a few friends that I have made and lost over the years people rarely ever like me. If I smiled and made an effort to appear endearing, people especially disliked me. A perky and pleasant personality that fits snugly into an office environment can hide an extremely vicious individual behind a cute demeanor but perky and pleasant never worked for me. Given a voice, I was more than likely to exhibit a bizarre and irregular sense of humor in polite company. Or to play it safe, I might keep to myself then be perceived as dull and sullen. Low self-esteem considerations were always a buzzword non-issue with me because I was already too deeply entrenched in my mental position by possible pre-natal discord.

A man who appeared to be the owner or the big publisher slash editor with overt editorial mannerisms like Perry White from the Daily Planet in Superman comics walked in to the room. Tracy and him argued about money and figures in matter of fact language like no one else was in the room.

"I don't care how you do it. Just fix it." he said.

"I can't do that Gabe. It's not legal. I could go to jail." Tracy was raising her voice somewhat.

"Just make the numbers work. I have to go now. I have a meeting." He had the ability to half-smile and talk softly when he argued.

"I won't do it Gabe!" she shouted as he turned to leave the room. He glanced down at me sitting there against the wall with a look of disapproval while Tracy seemed to catch his disdain for my presence. That cemented my fate. He hadn't noticed me in the room until just then. His reaction to me was most typical of the reception that I was accustomed to receiving. From the way that he talked I concluded that he was Jewish and from somewhere around New York City where they talk strangely, although I don't believe that I had ever actually encountered a Jewish person from New York City except portrayed by a character actor on TV or in the movies. I was really feeling like a white California boy from the burbs on this day. It was a big day of firsts, a dyke and a Jew who talked funny.

Gabe's clothes were from a different planet than my world. Beige polished cotton dress trousers with a permanent press seam on the legs and a subdued cyan blue shirt which betrayed the nascent pot belly of a compulsive worker who enjoyed dining out at fine Los Angeles restaurants and usually for free in exchange for preferred advertising placement on a right hand page. Holding those trousers up was a light brown belt with no decorative patterns, of modest width with a simple gold plated buckle. Down where the rubber hits the road, always a concern, he ran both feet inside umber brown loafers probably obtained through another favorable ad placement deal.

"Oh Gabe! He makes me so mad. I won't do some of the things that he asks. I just can't do that. I could end up in big trouble. I can't do something that is against the law. I could go to jail. Well that needn't concern you." she said turning to me. "I need someone to come in two days a week and fill out invoices for approximately eight hours each day. This is a terribly boring and tedious job but after a few months you'll probably end up in the art department anyway. Do you want the job?"

"Yes. I want it." I said. I sort of smiled, taking the middle ground.

Tracy hired me on the spot. It was like a miracle in real life. I gained a whole new appreciation for dyke lesbians. She liked me, the whole miserable package. My presence irritated the hell out of Gabe. Even today, I would take a bullet for her should the unlikely circumstance arise. I felt that Gabe wouldn't ever fire her because she knew too much about his sleazy under-the-table dealings. Gabe and a smarmy salesman the other employees called Screw-Your-Toes-Off were diverting money. That much I figured out. It was easier and more fun to say Screw-Your-Toes-Off than his true name which sounded eastern European. S–Y–T–O was a moniker only spoken behind his back, daily.

"Soon we won't be needing you anymore. In a couple of months there won't be anymore invoices to fill out. We'll be replacing you with a computer." Those were the first words that Gabe Klein spoke to me. In fact, those were his only words spoken to me and he repeated them often. He managed to remind me of my imminent doom at least one instance each week. I was not terribly uncomfortable with impending doom so I just kept my back to the room, looked busy and listened for tales of corruption. I loved corruption, it was completely entertaining. One week a black man broke into Screw-Your-Toes-Off's *casa de luxury*, robbed and pistol whipped the daylights out of him. His face was messed up pretty bad. The entire staff seemed to enjoy his suffering. In all probability it was because of his appearance, stringy long blond hippie hair cascading over a brightly colored cerulean blue business suit, coupled with the rumored lucrative side deals with clients involving Gabe, costly consumer goods, cash and services. In addition, S–Y–T–O evinced certain slimy, ingratiating, insincere mannerisms that went well beyond perky and pleasant. These mannerisms helped bring him some monetary success. Fortunately for the rest of the world, as a salesman he was limited in his dealings by the bounds of his sales territory.

The quiet accounting office was also occasionally visited by a kind of interesting looking girl. She had a uniquely different manner of dress exhibited through an eccentricity defined by its own fashion terms, combining images, characters and patterns, folk art and brightly colored fabrics into a strangely homogenous fashion statement of questionable intent. She wasn't punk but rather she was a new kind of unconventionality. In all likelihood she hadn't defined a distinct style that was likely to spread across the nation, although it was working for her. It was especially pleasant to observe bright non-fashion after long hours of bean counting so I looked forward to her visits to our back room. She had orphan Annie blond hair and a warm smile that lit up her face which was belied by truly sad eyes. There was a popular song on the radio in that era called Betty Davis Eyes and she wore them perfectly, pretty but sad and weary. I looked her up in the GO L.A. masthead. Strange sort of name. Zanna Puzio, art director.

The Asian merchants already knew me by my first name at the corner liquor store and I had been living there at the bridge dump for only six weeks. I put on thirty pounds seemingly overnight. My gaunt face filled out and my waist expanded. In time, I began walking without the aid of the crutches. Too much alcohol can make a person grow puffy and plump and this was my new condition. Booze blubber. It was like an instantaneous gelatin growth. I wasn't eating much food except the occasional burrito or burger from the street stands.

Danté found me to be entertaining in this condition and we were great buddies at this time. We continued ardently to pursue our goal which was to publish more greater P*NK Magazines. He was a little miffed that his career wasn't moving along more smoothly. He was unable to land the super kool freelance record industry jobs and slick magazine spreads that he wanted. Punk and New Wave rock bands that he courted and schmoozed selected other photographers for their promos and products. There was a short list of a dozen or more photographers running around shooting the scene and each one had a quirky persona and an trademark look to their work, some better than others.

This punk new wave era manifested a radical break in visual dynamics from the rock music photography which had preceded it before 1976. People were looking for a new vision to define the times, brighter colors and shapes, gritty street shots, bad attitudes, strange composition, macabre death visages, new fashions, radical make-up and hair. Art directors too were choosing other photographers ahead of Danté. Perhaps he had a problem with his interview manner or maybe they just didn't like his portfolio because he was torn between uninventive fashion present-ations and wild live stage shots of L.A. punk groups. As long as he was being rejected by others, he was mine to use. Ultimately, it was the eccentric punk work that provided him with a viable reputation. From his point of view, he seemed to enjoy observing my increasingly dipsomaniacal sinking lifestyle. My new part-time employment at GO L.A. surprised Danté a little bit, just about as much as it had surprised me.

I managed to meet Zanna Puzio one afternoon. I even liked the name itself on its own merit. We started talking on the stairs halfway between floors. One thing I omitted. She had a butt shaped like a black woman's tush. This was enough in itself

SUB-HOLLYWOOD — BRUCE CAEN

to make me come out of my shell and make that extra effort. If her ass was more modest I possibly never would have spoken to her and my life would have taken a completely different course. We decided to meet and go to lunch later that afternoon. She was going to lunch with guys all the time, I had observed that.

This is where something unexpected happened that was in some way of much greater importance to me than it seemed at the time. We walked out of the GO L.A. offices together and up to a crosswalk with the push-button light apparatus, then we waited for the walk signal. While we were waiting an agitated shriveled old man wearing an L.A. Lakers cap, not a day under seventy to be sure, came running up to Zanna. He appeared overly animated approaching us suddenly out of nowhere. He was talking loudly and gesturing at Zanna, not quite yelling but his speech was rapid and he was red in the face. His voice was strident, raspy and ear-splitting. He was a completely irritating cramped up man judging by his manner. For all his wild arm waving and vocalizations, he never spoke a word of English, which was my favorite language. Zanna stood absolutely still and calmly stared at him until he ran out of steam. Then she replied in a foreign language that I couldn't place.

"Oh Leo, di-mee spo-kwee. Di-mee spo-kwee Leo!"

She repeated herself again looking at him in the eyes. Then she added sternly a few more unfamiliar sounding phrases. The geriatric deranged man gestured and mumbled something foreign and hurried away up the street, whiz-zip from whence he came.

"OK, Zannushka-kohanna." He uttered as he turned and went on his way.

"What was the heck was that? A human tornado? Man that guy was perturbed."

"That was my uncle Leo. He is very upset. He wants to come into where I work and sit and cry but I won't let him come inside. So he sits in his car outside and waits for me to come out. He wants to go see my mother with me today but I told him that I just don't have the time to take him. We're on a deadline."

"Go see your mother? Where is your mother?"

"She's down in Inglewood in a hospital. She's dying from cancer. This is the end of the road. They can't treat her anymore. She's been in several hospitals the last few years. This is the last one, it's what I can afford now."

"I'm so sorry to hear that."

"Well you saw him just now. Uncle Leo is having a hard time of it. My mother has taken care of him his whole life. He is her brother and she has always specially looked after his well-being. He followed her here from Poland. He came here to America because he couldn't stand to be away from her. She has always loved him so much. She calls him her little black sheep."

"Was he speaking Polish? I've never heard anyone speak Polish before. I couldn't figure out what language he was speaking."

"Yes, we're Polish. I was a child when we came to America, ten years old."

"This is a funny coincidence but it's not funny. My mom's sick and I think that she's going to die soon. I'm not dealing with it so well myself. I've been drinking too much alcohol. It's my way of dealing with things. When my dad died, that was ten years ago, I didn't do so well with that either. I took a ton of drugs until I made myself sick."

We were walking up the sidewalk. By this point in time, I was newly free of the crutches. She stopped at an early model faded blue Volvo styled to mimic the '39 Ford Sedan but diminutive. We climbed in and drove off to find lunch.

"I was thinking of going to Anelcy's. It's a little Mexican place off Western on Melrose. It's really inexpensive and they make great carnitas."

"Sounds ok to me. Your uncle sure can rattle a guy nursing yesterday's hangover and working on tomorrow's. He's got such an irritating voice. And if you're from Poland why is it that you don't have an accent."

"I don't know. I learned English mostly off of the TV after we arrived. The first thing that I remember about America is all the brightly waving flags. There were all these flags everywhere waving over all the used car lots and they looked so pretty. They had nothing like that in Poland. And I thought that this must be a wonderful country."

"Where did you live when you first got here?"

"We have relatives here who promised my mother money and a place to live if she came here. So she put us on a plane, my mother and me and of course uncle Leo insisted on coming with us. We flew to America on SAS Airlines. I will never forget that flight. Then when we got here no one gave us any money or a place to live. None of the relatives did what they promised they were going to do. We lived in a cheap motel on Sunset Boulevard just a little bit west of Hollywood High School."

"Ooh! Up there where there's lots of hookers on the streets."

"My mother called them 'prostitutki'. That's the plural. A single one she called a 'prostitutka'."

"That's amusing, well, almost amusing."

"We lived there for the first two years. I used to rollerskate up and down the sidewalks on Sunset Boulevard. I'd just skate around the prostitutes when they were out there. My mom had to take a job at a dry cleaners sewing buttons. Do you know the place on Sunset with the dancing neon coathanger with little legs? By the

Ralphs market. That's the place. She was one of the most famous opera singers in Poland in her time and she had to sew clothes in a dry cleaners for seventeen years in America to support us. She wanted to take care of me."

"Your mom was a singer?"

"She was a wonderful singer. She had a beautiful voice. People loved to listen to her sing. She sang in our kitchen every day. Sometimes here in Los Angeles she had her friends come over and she sang for them."

"Did your uncle get a job too?"

"He took a job cleaning toilets downtown. He would wake up early and walk all the way to downtown Los Angeles every weekday. He worked in the film industry back in Poland, making movies, but he had trouble with the language here. He speaks German and Russian and Polish but he never got a handle on English. Later on, he got a job working in a camera shop fixing cameras."

Annelcy's was situated in a store front on Melrose in a neighborhood which was an enclave of mainly poor Latinos near to some landmark movie studios and sound stages. It was a high ceilinged, poorly decorated little restaurant with an amateurish tropical mural painted on one wall, a few tables and chairs and a juke box that had not a single selection of North American pop music. We dined and we both tried to make some light conversation on a different subject and I picked up some gossip about the people at GO L.A. As art director, Zanna was on top of it all. I told her about my personal publishing obsession.

"Oh, P*NK Magazine. I've seen that. Andrew Wolfram brought one in. We were all looking at it."

"My car is stuffed full of the back issues. I'll give you some. You can spread'em around the art department if you like."

"We headed back to the GO L.A. offices. Back inside on the stairs we ran into Andrew Wolfram coming down the stairs, a tall gaunt expatriate Englishman."

"Andrew," she said, "this is Ronnie Kale aka Ronnie Ripper. He publishes that magazine you were showing around the other day." All the punks were using street names and I had adopted Double R Ronnie Ripper in the pages of P*NK Magazine even though the nickname Liverhead stubbornly persisted. We shook hands. He had refined mannerisms and smelled a little bit poignantly overripe to the nostrils.

"P*NK Magazine!" he laughed. "I was sitting on a bus bench waiting for the bus and I saw one laying in the gutter. Someone had thrown it away. So I picked it up. It's disgusting."

"Yeah. I hear that all the time. Female circumcision isn't a popular topic in Hollywood. We're making a renewed effort to be loved by our readers."

Then I excused myself and made my way back to Tracy's office. I continued counting beans. At some point during our lunch conversation, I had offered to accompany Zanna to the hospital to visit her mother. That was the next activity that we did together. It was a deathbed date. It wasn't a typical first date and maybe it wasn't an actual date by definition. But that's what we did. We began our personal interactions at this rock bottom level of life and death reality.

It was two days after the carnitas lunch when we met to drive down to the Inglewood hospital. She warned me that it was not going to be easy to witness. She said that I could wait outside if the experience made me ill. I briefly told her about my dad's death. I told her how I had seen my uncle George laying dead in his coffin in his living room when I was eleven.

She parked the car and we sat there in silence for a moment. We were in a black neighborhood. Then Zanna said, "I am so angry. They've stolen her wedding ring at this place. I've asked everybody there what could have happened to it and no one has an answer."

"That's lowdown. Does this place have mostly black people working as nurses and doctors in it? Because I have a theory. I think they're waiting for us in the hospitals and nursing homes across the nation. They're waiting for us to get sick and weak and then they're going to exact their revenge one victim at a time for four hundred years of slavery. Do you think that's what's behind it?"

"No. I don't know. OK let's go in. She probably won't know we're even here. She hasn't been conscious for several weeks since I moved her here from that other hospital. There was a doctor there who tried an experimental technique where he cooked her. She never came back from that. He finished her."

"He cooked her? What do you mean he cooked her?"

"He cooked her. That asshole. He told me he wanted to try an experimental procedure that might kill the cancer where he raised her body temperature so high that it would kill all the cancer cells. That was at another hospital. I pulled her out of there after that and brought her here. I feel sick everytime I have to drive past that place. I hate that doctor. He treated my mother like an experimental lab rat."

"Oh god. That's awful. You've had a really rough time of it. How long has this been going on?"

"She got sick two and a half years ago. I had to stop my fine art career and get a serious job to keep her and my uncle going."

"But you've got an interesting job. It's a great job."

"But it's not what I wanted to do."

We wound our way through the hallways.

"OK prepare yourself." she said.

We turned the corner and entered a room. I seem to remember that the walls were white. On the bed was a figure that resembled an unwrapped ancient Egyptian mummy. A head was visible and the fragile torso and legs were wrapped in white clean sheets. The flesh was desiccated with sienna colored jaundice. It was hard to make out facial features except for an open mouth which was sucking air. Her mom looked like a B–horror movie prop, except that it was her mom and she was alive. Zanna didn't know what to do for her. She smoothed her thin hair and played with the sheets. The enshrouded lady must have weight sixty pounds or less. How can she still be living I wondered. We sat in silence while Zanna held her hands for a time.

"You see. It's bad." she said.

I wasn't able to speak. I waited there quietly.

After we spent a half an hour sitting with her, we left. I hoped that she knew that Zanna was there looking after her. Zanna went over to talk to the nurse on duty and then we walked out.

"I think that chemical they use at the dry cleaners to clean the clothes gave her the cancer. She sat in those fumes for ten hours a day for seventeen years. And then she came down with liver cancer."

"That's probably true. It's some kind of petroleum solvent isn't it?"

"Yeah, it is I think."

"That was a hard dose of reality Zanna. I don't think I can speak for a while."

Zanna's mom died three days later. She died alone in the hospital and Zanna received the phone call while at work on a deadline in the art department. She took a few days off to deal with funeral arrangements and console her uncle. When the funeral was held, I went with Zanna and her uncle Leo. I found myself right in the middle of her life. The funeral was attended by the whole natty crew from GO L.A., including Gabe Klein. He was probably a little surprised to see me there accompanying Zanna and her uncle. It was a Jewish funeral. Zanna had told me that she was Jewish but somehow I had not considered the formalities of a Jewish funeral. I tried to stay inconspicuous but I wasn't dressed appropriately. The only clothes I owned were my Hollywood punk rock street clothes. Spiked studded wristbands, Chippewa engineer boots, studded belts, the whole uniform often described. This was 1980. Both our mothers kicked the bucket that year when we first met.

I walked down to Zannas apartment on Oxford Street above Beverly Blvd. I had developed a love for walking after the swelling in my knee had eased up. The knee had cartilage damage that caused the joint to collapse occasionally but if I was careful I could get around normally. Also, some vestigial interest in physical fitness occasionally surfaced alongside my self-destructive habits. At this time of great personal stress, I was smoking Camel straights and Marlboros in the soft pack because they last longer than the fliptop hard box. To my surprise, when I arrived at Zanna's there was a large man in her apartment with her. He was playing music from his collection of old 45s. Playing old 45s is always fun. She introduced us but we already knew each other. My arrival blew the big man's rockabilly tune party to hell. His light-hearted demeanor grew downcast.

It was Arthur Adler. Danté had a fascination with this guy. Arthur collected old cars. Danté, as you know had the '51 Merc Ledsled. He admired Adler for his collection of several kool old restored classics. Adler also collected old motorcycles, Indians and classic BMWs dating way back to the 1940s and even the 1930s. He restored the old bikes to mint condition. He also collected old juke boxes and restored them. He had an admirable ensemble of multiple trendy kool hobby avocations. Plus, Arthur wore stylish antique clothing from the 40s and 50s, like beautiful vintage Country & Western shirts and boots. On the down side, Zanna later told me that he needed to bathe more. Apparently he frequently smelled bad. Be it noted herein, that we have an Arthur and an Andrew who exhibited strong characteristic body odors. Except for his insignificant personal hygiene problem, Arthur's bad daddy chic all fit right in with the roots music thrust that was driving the new L.A. music. He likewise played in a little Country & Western musical group that based its sound around the stylings of Lefty Frizzel. There was even a new musical groove called 'Cow Punk' that evolved in L.A., although Arthur never carried his musical pursuits that far beyond the pale of tradition.

More to the point, Adler and I had a little disagreement, either before my wrist and knee accidents or when I was between accidents, sometime before I met Zanna; maybe even as much as a year prior to me showing up at Zanna's apartment that evening. Danté had dragged me along to a Memorial Day celebration which included a reenactment of a Civil War battle out on the grounds of the Veterans Administration cemetery in West Los Angeles. I brought along this pretty redhead lady who was a singer in a punk band. Once we got there I found out that Arthur wanted me to put on an itchy wool Civil War Union Army military uniform and march around all day in the hot sun re-enacting his battle of Antietam. I was a horn dog for the girl. She was wearing a loose flowery skirt and white blouse and we two ran off under a tree in the grass. Arthur Adler watched us and he was not pleased with this. People on both sides of the national conflict continued to breed throughout the Civil War, of this much I was certain.

Danté came over to the where the girl and I were laying in the shaded grass under a tree and said, "Arthur wants you to put on a Union uniform and participate in the reenactment."

I said, "I am not going to do that Danté. Let Arthur have his war without me."

"He's gonna be pissed."

"War is hell isn't it. Tell Arthur that I'm not military material. I have a 4F deferment from the military. I couldn't be in the military if I wanted to be in the military and I'm not going to march in his army. Why don't you put on a uniform and go march around all day?"

"I don't want to do it either." he laughed. Then he went over to Arthur and blamed the whole thing on me. I turned my attention back to the lady's open blouse and her beautiful white breasts.

When I popped into Zanna's living room that evening Arthur was livid. It took him by surprise. He became all wide-eyed and nervous, then he came up with some excuse to leave suddenly. He shot off like a bullet from a Colt Peacemaker with his 45s under his arm.

Zanna made fun of me for wearing a leather jacket on a hot summer's evening. I hadn't even noticed.

The apartment was filled with smiling dolls and grinning toys, a myriad of faces frozen with happiness. Zanna owned designer nicknacks and collectibles like an Eames bent wooden chair and some wavy designer lamps and a Heywood-Wakefield piece for holding and displaying collectible china. I thought Heywood Wakefield was the name of a guy who made some chairs and tables which I didn't especially care for, but I was wrong, it's an entire furniture company from the 1930s era. She collected old Bauer Ware sets. Any direction you turned there were arrayed those umpteen scads of happy smiling toy faces. Below the mantle inside the faux fireplace, five little handmade folk art dolls about 24 inches tall sat at school desks with their arms and legs outreaching, all smiles. Three smiling brightly painted wooden mechanical fish lunged out from a painted wooden box with sparkly glittery highlights ready to swim in the air at the flip of a switch. She had several grinning Naugas; stuffed naugahyde grinning little monsters which were manu-factured by the artificial leather industry in the 1960s as promotional items. There were hundreds of items on shelves, counters and tabletops mostly all grinning. I immediately found this all to be uplifting to my spirit.

I said to her, "I am so unhappy where I live I just really want to move in here." This all happened with such whirlwind speed in the week after the funeral. We had even found some brief time for great sex during that week so we were on familiar terms.

Then I said, "I don't own anything that I want to move here. I can just leave the office on Hollywood Boulevard as it is and anything at the bridge apartment is too full of bugs to bring in here."

Zanna said, "Really! You want to move in here just like that? OK go get your car and whatever stuff you want and come back."

Back at the bridge pad, I telephoned Danté. "I'm moving into Zanna's place tonight. So I won't be at that apartment anymore."

He said, "Really? You're moving in with Zanna? You're kidding me. I'm coming right over."

I called Zanna. "Danté is coming over in an hour."

"Well I've made some goulash. We can have dinner together if he's hungry. Do you want some goulash?"

I wasn't exactly sure what that was but I knew it was real food. "Oh yeah. That sounds delicious."

A new place to live and goulash. Was this too good to be real? We all three dined together but Danté and I ate the larger portions of it. Real cooked food makes a person euphoric and dizzy in the head after a couple of years of beer and cigarettes and greasy burgers and tacos. We had a delightful evening.

... ❦ ...

Zanna had eight to ten production people working under her in the art department which was located in a second floor room to the front of the GO L.A. offices. This structure, which was a house before the neighborhood changed, was a common anomaly in the permutating Hollywood area. The reassignment of a home typically preceded its destruction and subsequent replacement by a fresh new mini-mall. The art department overlooked Santa Monica Boulevard, a popular street judging by the quantity of traffic, but not a charming panorama in this neighborhood. She arranged with Tracy that I move from accounting to the art department to work on the weekly production of GO L.A. It seemed an easy transition in theory because I had been doing most of my own production on my own underground periodical. Although

Zanna had an upbeat managerial style and she kept the mood of her group elevated in times of stress, the reality of hiring me aboard the art department proved to be more problematic than practical.

There was no time card punching and people were allowed to be responsible to report their hours. She should have been the perfect boss. In fact, Zanna could be downright comical in her imitations of the sales staff or Gabe when a deadline was looming. There was an X taped to the floor like a marker that they place for a movie or TV actor to stand on and speak when the cameras are rolling.

"Why is there an X on the floor there?" I asked innocently.

"That's where Gabe stands every Wednesday night when he comes in here after making the newspaper larger at the last minute. He walks in here and stands on that spot and says, 'Where do we stand?'"

About 8:30 that evening Gabe paced into the art department with a serious look on his face. He walked to the center of the room and stopped on the X completely unaware of it. "OK. Where do we stand?" he said to Zanna.

When I was a small kid I toured our hometown newspaper with my class and they showed us how type was set. Back then, which was a very long time ago now, type was set with molten lead and it was stacked in these clumsy trays to compose a page. By 1980 typesetting had technologically advanced into a photo process but the main production of a newspaper was still done manually. Type corrections had to be cut out of the body copy and corrections manually glued in place.

If a photograph had a black outline around it, that was done with black tape which was 1 point thick, one seventy second of an inch. You see, one point tape is very skinny tape at 72 points to the inch. The corners of the tape had to be cut at 45° angles with a blade to join up and then everything had to be lined up with a T-square. This minutiae of little details, sticky glues and waxes and right angles formed a difficult correlation with my cycle of drinking and hangovers. I got grouchy doing paste-up, and caught up in sticky strips of tape and bits of type and I would continually glue my elbow to the tabletop. Typesetting bits were stuck to my sleeves and hair and lining up the 90° angles was pure hell. Accordingly, I lasted no more than one week in the art department of GO L.A. and then Zanna fired me for being drunk, irritable and unproductive. It was like a soldier being killed by friendly fire.

"Go home and work on your own magazine. Just go now." she said. So now I had lost my part-time job but I had a nice place to work because she had an enormous wooden drafting table in her dining room that was maybe nine feet across with an adjustable tilting top surface and big multi-use drawers. I kept the Hollywood

Boulevard office but I didn't use it much for a time except for occasional photography and storage. Cowboy Brown had me on his official shit list down at the shine stand and he let me know it. Young CB had his back.

Zanna's uncle called her on the phone at least once every thirty minutes at work all day long. I soon discovered that he also called her at home every thirty minutes. She had an answering machine which amplified his irritating messages. Not only did he have an abrasive voice but his messages were an exercise in unvarying perpetual repetition.

"Hello Zanna? Za-na-na-ko-ko? (Insert thirty seconds of Polish saying 'How are you sweetheart. I am worried about you. When are you coming over to see me. I have some fresh vegetables for you. I got a letter from the government and I can't understand it. Do they want money? Call me back please.') Ko-Ko-hana." Click.

After five or six calls I picked up the phone. "Hello."

"Who is theez? Where is Zanna?"

"She's not here. She's at work."

"Who is theez? Why is Zanna not there?"

"This is Ronnie. Zanna is at work."

"Rondonny? Rondonny? Where is Zanna? Has something happened to Zanna?"

"Not Rondonny. My name is Ronnie."

"Where is Zanna? How come she is not at work?"

"She's at work?"

"There is trouble at work? Has she been fired?"

"No trouble."

"Has something happened to Zanna? Where is Zanna?"

"Nothing has happened to Zanna."

"Where is Zanna? Is she in the hospital?"

"She's at work."

"Who is this speaking? Who is speaking? Where is Zanna? She is sick?"

Click. I hung up the phone.

"I give up on that guy. He's nuts." I spoke to my audience of smiling dolls, all extensions of Zanna's personality. Then I calmly went back to my creative work ritual. I put on a 'Circle Jerks' album to create the necessary punk rock ambience then went back and sat down in the drafting chair at the drafting desk. Bam! Bam! Bam! The noise startled the crap out of me. Now I'm rattled. Bam! Bam! Bam! I'm even shaking a little and expecting to find a S.W.A.T. police squad at the door. I open the front door. Uncle Leo is standing at the door and he has a heavy-set angry Jamaican-Hawaiian-Polynesian lady standing behind him. They are both scowling.

"Where is my niece? What has happened to my niece?" he shouts as he pushes past me and hurries down the length of the apartment searching for Zanna. "Where is Zanna? How come Zanna is not at home now?" says the stocky Hawaiian lady with authority.

"Zanna is at work. Who are you?"

"So why are you in here when Zanna is at work?" she says with a Jamaican lilt.

"Where is Zanna? What have you done with my niece?" her uncle says loudly behind me.

This is crazy I am thinking. I'm sandwiched between a tough Tropical Island Mamma with a Jamaican accent and an ancient Polish crazy man wearing a greasy L.A. Lakers cap. I walked over to the stereo and turned off the 'Circle Jerks'. My punky ambience had blown all into a multi-national hell punkshit.

"Who are you again?" I asked the brown-skinned island woman. She is ageless, stocky, ugly and built like an Abrams M1 tank. She could be an ugly thirty-five or an ugly seventy years old. I'm thinking gorilla in a dress.

"I am the property owner here. Edna Mau. Zanna leases this apartment from me."

"There's the phone call her." I say. I'm trying to stay calm and kool but I am frazzled as hell. The big Hawaiian looks me up and down. She doesn't like what she sees. She goes over to the telephone and calls Zanna at GO L.A. They talk. Then she turns to me.

"She says that you are staying here. According to the lease it is legal for her to have one other occupant in this apartment so I have to let you stay."

She turns to the uncle and says, "Zanna is at work. He is staying here with her. It is all right. She is permitted one additional tenant on the lease."

"Zanna is at work then? Everything is OK?" replies the uncle. "Let me telephone my niece." Then he dials her number and chatters in Polish for a few minutes over the phone. I hear him enunciating Rondonny twice. He hangs the phone up. The three of us are standing in the living room facing each other.

"OK good-bye." he says. "Good-bye Rondonny." They walk out. The thickset lady walks four paces across the Spanish arched portico and enters the opposing door.

"Oh god. She lives here! This is gonna be interesting." And there I stood aghast as I watched the uncle get into an old green junker 1960s Ford four door V-8 and drive away. It burned oil leaving a trail of opaque white and grey smoke. I went into the back bedroom and watched cartoons for a couple of hours to clear my head. Popeye, Brutus Olive Oil, Spinach, Wimpy and Sweet Pea ready to do the quick repair job on my rattled brain. And Snagglepuss, "Exit stage right!"

I called up Zanna. "Where is that big Polynesian woman from? What nationality is she? She sounds Jamaican. The U.S. Special Forces needs her killing enemy."

"She's Hawaiian she says. But she owns property in Jamaica. She goes there to her ranch in Jamaica once a year for a month or two to oversee things. That's when Kelly really goes nuts. Have you seen Kelly? She has an Irish boyfriend who's a big drunk."

"So she's a Jamaican posing as a Hawaiian hulk with an Irish boyfriend."

"Yeah pretty much I guess so. She loves him. He passes out on the front lawn."

"Wow. She's a big strong woman."

"She had a husband who died. Every year she has a Christmas party where she invites the neighbors from across the street, they're Phillipinos, and everybody from the building here. There's a old retired nun living upstairs and she comes down and tells off color jokes. And upstairs is a black girl who was getting married and having a baby shower and then there was no baby and there was no husband. You wait. You'll meet them all."

"You're uncle. Does he always call that much?"

"He calls all day every day. You should pick it up more often."

"Oh sure. If I say you're not here he doesn't believe me and he calls me Rondonny. Could you tell him to get my name straight? And I can't stand the sound of his voice."

"Is that right? He didn't used to be so crazy before my mom became ill with cancer."

In late July, we drove up to the San Francisco Bay Area to see my mother. We took Zanna's Volvo up the coast Highway One, a wonderfully scenic five hundred miles. It was almost fun except that we were going to see my mom like I had never seen her. My mom had never been ill when I was growing up. Now, she had recently spent two weeks in the hospital and then they returned her home. She revealed to me that she possibly had some kind of systemic non-specific cancer. The doctors couldn't put their finger on a particular body part or organ. In the end the doctors never quite figured it out. She just died.

San Simeon, Big Sur, Monterey, Pacific Grove, Castroville the Artichoke Capital of the World, Santa Cruz, Los Gatos, a beautiful coastline plus artichokes. Simply breathtaking cultivated edible thistles and untamed ocean. So Californian. Farther north they do the same thing with pumpkins. Untamed ocean, rocky seacliff vistas and cultivated pumpkins. So Californian. Oh the wonder of it all! Thank God we have real estate developers anxious to divide up the land into rectangular grids and cul-de-sacs. Nature belongs in museums and dioramas. Build another golf course.

The children need culture. I insisted we stop at Santa Cruz to ride the old white wooden roller coaster on the boardwalk. The rollercoaster there is an antique wooden relic that appears unintimidating to look at, but it goes fast. Zanna had never been on a roller coaster. When the ride was over I turned to look at her and she was crying like a baby. Her face was covered with wet dripping tears.

"Why did you do that to me? That was horrible."

"It's a roller coaster. That's what roller coasters do. I thought you knew that."

"No I didn't know. It was terrible." She cried for fifteen minutes.

When we got to my mom's apartment, I let myself in.

"Mom." I yelled. "I'm here with Zanna."

She came out of the bedroom and turned the corner wearing her bedclothes and walking with a limp. She smiled. It was the beautiful loving smile that she gave me when I was a little kid. It sent me back to a beautiful place in the past. She gave me a big warm hug. She was full of love. I introduced Zanna. Send up fireworks! She actually seemed to like Zanna. This was a first. She liked a girl I brought home. It only took thirty years.

This is the last point at which I want to remember my mother because I feel she still had her senses about her. Still I only remember a few instances about the visit but mostly I have an impression of her warm and loving manner on this occasion. At one point she took me into her bathroom and opened the cabinet under the sink. She pulled out a silver metallic box about twelve inches square and nine inches deep.

"If anything happens to me, like if I should die, I have placed some things here in this box to help take care of you." she said.

I replied, "OK mom." Then she placed the box back in the cabinet.

The other thing I remember is that Zanna went into her bedroom and they talked for maybe as long as two hours privately.

I asked Zanna, "What were you two talking about all that time."

"Your mother said, 'You know he has temper tantrums. They can be pretty awful.' And I said, 'I know I've seen his temper.'"

Then as quickly as we got there we were back in Los Angeles and I went back to work with my publishing. Shannon phoned a few weeks after that and said that she would like to come over and talk to me about my mother's illness. She came over on a Sunday evening when Zanna and I were both there and we three sat in the living room. My sister sat on the Eames chair, an extremely comfortable molded plywood contraption. Zanna made her a soft drink and sat down with us.

"You know mother is going to die." my sister said.

"Yeah. It looks that way." I answered.

"Don't you care? Doesn't it bother you? Don't you have any feelings?" she said.

"Did you drive over here to find out if it bothers me if my mother is going to die?" I asked. Another typical family discussion was building.

A wave anger or anguish flushed Shannon's face. She was almost at the point of speaking.

Zanna, trying to reverse the direction we were headed, said, "Of course he cares. Maybe you two should just carefully start this conversation over from the beginning."

"Shut up you cheap fucking cunt!" my sister screamed. She stood up. "This is none of your goddam business you fucking whore. You're not a part of our family so stay out of our business!"

"Get the fuck out of here Shannon. You've got a lot of nerve coming over here and screaming. Get the hell out!" I shouted. "You remember where the door is."

"I hate you you little bastard!" Shannon screamed and she ran out the door slamming it.

"There now you've met my sister. You thought I was exaggerating when I said she was nasty. What a bitch. She still looks good though. Fucking cunt bitch-in-heat."

"She's upset about your mother." said Zanna.

"So she insults you. You didn't say anything wrong. The two of them always enjoyed attacking my girlfriends. They always have done that. The last time I talked to Shannon was over the intercom at her apartment on that Thanksgiving when my mom came down to visit. Remember I told you. She told me off over the intercom on Thanksgiving. Another warm and fuzzy family get together."

"Yeah. I remember. Just let it go. There is nothing you can do about her behavior."

In early September, I booked a flight up to San Francisco. It was Croak City for mom or getting close to it. Shannon was scheduled to pick me up at the San Francisco Airport and drive me down to the hospital. This was the same hospital that my father had died in eleven years before which brought back to my mind Shannon's conspicuous absence from that family transition. This time was different in that this time Shannon was deeply entrenched in the front lines. In fact she was all over it. At the time, I thought it was because she loved my mother more than my father. But no. She didn't like either of them much as it turned out. She was in therapy for life. It was a lifelong process fattening the wallets of a concatenation of shrinks. There's a long dictionary word. I finally fit one in. It simply means she sought help because she didn't love anyone but herself and she didn't love herself much. So she went from headshrinker to therapist to psychologist to psychiatrist. They have trends and fads for the psycho-obsessed, therapy dependent, psychologically needy just like dieters have fads and trends.

I missed my flight and arrived an hour later than scheduled. No one was there to pick me up so I called the hospital. Shannon was beyond irate. She had transcended anger. She was raging.

I said, "Shit happens. I missed the flight and so I got on the next one. Get over it. I'm only an hour late. Are you going to pick me up or not?"

"I'll be right there." Click. A hour later she arrived with a fresh faced boyfriend in tow named Henry and we three drove back to Stanford Hospital. Henry offered to ride in the back seat. Up front, Shannon gave me an animated sermon on the virtues of punctuality and the vexations of sibling assholes as she drove.

When we arrived at the hospital, Henry sagely opted to stay in the car and nap. Shannon and I entered the hospital and took the elevator upstairs. When we entered the sick room, I could immediately see that my mother was never going to rally her strength. She was only partially in control of her mind and thought processes, losing her grip on reality, physically distorted and shrivelled up, chemotherapy ravaged and drugged. Croakatoid. In the death grip.

My mother looked at me and said, "You got fat!"

"I've been drinking too much. It'll do that to ya. How do you feel mom? You don't look like you're doing so good yourself."

"Oh, I feel better today. The nurses have been so nice to me here. They moved me into this bright room with a window view. And the driver who takes me to my chemotherapy treatments twice a week has been so kind. Shannon will you get me my Metamucil. It's time for my Metamucil."

Just then a fresh faced college girl entered the room. "Excuse me," she said. "I am a Stanford University Graduate Student and I am writing an investigative paper on the development of bedsores in longterm patients. May I use you as a case study for my paper." She said this directly to my mother and she smiled.

"Oh well honey, I don't see why not. It's ok with me. I'm not going anywhere." my mother replied through her distorted wizened visage.

"Hell no! You can't!" shouts Shannon. "Get out of here now and don't come back."

My mother turned to me. "I have made Shannon executor of my estate. She will handle everything when I am gone."

"I see. You and Shannon have worked it all out. It's the girls club."

That comment did it. Shannon raged. The vitriol spewed out of her mouth so rapidly that the meaning was clear although the words, mostly indistinguishable, were strung together so densely that they struck me like brick shards. She was on one side of the hospital bed holding onto those metal supports on the sides and I was on the other. She was screaming a red-faced motormouth tirade of hate over the poor sick confused woman, our mother. I grabbed my leather punk rock motorcycle jacket from the courtesy chair and threw it over my shoulder. It felt like an awkwardly theatrical gesture.

"You won't ever see me again. You two deserve each other." I said. I looked down at the dying old woman and walked out.

"I hope you two can be friends one day." My mother softly uttered. Her last words to me.

I had enough of the two of them. I couldn't stand being screamed at again by the blond. The mother seemed helpless, drugged and unable to comprehend reality. It was impossible to figure out their interlaced connection. It felt creepy to fight like rabid hyenas over my mom's wide-eyed carcass in a hospital. Shannon was playing the role of the alpha dog, a much different persona than her conspicuous absence from my fathers final days. I didn't know if I did the right thing. Probably not. I walked to the El Camino Real and hitchhiked to my mom's apartment. She would probably never return here again. I knew where mom kept the Johnny Walker Red. I drank a couple of doubles and then I called Zanna. I was crazy nuts with it all at this point. Shannon's jeremiad started the minute I got off the plane and placed the phone call to the hospital.

I went into my mother's bedroom and opened the drawer where I knew her to keep personal memorabilia and my childhood Nazi wooden ruler. She had kept all the letters I had written to her from England when I was in art college. They were written on those cyan hued light-weight European style air mail envelopes that you write on and then fold into shape and just mail. There was over a hundred of them and they were penned in my clumsy handwriting over every possible space on which it was possible to write. I had so much to say, so much optimism. I had the liberty and the sanity then to read Proust, Joyce and Beckett and write long letters to my mother. It was the freedom to study art that my mother had given to me by her support. I had no reason to be bitter about my mother. However, I was deeply angry from whatever it was in life that was driving me, a multi-faceted sort of chimera. Then I pushed the drawer shut and went to the living room and sat on her sofa. I simply stared at the walls and sparkly ceiling glitter feeling the warm alcohol in my body and pondered the ravages of the passage of time on humans. My mother will not die young and she will not have a beautiful corpse, I thought. Then I drunkenly pondered Sartre's 'Nausea' from the perspective of an unhappy American living in California.

Crash! Bang! The back door from the swimming pool side leading into the kitchen flew open. Shannon charged through the door like it was first down and goal to go. The Oakland Raiders. With her head down and moving fast she was followed immediately by a blocker, the young actor boyfriend of hers, Henry. He was kind of a generic fair and fresh all-American looking young man performing in the characteristic manner in which many aspiring actors carry themselves. Today, Henry was doing double extra duty. Now he appeared more awkward and uncomfortable than in the car. Shannon disappeared through my mothers bedroom door. Henry followed her avoiding eye contact with me. When she reappeared a mere fifteen seconds later she was carrying the silver metallic twelve by twelve by nine box under her arm. The two of them ran out the rear door they had moments before entered. Never a word was spoken and they left the back door open while the screen door closed slowly by a spring mechanism of its own accord. I heard the muffled rumble of their car leaving. Henry was more nonplussed than aggressive. This was all beyond his comprehension. Shannon characteristically demanded macho demonstrations from her boyfriends.

"The element of surprise is extremely effective in a tactical situation." I mumbled or something to that effect. "Touchdown!"

I got up and went to the phone and called Zanna again.

"Shannon came running in here and took the box that my mother told me to look in if she died. She ran away with it."

"Just get on a plane and come back here. Don't drink anymore. Can you get to the airport?"

"Yeah sure."

"Call me when you find out your flight and I'll come and pick you up." said Zanna. I called a shuttle and made my way back up to the SFX airport and I caught a late flight back to L.A. No goodbyes left to make. When I arrived back in L.A., I came back more fucked up in the head than before I left. That little hospital day-trip shook me up.

I caught a shuttle from LAX back to the apartment. I arrived back at Zanna's after midnight. A lady neighbor, a retired hairdresser from the adjacent four-plex was standing in the driveway holding her toy poodle Bubbles (petite Bubbles feet rarely touched the ground). The lady's perfect silver bubble hairdo seemed to glow in the moonlight. The space orb bubble hairdo instantly identified her to be a lady from my mom's generation. She was staring at a tall grey-haired man in a polyester leisure suit who was standing on the grass in front of Edna's fourplex loosely holding his large penis, urinating on a palm tree and talking to Edna who was inside her ground floor apartment with the window open.

"Go inside. Kelly. Go inside the apartment. Kelly. Kelly." The silver haired lady spoke calmly. She was wearing a sheer feminine bathrobe and getting a good long eyeful at what Kelly was manipulating in his hand. Tube steak. Schlong.

I opened the gate on the chainlink fence and entered the yard. "Hey Kelly. How's it hangin'?"

"Can't complain." he said with a chuckle through a cloud of cigarette smoke.

Edna came out. "Kelly. Come inside here right now." she insisted.

"He needs to stay indoors when he's like this Edna." commented the silver bubble-haired lady.

"Poncho! Poncho is still inside the van." Kelly said. He shuffled over to a white Ford van parked in the driveway, opened the door and released a German Shepherd. "C'mon Ponch!" The three of them Edna, Poncho and Kelly disappeared inside her apartment in that order. Kelly was a big brawny old Irishman, at least 6' 2" but Edna could handle him and then some.

"He gets so drunk that he urinates in the front yard. When I saw him wandering out there with his trousers open again I called Edna." the concerned neighbor commented to me.

"It's disgusting behavior for a mature gentleman." I said and walked up the three white painted steps through the arched double doors and turned right into Zanna's apartment. Edna had a green thumb. The front yard was full of beautiful lush plants, flowers and green grass. Kelly did his part watering the palm trees.They grew rapidly. Zanna was standing at the window peeking out.

"You met the Super Snooper." she said. "She lives next door. She keeps a close eye on everybody."

"She's still standing out there holding that poodle. She definitely kept an eye on Kelly's dick. Skin show's over. Now I know what they grow in Ireland."

217

Danté phoned. "Buck and Lana have a new place. They want us to come over and see it. It's a small Spanish style house."

"When today?"

"Yeah this afternoon."

"Well, come over and pick me up."

"OK. See you in a bit."

"Zanna!" I yelled down the hallway. "Get dressed. Do you remember I told you about Buck and Lana?"

"Yeah."

"They moved into a new place. Dante's coming over and we're going over to look at it. Get dressed and come with us. They're really kool. It'll be fun."

"OK. How long do I have to get ready?"

"He'll probably be here in an hour."

"OK."

Danté showed up and we all three piled into the front seat of the Merc. Danté drove down Crenshaw a couple of blocks below Wilshire Boulevard and then wound around a few neighborhood blocks and he eventually pulled up in front of a white Spanish style one bedroom house sitting on a dried up little lot. It had those orange semi-circular clay tiles around the eaves.

"That's it. Pretty nice." Danté said with a smile.

The three of us exited the Merc and walked up the sidewalk to the front porch. The warm midday had passed into a typically hot and sunny Los Angeles afternoon. The screen door was closed but the front door was open and we could see Buck and Lana sitting in a nearly empty large room beckoning us to come inside. Inside the front room was furnished only with an old couch on a hardwood floor. I introduced Zanna to Buck and Lana.

"Isn't this great." Buck said standing up. He briefly showed us the kitchen with a wave of his arm. "It's a nice little kitchen with built in cabinets." says Lana.

"Do you want a beer? Buck opened up the fridge and handed us each a cold bottle of beer which he opened with a gadget on his belt.

"Let me show you the bedroom." We walked casually as a group across the wooden floor past the couch and then filed one by one into the bedroom. The only pieces of furniture in there were a king-sized bed with a white bedspread and a stained walnut wooden dresser. Over the bed was tacked up an unframed full-sized colorful silk-screened nineteen by twenty five inch white supremacist poster. I remember thinking at the time that it appeared to be a representation from a South African apartheid group. The entire bedroom was decorated with similarly slanted emblems and paraphernalia, a Confederate flag, Nazi swastikas, an image of Adolf Hitler, a Nazi dagger, possibly a knock-off replica.

"Wow." I said. "You've got a lot of Nazi shit."

"Yeah. Lots of it." said Lana.

We drank a beer in the front room and talked about the punk rock shows that we had recently attended. Then it got awkward as the conversation slowed and Zanna said that she had to get back so she could go visit her uncle. Danté drove us back to the Oxford Street fourplex and dropped us off.

As Danté drove off, we went inside and sat across the angular designer table from each other in Zanna's living room. I said, "Did you notice anything unusual about that visit? I never know what to say when I run into shit like that. I didn't know that they were like that. I thought they were just your basic rock 'n roll biker punks."

"You mean the Nazi posters? I'm not surprised by anything. Were you surprised?"

"Well yeah. I've never had friends like that."

"That's how it happened in Poland. Jewish people were turned in to the Nazis by their neighbors and friends, by people they had known since kindergarten and grade school. At first the Jews were made to wear armbands that marked them as Jewish and then they weren't allowed to walk on the sidewalks. They made my mother walk down the middle of the street where all the horseshit was. Then they threw the Jews out of their houses and apartments, took everything they owned and fenced them into a ghetto. Then from the ghetto they sent them to Aushwitz."

"Where exactly are you from? I can never understand what you are saying."

"Wooje. It's pronounced Wooje. But it's spelled L-o-d-z. My mother was forced by Nazis into the Lodz ghetto. They were going to kill her. The rest of her family was buried alive by the Nazis. They killed all the Jews in Poland. There were no Jews left after the war. Just a few thousand survived out of two million."

"Jesus. How did your mom get away?"

"Back then, my father worked for a baker and he delivered rolls into the ghetto. He saw my mother imprisoned in there and he had been in love with her since they were little children when they were schoolmates. She was always a very popular girl because she was such a beautiful singer even as a child. My father helped her to escape but he wasn't my father yet because I wasn't born until 1952."

"How come he wasn't caged in there?"

"He was Roman Catholic."

"How did he get her out?"

"He bribed a Nazi guard with gold. That's the only thing they would accept back then. Money was worthless. Gold. He slipped her out and he took her to a farmhouse in the countryside where he had paid the owner with a chest full of gold to hide her inside a large hollowed out couch which was in their farm house. She lived inside the couch for five years until the war was over. Sometimes the Nazi soldiers would come to the farm house and stay over. Naturally, they would sit on the couch when they were there."

"She never came out of the couch?"

"No. She couldn't come out. If anyone saw her she would be turned in and killed and the farmer would be killed."

"Didn't she have to shit and piss. Didn't the couch begin to stink or something?"

"When you don't eat and you don't drink, your body functions just slow down to nothing and virtually stop. The deal my father made with the farmer was that she could hide inside the couch. There was no agreement to give her food or water and the farmer gave her nothing."

"How come she didn't die? She had to eat something in five years."

"My father would smuggle food out there late at night when he felt it was safe, maybe every couple of weeks. He would lift her out of the couch and carry her out of the house because she was too weak to walk and lay her down outside in the grass in the moonlight and he would give her some food and water."

"And they weren't married yet?"

"No. He just loved her."

"That's him in the picture? Your dad, he was very handsome. Where was your uncle?"

"He was enlisted in the Polish army. He was captured by the Russians and he spent nearly the entire war in Siberia in a gulag. They survived by eating tree bark and boiling it to make tea."

"Your mom's name was Nora?"

"Yes. Nora."

"Boy Nora sure had a strong will to live. My family members give up the ghost without much struggle. We're a family of wimps. At the first sign of trouble we drop and die. That's quite a story Zanna."

"I'm going over to my uncle's to pay some of his bills and pick up some vegetables. Do you want to come over? I'll only be there a half an hour."

"Uh. Yeah. I guess."

She telephoned the uncle and talked in Polish for a few minutes. Then we got into her Volvo and drove off. Zanna's Volvo was parked on the street as was my '52 Ford. There was only street parking available at the fourplex because Edna needed all four parking places in the rear and the entire backyard to turn around her car. In my opinion, Edna had a spatial visualization problem. Tenant parking was not included in the lease agreement and therefore the property owner exclusively had the usage rights to the entire backyard. No tenant was ever allowed usage of the backyard for any reason, although burglars found the rear access convenient.

Uncle Leo lived immediately off of the corner of Edinburgh and Melrose Avenue in a fourplex but Zanna drove down to Beverly Boulevard and then headed west. He lived where the Jewish immigrant apartment houses abutted on the trendy Melrose Avenue shops. Down Fairfax Avenue, one block to the east were the many family owned vegetable and fruit stand shopfronts where uncle Leo shopped. The area was full of little Jewish elderly people of uncle Leo's generation. They were generally physically smaller than typical Americans.

"Why aren't you driving down Melrose. He lives off of Melrose not Beverly." I remarked.

"I have to drive this trip to my uncle's seven days a week," she said, "I don't have to drive it the same way every day. You can't imagine how sick I am of driving up and down Melrose Avenue year after year."

In a couple of minutes we were driving through a Hasidic Jewish neighborhood around Beverly Boulevard and Highland. I see a fellow wearing a black hat with a broad flat brim trimmed with fur and dangling balls around the edges.

"Well, these Jews certainly do dress funny Zanna. Look at that guy's hat."

"That's why they come here. It's OK to be Jewish in America and its OK to dress funny."

"The little boys have sideburns."

"Yeah. So what?"

"So nothing."

"How come you don't dress like them?"

"Because I'm me. I dress like I want to dress."

"I can't recall seeing any neighborhoods like this in northern California come to think of it. You know, an American kid would never pamper an old fart uncle the way you do uncle Leo. An American kid would move to another city to get away from him."

"Yeah, well I can't do that. My mother loved him. I have to take care of him."

"Why didn't your father come to America."

"He's dead."

"Was he dead before you came over here?"

"No. He died after we moved here. He was cheating on my mother with his secretary. That was when mother decided to just pack it in and come to America."

"You mean after they went through all that horrible stuff during the war? So that was way long after the war in the late '50s?"

"Yeah. They were such great friends my mother and father and my uncle. And I had a little dog called Bambka. My uncle and my father were the very best of friends. They used to drink vodka and smoke cigarettes and talk and laugh all night long."

"How did he die?" Zanna went silent. "How did your father die?" I repeated.

"He had a heart attack. Well, he had a few serious heart attacks when we were still in Poland. His heart condition kept getting worse; what he had was called congestive heart failure, I think. They all smoked too many cigarettes and drank vodka. He died after we came to America the first year. He had a heart attack while he was having sex with the secretary. He died right on top of her."

"Oh my god!" I went silent. "Oh my god!" I repeated.

"My uncle used to smoke cigarettes like a chimney but we had a car accident at this intersection at Fairfax and Beverly in the 1960s and they X-rayed his chest and found that he had lung cancer. They removed one lung and he quit smoking." Zanna says this as she downshifts into second gear and turns the old Volvo to the right onto Fairfax Avenue.

"Leo's a tough old codger ain't he? He's survived a Nazi invasion, Siberian gulags and lung cancer and he's still running around like a crazy man. My dad got lung cancer from Camel cigarettes but he died." I replied.

We pulled up in front of the apartment on Edinburgh. Zanna used her key to open the door.

"If I knock, he probably won't hear it. He's almost completely deaf."

Inside the door was a set of wooden stairs leading up to the second floor apartment. The top of the stairs opened into a dusty living room. I could see the back of the uncle's dirty and dented L.A. Lakers cap rising slightly above the rear of a tattered armchair upholstered with a soiled embroidered floral pattern. Three televisions were turned on to the same sports event. They began advertising athletic shoes in triplicate. Two of the TVs were stacked one on top of the other and then a third was placed next to them on its own small wooden table and each one had a corresponding set of rabbit ear antennas. The sound was off on all three TVs.

"Where's the sound? He's got three TVs going and no sound."

"He can't hear them so he leaves the sound off."

Zanna walked around in front of him and said hello. He immediately stood up.

"Ronnie is here." she says.

"Who?"

"Ronnie. Ronnie is here."

He turned around. "Oh hello." he says. He managed to sort of smile through all his wrinkles. He was immaculately clean shaven.

"Are you watching the Dodgers? Who is winning?"

"What?" he says.

Zanna repeated what I said to him in Polish.

"Oh. It's that game they play with the stick. I don't like the game with the stick. I like The Lakers. Magic Johnson is a very good player."

We go into the kitchen and sit around a worn '50s style bent chrome tubing and formica table with a swirly patterned yellow top surface faded white from use.

"Do you want some potato soup Rononnie? I will heat you some soup. Very good."

"No thanks." I look at Zanna and she nods approvingly.

"Well, OK. Sure."

He lights the gas stove with a match and begins warming a pot.

"You like pickles? I have a jar of pickles for you."

"I don't like pickles."

"Bread?"

"It's a corn rye bread. It's good." says Zanna.

"OK I'll have a slice of rye bread."

I notice that the linoleum is completely worn through to the wood in the most frequently travelled areas of the kitchen. The paint on the ceiling is peeling. The living room is weary-worn. All the mementos and family portraits on the walls are slightly off the right angle. Zanna sees me looking around.

"He collects grocery bags. I discovered an entire closet crammed with them and all the lower cupboards and the laundry room is completely filled."

"Your mom used to live here too?"

"This is where we moved to from the motel on Sunset Boulevard. My mother's bedroom is left untouched. Uncle Leo won't move a thing."

"Why don't you pick up the phone when I call Rononnie?"

"You're not calling me, you're calling Zanna."

"I will call you specially. Then you pick up the phone."

"OK."

"After we eat I will show you some pictures. I had many girlfriends in Poland. You will see. Ha! Ha! Very beautiful."

When the food was cleared away, Zanna started going through his bills and writing checks. Uncle Leo shuffled off into the rear of the apartment and returned with a yellowed old shoebox. He showed me old photographs that were stacked carefully within the vintage box. There were photographs of him when he was a much younger man with attractive women. He was dressed up in sharp fashionable clothes, wearing tailored suits with a tie. The women too were fashionable.

"We were very much in love." He remarked repeatedly.

There was a photograph of him turned out in a suit and tie sitting elevated behind a 35mm movie camera on a crane with an entire film crew around him.

"Man! That's a serious movie crew and camera set-up!"

"In Poland, I was in the film business." he said. "Ha ha. I was sitting at a café with my young friend and I said to him, 'Polanski is casting his movie. Why don't you go over and see if you can get a bit part in this movie?' So I sent him over to where Polanski was casting. I thought he might only get a small part. He was new to acting and they put him in the lead role. It was called 'Knife in the Water.' Have you heard of it?"

"Is that true?" I asked obliquely to Zanna.

"Yes." She said.

I saw a photo in the box of two Nazi soldiers with submachine guns marching a civilian up the center of a street. The photo was taken looking down on the street from a second floor window. It looked like a theatrical shot from a movie set.

"What's this?" I asked.

"What's this?" Zanna repeated in Polish.

"I took that from my window. They took that man into the alley and shot him to death right after I took that picture."

As I looked back over the photos, I tried to imagine how a handsome successful stylish man could have devolved into a crazy wrinkled compulsive little curmudgeon with a dirty L.A. Lakers cap.

"I still write to this one." He said pointing to a photograph of a young lady. "And this one died two years ago."

"Ask him about Stalin." Zanna said. "Because he's going to tell you anyway."

"What about Stalin?" I said.

"What?" he said.

"Tell him about Stalin." Zanna said loudly in Polish.

"Oh Stalin. In Siberia we were very miserable. There was this one man who had a large picture of Stalin tattooed on his ass so when he pulled down his pants to shit it came out of Stalins mouth. Very funny." he laughed. "Very funny."

Apart from his dirty hat, Uncle Leo typically wore a permanently pressed royal blue shirt with a ballpoint pen clipped in the pocket. I noticed upon close observation over time that he was always clean shaven and well groomed. Outdoors he wore a maroon Members Only jacket, possibly a JCPenney product. In place of sunglasses he carried clip-over bargain sunglass substitutes that fit over any pair of regular corrected lenses. Occasionally he alternated from those clip-overs to an oversized wrap-around sunglass brand that universally fit over any standard pair of corrected eyeglasses. Each of these products were readily available at any local drugstore chain such as Osco, Savon, or Thrifty Drugs. These brands were popular geezer fashions with numerous immigrant septuagenarians in the Fairfax District.

Uncle Leo regularly visited these drug stores in the neighborhood at least twice a day to check his blood pressure on the free-to-the-public machine. He would often hold his wrist and count his pulse while staring at his watch at any location such as a restaurant. He ate the Number 9 Meal Fish Sandwich at McDonalds once a week. He had a blurred prisoner number tattooed on his forearm. He drove to his doctor down on Wilshire Boulevard no less than three days a week and appeared in the waiting room unannounced. His doctor's visits were covered by Medicare, Medicaid, Medical or whatever government program it is that pays for old geezers. Each visit he wanted to know only if he would live one more day. He was always disinclined to believe the doctor's prognosis.

"He's in great health for a man of his age." the doctor would tell Zanna over the phone. Uncle Leo called the doctor a flatfoot.

Uncle Leo had a direct line to Jerry West's personal office telephone. Jerry West was a record breaking star player who moved up to Coach, then later West became General Manager of the L.A. Lakers. According to Zanna and Leo, Jerry took his personal calls frequently and he listened to Leo's basketball criticisms through the thick Polish accent and they discussed how to better the Laker team.

Uncle Leo's generation of filmmakers was a generation senior to Polanski in the 1950s and the great Polish directors of Leo's generation who were still working in film stopped in to visit him whenever they were in Los Angeles. With all this variety and sophistication to his personality, he still irritated the hell out of me. He was petulant and quirky and it was difficult to find the sophisticated man hidden within the cantankerous old Polish codger.

From this point of view notwithstanding, he was more suited than most people to comprehend the sort of off-balance anti-social creative compulsive psycho-dramatic personality who was now sitting at his kitchen table and who was ruining his niece's life daily. He was endearing when he was giving me a gift of lemons or pickles, neither of which I liked. Zanna would buy him a new winter jacket and slacks every autumn. She would clean his apartment as best she could and cover all his expenses beyond a meager Social Security stipend. Uncle Leo had taped a

SUB-HOLLYWOOD —— BRUCE CAEN

fragile creased black and white photograph of an old girlfriend to the living room wall with Johnson & Johnson flesh-colored Band-Aid Plastic Strips, the kind used across America for dressing small flesh wounds and scrapes. There was a wooden chair with a cushion on it placed in front of the four by five inch photograph where he used to sit alone and stare at it and reminisce.

"Take some lemons home Ronnonie. They are very good." He handed me a small bag of lemons. They would go perfectly with tequila and methadrine. So, I took 'em.

... ♪ ...

The next night Danté and myself were off to Chinatown. L.A. Chinatown had become punky. The Hong Kong Café and Madame Wongs put on a series of shows featuring bands like The Germs and The Blasters and many others. At the Hong Kong Café, the stage was elevated maybe two feet above the floor height so that the musicians and the audience rocked out united as one. Late that night, a group of us were hanging around in the area delegated to the bands and their equipment when the musicians were off-stage and between sets. Lana and Buck were mingling around in the crowd. Lana came over to me and made small talk for a while.

"You know that girl you were with the other day is Jewish." she said matter of factly. Lana had refined features with a shock of trimmed brunette hair and fair skin with freckles.

"Lana. I don't make friends with people based on their religion. Is it bad that she is Jewish?"

"Well, yeah. I think so."

"I just don't give a shit. This is America. People can be any religion that they like. Any religion. They can wear little bells in their noses and chant rama-rama-ding-a-ling all day and night. So what is so bad about Jewish people?"

"Well. They killed our lord."

"That is so stupid and crazy a thing to say. You're saying that my girlfriend Zanna Puzio killed your lord."

"Her people did."

"OK. We're through talking. End of conversation. You're a bigot. Have you ever read the American Bill of Rights? I can't talk to you anymore. I don't want to get angry. I can enjoy a good joke at the expense of any religion, but you're pushing hatred."

"I'm just trying to tell you something." she said. Then I walked away from her.

Me, Ronnie the Liverhead, just wanted to be a punk rocker. I loved the bands like Social Distortion and The Circle Jerks. For me, their music made life worth living. This cliché dialogue was rehashing World War II Naziism all over again but it wasn't dull or humorous. I couldn't believe I was hearing Lana say that even after observing their decorations in the bedroom. Since there were Jews playing in punk bands, logically the next step was to boycott those bands. Racial or religious bigotry was not something I had ever encountered working with artists and artistic people. Fortunately for the world at large, I felt that Buck and Lana were lacking the intellectual and social skills to organize anything larger than small drug deal.

On the drive home that night around 2:30 a.m., I made a remark about Buck and Lana's use of Nazi symbols as home decorations to Danté who was in cheerful spirits.

"Lana told me that Zanna was Jewish and that was a reason not to date her. So does that mean that Buck and Lana are bona fide Nazis? How long have they been going down that road?" I asked.

"Well there are a lot of people on the scene who feel that way." Danté replied.

"On the scene? On the punk rock scene? There are not. 'Gabba gabba hey. Your one of us.' Heard of the Ramones? Duh."

"A lot of people who hang around our club scene and the Taco Stand parties and stuff think that way."

"You mean people like Big Billy? Big Billy loves black people. He loves their culture. He can't be a Nazi. That's an oxymoron. Somebody's a moron."

"And Jews control the entertainment industry."

"OK. Danté. In America, people can go into whatever line of work that they wish. Jews can go into the entertainment business if they like and so can Transylvanians. Do you think Jews are keeping your career down as part of a plot?"

"Well possibly yes."

"Possibly P*NK Magazine is ruining your career goals. And possibly Jews are systematically keeping Italians who like photography from participating in the fashion industry. But, I thought that Italians always were the hot shit in the fashion industry. Then that makes you the one poor Italian sucker who has got Jews breathing down your ass, turning you away from jobs. So start your own damn company and hire yourself. You're in America. Don't you see how crazy it is to think that way?"

"Listen, I'm Sicilian. It's a tradition with us."

"In New York City, there's Jews in the Italian mafia. That's America. And I thought Rossetti was a name from northern Italy. Milan not Sicily. Besides you weren't born in Italy. You were born in America. That makes you an American." I made that Milanese remark up off the top of my head knowing absolutely nothing about Italian name etymology.

"I'm just saying that a lot of people on the scene feel that way. We call ourselves the Hollywood Wolves. You're a Hollywood Wolf too. You're one of us. Didn't you know that?"

"I'm a Hollywood Wolf? Me? I didn't know that. Well thank you. I am very flattered. You do know that the magazine we have been publishing is a satirical magazine. It's tongue-in-cheek dark humor."

"Oh yeah. I know that. We're just having fun." Danté pulled his Merc up in front of Zanna's Spanish fourplex.

"OK then, I'll talk to you tomorrow. And I'm a Hollywood fuckin' Wolf too. Do you have any badges or anything?"

"Well some of the guys and girls are getting FTW and the number 13 tattooed on their arms."

"FTW? What's that mean?"

"Fuck The World."

"Well, I've had enough trouble hiding this dragon tattoo from my dying mother. I'll hold back on the FTW for a while. I notice you don't have an FTW tatt. Maybe you should go all the way and get F-U-C-K tattooed on your knuckles. Later on man." I slammed the door and he drove off. Then I went inside and woke Zanna up and told her all about the Hollywood Wolves and the Jews controlling the entertainment industry.

In the next month, I completely obsessed, more that my usual obsession, over P*NK Magazine projects. We produced and pressed a punk band flexi-disc record to insert inside the publication. I was running off to the UCLA medical student's bookstore buying armloads of books about facial deformities and diseases for use in fictional reader testimonial articles. I desperately needed a great writer in the magazine; but in the absence of a dependable modest genius who would work for almost free of charge, I did most of the writing myself. I would often write all night until I fell off of my chair about 5a.m. stoned and drunk. That was my unique way of developing a writing style. Zanna would wake me up on her way to work.

"Get off the floor. Clean this place up. You've turned it into a pigsty. It stinks of stale tequila, cigarettes and rotting lemons. Open some windows. How does this look?" She would say modeling a stylish outfit and smiling.

"I love that sweater thing you're wearing but the shoes look funny. Find some different shoes." I would say from the floor.

"Shit. I don't have time for this." She would mumble, then she would run down the hallway into the back and return with new shoes.

"That looks good. See you later." I'd say typically. I was developing a horizontal literary style drunk on the floor technique quite a bit back then.

One evening around this time period, late October 1980, Zanna and I were sitting in the front room. I was cutting skeletal deformities manipulated through a stat camera into a horrid little graphics when the telephone rang.

Zanna picked it up. "It's for you." she said.

"Hello." I answered.

"Hello. Is this Ronnie? Ronnie Kale?"

"Yes."

"Ronnie. This is your aunt Grace."

"Aunt Grace. What a surprise to hear from you. It's been a while." She was one of the estranged family members that Shannon had raked over the coals on general principles. My mother had been very close with her.

"Ronnie, I just wanted to say that I am so sorry about your mother. We wanted to send our condolences, some flowers or come together as a family but there were no funeral announcements."

"Funeral announcements? What are you talking about?"

"Oh Ronnie. I just can't believe you two children. What happened in your family that went so terribly wrong with you two children? Ronnie your mother died three weeks ago. Aren't you even aware of it? I just can't believe this. Aren't you even aware that your mother is dead? You're mother is dead Ronnie."

"I'm sorry Grace. This is the first I have heard of it. Thank you for calling me. I don't mean to be rude but I've gotta hang up." I hung up on her.

"Zanna. That was my aunt Grace. One of the many relatives that my sister attacked and alienated with her nasty mouth. She said that my mother died three weeks ago. There was apparently no funeral services and no wake of any kind. No fucking good-bye announcement. Godammit. You would think that my sister could have called me. Imagine not giving your own mother a funeral. Godfuckingdammit. I just kind of hung up on aunt Grace. I didn't know what the hell to say."

"Your sister will call you when she is ready to make the call. That's just the way it is. There is nothing you can do about it."

"Bitchcunt from hell."

"Yeah well so."

"I hate to imagine the rock bottom bargain deal she got for disposal of the body. They probably tossed her off the back of a rowboat into San Francisco Bay into the tule reeds fifty feet from shore. My mom's floating in the mud at the bottom of the San Francisco Bay with a sack of bricks tied around her waist and neck."

"It's possible."

"She's probably got hermit crabs living in her eye sockets and her toes have been nibbled off."

It was mid-January. Eight or ten weeks had passed since aunt Grace had phoned me about my mother's death. I had just published the new issue of P*NK Magazine. It had a diseased skull on the cover that was taken from a medical photo and then drawn over; a white grinning skull on a solid black background, the P*NK logo ran in a process blue banner across the top knocking out in white and yellow. I was now switched into my marketing mode. I was Mr. Personality. The distributor in NYC had admonished me to always do the magazine banner in red. She had no problem with the skull. It looked awesome at the newsstands. Plus, in addition to the free inserted Punk music disc each edition was cut, trimmed and stapled at the printer. Fancy. Now, to my surprise, I received a phone call from Shannon.

"Ronnie this is Shannon."

"Hi Shannon."

"Ronnie. Mother is dead."

"Shannon. This is so terrible! She's dead, mother is really really dead?" I lived in Hollywood where some highbrow acting skills have to rub off on you just through environmental contamination. I had gotten drunk with a pretty girl on Tyrone Power's tomb in the middle of the night at that old cemetery near Santa Monica Boulevard and Van Ness. That kind of behavior will put the thespian spirit in you.

"Yes. After she left the hospital I put her in a nursing home. She just kept getting weaker and weaker and then she died. She had cancer you know. I asked her where it started and she just rubbed her stomach. She told me that having children ruined her life. She said she wished she had never had children. Isn't that terrible?"

"How awful. That'll put a person in therapy. When is the funeral service?"

"Uh, mom didn't have a funeral. I decided against it. All those horrible friends of hers, Aunt Grace and Margy, Fred and Bob would have come and I hate them all. Don't you hate them? I just couldn't stand to see them again one more time."

"Yeah. They're unbearable. She had an enormous number of friends. Well, thanks for calling me." I said avoiding the possible argument.

"I have some stuff for you. You remember that I was made executor of her will."

"Oh yeah. Stuff."

"You're going to receive $2500 in cash and her 1971 Dodge Demon. Plus, I have a few personal items like Dad's ivory ash tray and some Marine corps items of his."

"No thanks on the small items. I'm not able to hang onto anything. My life is too unstable. But the Dodge Demon is a big yes. That's a slant 6. It'll run until the body rots off. I helped mom pick out that car in 1971. We drove it off the lot."

"Come over Saturday at noon. Do you remember where I live?"

"Yeah. Colton in Studio City. What number do I buzz?"

"Twenty one."

"OK. I'll be there."

I picked up the flimflam inheritance at the appointed time and place. We did our business in the parking lot. Shannon never invited me in and she never offered to show me the will. I didn't ask to see it. I gave the car to uncle Leo for free initially, until about a month later when I met Marco, a methamphetamine dealer who had moved to Hollywood from the Bay Area with his half brother Royal. They came to L.A. to make a killing in the rock scene and to party. Soon after I met Marco, I asked Zanna for five hundred dollars for the slant six Demon. She was not pleased, considering that my contribution to the household rent was near to zero. Judging by my personal arithmetic, I had the Pioneer Spirit Building office to maintain; that was my back-up space, then there were the necessary private lifestyle considerations. The cost of living just keeps rising.

Dealing high quality narcotics to musicians and their in-crowd exclusively, meant that the risk of selling to a narcotics agent was nil. The L.A. punk scene had grown massive enough to keep any pair of industrious small dealers in chips with enough green left over to pack a tidy nest egg away for a rainy day. Rock musicians are extremely clan-like and self-protective from outsiders. No narco-cop can play a guitar or perform with the skills and creativity needed to penetrate into the metal or punk rock scene with a new sound. They say that Elvis wanted to become a narc, so he's possibly the one historical exception to the rule. Besides, that's an unusual profession for a rock star addicted to the very same illegal narcotic substances.

With the $2500, I bought a new Nikon 35mm camera with an expensive lens. I

SUB-HOLLYWOOD — BRUCE CAEN

also intended to take care of Danté, who felt that he needed a larger format Hasselblad camera to compete with every other trendy fashion photographer in Hollywood. He rationalized that they were getting all the jobs that he wanted because they used Hasselblads as portrayed in Antonioni's 'Blow-Up'. I planned to buy Danté a Hasselblad body. Between his roommate and himself, they had all the necessary lenses and other paraphernalia.

I got a phone call from Danté. "Hey Ronnie. How's it going. Buck and Lana got a new place closer in to Hollywood. It's kind of in your neighborhood. Do you want to stop by there with me tonight?"

"They moved again? Yeah, I wanna go. I've been missing Bucky."

"Yeah, now they've got an apartment."

"Sure, c'mon over. Pick me up, OK? I'll be home." I didn't hold any grudges about Buck and Lana's skewed politics. Everybody was crazy; it was just a matter of genre, intensity and style. There was no point in avoiding people for being despicable eccentrics in my line of work, since I wasn't promoting their biases. Obviously, the whole notion hit Zanna closer to her heart because of her family's experiences in genocide but Zanna certainly wasted no thoughts on the two of them. My mother's attempts to bury forever her family heritage in the soil of America with the death of my grandmother were for the most part completely successful.

Zanna said, "You're a Jew. You can call yourself anything you like."

"OK. I'm a Zen Buddhist. Tell me I can't be a Zen Buddhist in America."

Danté came over about 8 o'clock. We drove east down Melrose and then north into a zone with cheap apartments mostly occupied by Latinos. He parked the car. We got out, crossed the sidewalk, climbed some stairs, entered a big door and proceeded down a gloomy hallway. Danté located the appropriate door and knocked. Zanna had chosen not to come with us.

Lana opened the door. "Hi guys. Come in."

The place was a studio apartment completely devoid of furniture except for a small cheap wooden table and two wooden chairs picked up at a second hand outlet or throwaways left on the sidewalk. One of the chairs was occupied by Buck who was sitting on it limply wearing a white t-shirt with cut-off sleeves and blue jeans with black engineer boots. This new place was even devoid of their fascist decorations.

"Hey there Buck." said Dante with a wide grin. Danté worked hard on his grin daily. "Always smile." he said to me. "Never let them know that your life if going all to shit. If someone asks you how you are doing, tell them you're great. Everything is great. And flash a big smile at them."

"Hi Buck. What's goin' on." I said. I nodded.

Buck was speechless. He sat with a frozen smile, quietly, glassy-eyed, with his arms dangling loosely at his sides. As a form of greeting, he looked over at us with bleary subdued happiness. He had needle tracks in each arm. What was striking was the number of injection marks that trailed down each arm from just below his shoulder deltoids to the wrists. He had by my rough estimation one hundred marks on one arm alone. The other arm looked like he was busy working his way down and it had telltale small injection bruises and scabs possibly two thirds of the way down to the wrist.

"That's the most tracks I've ever seen on one individual. It must be some kind of Worlds Record for Arms." I said in astonishment. No one heard me speak.

Lana and Danté made some small talk about somebody talking shit to Lana that she couldn't tolerate. She was still a delightfully pretty girl even with the excessive drugs and all. We didn't stay long, maybe fifteen minutes. There was nowhere to sit except opposite to Buck in the second wooden chair. Lana, Danté and I stood awkwardly leaving the second chair open. They didn't offer us a beer or a soft drink. Then Danté and me left.

"It's nice to see that Buck's keeping busy." I said when we were back in the Merc.

"Yeah right! He's sure busy." laughed Danté.

"Where is Buck from originally? Where did he grow up poor white trash?"

"Poor white trash! His parents live in a big mansion in Beverly Hills. That's where he grew up." Danté chuckled. "You should see his parents place. Very pish-posh expensive with grounds, waterfalls, a pool, tennis court. His mother is beautiful. I'd like to fuck her."

"What? He's a rich kid? I don't believe it!"

"It's true. His parents live in Bel-Air Beverly Hills. What's the difference. I've been over to his house and met them. His mom and dad are very nice, very rich parents. They don't know what to do about Buck. He's so damaged."

"I can't believe it. I put him up in my fucking office for a month for free because I thought he was on the streets. That's so typically L.A. You never know what or who you're dealing with. You can't believe your eyes. Some hardass biker. Why didn't you tell me?"

"I don't know. I didn't think it mattered. And you never asked."

Then after I sat in silence for a while..."Danté, I've got a little bit of money left from the inheritance. I thought I might use it to buy you that Hasselblad camera."

"Oh thanks Ronnie. That's really nice of you."

"Do you want to go down to the South Bay and see Social Distortion on Saturday? You'll have to drive because I get completely lost when I leave

Hollywood and downtown."

"Yeah. Let's go. I can drive."

A week later, after the Social Distortion show, I accompanied Danté to Samys Camera store and he picked out his Hasselblad for around nine hundred dollars. The following week, we were driving around Hollywood in my '52 Ford during the afternoon, as we often did and he said something that took me by surprise.

"Ronnie. I want to quit the magazine." he said. I was blindsided.

"OK Danté. So quit." I said. Bing bang boom, it was happy trails.

We drove back to Zanna's apartment and I parked the '52 Ford in front along the curb.

"Bye Danté." I said.

"Bye Ronnie." he said. Then he got out of the car and left. He drove away in his silver Merc, a classic shot of one point Renaissance diminishing perspective, then turned the corner out of sight.

That was the last I saw of Danté. L.A. is a big place and it's easy to never ever see someone. I heard through the grapevine a year down the road that he had gotten hepatitis. His particular brand of hepatitis was unknown to me but it was potent. He was near death for a year. I never called him. I don't know if it was contracted from intravenous drug use or some other way. I never even imagined that Danté was a man who would shoot up narcotics for entertainment and pleasure. It takes a major compulsion for excess to lead a soul to the needle and the dance with death. Then again, the practice seemed to be ubiquitous in Hollywood in those days before HIV. People partied hard. I also heard that Danté had met a fashion retail shopgirl who had a baby by another man. The father abandoned them and Danté moved into a living situation with the mother and child.

CHAPTER 13

*"It was after I got to Boston that I went
into the anechoic chamber at Harvard University.*

*...Anyway, in that silent room I heard two sounds,
one high and one low.*

*Afterwards, I asked the engineer in charge,
'Why if the room was so silent I had heard two sounds?'*

*He said, 'Describe them.'
I did.*

*He said, 'The high one was your nervous system in operation.
The low one was your blood in circulation.' "*

(JOHN CAGE, 1959, reading from INDETERMINACY)

Zanna won a national award for newspaper design. She received a trophy plaque
that was made out of wood and embossed metal and meant to hang on the wall but
nonetheless by summertime, Gabe had her fired. He wrote her a long letter full of
contrition and convoluted reasons but primarily he seemed to object to what he
termed her rock and roll lifestyle. This wasn't an entirely valid reason because I
almost never took her with me to the punk shows. She had her own life which was
more normal than mine. I had learned from experience with previous girlfriends
that if I felt I had something good going on that it was to my benefit not to parade

it around because unscrupulous people would try to steal it. Hollywood is full of starstruck losers who want to take what others have. There is a huge population of untalented hopeless hopefuls desperately trying to get something and to go somewhere in order to be somebody they will never be; and there is another cross-category contingent of just plain low-life scenemakers attracted by the specious glamour and the fey lifestyle. Zanna was sweet and generous almost to the point of naivete. So as I rationalized about my situation, I kept her partially tucked away from my scene. That was one reason and the other was that I just couldn't stop cheating. I just wasn't capable of love even if I loved someone, Zanna included.

Now, after her termination, she was suddenly home every day and with no job she became more observant. She found things about me to criticize which had previously gone unnoticed. All her critical and organizational skills which had been so adeptly applied to newspaper art direction were now in turn focused on homemaking. We started fighting. The delicate balance of our interactions had been altered by dint of her continuous domestic omnipresence and her critical eye for detail. She definitely noticed that I was personally quite unkempt and I was egregiously competent at making a mess in the kitchen, the bathroom, the bedroom and the living room. I entertained strange visitors although she was more at ease with the visitors than my lack of domestic discipline.

One afternoon in late spring Zanna and I had a blowout fight which was so magnificent it was deserving of a name, The Dancing Gypsy Bear and Twirling Monkeys in Tou-tous Fight. It was one of our better fights from a series of fights that occurred during what I term my alcoholic period which continued throughout her unemployment. For this fight, I was wearing a gypsy clothing costume like from a Hollywood movie depiction. Accompanying me, twirling with flamboyant skill and bravado was a full grown dancing black bear with a link chain attached to a brass ring in its nose. Surrounding the bear and myself were six dancing chimpanzees wearing tou-tous twirling on pedestals painted circus style in red and white horizonal stripes. It was a joyous and amusing performance. Even stranger, cold water began splashing on my feet and the bear and the chimps became transparent and then disappeared altogether. I saw that I was holding one of my used wooden crutches into the water of an overflowing bathtub, the faucet on full, and stirring feverishly at a wooden Thonet chair that was floating and whirling in circular rotations caused by the movement of the crutch and water. The monkeys dissipated completely into the splashed dripping wet plastic shower curtain with geometric patterns on it. There I was standing in the flooded bathroom behaving like a madman.

"I've lost my mind." I said aloud. I turned out the water which had flooded the bathroom and was flowing rapidly down the wooden floorboards of the hallway, then I walked into the kitchen. Zanna was standing in the center of that room which was covered floors, walls, countertops and even the ceiling with pungent far eastern spices like marsala and curry powders. She was crying. I recalled at this point that I had been throwing spices only a few minutes before the bathtub flooding. The spices were all in Zanna's hair, covering her face and clothing.

"Zanna, I just had a psychotic interlude in the bathroom. I need help of some kind. I've started to go crazy. When I'm awake, I am living in a dream that isn't reality. I need to stop drinking but I can't stop it. I blacked out into another reality." Then I explained to her about the bears and monkeys.

"It's worse than that." She said. "This has been going on for quite a while. You have been crazy for a long time. You just haven't been aware of it."

"I can't quit the juice. I'm in its grip. It's got a hold on me that I can't break. I need liquor twenty four hours a day. Beer for breakfast, Old Bushmills or Canadian Mist, Cold Duck and then late at night Gin. Can you help me? I'm sorry. I didn't know it had gone this far unzipped on the Circus Train."

"I might know someone who can help. Denise knows a wholistic doctor who helped her gay friend Eddie quit drinking. The doctor uses diet and herbs. He's supposed to be very effective. I'll check into it and get his phone number."

"I'm really sorry. I didn't realize that I had become this much of a complete lunatic."

"Well you have. If you're sorry, you can start by helping me clean up the kitchen and the bathroom right now."

"Yeah ok."

DUAL PRONG MEDICINE: This was the beginning of my new program to rid myself of the terrible scourge of alcoholism in my life. Surprisingly, it was entirely successful within a very short period of time. In order to achieve these rapid results, I employed a two-pronged approach. The first prong of attack was the new age healer recommended by Zanna. The doctor was an Englishman who was a chiropractor and acupressure professional as well as a dietician who based his practice in the alternative organic foods and herbal medicine awareness which had found its inception in American popular culture during the '60s Haight Ashbury era. He called himself a wholistic doctor but he wasn't an actual M.D. He preferred to be called Dr. Bob in casual conversation and his demeanor was that of a medical professional.

Dr. Bob examined me in my underwear for about fifteen minutes. He had me recline in various positions on a black naugahyde covered examination table while he pressed my organs and performed minor chiropractic adjustments.

When he had completed his observations he had me sit up on the table and he addressed me face to face making eye contact. "Don't worry Ronnie. You don't have cancer. Your problems with drinking alcohol, we should be able to completely eliminate within one week. This does require that you make the effort to quit alcohol and to follow the program that I provide. You quite simply are hypo-glycemic and if we treat that condition through your diet and acupressure stimulation you will lose all desire to drink within a few days."

"Are you kidding me? That sounds too good to be true Dr. Bob. What does this treatment involve? What do I have to do?"

"Some people's body's have more difficulty assimilating protein through the digestive processes than other people. I am going to place you on a regimen of high-potency protein powder in which the amino acids are pre-digested. You can add this powder to a milkshake in a blender or mix it with some fruit juice and some of your favorite fresh fruit. Experiment with the blender drinks, mix the fruits and juices that you like for taste and add in the protein powder. In addition, I want you to begin taking packets of high potency multi-vitamins along with the protein shakes. I guarantee you that you will no longer have any desire to drink alcoholic beverages within just a few days. Come in and see me once a week for the acupressure and chiropractic adjustments and we'll monitor what kind of progress you are making."

This successful treatment came at a cost of three thousand dollars and the bills were paid for entirely by Zanna. After about six weeks of seeing Dr. Bob on a weekly basis, he began to move his practice in its entirety up to the northern California city of Sausalito, a much lovelier location than his current neighborhood off La Tijiera Boulevard near to LAX. After a short time he began not showing up for my appointments and his offices were soon to be occupied by an unsatisfactory inferior substitute for Dr. Bob. Then basically, I was given the message that Dr. Bob was gone for good and was never coming back. A drunk tossed in the trash cure all.

I must admit to developing some personal emotional issues in dealing with my abandonment by Dr. Bob, nevertheless through the dietary disciplines which he inculcated into my lifestyle, I was freed of alcoholism completely for the rest of my life (except for rare special occasions, major holidays, weddings, birthdays, and gala toasts).

Unpredictible circumstances such as the preceding example were the basis of my two pronged offensive (a duality of techniques creating twice the positive results) against alcohol. Although the second prong of attack had its foundations in a personal theory of mine about drug addiction and mental and physical health, it could best be summed up in three words — Marco and Royal. My working theory was basically that if you got into trouble with one drug the correct maneuver was to switch to the use of another alternative substance entirely. I recalled that I had spent most of my life intoxicated from alcohol, since I was a pre-teen to some degree and that it was not altogether a bad way to live if managed properly. Accordingly, it was from this philosophical standpoint that I switched almost entirely from alcohol to methamphetamine around the time that Dr. Bob moved to Sausalito. Still, I kept on taking the protein shakes and vitamins and dropped the fake Dr. Bob duplicate. Substitute wholistic pseudo-doctors have their place. Let the reader make that call.

PRONG TWO MEDICAL PHASE: Marco (in concert with his partner big brother Royal) sold speed, not benzedrine or dexedrine or crank. His product was pure crystal methamphetamine. A lovely and exquisite product to behold. White rocks that when cut apart and dropped in a quarter teaspoonful of water disappeared without a trace of impurity. The substance didn't even need to be cooked before it was strained through a little cotton ball and sucked into a disposable insulin syringe. When the heart muscle first pumped the chemical through the lungs a burst of ether tinged air would rush from the exhalations to the back of the throat. From that point on, it was no problem to keep busy for a day or two. It was a long smooth ride on a fast rocket, a refreshing liberation from the alcoholic doldrums.

I was one of the first acquaintances that Marco bonded with when he arrived in Los Angeles. His benefit to tagging around with me initially was that I was a working link with almost every punk band in So Cal. Once they were on the scene, the nightclubs, gigs, after hours parties and clubs, Marco and Royal were impossible to ignore, even in a counterculture setting where nearly everybody was cut, trimmed and attired for maximum eccentricity. Each brother cut a stunning figure in a crowd together or separately. As a matter of strategy possibly, Marco and Royal made an effort it seemed, from my point of view, to be seen in public not as a pair but separately. I believe that Marco informed me one long night that in terms of their genes they had the same mother and two different fathers. They had similar overall appearances, some Eastern European tribe, but there was most noticeably an enormous size difference between the two men. Marco, my closer drug buddy friend of the two, was nearer to my size, possibly an inch or two taller than me making him about six feet tall with a heavier bone structure than mine. He often dressed effeminately but not as if he was gay. He wore black spandex tights and black pointy-toed rocker boots and had closely shorn appropriately tousled brown hair with the color overtone highlights of patinated bronze; Adonis-like and sleazy all in one package. He fucked the most prettiest of girls on the L.A. punk scene, one of the perquisites of drug dealing.

Both Marco and Royal exuded an aura of real freakish danger. I often wondered did anyone else notice that? The punk scene was full of people styled to exude strange danger and street toughness but most were not truly violent toward others except as an image in the mind of society as a whole. Punk rockers were xenoliths in the homogenous social whole and bonded together as a group by their music. However, I felt that either of these brothers may kill you without remorse if you crossed them; but of the two, Royal was more apparently a walking living terror. Royal dealt heroin in addition to speed but Marco kept away from the junk as far as I knew. And then again, I really didn't know much. For example, consider surnames. I never learned their family name or names even though I was routinely stopping by their crib in the Fairfax District three and four days a week for a couple of years. They were very good at control. They worked out of a duplex a couple of blocks from Canters Delicatessan in the Fairfax District, a mostly Jewish neighborhood nearby in actual fact to uncle Leo. Jews, at least this group of L.A. Jews in the Fairfax area, kept to themselves and tolerated diversity without question. It occurs to me today that Marco and Royal probably occupied the entire building, although my experience was cautiously limited by them to a few rooms in the bottom apartment. In my years of foot traffic to their place I never once rubbed shoulders with a neighbor utilizing the shared entranceway.

Royal was a tall heavy framed imposing man but he wasn't heavy from bodyfat; he was just one exceptionally large muscular man. His hands were so large that I estimated that it would take five or six of my hands combined to equal the mass of one of his knuckle busters. His big boned fists inflicted serious damage when those giant knuckles collided with an unlucky face. I saw the results of that action on a couple of broken up guys who crossed him. His mouth had long thin dark purple lips sculpted with a cruel twist like something imagined by Mary Shelley. Except for their size difference, he resembled Marco in the facial features. Although Royal was a couple of years older than Marco, his wrinkles and facial characteristics appeared to have been etched by jail time. Jail time can spell itself out indelibly in a man's face.

I recall now that I even got high with Royal a few times but we never struck up a druggie friendship. He was difficult to talk to and he didn't appear to like me much. Royal had a Bird of Paradise tattooed on his right arm. It was a pretty piece of ink that ran the entire length of his enormous limb, from the shoulder to the wrist. He would shoot up in that arm, piercing the needle through the exotically colored plumage and it never left a visible track. Royal was capable and willing to carry out any enforcement duties for the business should they be necessary for whatever reason.

One time I went down to East L.A. with a couple of friends, Mickey Mike and Tina Tupelo, and Royal. Royal maintained a stuccoed small house behind another white painted small house which was occupied by Mexican gang members. They can be unneighborly when collected together as a group as they were on this particular afternoon sitting on their back porch when we passed by them in a line on foot with me taking up the rear. Marco up front ignored them with indifference, Tina smiled and said hi, she was pretty, Mickey Mike looked straight ahead in the direction of Tina's ass, then I took up the rear and risked a quick glance at them. They were maybe eight in number. They were all eight frowning in unison. One in the middle toward the front looked down at me from the porch and into my eyes.

He said, "Get out of here or I'll kill you." I immediately picked up speed in my step and followed my friends into Royal's retreat.

Royal had methamphetamine and one syringe. We paid him for the drug and split it up. We sat around a low coffee table while Royal gathered together a cotton ball, a spoon and a glass of tap water and proceeded to immediately inject the drug into the plumage of the bird. He passed the needle to Tina and she cleaned it by filling it with tap water and squirting it on the floor; then she pulled out the plastic plunger and rolled the little black rubber tip inside her ear to pick up some earwax and then she rolled it along the outside of her nostrils.

"I've gotta get this sucker lubricated with my earwax and nose grease," she laughed, "so it'll work smooth." Then she injected herself. Then Mickey Mike followed suit. Tina and Mickey Mike just continually rocked and rolled all day and night. No gang guys would want to shoot them for crossing their turf. Mickey Mike could make a rhinoceros chuckle. He kept the mood elevated. He told Tina a joke about a leprechaun who went into a bar with a large hemorrhoid so he couldn't sit down. And the two of them kept us all laughing with their easy lowbrow back and forth banter.

When it came to my turn I said, "I'll just snort a couple of lines. Save your needle." Royal took it back and I cut up a couple of lines with a blade and sniffed it. Royal was not a loquacious or jolly big man. He was a man of few words, generally softspoken, and most of his conversation this day was procedural but he had a pent up fire inside that gave him a kicker of a presence. This was by no means a big awkward shy man who was harboring anger at the world. He was able to come off as uncannily complex and on the few occasions whenever I happened to stumble onto the subject of fine arts or mention literary references in conversation, he talked with well-informed repartee. It's like the Bo Diddley song says, you can't judge a book by looking at the cover. I never figured him out except that he was a killer-diller with a cobra snake for a necktie, that is describing him with more Bo Diddleyisms. We left the back house about thirty minutes after we arrived; the eight Mexican gang members were still sitting back there. We walked past them a second time. Royal again walked past them indifferently without acknowledging them. They didn't shoot me. They were completely silent but gravely focused.

Mostly we (Zanna, myself and friends) snorted the meth we purchased but on more special occasions we injected it. Zanna hated the injections and she only did it once or maybe twice. Then she forbade it in her flat but we just did it anyway. For the most part my casual friends of the period and myself didn't share needles or turn ourselves into pincushions like Buck was inclined to do. Also, it was about this time in the early '80s with the rise of Ronald Reagan, that the articles first began to appear in the national news magazines and television broadcasts about a new disease which was initially termed by the popular media as The Gay Flu.

I shot up crystal meth with Marco one saturday evening about 8 o'clock in his apartment kitchen around the period of the start of the Reagan presidency which marked the peak period of my publishing popularity with P*NK Magazine. New readers were finding the satirical articles and drawings humorous. The established print media in Los Angeles and New York City were giving us accolades and writing small accounts of their enjoyment of P*NK Magazine's idiosyncrasies. A famous Brit rock band posed with a member reading the magazine on a record jacket. People were impressed by that. Logically, from Marco's point of view I was a good guy to know inasmuch as I was socially fluid, counterculture oriented and yet making a small living at it, which in those days was the exception to the rule.

That same evening, when I ran into Marco around midnight at an after hours art opening at Club Seven, he said "Do you want do go out to Darwin with me tonight?"

"Darwin? What's Darwin? Sounds like evolution. Are you an agent of a mutant species that is is seeking contact with the human race? Why would you contact punk rockers? We can't help you. We got bad haircuts. You probably ought to go directly to the military. They know how to handle aliens and mutants."

"Darwin is an abandoned mining town near Death Valley. Royal and me bought an old station house that used to be part of the mine; it's on several acres of the hottest desert land you'll ever see."

"It's located on several acres of hot desert? What happens beyond the several acres."

"More endless desert. Bureau of Land Management property and National Park Lands. The house is a really kool old hot train station and residence that was attached to a railroad spur until the mine shut down. I just want to go out there to check out the property and watch the sun come up. You'll really dig it. Then we'll come right back in the morning."

"You say it's kool and it's hot? Yeah I want to go. You probably want me to drive. You don't even own a car right now do you?"

"No, I'm taking cabs to get around. You drive and I'll pay for gas and the other items we'll be needing." I thought that possibly Marco never drove a car in order to run under the radar, keep his name out of government information systems.

"This location is really out in the boondocks. Is that correct?"

"Very obscure. Will your old car make it? A breakdown could be serious out in the desert."

"Yeah. It should do just fine. We'll be travelling at night when it's cool outside so it shouldn't overheat. It's nearly all new and completely rebuilt under the hood. It's like a new old car. The upholstery still needs some work."

We took our time to say our goodbyes around Club Seven and then we rode my '52 Ford to the 24 hour market at Vine and Melrose. We bought a couple of gallons of water, Hawaiian potato chips, barbeque potato chips, chocolate bars, Coca-Colas, chocolate chip cookies and pre-popped popcorn in a bag; then we stopped for gas at Melrose and La Brea and then we drove over to Fairfax Avenue. Marco ran into his apartment to change into some jeans and athletic shoes and bring the extra stuff he mentioned, none of which was visible when he came out except for the shoes and jeans; except he also carried a couple of jackets with a small soft briefcase style bag tucked inside one of the jackets hidden inside pockets.

On the ride out, we talked about what seemed like every possible worldly topic, and it was a long ride indeed from Los Angeles into a strange mystical landscape of severe geological contrasts, more than 3 hours running. Darwin is probably one of the most obscure small towns in the United States. Darwin lies in the lee of the eastern Sierra Nevadas highest peaks, the Mt. Whitney and Olancha pinnacles, sheer granite rock rising to nearly three miles above sea level. Buried in an extreme desert landscape, Darwin then had a population of no more than 100 souls, no police department and a post office the size of a men's toilet in a roadside gas station. After riding parallel to the eastern backside of the Sierras along Highway 395, we entered the town of Lone Pine, then we doubled back slightly as we veered eastward toward Death Valley riding swiftly on a seemingly endless two lane road. These locations, in which the raw strength of the landscape itself contributed to the content of the scene like a great dramatic actor, were utilized in many Hollywood films, both westerns and film noir masterpieces like High Sierra starring Humphrey Bogart and Ida Lupino.

Our drive was illuminated by a gibbous moon hung in the sprawling milky way. Country music gave way to jumbled static on the AM radio as we drove north. Speeding beneath the craggy spines of the Sierra Nevada range we talked about the punky girls in the San Francisco scene versus the L.A. punkettes of Hollywood and the beach towns, every punk rock band in the world, punk rock singers and guitar players, music magazines, New York City, No Wave, James Chance, Debbie Harry, SST Records, Mink de Ville, Johnny Cash, Survival Research Laboratories, space aliens and UFO abductions, the nature of money, beat writers, LSD, The Gun Club, the 1960s vs. 1970s, Throbbing Gristle, Jimmy Carter and Ronald Reagan, music television, reincarnation, Raymond Pettibon, Gary Panter, Darby Crash, Oki Dogs vs. Pinks Chile Dogs, the ancient Egyptians, Bobby Beausoleil, Charlie Manson and his apprehension by police at the nearby Barker Ranch, and soon we found ourselves singing together a patchwork version of 'Cease to Exist', the Charlie Manson song that made its way onto a Beach Boys album. This night was the nearest I came to having a close friendship with Marco. He seemed to emanate a kind of power and radiance or charismatic quality at times. At other times, I thought his unique energy and force was just the magical hold of his narcotic chemicals on my senses.

Somewhere in the middle of the desert almost midway between Lone Pine and Death Valley, a narrow modestly neglected two lane slip road almost invisibly veered from the main highway like an hallucination of sand and stars and faintly glowing horizons steeped in the pure and absolute silence. It was so quiet outside the Ford when we stopped the car for a leg stretch, a smoke, and a pee on the sand, we thought we could hear the blood pumping through our veins and the electricity flowing in the synapses of our brains racing from amphetamines.

'Submission is a gift, go on give it to your brother.'

The outside air was chilly but we weren't penetrated by the cold. Scarcely perceptible, traces of dawn were beginning to appear to the east. Several Joshua trees in deep shadow seemed to haunt the landscape with twisted anthropomorphic forms. We piled back into car and crept forward at a leisurely pace down the ribbon of road toward the southwest horizon. Soon we found ourselves creeping through the sleeping desert micro-town aware of the sound of gravel under the tires.

"This looks like the little shit town with the dilapidated gas station from Wes Craven's 'The Hills Have Eyes'. Are we driving into hell? I don't even see one single gas station here."

"No. No. No." Marco spoke. "This is a quiet little isolated town full of regular people who just want to be left alone and live beyond the hassles of society and the population explosion."

We were driving past inhabited tar paper shanty shacks and abandoned one room house frames with entire walls blown away by the fierce high desert winds and consumed by the oppressive sunshine, several dilapidated RV trailers up on blocks with their tires missing with crooked porches, small desert houses patched with plywood and variegated siding, an occasional nicely kept domicile; up on the hill to the east were approximately twenty derelict and abandoned buildings fenced behind cyclone fencing and barbed wire. This was the remnants of the mining company no longer in business.

"My station house is up the road that goes behind the hills. It's on the other side of this hill that overlooks the town."

There was only one crossroad in town without a stop sign on what had now become a washboard and potholed dirt and gravel road, leaving the paved ribbon behind where the town amorphously had started. This was the intersection of Main Street and Broadway, downtown Darwin.

"I have to go slowly. I don't want to break an axle out here." I said.

"It's not a good road but you can make it." Marco said.

We proceeded over the crest of the hill and Marco directed me to the left up another dirt road. I drove about a mile through the desert until a structure appeared nestled against the hillside in shadows. The 1950s automobile suspension was groaning and squeaking.

"We better walk the rest of the way. I'm going to park it here."

"Let's boogie."

We gathered the clothes, potato chips, bottled water and whatever else we could carry and walked the 100 yards or so up to the old house. It was a faded dusty beige wooden structure built in the early-1920s. We climbed five wooden steps which led onto the front porch. Marco began groping around on a wooden beam which required him to stand on his toes and stretch to his full length. His ballet moves yielded a single key which he used to open the front door. We dragged our stuff inside and dropped it on the floor. Marco produced a miniature pocket flashlight and he began shuffling around randomly from room to room.

"How about I light a fire in the old stove. It's actually pretty damn cold in here. Are you cold?" he suggested.

"I like a good warm fire. That's a beautiful old stove."

The old potbelly stove was made of cast iron with decorative flourishes patinated with black and brown rusted surfaces created by time and usage. The surface proudly read 'FATSO' on an air vent, then 'King Stove Co. Sheffield ALA.

"I've got some old newspapers in the car. I'll go get 'em."

When I returned Marco had a pile of kindling sticks and small logs stacked by the stove. He had lit a short white candle mounted on a discarded tuna fish can. I started wandering about the place from room to room in the dim predawn half light. The back rooms were devoid of furniture.

"There's a secret door in the large room back there. See if you can find it." He said. I looked all around for a hidden door but I couldn't find it. Marco appeared in the doorway holding the candle, laughing, his wavy hair jiggling.

"Here look at this." He said. He walked over to a wooden panel in the middle of a north facing wall and pushed it slowly. It opened inward to a small wood paneled bedroom with a single wood framed bed, covered with a Navajo blanket and a sheepskin, topped with three or four multi-colored pillows. There was a chest of drawers and a floor lamp and a small hardwood table with two chairs; an entire matching set of antique Stickley Craftsman furniture. A single window with Venetian blinds half-opened revealed the rapidly arriving dawn.

"Nice huh? I picked it all up at an estate sale in Pasadena. There's another hidden hidden entrance out there. I'll show it to you."

"Does this place have electric power?"

"It does. It's turned off at the main fuse box outside which has a padlock on it."

He walked over to the door leading into the big empty room and retrieved a kind of broomstick with a hook on the end, walked across the room and hooked a ring in the ceiling and pulled downward. A wooden ladder staircase dropped down from the ceiling. He climbed the ladder and I followed. Upstairs, he was standing in the middle of the space smiling.

"Isn't this great! There's a bathroom up here through that door. It's going to take a little work to get it up and running but the septic tank is fully functional and the water tank and pipes are all in working order. There's a water truck that comes out from Lone Pine once a month and the guy fills all the water tanks in town for ten bucks a pop."

"You don't have a bathroom that works?" I felt my mother talking through me.

"Oh yeah. The downstairs bog works. There's an outhouse out back which is fun. You can open the door and enjoy the desert landscape while you crap but watch out for black widows crawling on your nads. They crawl in there, spin webs, and then they kill their men."

He glided back down the steps and I followed. We went back to the front room with the stove now burning hot and pulled up chairs, two old chairs with well worn cushions.

"These old chairs came with the place. Aren't they great. So comfortable."

I started in on a oversized bag of popcorn and a bottle of Coca Cola.

We sat quietly and stared hypnotically at the flames through the partially open door of the cast iron stove. The crackling sounds and the redolent fragrance of the burning wood completely absorbed us for a time.

"We have to go into town at eight o'clock. I want to meet with Derek. That's his hour to be around the house."

"Who's Derek?"

The sun was now gaining in dominion rapidly over the darkness. The grey dawn transformed into raw intense daylight rapidly in the high desert.

"Derek is a mentally retarded man who lives in an old trailer over the hill in beautiful downtown Darwin. Royal found him hunting jackrabbits around the house here with an air rifle. He was so poor that he was eating them and any other rodents he killed. Royal offered to hire him on as a security man to keep an eye on the house here. So we've arranged to pay him seventy five dollars a month to watch the place."

"Is he going to live in here?"

"No. No. He lives in the trailer with his wife. He's a kind of packrat. The yard around the trailer is fenced in with rusty wire fencing and it's full of a hideous assortment of worthless junk that's broken and destroyed by the blowing sand, junk cars, washing machines, old boats, engines and electric motors, toys and parts, parts to who knows what. His wife is retarded too. She has Downs Syndrome. Anyway, they can't live in here 'cause we have plans to use this place for our own business and pleasure. They have a nice large trailer but its old. Derek's dependable and smart enough to handle the security job. Royal is having a telephone installed at Derek's place so he can call us. He takes his duties very seriously. He's a really big guy, almost as big as Royal but you realize he's retarded immediately when you talk to him. He's good at doing some things like chores and not good at other stuff. He has a driver's license and drives his own pickup truck and rides a bicycle too but he can't tell the difference between a twenty dollar bill and a ten dollar bill and a one dollar bill. Derek told Royal that when he used to get his welfare check they would give the money to him in all different denominations and then guys at the market would short change him when he made purchases as soon as they realized his deficiency. So Derek asked us to pay him in one dollar bills because he can count out the ones correctly. I brought along six months advance pay for him in one dollar bills in my bag. That's big money in Darwin."

"How'd he ever get a driver's license? I mean if he can't even count."

"Anybody can get a driver's license."

Marco picked up his black soft briefcase and opened it on the small wooden table between our chairs. He pulled out a wad of one dollar bills from a side compartment and thumbed through them and laughed.

"Payday!" Next, he pulled out two disposable syringes and a small plastic bag with a white rock nestled in the corner. "Should we mix some rocket fuel now for the trip back? Are you feeling a little bit tired?"

"You know I'm not going to turn down that offer. You don't want me to get drowsy and drive us into a sand dune. So do you really think that you need security in this out-of-the-way place?" I said.

"Oh yeah. We always need security. We'll install some electronic alarm stuff, video and a two thousand pound vintage safe once we settle in and get ourselves set up. That's Royal's job. There's a company that sells used and antique combination safes in downtown Los Angeles. They're impregnable."

His eyes froze. He didn't want to talk about security any more and he changed the subject succinctly. I was left to imagine what the nature of their plans were in this desiccated landscape. Everyone always talks about the desert being a haven for speed dealers and improv labs. I made my assumptions along that line of thought. If I asked him about that directly he would have gotten pissed off at me and the ride back to L.A. would have gone to hell. Marco was living a criminal lifestyle with his half-brother. It was so easy to overlook that consideration in punk rock L.A. where so few people seemed to hold a real job. Marco's life was defined by a materially different set of social terms of conduct than mine. Then again, if I thought about it, nearly everybody lived under a variety of materially different circumstances than myself, musicians, lawyers, waitresses. There was no point in spoiling the fun.

An hour later, when we went to the front door to leave, there was a snake in the doorway that wouldn't move. It was curled back on itself. It appeared to be about six feet long. I threw some water on it and it bolted off across the porch and disappeared into the landscape, streaking to the top of a scrimpy salt cedar tree.

"Shit! That scared the hell out of me. I've never seen a snake move so fast!" I shouted. My heart was pounding.

"Racer snake." said Marco dryly. "They usually run."

CHAPTER 13.5 UPGRADE–KITTEN'S HARD DRIVE: I took the initiative to change banks. In an irrational surge of pure moxie, I moved the business account to the posh Beverly Hills Bank and changed the company image on the official P*NK Magazine checkbook to a black ink skull. In order to drive my '52 Ford into Beverly Hills routinely with impunity, taking into account the needle marks in my arms from crystal meth usage, I needed to come up with a whopper of a justification to bolster my self-confidence and more importantly to protect me from a curious police patrol cruiser accustomed to upscale automobiles. My '52 Ford was as mechanically sound as a new car I reckoned, but cosmetically it wasn't quite a show car. It had a characteristic white trash appearance to its exterior, a magnet to police black and whites in a wealthy neighborhood. As a counter to these negative psychic and mental emanations, I rationalized irrationally. An extraordinary Being had been placed on Earth on a special mission which was ordained by Holy God and this mission would consequently be protected from police interference. That special Being was me.

My bi-weekly trips from Oxford Street in Hollywood into the venerable vulnerable swanky sparkling heart of Beverly Hills to do my banking were a challenge and a test of my faith in the power of God to protect me from harm so long as I continued to publish P*NK Magazine. Consequently, somedays I negotiated my way through the lunchtime Beverly Hills and Hollywood traffic after having stayed awake, strung out, a long way out, for two or three weeks with no zees cut, sleepless on speed. The longest length of time I stayed awake was for the duration of a month. Busy as a bumble bee, I functioned efficiently for nearly three weeks, but after the third week I was unable to drive or do much of anything except talk on the phone, sit around after-hours nightclubs, and think occasional great thoughts befitting an enlightened mind.

When my starter motor broke, I made a phone call up to my new temporary female starter motor and driving buddy, lovely Kitten with pink pubic hair. A man couldn't ask for a better starter motor. She would say, "I can be down there in a half an hour Ronnie." Then she would jump on her moped and drive down the hill to Zannas from her cramped two room courtyard apartment. Kitten was now nested on an unattractive hillside in south Silverlake up near the east end of Melrose Avenue where the street seemed to melt into the low rent neighborhoods below Sunset Blvd.

Kitten had been dating Andrew Wolfram when Zanna was art director at GO L.A., and he had arranged for Kitten to go to work for Zanna in the art department doing paste-up. It was Kitten's first real job that was not preceded by 'blow'. But now Zanna had moved on and I was alone in the fourplex during the work week.

Zanna was now working at Worldwide Films in Hollywood. Zanna's spanking new job was as Art Director of Advertising for the heavyweight film company. Curiously, she chose to surrounded herself in her personal life with people like Kitten and myself. Kitten, petite as she was, was able to push start my old Ford with the strength of a 200 lb man.

"I'll help you push Kitten." I said and I jumped out of the drivers seat and leaned my shoulder into the door jamb. You had to love her.

"Just get in." Kitten shouted. "I can push it." She pushed the car and her firm nipples pushed earnestly against her tight cut up Black Flag t-shirt.

So I jumped back into the drivers seat and popped the clutch, the engine rumbled and we'd ride off to the Beverly Hills Bank protected by God from the roaming police cruisers. Banking in Beverly Hills with Kitten was a delightful good time. She was so beautiful and damaged, a one hundred percent pure and perfect rock and roll girl. Like my car and me, a.k.a. Liverhead or Ronnie Ripper, Kitten was completely out of place in Beverly Hills.

I always kept my mission from God a secret from everyone including Kitten because I knew that even she would laugh at me out loud. The notion specifically, that I was given protection from certain perils on earth by God; and my insight that as a publisher I was aided by God so that I could continue to create an aberrant punk rock magazine; these considerations I felt would draw earthly human ridicule down upon my head, even from my own kind. Without protection though, I would have been unable to continue to publish and my proof of this protection was made evident by my unimpeded bi–weekly runs to the Beverly Hills Bank. My car became invisible to police. Of course, I only used my protection for official magazine business.

When she first arrived in L.A. from Sacramento, Kitten was captured and kidnapped by three men (two black and one white) and imprisoned in an abandoned house in Compton or Watts, an area sometimes called by the misnomer Wompton. They raped her for three days until she escaped. She in turn had them captured by the police, and then prosecuted and imprisoned.

With these facts in mind, it might seem an incongruous statement to note that Kitten had earned a reputation as a blow job princess around the Hollywood nightclubs. These blow jobs were given of her own free will. Men and boys, including me, really liked Kitten and she liked them in return. After a blow job some girls spit the semen back out onto the floor and make ugly faces. Some girls won't let a man hold their head and give them the heave-ho pump-and-thrust but Kitten wasn't like that, she wanted to take it all, every hard inch and slimy gob droplet. Kitten always gave her man of the moment a great ride. Sacramento suffered a terrible loss when Kitten ran away from home to go live in Hollywood.

... 𝄢 ...

Zanna was now working at the tippy-top penthouse of a high rise located on Sunset Boulevard in Hollywood. She had literally risen up to a more prestigious job than her GO L.A. position but she worked longer hours, often seven days a week producing an abundant variety of ad campaigns for new movies and even for movies which hadn't yet been put on film. Worldwide Films was a new and aggressive entrepreneurial film company owned by two obese Israeli businessmen. It was rumored that they had made their initial fortunes running guns to South Africa. True or not, it made for interesting gossip. Their strategy in Hollywood, as Zanna perceived it from her catbird's seat, was to lure major American movie stars into low budget B-movies in order to increase box office draw. This tactic seemed to be working quite well. Their ever growing list of movie stars was impressive.

Zanna ran an even larger art department than the one at the newspaper. She had a staff of at least twenty five designers, generic art helpers and various cocaine addicted assistants. I suspected that at least two or three members of her staff maintained their job status by fucking Zanna. Uncle Leo, when he wasn't calling his niece compulsively on the phone, repetitiously like precision clockwork, every fifteen minutes and tying up the switchboard, could be seen daily driving in circles around the highrise building in my deceased mother's old red Mopar bomb. Zanna's staff was alerted to report any encounters around Hollywood with a red 1971 Dodge Demon driven by a disgruntled senior citizen. In this way Zanna was kept apprised of his movements on the streets. As a point of detail, uncle Leo displayed a full head of genuine white hair on the rare occasions that he was without his L.A. Lakers cap.

Uncle Leo learned to improvise a variety of techniques for drawing attention to himself. Apart from the obsessions of Lakers basketball and monitoring his blood pressure, he had a singular loving compulsion to infringe upon Zanna's work day, especially under the fiercest deadlines, like Cannes. One busy afternoon he was arrested at the Bargain Clown, a local discount supermarket with a giant colorful fiberglass sculpture of a happy clown situated on the roof, a popular emporium among septuagenarians and other neighborhood thrift shoppers on restricted budgets. He was caught leaving the premises with a brick of cheddar cheese tucked in his coat pocket. The management called both the police and Zanna. She rushed segmentheaderSUB-HOLLYWOOD —— BRUCE CAEN

down there from Worldwide Films headquarters in order to prevent uncle Leo from being promptly jailed. She found the fuddled uncle weeping and under house arrest in the rear upstairs Bargain Clown business offices. The salty old dog was set free after an hour of cajoling those in authority, and all differing points of view were laid on the table, with a punishment much worse than a mere slap on the knuckles. Uncle Leo was forced to suffer under the yoke of an official lifetime banishment from the Bargain Clown. Uncle Leo's polaroid photo was placed permanently in the BC persona non gratis mug shot archive. The Bargain Clown knew how to deal with his type. He continued to assert repeatedly with tear moistened cheeks that he had simply forgotten that he placed the cheese into his coat pocket as he departed the store in tow behind Zanna.

Soon after that incident, my mother's former car was spotted rolled over on its roof in the middle of Crescent Heights Boulevard by one of Zanna's employees as she was driving into the Worldwide Films offices at eight thirty on a Monday morning. There were police and paramedics on the scene but uncle Leo had apparently already been transported to a hospital. Zanna spent that day calling the police and hospitals trying to locate uncle Leo, crying with anguished red puffy eyes while proofing artwork, imagining that the worst fate had befallen him. By afternoon, she located him at Cedars-Sinai Hospital. He had been admitted with a broken rib and a case of walking pneumonia. The other parties from another vehicle involved in the accident had received much graver injuries.

And so events rolled methodically along with Leo. He had a half dozen automobile accidents in a short two year period. Although he rarely actually stopped into the Fairfax District Senior Citizen Center to socialize because he found the behavior of the elderly people too stilted, and the old ladies were no longer seductive enough for his tastes, he managed to run his car into two senior citizens crossing the street in front of Fairfax District Senior Citizen Center. The geriatric pair were hospitalized for an extended stay. He took the driver's door off a car parked in front of the newsstand located across Fairfax Avenue from Canter's Delicatessen, a drive-by sideswipe which occurred not more than two blocks from Marco's duplex. He had developed an almost J.G. Ballard style of symbiotic relationship with his car, his body and the external world. Now, Leo and I both had incurred Ballard style crashes.

The DMV frequently forced him to pass a new driving test including a written exam and a vision test. He needed to rent a vehicle to test in because his own vehicle, my mother's former red Dodge Demon, was scarred and battered from his various collisions. He would become extremely nervous before these exams and then pass the tests swimmingly. Soon after the roll-over accident, he took a solo

252

header down the staircase in his apartment. This occurred on the eve of a romantic trip Zanna and I were planning to take to Palm Springs. The next time we scheduled a short trip we simply arranged to bring him with us, not quite so romantic. When we three travelled, he would fractiously speak solely in Polish for extended periods of time (fractious was Word of the Day on November 26, 2000). This made for clumsy three-way conversations with Zanna caught in the middle especially in restaurants. He often stayed in character by communicating with the waitresses and any other typical Americans within earshot in fluent Polish. At this point, I found him to be as entertaining as he was irritating. He threw his corn-on-the-cob high into the air out of the booth in a family diner in Desert Hot Springs.

"No good!" he grunted in English through his dentures. "Terrible!" He seemed to be warming up to me a little.

In the void left by Danté's unanticipated departure, I picked up three new photographers; to be precise, there was an additional fourth photographer named Ian who enters into this story line but he proved to be extremely irritating, so therefore I tend to blot him from my memory. Included in this group was Danté's perceived creative nemesis from the Art Center College, the renowned and esteemed new wave lenshead Conrad Miller. Danté had been green with envy over the professional career that Conrad Miller had built for himself with an apparent ease and grace. In actuality, I had never known who the heck this Conrad Miller fellow was that Danté obsessed over repeatedly. After the split with my senior executive and photo talent Danté, I ran into Conrad Miller almost in the obtuse way that a distracted person might walk into a telephone pole. Our meeting was completely unpremeditated. By that I mean we didn't seek out one another.

Firstly, Conrad was a friend of Zannas so he was to be found in our kitchen or front living room drinking liquor socially. Zanna's was a watering hole that he frequented when he sought a bit of conversation and gossip with his cocktail. Secondly, he was also to be found on Oxford Street almost daily during afternoons about three quarters of a block up from Zanna's, working on his cherry Austin Mini Cooper. I couldn't miss him because he was standing on the shining path which led to the 7-11 Market, a road which I travelled as a pedestrian a couple of times daily in my quest for candy bars, soda pop and one dollar cheeseburgers.

We got to talking. He wanted to work on some new magazine projects with me. In particular he was interested in photographing some of the artists involved in the Industrial Movement in San Francisco. We planned a field trip. Conrad was sophisticated, comical, handsome and prematurely balding. He had a sense of humor which frequently caused him to smile and laugh at common topics presented from an offbeat point of view. He typically wore only gray and black clothing but he liked to dress in slacks, designer shirts and dress shoes rather than punk rock denim and leather.

In the early '80s, for those who enjoyed the austere and harsh thrills, San Francisco had an exciting and vital Industrial creative movement, influenced by England's 'Throbbing Gristle' and the German group 'Einsturzende Neubauten'. In SF, this obsession included local rock bands and unique fabricators of bizarre and dangerous remote-controlled kinetic machines constructed frequently with the addition of explosive devices which were deployed in public performances which replicated mechanized warfare. Undoubtedly, these machine performances were totally illegal if only for the firing of numerous potentially lethal explosive rocket devices through remote technologies. These mad machine creators performed for large audiences worldwide yet remained underground and secretive. Much of their technology was stolen the old fashioned way and other high-end gadgets were illegally fleeced and donated by employees in the war industries. Included in this movement were musical bands such as Factrix, Minimal Man, and Tuxedo Moon.

The crew of ultra-violent machine fabricators worked under the umbrella name Survival Research Laboratories. Conrad and myself arranged to stay in San Francisco with an afficionado of this movement, a guy named Fritz who lived in a junkyard located in the Mission District. Fritz was blond, Germanic looking and missing one eye, lost to a piece of flying metal. This made for an instant bond between Fritz and Conrad. Conrad was missing two fingers on his right hand, lost in a teenaged pipe bomb mishap. We stayed in his junkyard and Fritz spent a week showing us around and aiding us to initiate projects involving written document-ation and photography.

A second photographer I began to work with was a San Francisco expatriate, now living in L.A., who made his reputation during the Summer of Love and the rush of creativity that exploded from that scene in the late '60s. He had produced some of the truly famous rock photos of that era. Sporting long bushy hippie style hair now turned white, he was delighted to begin working with punk rock musicians. Herbert Wallach, in his full post-grey maturity was taking on the look of an out-of-work Santa Claus wearing tasteless tourist street clothes, baggy multi-pocketed beige short cargo pants, brightly colored Hawaiian shirts, brown leather sandals worn over white athletic socks pulled up to mid-calf on spindly sun-deprived legs, and enormous black-framed rectilinear eyeglasses that distorted his upper facial features. Beyond the full beard, his full head of white hair was tied in no less that four wildly frizzy thickly matted pony tails resembling an unshorn white Chilean Alpacan llama.

We mostly had a blast. Artistically, Herbert was a photographic master with light and scale. He was interested initially in taking the punk group Social Distortion out to the Mojave desert for photos. Herbert and myself zig-zagged the Mojave exploring locations ranging from remote junkyards with giant airplane carcasses, through the towns of Boron and Randsburg, then out into to Edwards Air Force Base and on down southward into the Mitchell Caverns. Herbert and I ingested either LSD or methamphetamine for entertainment and travel and occasionally we sampled some food. The military was extremely hospitable to us even when we were accompanied by the most hardcore of punk groups. We saw the X-1 in which Chuck Yeager flew to first break the sound barrier and we viewed up close the NASA space shuttle parked in a giant aviation hangar. An Air Force pilot, a handsome young officer he was, offered to let a few of the punk girls use the toilet in his private quarters. They stole his tooth brush and tooth paste.

A third photographer, Ray Trend, who was an extremely tall man towering over audiences at live shows, expressed an interest in contributing to P*NK Magazine. He was a self-promoting machine in a human form. Ray carried his portfolio book of photos of hardcore punkers and death ritual obsessed rockers everywhere he went and he always showed it to me once or twice every time we got together; then he also showed the portfolio to all others who expressed even the remotest minutest atomic particle of interest anywhere he happened to be at the time. A passing glance was sufficient to draw out his black photo books followed by a deep bass intoned grave chuckle. He was extremely prolific. Possibly due to his towering height Ray was able to get interesting angles on live hardcore perfomances. Ray-T was somewhat death obsessed himself and this complemented the ritualistic dark obsessions of his young subjects both male and female. Ray-T made Metal Punk necrophiliac rituals and the obsessed living-dead Gothic Rock genre his meat and potatoes and surprisingly enough, he was perpetually sober as a tombstone. I was always a little mystified by his sobriety but I always suspected his veins were flowing with liquid nitrogen, running super cool as a frigid corpse dressed in black. Ray purchased a 1960s vintage hearse in order to arrive at punk shows in funereal style. He drove it always with a black coffin in the rear. Tod Browning's 'Dracula'. Munsters. Addams Family. Death Ray Trend. Death has never been boring. Even dung beatles avoid its pall.

DEATHROCK SUPERMARKET: I took a dropdead beautiful Deathrock girl who was a singer in a new Deathrock band to a giant Ralphs Supermarket. We systematically walked around the aisles of products and I asked her questions apropos to our environment.

"Do you like Ralphs Supermarket?" I queried.

"Um. I usually leave the shopping to my family because I hate supermarkets. I mean, they're ok. I figure they're more interesting in Hollywood though because you get a wide selection of weird people."

"Do you like salads." I asked as we passed the vegetables.

"I love salads! Radishes, lettuce, celery, cucumbers, tomatoes."

"Do you like red potatoes, white potatoes or the brown ones?"

"I usually eat these kind. Russet. Oh, I like them fried and mashed, anyway."

"Do you like eggplants?"

"I've never had them." She confessed.

"Cauliflower?"

"Yeah. I like cauliflower. Let's go to the cold part. I like the cold section."

"Do you like Tater Tots and frozen stuff like that?" I asked.

"I guess." She replied.

"Aunt Jemima Frozen French Toast?"

"I don't eat french toast too often."

"What do you usually eat?"

"Chinese food."

"Do you eat it at home or do you go out?"

"I eat it or I make it."

"Can you cook Chinese food?"

"Well, mainly rice. Or I'll buy something and I'll make it."

"Do you like the frozen food section simply because it's cold?" I asked, feeling I was getting to the essence the matter.

"Yeah. I like things that are cold. I hate heat. That's why I like the nighttime, because it's cooler than the daytime. I don't like the heat."

"Do you have air conditioning in your car?"

"No. It broke."

"Do you like ice cream?"

"I don't like ice cream! Ask me morbid things then you'll find good answers out of me."

"Do you like milk?" I asked doggedly.

"What? Uh. A little bit. I don't like milk as much as I used to."

"Do you ever wash the dishes?"

"When I feel like it. I hate washing the dishes."

"Do you get the cheap stuff or the thick stuff that washes more dishes?"

"Well, I don't buy it but I think it's the cheap stuff because the bubbles don't last too long. And I don't wash clothes! We should have gone to the graveyard. That's more like home. I used to go to the graveyard a lot at night."

"When you're taking a shower?" I redirected.

"What kind of soap do I use? I personally use Ivory Soap because it's clean. I just like it."

"Do you take bubble baths?"

"Once in a while. I like perfume baths that make your skin real soft. I get the good stuff."

"Where do you get it?"

"Through Avon or something, maybe Thrifty Drugs."

We turn the corner and confront new genres of products. "Do you have a cat?"

"Yes. I have a black cat named Damian."

"Do you use Tidy Cat Kitty Litter?"

"I don't know. My mom buys the cat do-do."

"What kind of food does your cat eat?"

"I don't know. My mom buys the cat food." We walk to another aisle passing feminine hygiene products. "Don't ask me these questions because I won't answer!"

"What toilet paper products do you prefer?" I ask mildly.

"I don't care as long as it's there! Aren't you going to ask me anything about my band?"

"If you came here to get something to eat what would you get?"

"Ummm. Maybe some donuts. I don't eat sweets too much because sugar gets me all freaked out sometimes."

"Have you ever had pickled onions?"

"No. I don't think I'd like them."

"What about Hostess Sno-Balls?"

"No. I don't think I'd like them."

"Do you like Arrowhead Drinking Water?"

"Yes!"

"What do you like about it?"

"Well, you know, it's got this neat taste to it."

"Mountain Dew?"

"Yeah. It's ok."

"Sugar Free Dr. Pepper?"

"No. I hate Dr. Pepper."

"Coke? Tab?"

"I don't like Tab."

"Pepsi Free?"

"I like Pepsi."

"RC Cola?"

"Yes."

"Do you like 7-Up?"

"I like 7-Up."

"Do you like 'Like'?"

"I've never had 'Like'. I don't keep up with these new latest things."

"Do you like Perrier?"

"No, I don't like bubbly water."

"Potato chips?"

"Yeah. I love potato chips."

I felt that I was making some small intellectual progress with the lady.

"Do you like pancakes?" I asked.

"I love pancakes."

"Do you like 'Aunt Jemima'?"

"Yes."

"What kind of syrup do you like?"

"Aunt Jemima."

"Do you like 'Mrs. Butterworths'?"

"I don't think I've had that. I usually buy one thing and stick to it."

"Baloney? Hot Dogs? Velveeta Cheese?"

"I hate cheese! Of all things I hate the most, I hate cheese."

"Have you ever had Ragoo Spaghetti Sauce?"

"Often. I like Italian food."

"Do you like Italian salad dressing?"

"I love Italian dressing. Italian and Thousand Island."

"Ech! Italian and Thousand Island?"

"Not together!"

"Would you eat this stuff? Canned squid?"

"No!"

"For twenty five dollars?"

"No. Maybe for a hundred."

"Do you wear L'Eggs Pantyhose?"

"I don't use pantyhose. I only wear black tights or purple ones."

"Do you dye your hair?"

"Yes."

"What product do you use?"

"Miss Clairol."

"Do you like that better than Nice 'N Easy?"

"I don't know."

"So you don't shop around too much?"

"No. I usually leave the shopping to my mom. I only go shopping if I have to, and that's not too often."

"Fresh fish?"

"I think it looks disgusting. I wouldn't eat that. I wouldn't eat it!"

"So you won't eat fish?"

"Yeah, I like fish like fishsticks where you squeeze on lemon and eat it with ketchup. I use Crest toothpaste."

"Do you like steaks?"

"Yeah. I like meat to an extent but I don't overdo it. After a while it's kind of disgusting."

"Do you eat a lot from fast food places?"

"Once in a while, mainly at McDonalds. I eat at McDonalds or I like Taco Bell."

"Do you think this is a nice supermarket?"

"To me every market is just the same. It's not a place where I would want to hang out every day."

"Do you want to buy anything in here today?"

"In here. No. I'm going to buy something later after we leave. I have to go to the occult shop. I'm into that kind of stuff, so is our guitarist. That's why we work well together. Are you interested in our band at all?"

"You're wondering about all of these food-related questions I guess. Do you read The National Enquirer?"

"Sometimes. It's just a stupid gossip magazine really."

"Don't you think that if I ask you questions about supermarkets that it will reveal something about the band?"

"What does a supermarket have to do with the band?"

"What does the band have to do with anything else?"

"Well I know they have no connection with a supermarket."

"Ok then. How does the band come up with ideas?"

"Well, this may sound a little bit cliché, but a few of us go to the Hollywood Memorial Graveyard. Sometimes we just sit there when it's real quiet. We sit and we just talk about anything that comes to mind; sometimes what we're surrounded by inspires us to write, because that's about the only thing that really inspires us. I know to some people it sounds morbid, liking graveyards, and always thinking really strange morbid things, but that's just the way we think. Sometimes our guitarist Dustman, if he gets real upset about something and he hasn't been rehearsing, since he's into magic, he like tends to ask a lot of things for what he wants and it just happens. It almost seems like we have some sort of connection with something 'out there'. It's hard to explain stuff like that if people don't understand. Some people just think we're weird. They think we're Satanists, which we're not."

"What's your favorite movie?"

"I was going to say 'The Exorcist' but I saw it for the second time the other night and when you see it for the second time, it really is stupid."

DEEP INTO THAT DARKNESS PEERING: Death moved among us, that fucking son-of-a-bitch with the scythe and filthy hooded garment. He is always coming, for him, for her, for you. Germs singer Darby Crash, once the prime mover of the L.A. Punk scene was a drug suicide. His death which occurred prematurely in the timeline of L.A. Punk, had been mostly overlooked even by the local press because he inadvertently chose to overdose on heroin on the same day that John Lennon was murdered in NYC. 'X' took a hit. Exene's pretty sister was killed in a car crash in Los Angeles. The band was informed while they were performing onstage at the Whisky. The show went on in brutal sadness. Will Shatter of 'Negative Trend' and 'Flipper' overdosed. Rob Graves, late of '45 Grave' overdosed. Bobbi Brat, cancer victim.

AIDS began killing long before scientists labeled a virus HIV as the primary vector of the disease. Many rock musicians met the reaper around the same period that movie star Rock Hudson became emaciated and passed on to Hollywood heaven. The tabloids ran wild with splash headlines all over the Hudson story. Little attention was given in the local press to the deaths of miscreant creative L.A. punks. The epidemic was worldwide. Some people knitted giant quilts in memory of the dead and in hopes of influencing the U.S. government to commit funds for research to end the epidemic. Soon everybody was touched by a personal loss.

There were other losses of life. Read the damn obituaries if you need some cheering up. A salient message from Larry Benton appeared on the answering machine at Zanna Central Headquarters. The phone was near to the new Sony television in the bedroom. The previous Toshiba TV had gone out the window wrapped in a bedsheet heisted by some local daytime drug burglars along with some of Zanna's mother's gold jewelry carried over from Poland.

Although he had moved away from the Arcade Theater lofts, Larry was still living in a downtown Los Angeles studio loft and he grew to hate the inner city ambience. Downtown L.A. living had lost one hundred and one percent of its romance for him. On a sunny Saturday morning, he had stumbled upon the barbaric bludgeoning murder of his music business friend in a downstairs loft. Larry discovered the body of his friend in bed with his head split open like a squashed pumpkin. Eliminate Death Nurse from our previous chapter as a suspect because this victim was killed in his sleep. No screaming whatsoever. Just one squishy thud in the night with a sledgehammer to his sleeping pumpkin. Well, the deed lacked finesse.

On the lighter side, Larry was touring sporadically creating light shows for electronic new wave bands and around the studio he was painting pedestrian Pop Art images. Maybe it was just me, with my perennially soured point of view but I saw nearly all the art coming from the downtown loft scene as occupying the general aesthetic territory of clichéd modernism, Bank of America art, bland modernism and conventional soporific pop. The lesson I had taken from the greats of modern art was that art was about ideas. Here was a vast void that could be measured not with a mere carpenter's tape measure but in light years and parsecs of dead air, the empty space between the ears of most of the artists living in downtown L.A. Perhaps that's exactly what troubled this head-crushing murderer? My opinion was culled from multiple experiences at openings and wandering around studios and lofts. Any art that was great, in my opinion, never attracted NYC style whiz-bang bling-bling gallery money and died languishing under somebody's bed or eventually found a new home in a dumpster.

I returned Larry's call. Naoko was dead. My foxy wild Japanese girlfriend. Larry and me shared an accurate mental database on all our past schoolmates. Larry made me swear to secrecy under penalty of death, his death and mine, never to reveal these details to another living soul. This penalty of death was no idle threat from Larry. It was a calculated business statement intended to generate the fear of a knifing in an associate spreading gossip about the suspected perpetrator. If this person who offed

Naoko picked up an earful that you were talking trash about him, you were finished. According to Larry, Naoko was seeing Royal. On Saturday night, Royal had shot her up with an overdose of heroin. Sure, it was accidental. Sunday morning her body was found tossed out onto a lawn in the well manicured estates off of Larchmont Ave. I didn't even know they were dating. Was this the contemporary state of heterosexual dating today? I told Zanna and then I told her to keep her mouth shut tight so Royal wouldn't kill us and throw us in a dumpster like some hard-boiled noir death scene. Besides, I continued habitually to buy high quality drugs from the sibling dealers. No one wanted to lose a good drug connection.

I was informed through nightclub barroom chatter, a uniquely reliable form of up-to-date info depending on the source, that Buck, my former drug buddy, had contracted AIDS. For a year or so after I heard that gossip, I saw him frequently hanging at the usual Hollywood bars, late nights after shows, and he smiled at me now and then across a row of last call drinkers, but I strictly avoided him. He was so fast with the hypodermic needle that I harbored a fear that he would find a way to surreptitiously stick his diseased syringe in me. Then some months later on, I heard through the barroom grapevine that Lana was pregnant and that she too had contracted AIDS.

My punky friend Tina Tupelo, an erotic and wild southern woman, extensively tattooed with personal fetish images, was seeing them. Tina was on their circuit, living in a old landmark Hollywood building that was populated with musicians, scenemakers, odd characters and peripheral hangers-on. Peripheral hangers on is a category that would include unemployed drummers who sewed glitter G-strings and kinky underwear on a pay-per-piece basis, girlfriends of rich musicians who were married, aspiring actors counted in quantity not quality, and a building manager who flashed his genitals at female tenants and routinely attempted to gas himself to death by putting his head in an oven. When Buck and Lana's baby was born, it was a boy. Their son was born with AIDS and the three of them died.

Tina and I did methamphetamine together now and then. She could be a genuine asset at times. I loved her wild mannerisms and cartoonish hilly-billy character-istics. She made me a fan of the South. She had a black sheep tattoo on one shoulder and a hanged-dead Raggedy Ann doll tattooed on the other; several more tattoos, long beautiful legs, a fine high ass, a pair of lovely silicon enhanced trailer-park Winnebagos and cat scratch street savvy gleaned from a million late night romps through urban after-hours revelry. You just had to love the girl, that is if you didn't hate her type on a general basis; and if your eyes went for the torn fishnet tights protruding from a micro-miniskirt and your ears loved her sing-song endless

Southern drawl, she owned your ass.

The Cathay de Grande had a '12 Punk Bands For A Dollar Night' and great bands like 'The Blasters' and Brit punk rockers 'GBH' played on the floor downstairs other nights. Five aggressive drunk pimply rednecks followed Tina Tupelo, Kitten and myself after we spilled out the side door of the Cathay De Grande off Selma Avenue at Argyle in the wee hours before sunrise. They were closing in on us to the sound of stomping macho boots from about a city block up the street. We three had no wheels and no strong concept about what to do except that the night was over and we were more or less walking up to Tinas flat to cut some Z's. Kitten and I looked at each other like we were two defenseless peewees in the sights of the wild barbarian huns and we were too stoned to be conjuring up a self-defense strategy. When the bootboys got within spitting distance, Tina spontaneously let out a rodeo inspired "Hee-yaw! Come and get it boys!" and she hiked down her micro-mini-tube skirt, located a dangling string protruding from her vagina and gave it a tug, revealing a soiled and bloody supersized Tampax tampon which she whirled and whipped about her head in a lasso inspired circle in front of their frozen faces. Instinctively, the killer rubes as a group turned and ran the other way and never looked back. I was extremely impressed and so too was Kitten. One of the first maxims of self defense is that virtually any object can be turned into a weapon should the urgency of the situation require improvisation.

The photographer named Ian Wright, number four in my informal list of new visual talent was a garrulous street photographer. Ian was one of those photographers who had an obsession with documenting Big Billy's activities, certain that these were the early years of a music legend. Billy's area of expertise was essentially perpetuating the legend of the excessive lifestyle of the contemporary white bluesman, alcoholism, heroin, electric guitar blues, Muddy Waters nostalgia punctuated by an occasional street fight. Guitarist Mike Bloomfield's end was a paragon, found dead in a car in San Francisco of a heroin overdose, he helped create the sound of Bob Dylan's amazing transition to electric rock and he played many of the genius magic blues riffs that drove the Paul Butterfield Blues Band, a cornerstone of the 1960s musical edifice. With Billy, Ian believed he had a young Paul Butterfield in his sights complete with the drama and excitement of a self-destructive talent.

Ian Wright owned a house at the top of Echo Park on a cliff overlooking Frogtown, a local street gang epithet for a rival Latino neighborhood section, located below the cliffside, which runs along the L.A. River next to the 5 freeway. We discussed the possibility of my making a move up to Ian's house. He was possibly looking to rent the bottom of the house which was a high-ceiling studio perched on the side of the cliff. The availability of the studio was contingent on whether a young guitarist who was living there moved away. The musicians girlfriend was pregnant so he needed to move out.

It was perfect. Ian needed the extra income. Zanna and I were having weird fights. I broke the back window when I tried to kick her in the butt and missed and my boot flew off and broke the glass. Kung-Fu stupid. Amphetamines, my solution to alcoholism, were taking their toll on our friendly dispositions. Zanna was having convulsive crying episodes which occurred when she had her period and used speed together in the same time frame. Her crying spasms scared the hell out of me.

Zanna made an accusation to me and in turn to her girlfriends that I beat her and kicked her during a fight. This was not accurate as I accurately recalled the incident. I responded that she was mistaken. Zanna had simply imagined the kicking and punching. The truth was that when we were fighting, we were extremely animated. We were engaged in frequent screaming, running, throwing objects at one another's heads twenty-four hours of the day and night. Zanna punched me in the head. I know that for certain. That girlpunch was a left hook that landed solidly to my temple but there was no point in me complaining to anyone that a girl punched me.

Edna, the landlady routinely was sicking the German Shepherd Poncho on me anytime I entered or exited the building, so I acquired the habit of carrying a heavy four foot long steel pipe wrapped with duct tape at one end for a non-slip hand hold. This heavy steel pipe added to my unpleasant demeanor. Zanna's girlfriends all believed that I was beating her with regularity. There were of course periods of time when we were perfectly happy together. Shorter periods than before. It shouldn't go unmentioned that I was experiencing a few personal problems that were exclusive to my own troubled mind. Dreams. Dreams of murdering the dead.

There were several bad dreams which haunted me when I managed to get some sleep. These were repeating dreams of terrifying images. Their content could only have been generated by unresolved caustic nuclear family issues traced back to my childhood and adolescence. There was no particular terrible incident from the family history that I could pinpoint as a prime cause. I was never raped or sodomized by a parent or relative. The worst repeating dream was a short sequence where I poured gasoline on my father's head. Sometimes he was sleeping or in other dreams he was sitting in a chair, and then I lit his head on fire with a disposable cigarette lighter. His head exploded into flames. He ran around the confined space of the room screaming in horror with his head aflame. His flesh would turn red then blister and sizzle as he suffocated to death by inhaling the scorching fire into his lungs. I made no attempt to extinguish the flames. In the dreams where my father was the victim, my mother was always present and frozen in terror. Sometimes Zanna was present in the scene as an observer. When I awoke from one of these hideous family murder dreams I would often be angry with Zanna. Most importantly, if I didn't directly conjure the dream images up into my awakened consciousness then my anger would remain all day unfocused just below consciousness but inclusive of Zanna. It was distressing to be murdering deceased family members. I also murdered my mother in dreams. Forget the dreams, try. Besides, I should have burned off Shannons head, but she wasn't dead.

I told Zanna about her involvement in these dreams. I cautioned her not to wake me suddenly, that I could become dangerous. Zanna said, "God damn you. You asshole." in her dry half joking manner of speaking. Still, I was looking for the opportunity to move away from her until my troubled mental state calmed down. My conscious self was disturbed by these spontaneous images of hate toward my deceased parents from REM hell dreamland, and of course with Zanna's inclusion, but my parents continued to be murdered with regularity in strange slaughter scenarios after I shut my eyes. I didn't hate my deceased parents.

Zanna and I had a nasty fight just prior to meeting the famed Los Angeles 1960s LSD trip doctor-cum-guru Oscar Haas over at Herbert Wallach's downtown photo studio. It was to be a civilized conversational evening with Herbert and his wife, the Acid Master Dr. Haas, and we two, the modern couple Zan-girl plus Ronnie Robot. Zanna and I were completely annihilated and exhausted from overwork, amphetamine abuse and cat fighting when we showed up at Herberts loft. We should have stayed at home but we were unable stay in one place. Herbert and his wife were prancing around on the balls of their feet with excitement over the doctor's impending arrival and it appeared that we were invited there to represent the trendy new generation literati of the drug culture. There was fine wine and exquisite hors d'oervres prepared. Zanna and me were a poster couple for the pissed undead.

"Don't they ever fight?" I whispered to Zanna. Herbert had bought his wife, Annelie, a Polish meat grinder as a gift for the Christmas holidays some months past and I pictured Annelie gleefully grinding Herbert sausages of every variety for his breakfast and his dinner, dressed like Bettie Page in skimpy black bondage gear.

I said to Zanna, "If this Dr. Psychedelia walks in here grinning from ear to ear like he's on some '60s acid high, I'm gonna shit in my pants in the middle of the room. I'm in no fucking mood for happiness and I don't want to see happiness parading around the room. I just know he's gonna be happy as Captain Kangaroo." I called Herbert over.

"Herbert which sausages are the human meat? We only eat ground children."

"Ha! Ha! That's very good. I'll check with Annelie." I waved for him to come a little closer so that I could speak softly.

"Herbert, we're really not in a very good way today. We're strung out, exhausted, and overworked. Maybe it would be better if we left. I just know the doctor is going to be too fucking happy for me to bear. It might kill me to be too near to his astral glow and cosmic radiance."

Herbert laughed. "No, you'll love him. He's a great guy. Don't worry about it."

Dr. Haas arrived solo. It would have made the night more interesting if he had arrived with an escort service whore. He looked older and somewhat heavier with considerably less hair than his 1960s images which made their way around the mass media; he also displayed a cheshire cat grin accompanied by sparkling lively blue eyes. He immediately started talking with enthusiasm about college hoops. There was a big UCLA Bruins game on TV and he wanted to turn it on and watch it just for starters while he devoured a few pounds of hors d'oervres.

I turned to Zanna and said, "This is going to be a long night. It probably takes him a few hours of wine and snacks just to get his engine going."

She said, "We could just get up really fast and sneak out of here. They're not watching us now. We can explain later."

"OK. Let's go. I just knew the Doctor was going to be smiling like that." So we got up off the studio couch and ran for the door while the others were talking about sausages and wine vintages in the kitchen.

We returned directly to home. Zanna began playing piano. She was classically trained and had a baby grand in the front room. For three months she had not been playing tunes (for lack of a better word). She had formerly liked to play a few Scott Joplin ditties, although she said that his hands were large and his work was difficult to play. Chopin, she played. Only recently now she played scales, only scales, with demonic speed, repetition and precision, sometimes for two or three hours at a stretch. I went into the back room and watched cartoons for a while. Ian Wright phoned just then and said that the little studio was available in Echo Park. It was inexpensive and I made plans with Ian to move up there soon. I planned to move at least on a part-time basis and keep my roiling confused hatred away from Zanna. I made the supposition that my dreams were an expression of hatred, burning up my parents heads, but I couldn't understand why my mind was repeatedly killing people who were already dead. Zanna's uncle called with his usual redundancy.

"Ronnie. Pick up the phone Ronnie. Ronnie I want to speak to you. Pick up the phone." The answering machine broadcasted his voice. Occasionally, he asked for me. Once in a blue moon, I picked up the call. This time I answered the phone.

"Ronnie. Hello? Who is this?"

"Ronnie. It's Ronnie."

"This is Ronnie? Is this Ronnie?"

"Yes! This is Ronnie."

"Ronnie. How is my niece doing? Is there trouble at her job?"

"She's doing fine. No trouble."

"There is trouble Ronnie?"

"No. No trouble."

"Is she sick? How is her health?"

"She's not sick?"

"She is sick? What is wrong Ronnie? You can tell me."

"Nothing is wrong. Nothing is wrong."

"Nothing is wrong? Ronnie you must come over for lunch. I will make you a vegetable soup for lunch. Come over Ronnie."

"Sure. I'll come over for lunch. Next week maybe."

"You will come next week?"

"Sure. Next week."

"OK Ronnie I will see you then." Click. He hung up. I got up and went to the sounds of piano playing. I waved my hands up in the air in front of the piano.

"Your uncle called."

"Yeah. So what."

"I told him that I would go over there for lunch next week. Now I'm sunk. He'll fixate on it. I can't get out of it."

"He'll make you vegetable soup. He makes a really good vegetable soup. It won't be so bad."

"Will it have legumes?"

"Legumes?"

"Ask Leo if he knows what a legume is. You're family is making vegetable soups and you don't even know what a simple legume is. A legume is a kind of vegetable in America. That's not very comforting. I told Ian Wright that I would take that studio in Echo Park."

"OK. That's not such a bad idea."

So, I maintained the office at Hollywood Boulevard and I took Ian's studio rental. I enjoyed the cliffs and green plants so initially I spent my work time at Ian's.

Nervous Breakdown
Fix Me
I've Had It
Wasted
Jealous Again
Revenge
White Minority
No Values
You Bet We've Got Something Personal Against You!
Clocked In
Six Pack
I've Heard It Before
American Waste
Machine
Louie Louie
Damaged
Slip It In
I Don't Care
I've Had It
Annihilate This Week
Loose Nut
Gimmie Gimmie Gimmie
Drinking And Driving
T.V. Party

BLACK FLAG, song titles

CHAPTER 14

THE BIG MICKEY FIX: I had an irresistible craving for 'Mickey Cakes' which taste like a cheap poor man's 'Twinkies'. When your bloodstream is riding the sugar rollercoaster 'Mickey Cakes' cut through like an uncut upper. My nerves were jangled so I ate them hurriedly as I was driving my car. I feel they cheated me this time around on the banana cream filling. There was just a little bit of cream at the bottom and little to none inside. Plus, I was handling a car battery and I had battery acid on my fingers which rubbed off on the cake so that they tasted like chemically hot cheap 'Twinkies'. My tongue is still burning an hour later.

I have just returned from an appointment where the other party didn't show up. I will soon be changing my place of residence at least temporarily. All residences in life are temporary homes. I've slept in my clothes for three days because I have been so very busy. One thing I did was to go to traffic court to protest a parking ticket. I went in there looking like a total sleazeball. My hair was all greasy and stringy. That's what they expect to see when they look at the general public. Wear soiled underpants.

I put a crush-proof box of cigarettes in my back pocket and sat on it for a good half an hour and rediscovered it back there crushed. I am smoking flattened cigarettes today. Nevertheless the 'Mickey Cakes' have put me in a good mood even without that big wad of banana cream which I was anticipating. Also news, the landlady's German Shepherd Poncho didn't try to bite me. It just stared at me with my steel pipe. The dog is playing psychological chess. Connor, our new upstairs neighbor who replaced the black girl who didn't have a baby, was robbed yesterday by the unfriendly neighborhood drug addicted burglars. They tied him up in the bedroom at knifepoint and for good measure they put a hood over his head. A small gang of burglars entered his back door on the second story about 6 a.m. this Monday morning. Once Conner was hogtied, they methodically spent the next two hours emptying out his apartment of valuable possessions. Prior to the robbery, Conner had owned some costly collectible items. They loaded his domestic booty into their van located in the alley. They had him dressed up like a holiday turkey. This group was cool-headed and they took their sweet time. Conner had more valuable things to take than we have downstairs and the burglars should know, because they got our stuff a few weeks ago during a previous daring daytime heist.

About 9 am Connor popped his head out the front door and said to me as I was groping for the morning newspaper, "I was robbed! Just now. I was robbed!" Edna was standing out on the front lawn with the garden hose in her hand watering the flowers. She may have heard Connor's SOS but she continued spraying water.

Well Mr. Fancypants, I was at home downstairs all morning with nothing to do and no one bothered to invite me. Hood party at Connor's! There's a reason besides her dog Poncho, the German Shepherd, that the bad guys don't attack the big Hawaiian landlady. She looks ugly, massive and pugnacious like she could wrestle a grizzly bear by herself and win. Actually, a Black man did follow Edna home from the bank one afternoon after she withdrew a large sum of cash. He confronted her when she got out of her car in the fourplex driveway. He tried to grab her purse away from her but Edna took the offensive; she wrestled him to the ground. His remaining efforts were spent trying to escape. He had suffered enough pain in her grip that he ran away with nothing and he was probably happy to have survived.

... 𝄢 ...

FINE DINING IN L.A. First off, we began our day late in the morning near downtown, in Chinatown with two Phillipe's French Dipped Sandwiches for breakfast. We took an hour or two off to play miniature golf in The Valley. Then we made the complete break with Western Civilization and we cruised again back down into the real Los Angeles Chinatown, not as romantically scenic and extensive as the San Francisco Chinatown. This was the same Chinatown as the one we just left.

My girlfriend said, "These people are the most ancient civilization on earth. They are as old and timeless as the dinosaurs. In fact, they came in around the time when the dinosaurs went out."

"Oh yes. I have seen the terrifying Fortunecookiesaurus bones in a museum." I repied. "A giant lizard cookie monster."

Before lunch we stopped in a crowded shabby Chinatown mall where we picked up a few cheap imported plastic battery operated fantasy massacre toys. Then we headed for a greasy chopstick down a sidestreet.

"Look at the distorted geometrics in this smashed up run-over Marlboro crushproof box." I quipped, picking up a piece of garbage from the street. "It appears to have been run over several times. Do you realize that you will be dining with a connoisseur of ordinary garbage?"

"I wish you'd bathe sometimes. You look like a bum." replied Zanna.

After dining on slimy greasy noodles and playing with our toys on the restaurant table, we conjured up another adventure.

"Let's go to Koreatown and see how they congregate!"

So off we went to Koreatown but we got lost and then seriously sidetracked by an ice cream parlor rising out of the shimmering monosodium glutamate induced psychedelia distortion fog. We stopped to eat homemade ice cream at a small family owned ice cream shop in a Mexican neighborhood bordering on Koreatown, as near as I can reckon. After the ice cream, I felt the need to go straight home Code 10 for a long nap and inevitably a nightmare. A few hours later I awoke in a foul mood.

"I'm in a bad mood from my dream." I said to Zanna. "Let's go get some ribs at Greece's Bar-B-Q."

Greece's Bar-B-Q was like a sinister dream fragment on its own merit because it had an absolutely indefinable anti-ambience in part because it had no furniture. It had a counter where orders were taken and picked up and a brick oven where delicious ribs were cooked. Instead of eating on the hard cement floor, ninety-nine percent of the customers opted to take the ribs home to eat them. Greece's was cozy like a prison cell in County Jail. Greece's was an establishment that appeared, through logical deduction by observing the skin color of the servers and patrons, to be owned by African-Americans. Greece's was unique in that it was a restaurant that moved around from location to location frequently. If you went there one time, it might not be in the same place the next time you visited, but if you drove around the neighborhood a little you could usually find it again. It was located more or less in the area down by La Brea and Washington near the Santa Monica Freeway.

"There it is. It's up on the next block."

"It didn't used to be there."

"It moved again. But I bet it's the same guys."

A FASHION MAKEOVER. Today I plan to completely transform myself into an Elvis Zombie, having just read Gary Panter's new book 'Invasion of The Elvis Zombies'. It has become my new Bible. Once the physical and spiritual trans-formation is completed, I will seek an audience with the great one and ask him many probing questions. I anticipate that we will sit face to face and exchange intellectual mysteries. Right now I am a mere wannabe. I wish to become a totally evil Son-of-Satan Elvis Zombie, not simply another generic stamped out Las Vegas style everyday variety undead E-Z.

First there is a question of style. I have chosen to become an obese transvestite Elvis Zombie shooting seconols, my shirt pockets packed with amyl nitrates, with sadistic strap-on genitalia accessories tucked in my handbag for easy access. Elvis was a sex symbol for every boy girl man or woman in America and beyond. In that light he must be considered a huge mass media homosexual phenomenon, as well as bi-sexual and heterosexual. In those primordial times of the 1950s, when sexual repression was rampant, Elvis served as a safe outlet in the new media for American male homosexuality and much later in his life he became the kingpin of the avant-garde of American male erotic obesity. Elvis was not only the King of Rock and Roll, he was also in some respects the Queen. In 1957, when he penned Love Me Tender and recorded it for RCA Records, the gorgeous, sensual, volatile young vocalist with the sneering puckering lips admonished both males and females to be more gentle.

I imagined an American horror. A dishevelled overweight dusted gang sodomized HIV-positive bi-sexual toupéed middle-aged Elvis look-alike weekend zombie staggers down a long deserted inner city alleyway leaning a shoulder into the dirty red brick wall every few broken steps for support. Stopping abruptly, this Elvis copycat plunges a gangrened hand into his pocket retrieving a Bic lighter shoplifted moments before from a Thrifty Drug Store after eating the head off the neck of an Arab sales clerk. Behind this amateurish makeup lies a filthy father of five (two boys and three girls) who, thrusting his head between his legs looks backwards through his sweaty crotch dropping the black-haired toupee onto the pavement several inches below. The inebriated zombie thrusts the flaming Bic cigarette lighter into his buttocks and farts loudly shooting an eighteen inch long firejet into the evening air burning a one inch circular hole through his soiled and ripped white rhinestone studded polyester Hawaiian Concert suit. Then he continues stumbling along and dancing and he begins to sing uncharacteristically out of tune.

"I don't want to be a vampire zombie lion because vampire undead power cats play too rough. I don't want to be a cyborg predator tiger because titanium nuclear powered robot tigers ain't the kind you love enough. I just want to be your melting chocolate marshmallow dead fleshy Plushy Bear. Drill a hole through my neck and drag me anywhere. Oh let me be your dead Plushy Bear."

Tonight, a new generation of adoring eyes are going to feast on this Elvis imitator, me. They will be driven of their minds with desire, with primitive carnal hunger except that I am obese and being a zombie, I am dead, stinking and mouldy. My sinister flesh houses an enormous population of writhing maggots. If any unwary person comes within my grasp, I plan to bite off a giant chunk of their living flesh because I hunger; and then sing a little "All Shook Up Dead Guts".

I want to jab my fingers into the eyes of a loving fan and pull their eyeballs twelve inches out from their head and then sign my autograph in blood on the wall. I want to rip my fans' arms free from their sockets and tear my long red fingers into their quivering abdomen until I am swimming in hot living guts and partially digested pepperoni pizza. Grr–r–r–r! I'm a zombie, but a singing and dancing zombie not without raw talent. I like, even love, my new Fredericks of Hollywood bra which houses my ample hirsute male breasts because Elvis had a very strong feminine persona. To borrow a refrain briefly from Allen Ginsberg, Holy Elvis Zombie. Holy obese homosexual Elvis Zombie with maggots!

Later that night, I took a cab over to Disgraceland, a punkster house located up in Hollywood between Selma and Sunset owned and operated by two pretty punkettes, the Pep Girls, Cherry Blood and Ida Libido. My friend Mickey Mike, guitar player extraordinaire had called to invite me to the late night party. It was a sloppy potty soiled imitation of an Elvis which I had created, but it was uniquely mine.

The cab stopped. "That's $18.50 Elvis. You can afford it." barked the cabbie. I could have decapitated him on the spot but my attention was distracted. The front porch of the house was dominated by a darkly clad figure posturing with a guitar. The sinewy guitarist was dressed entirely in black patent leather. It was a knock off of the leather suit that Elvis wore from the 1968 TV Special. It was the youthful Elvis, the erotic untamed persona as it last appeared to the public before the transformation to obesity and the nightmare of his death toiletside nude at Graceland Mansion. Only the hair and make-up of this imposter were incongruous. I could see in the shadows that this Elvis was a platinum blond with make-up done in the manner of a 1950s sex starlet, reminiscent of Jayne Mansfield even to the exaggerated outline of the deep red lipstick. This made for a cloying combination of personalities in one individual.

Attention to detail was everything. Did he, or she know that Elvis was an uncircumcised hipshaker? As I approached the porch I noticed that his neck was ringed by a deep wound smeared with partially clotted blood. In fact his head had the appearance of having been severed and then whimsically stuck back in place by a B-movie prop guy. In the driveway, under an overgrown shade tree was parked a dusty wrecked pink early 1960s Cadillac. Some weird hybrid American archetype personality death fetish Jayne Mansfield Elvis fusion, I thought. Clever.

"Is this the party?" I queried just to say some little something. My voice seemed to rattle in my throat with insecurity. I was out-Elvised. "Be strong, Elvis Doesn't cry!" I thought. I soiled my boxer shorts.

"Hi. I'm Elayne. The party is inside."

I crossed the porch and opened the door without knocking and then entered the house. Inside, I entered an anteroom which had a bunkbed on the left and some plushy tattered furniture on the right. The bunkbed, I knew from previous visits was for guests. The house had two bedrooms in the back arrayed down the long hallway. Interior to the anteroom was a living room with an empty fireplace facing the front door. In the living room was a small boisterous crowd sitting and standing around in a circle. Charlie, the singer in Mickey Mike's band was either peacefully unconscious, dead or deeply asleep on the floor with his head stuck completely inside of a cardboard box, formerly used for consumer electronics. Charlie chilled undisturbed in the midst of the effervescent group. He never moved a muscle all night. Mickey Mike and his friend Smarty were sitting and standing, animated clownish in the middle of the group, loosely entertaining the small crowd who were comprised exclusively of perennial after hours punk nightclub habitués. For such a small room it was filled to capacity; people were sitting, standing and leaning on walls with all the exuberance of fight night at the Olympic Auditorium, except for Charlie with his head in the box. A couple of Z-Boys came in the door with skateboards slung on their shoulders and stood in the crowd wide-eyed.

Smarty and Mickey Mike started watusi boogaloo dancing naked in the middle of the room with their pants around their ankles wearing technically only their cowboy boots shouting, laughing and jeering at the crowd circled around them. At the point I settled in, Smarty held open a Motorhead album jacket and Mickey Mike sexually assaulted it with an erect penis. Mickey Mike then began breaking furniture pieces in the middle of the floor, throwing wooden chairs down against the hardwood floor with an uncommon admixture of violent rage combined with hilarity. He then threw the broken chair parts into the fireplace until it was mostly filled up. The Heavymetal Punk crazed crowd adored the pantsless daft destruction. So he broke more stuff.

"Let's have a little wine. What do you say." said Smarty, a working class American Irish youth with a great shock of naturally wild hair on top of his head.

"Tell me about that retarded chick you fucked in the puddle." Mickey Mike taunted.

"She was blind and deaf. We fucked her by Braille. Truthfully she was not retarded. She was severely handicapped. Retarded had nothing to do with it. And it was her fur jacket not mine that I fucked her on. I'm in love. I have an erection and I have nothing on it except skin. There's nothing crawling on it except my fingers. I'm the happiest dude in the whole world. I'm so lazy, I married a pregnant girl." said Smarty.

Someone from the crowd yelled, "Hey, that's my joke."

"Oh fuck off Rory! Why do you fuck with your cock instead of mine?"

"So my balls don't blow up."

"Ohh-h-h! An intellectual." Smarty came back. "OK. I am having deep thoughts. Mickey you definitely have the biggest cock of any man I know. He's got a big ol' dick. Hey Mickey let's see your dick now."

"Is it expandable?" A familiar voice shouts. I looked around to see Kitten nestled among the crowd.

"If Irishmen didn't love to drink, we'd rule the world. You're somebody's dick now." Rory proclaimed.

"I'll suck it." announced Smarty.

"OK suck it." echoed Mickey Mike.

"Oh no!" a girl shouted. She had a voice much like Kitten.

"Hey! Kitten wants to see your dick."

"Kitten's seen my dick. Hold on I'm going to pee on the record player." snapped Mickey Mike.

"This is ridiculous. I'll go home." said a punk guy as if he'd paid for a ticket to the show.

" 'Oh! Oh! I'll go home!' So go home!"

"Hey dude. Go down. Go down. Go down!" shouted a young man wearing a black leather motorcycle jacket, holding a skateboard across his shoulder.

"Let's have an orgy. Let's all take our clothes off and fuck. C'mon, let's all get naked. We're going to all get naked. Everybody, clothes off! I'm embarrassed. Mickey Mike's got a bigger dick than I have." Smarty shouted. Mickey Mike and Smarty began walking around in small circles waving their t-shirts in the air with their pants still dropped around their cowboy boots.

"It's a naked night from hell!" whooped Mickey Mike.

Smarty shouted again pointing, "Hey Mickey. You don't fuck with that thing do you? Do you fuck with that?"

"You suck this while I suck yours. OK?" replied Mickey Mike handling his penis.

"I want to have sex with her not with you." Smarty testified pointing at a pretty punkette.

"Shed all of your inhibitions Smarty." Mickey Mike roared, "It's the California lifestyle. Hot tubs, yogurt. (kiss kiss) You lovely dude you."

"I want to say that my friend Timmy fucks fat women." chortled Smarty pointing into the crowd. "How do you like me sucking your dick?"

Mickey Mike said, "It's cool."

A punker from the crowd yelled, "He still hasn't got a big enough boner. I want to see a blow job with a huge boner. Get it?"

"I love that. Do it again." murmured Mickey Mike.

Smarty stated scientifically, "I've just injected wine into Mickey's prick."

"C'mon Smart Boy. Put it in your mouth again." pleaded Mickey Mike.

"It's a dirty job but someone has got to do it."

Smarty picked up the Motorhead jacket and beat on Mickey's penis with it. "Die pig! Die pig!" Then Smarty rubbed his ass up against Mickey Mikes cock.

"He farted on my dick! I'm pulling up my pants." shouted Mickey Mike. "Here's a couple of pubic hairs for you Smarty. You sweety little guy you."

Leaning up against the wall, I completely forgot that I was a dead Elvis. The activity in the room degenerated into a teeming swirl of black leather and wild hairdos, unrestrained voices and laughing. Around 4 am I left the party. I walked alone up to the P*NK Magazine offices at Hollywood Boulevard and Las Palmas. Keeping in the deep shadows away from streetlights, I hoofed up Hudson Street toward Hollywood Boulevard. Unexpectedly, a black man in dark gym sweats, athletic shoes and a hooded sweatshirt came out of a cheap hotel, Hudson Hotel. He turned and walked toward me on my side of the sidewalk.

I muttered to myself "Be loose Ronnie."

I was thinking that when black guys dress in the loose sports gear with their hoods up it's nearly impossible to make out their features and read their body language. I felt that I knew what was coming. This man would be impossible to avoid on the sidewalk. I could cut and run or I could stop and talk to him and risk getting stabbed and murdered. Hell, this was my neighborhood so I kept walking on. In seconds, we encountered each other on the sidewalk in the night shadows. There was no automobile traffic on the streets at this hour.

"Hey my man. Can you help me out here. Give me a few seconds of yo' time. Jus' talk to me now. I want to give you a gift."

"I don't want anything man." I said.

"Here, take this home for me."

"No. No. No thanks."

"I can tell by lookin' at yo' eyes that you want dis and you won't tell no one 'bout us talkin' here." He stealthily pushed a small revolver into my hand. It was warm. "Keep it. Keep it secret. You own it now. Thank you brother man. Don' show no policemans now."

Then he hurried on down Hudson and disappeared around the corner behind Grandma's Kitchen a little hole-in-the-wall lunch place on the corner at Selma. I stuffed the revolver in my pants and pulled my shirt over it.

I shambled up to Hollywood Boulevard stepping on all the stars in the sidewalks with movie stars names embedded in them. Even the famous boulevard was nearly emptied of traffic after 4 am. At night, the darkened office building with the patriotic name, overlooking the intersection of Hollywood and Las Palmas, had to be entered from the side entrance on Las Palmas, the same damn entrance where I fell down the stairs a few years earlier. The heavy wooden framed glass door was tucked back into a darkened alcove shaded entirely from the streetlights. I fumbled with my keys.

Inside the building, I pulled out the handgun. I studied it myopically as I walked quietly up the interior hallway. It had a black handgrip. It was a clean piece. Black metal J-frame Smith and Wesson, two shots fired and three live bullets left. It was almost the same gun that my father had owned except that this was a smaller frame .38 with a shorter barrel. I hid it inside my office in the back of a drawer full of art materials. I could see the headlines. Elvis Bandit Robs Bank of America. Elvis Imitator Shoots Bob Hope. I could become famous.

I loved the office late at night when the streets were relatively quiet. Hollywood Boulevard was never completely silent. When the activity of nighttime slowed there was a brief period of inactivity before the early morning arrivals began, street sweepers and sidewalk washing, buses and pedestrians gradually increasing. Despite what the Chamber of Commerce would have you believe, Hollywood Boulevard was a magnet for weird snakes after midnight.

I climbed up the ladder to the sky high bunkbed that I had built. I masturbated and then lay quietly listening to the rustling silence of the boulevard. I imagined that my chest muscles were paralyzed from polio and I was breathing in an iron lung like hospitals used in the 1950s.

"I feel as though I am dead in my coffin. Over my head separated by six feet of earth is a tombstone that reads 'Elvis Aaron Presley'. This stuffy coffin leaves me no wiggle room for dancing." Then more blackness followed.

"I mighta had a better time as a Sid Vicious zombie." I thought.

I reluctantly went over to uncle Leo's for lunch after I had caught up on my sleep for a few days. I wanted to slow myself down before our visit because my heart was continually racing and my breathing was exaggerated from amphetamines. I had become highly sensitive to sunlight, it made me feel faint and ill. When I slept I would wrap my arms and legs around Zanna and feeling her warmth, then match my breathing to hers. She consumed much less drugs than myself. I would sleep for maybe three days at a stretch when I managed to sleep, then wake up and purchase a quart or two of Dreyers Rocky Road ice cream and eat it in one sitting.

At uncle Leo's I had to knock on the door repeatedly for nearly ten minutes until my knuckles hurt before he responded. He was deaf. Sometimes more deaf than other times, depending on his mood and the circumstances. He was also prone to turning his hearing aid off if he was uncomfortable with the company; for example if a lady near to his own age, which was mid-70s flirted with him or even spoke to him with a smile, it was off with the hearing aid. He saved his sugar for the young ladies. I heard him descending the wooden steps and I braced myself for the unknown.

"Ronnie. Hi Ronnie. You came over. I am glad to see you Ronnie. I have made vegetable soup. It is very good. You will like it. Did you watch the Lakers yesterday? Terrible. Shameful." He was wearing his battered Lakers baseball style cap and a slate blue Members Only jacket. He was as constant in his attire, which was the fashion among Jewish immigrant senior men seen walking up and down Fairfax Avenue, as I was in mine. His deeply wrinkled face was clean shaven.

"Naw, I didn't see it. Bad game huh?"

"Ronnie, can you help me? There is a bird living with me." We ascended the wooden uncarpeted stairs. I was thinking that this was the apartment where Zanna lived with her mother and uncle after they moved out of the motel on Sunset Boulevard; through elementary school, junior high school and high school. I looked around specifically for vestiges of her mother's life. Not much. A few old photos of Zanna's father who was a well-groomed businessman, her father and mother together, and Zanna's formal high school photo, all placed in cheap frames, still off the perpendicular as they were on the previous visit. There were several pieces of old dusty furniture that no sane man would have purchased, with elaborately scrolled and scalloped wooden legs, budget rococo probably acquired by Zanna's mom.

I looked around in the kitchen to see how uncle Leo's collection of grocery bags had grown. He collected both the plastic and the paper types, separately and together with the paper bag inserted into the plastic bag. The entire laundry room was filled so full with bags that it was nearly impossible to see the washer and dryer. I assumed that several cupboards in the kitchen and the closets around the apartment were filled with grocery bags but I wanted to see for myself. I opened a lower cupboard. It was completely filled with paper-in-plastic grocery bags. The customer usually has to make a special request for double bagging.

In the living room, there was a framed pencil drawing of Pablo Picasso's face and head, drawn on bond paper taken from an art store drawing pad, made by Zanna when she was in high school. There was the same well-worn cushioned chair with the three TVs in front of it, all turned on to the same channel with no sound. The TVs were stacked in the same manner as my previous visit. Two TVs were stacked one on top of another on one table and the third was sitting on a darkly stained wooden small table with the scrolling and scalloping theme.

"I am looking for this bird Ronnie." Uncle Leo began searching randomly around the living room for his quarry. "Where is that goddam bird? It is living in here. Can you get rid of this bird for me Ronnie? It flew in the window and it stays and stays. Oh I give up! I will make you some soup."

I got a close-up look at the old creased photograph taped to the wall in front of the cushioned wooden chair. This was the one specially taped to the wall with Johnson and Johnson flesh-toned adhesive bandages, a photograph of a young lady fashionably dressed from another era, a bygone place and time.

"Who is this lady in the photo?" I asked loudly but uncle Leo didn't hear me. I followed him into the kitchen where he had the soup in a pot on the stove. The linoleum floors were in need of a scrubbing except in front of the stove where they were worn through to the wooden floorboards; same as the linoleum in front of the kitchen sink whose window faced the nearby windows of the adjoining apartment building where another family lived in spatially similar conditions. He lit the gas fire under the pot and shuffled over toward the kitchen cabinets.

"There is the bird!" he said with animation. "Get out of here bird. You cannot live here!" There was a pigeon sitting high up on the shelving where two cabinet doors had been left open. It fit right in. I hadn't noticed it. Uncle Leo grabbed at the pigeon with both hands. The pigeon adroitly moved a foot to the left and stared at him unruffled and curious. Uncle Leo grabbed at the pigeon a second time and the bird moved to the right back to its original perch. A cheap hustling, street smart, filching unwashed bird.

"Ronnie can you catch this bird?"

"You gotta broom? I'll beat the hell out of it."

"What?"

"A broom?"

"What is it that you want?"

"Nevermind. I'll find it." I rummaged around the laundry room among the grocery bags and came up with a broom. I measured my distance to the bird so that I could get an accurate swing and whack it. The bird took one look at me with the broom and flew out of the kitchen through the living room and out the open front window.

"You might want to keep that front window closed. If it comes back, hit it with the broom." I said in an authoritative masculine manner. Ronnie birdwhacker. Just then the front door slammed and I could hear Zanna's footsteps coming up the stairs. She was carrying a load of dry cleaning. I was relieved that uncle Leo wasn't able to find the opportunity to unload a fusillade of questions on me concerning Zanna's employment and her health. We three ate lunch together then Zanna opened his mail and paid his bills. It was nice.

"Tell me again.What is the deal with the photo stuck to the wall in there with band-aids?" I asked directing my question to Zanna.

"You see what I have to deal with? She is an old girlfriend from Poland. He sits in front of the picture and stares at it. He phones her from time to time."

"He phones her in Poland?" It seemed incredible to me that he could phone Poland from America. Poland seemed to me to be less real than Snow White and the Seven Dwarves. It was like an abstraction of a place.

"Yes. But most of his girlfriends have died. Most of his old friends are gone. They're dead."

"It must be tough outliving your friends. And then living here in Los Angeles must make it even worse. L.A. isn't kind to old folks."

"Do you want some pickles Ronnie? I have a jar of very good pickles."

"Pickles? No thanks. No pickles."

"Take some lemons. I have a whole basketful of lemons. They will spoil if I keep them all. I will make you a bag of lemons."

"OK. Thanks Leo. I like lemons." Then I turned to Zanna. "He misses your mom I bet."

"She looked after him his whole life. She loved him so much. Their parents and two sisters were killed in the war. She called him the black sheep but he was her older brother. I miss her. She was wonderful to all my friends. They used to love to come over and visit with her. She used to sing when she was in the kitchen. She would serve them apple strudel cake and tea. She always had a cake here to serve to guests. She was a beautiful singer. Everyone loved my mother."

"The Lakers and the Kings play tonight. Are you going to watch the game Ronnie? I am going to call you. This time you pick up the telephone. When I call you, you pick up the phone Ronnie."

"OK. If I'm there, I'll pick up the phone." A few hours later he phoned. I ignored it.

CHAPTER 14.2–DOWNGRADED TO JUNK: P*NK Magazine put on a super party in Hollywood, not a benefit but a free party. Maureen, a former girlfriend of Larry Benton had taken up tasks on the commercial end of things, PR, advertising and distribution duties. She came fully loaded with female assets. In addition to her eye-catching curves and pretty face, she was a chatty-chatty mouth, perfect for advertising and promotions. She came equipped like all human beings with her own special characteristic personality flaws and foibles which at the time of the big party were less apparent to me than her assets.

She found a wonderful little venue tucked away in the heart of Hollywood with a perfect small raised stage that had not been used previously for rock scene parties and she launched a scintillating buzz around L.A. The night of the party a numerically massive punk in-crowd packed the place. It was exciting. I sprung the Benjamins for several kegs of free beer. All night, the hottest Punk bands in town shredded on stage for the entire evening. The bands ran the stage, shared equipment, mixed the sound and decided what act played next.

Before the party, Zanna and Conrad did heroin together in our kitchen and I was responsible for the consumption of multiple toxins and managed to remain on my feet all evening and never slurred my speech over the din of the crowd and the guitars.

Mostly I said "Hey what's happenin'? Are you having a good time? There's plenty of free beer at the bar. You look great." Nothing too grammatically challenging. I was after all, the host. I kept a booklet of host jokes in my rear pocket.

There was a major contingent of South Bay punkers there from the SST stable, Hollywood veterans and other So Cal areas were represented in metal studs, radical make-up and leather. The unpleasant stress was taken away from me because I really did none of the hands on organizing of the event. Plus, most importantly, there would be no need for me to run away with the cash box because this was a free party. Running with the money was my talent. Maureen had simply put her red talkative lips to the telephone mouthpiece. She was capable of talking on the phone twelve hours a day and loving it. The magazine grew even more popular with her onboard.

To the outside world of the casual viewer, occasional participants in counter-culture events and uncommon extraordinary aesthetic deviance, as well as individuals interested in West Coast punk music, P*NK Magazine had become an impressive cultural statement. P*NK Magazine itself got press in major establishment publications, even overseas. My photograph was taken formally and candidly by people hired to do that. It made me squeamish. I typically felt a revulsion upon viewing a photograph of myself. I was not a media personality performer so much as an unstable borderline threat to society. My living quarters today are filled with several pounds of explosives, loaded firearms, incendiary devices and booby traps. It's all legal. Just make sure you give me a phone call before you visit. Five hungry pitbulls can consume enormous quantities of ground beef. I've named them all five Ronnie, so that if you call my name, all five dogs run at you.

As you might guess, something inevitably went wrong with Maureen's tenure. Her time in the underground publishing world was short-lived. It was patently obvious that Maureen was plotting in her mind to take over P*NK Magazine and commercialize it, but she was running more on a head of steam than business acumen. Although it wasn't her job to be intellectual, Maureen simply had no great intellect, below average possibly in some salient areas. It's so hard to feel sorry for any person who aspired to take-over P*NK Magazine. Feel charity for her.

Maureen was busy schmoozing with the newer subsidiary sub-labels of the major labels, which in Los Angeles tentatively promoted West Coast Punk and New Music Pop sounds, Electronic New Wave and the Paisley Underground, which was stylistically Punked up Psychedelic music. Got that? Pop Punk Rock was put in fresh diapers by cheap babysitter subsidiaries. Maureen was drawing her new found energy like a cartoon superhero from her position at P*NK Magazine. In turn, looking on the plus side, she found several new exciting musical groups we could work into our pages. Her job at P*NK Magazine gave her the ability to gain access to people who would never have spoken to her otherwise. Then she landed herself a job at a genuine subsidiary sub-label Faultline Records owned and sponsored by a major record label. She felt no ethical qualms about performing both jobs, the magazine and the record company simultaneously. P*NK Magazine certainly couldn't pay all of her bills.

On a pedestrian day-to-day level she often lacked even the smallest bit of tact and grace. She went after my little Zanna, a vastly unpretentious talented big cheese art director working at the top in the real world of Hollywood movie making, with the cutting edge Big Boys. A woman succeeding in a man's world in 1981-82.

"How is the housemaid today? I see dirty dishes in the sink. Better get busy cleaning up." Maureen would say face-to-face as a greeting to Zanna at our apartment. Zanna, who could trade repartee with the best of them and do hilarious stand-up impersonations of nearly anybody to perfection would simply walk away and ignore Maureen. When I inevitably fucked Maureen at her apartment, Zanna phoned around seven in the morning. Maureen passed me the phone in bed. We two smelled like sex.

"He's right here." Maureen said gleefully. That pissed off Zanna but it wasn't going to break us up. That was Maureen's probable intent. Zanna and I had a remarkable bond. Zanna had boyfriends. We were loosely knit in some ways and tightly bound together in other ways that people from outside were unable to perceive.

There was the greater problem of alcohol with Maureen. She was a person whose personality split almost like two people inhabiting one body. After just one drink the daft obnoxious minx surfaced. This was not a recipe for success. Functioning alcoholics and addicts seemed to be a normal human condition around Hollywood but Maureen was incapable of achieving the intoxicated Zen of normalcy. She was completely unaware of her drastic character change. I certainly wasn't going to inform her and apparently no one else cared enough to make the effort. After a half a glass of wine she rapidly developed a loud case of B-movie tasteless bitch tramp insanity; two thousand maniacs in one beautiful girl. We had a few wild business meetings at respectable Musso and Franks Grill on Hollywood Boulevard. With one glass of red wine accompanying a small lettuce, tomato and cucumber salad she would lose control. She was engineered like fine Bavarian clockwork, a tiny door in her forehead would spring open and the little bird would pop out of it.

"Cuckoo! Cuckoo!"

It was in this manner that she burned her way through the underground publishing industry and the cutting edge recording industry in the short space of a year give or take a month. Faultline Records wasn't bringing in the kind of money that the big boys at the top of the heap respected and they closed it down. Punk Pop pooped in its subsidiary label diapers. L.A. Punk Rock still looked, smelled and sounded like shit when it came around under the noses of the major labels. Black Flag had been labeled anti-parent by the major industry labels and refused a recording contract. They were the essence of L.A. Punk Hardcore. Not to worry, parents could always advise their thirteen year old teens to purchase Circle Jerks, Social Distortion, and T.S.O.L. recordings.

Maureen left her skidmarks on Sunset Boulevard when they booted her fine ass out and closed the place down. They brought the one or two real company execs back into the main office complex and left Maureen with nothing but a bad reputation and some difficulty sitting on a chafed crack as those abrasions healed. That was about the same time that I was done with her. It's possible that I was told by Larry Benton that Maureen got religion of the born again kind, but I may have imagined that. People were coming and going so rapidly for me at this point that I often missed the details.

A DREAM WITHIN A DREAM

Take this kiss upon the brow!
And, in parting from you now,
Thus much let me avow-
You are not wrong, who deem
That my days have been a dream;
Yet if hope has flown away
In a night, or in a day,
In a vision, or in none,
Is it therefore the less gone?
All that we see or seem
Is but a dream within a dream.

I stand amid the roar
Of a surf-tormented shore,
And I hold within my hand
Grains of the golden sand-
How few! yet how they creep
Through my fingers to the deep,
While I weep—while I weep!
O God! can I not grasp
Them with a tighter clasp?
O God! can I not save
One from the pitiless wave?
Is all that we see or seem
But a dream within a dream?

– EDGAR ALLEN POE –1827
Edgar Allen Poe (1809-1849)
Poe died of an unknown cause,
fallen on a Baltimore street.

CHAPTER 15

Conrad Miller and I had some fun. To my surprise, he was crazier than me. We picked up a military smoke bomb up in San Francisco from the wild machine creators. It looked like a stick of dynamite. It put out ninety thousand cubic square feet of smoke. One night we sneaked it into a nightclub on the Sunset Strip, lit the fuse and the place filled with opaque white smoke. It was a stupid act that could have caused a deadly stampede. It was fun for us and shut the club down for the night. Confused people poured into the streets, fire engines arrived, cops. We had big laughs, then Conrad and me, we scrammed. We took some drugs together now and then, needless to say, but he mostly went downtown and I mainly went uptown, so that was that. On the creative end of it all, Conrad's work made P*NK Magazine look beautiful and brilliantly ugly. The magazine was arriving aesthetically at that Jean Cocteau tenet, "Astonish me!"

Conrad was widely considered by clients around the world, other visual artists, and performers to be a genius with the camera. Rock bands hired him to acquire a daring new exciting image. He employed unorthodox development techniques in the darkroom to enhance color intensities and united his technical chromatic skills with the flattened aesthetic color space of modernist twentieth century painters. In addition, he employed experimental make-up designers. Art history buffs could read influences from Rodchenko, Malevich, Mondrian, and the German Expressionists admixed with high fashion glamour, reductive and visionary. Conrad had no reluctance to descend into the P*NK Magazine pit and reconstruct its parameters.

There was a small clique of young L.A. photographers who shot the hottest jobs in fashion, rock and celebrity glamour for magazines and record jackets. Conrad was among them, maybe at the time he was 25 years old, the best of the group. It was popular among those photographers to have Asian girlfriends; perfect petite beautiful Asian girls. Strangely, as a group of artists involved with fashion, they mostly weren't gay. They lived well.

Then Conrad Miller got himself killed, a sudden violent death. Sometimes those of us who remain among the living seem to be the unlucky ones. He died at night riding on his newly restored antique BMW motorcycle. Conrad's African-American buddy Jack called over to Zanna's. I picked up the phone.

"I just called to tell you and Zanna that Conrad is dead." Jack said. "He was killed on his motorcycle about an hour ago. I can't tell you anything more right now. He was declared D.O.A. at Queen of Angels Hospital." He hung up. Jack was too rattled to carry on a conversation.

"Zanna, that was Jack. Conrad is dead. He was killed on his motorcycle an hour ago." Zanna was devastated. She loved her friends. She had no family to fall back on. Her friends meant everything to her. Her friends were her family and she cherished them.

Conrad's BMW motorcycle was made in 1963 when they still looked kool, before the design of the bike became hideous modern. The restoration didn't last long. He was struck by a car in the Cahuenga pass about 10 pm, hit and run, L.A. style. They found heroin in Conrad's blood at the hospital. People were coming and going too fast for me. Neither Zanna nor myself absorbed his loss with a sense of deliverance and grace, the suddenness of the loss, the open casket funeral with a partial head showing, the unfocused mourning crowd of numerous friends wearing black, and grieving relatives to whom we were strangers. It was a Jewish funeral. I never knew that he was Jewish. Jewish funerals are pretty much like other funerals. There's a dead person and a eulogy.

Other friends who knew Conrad intimately seemed to be aware of a different facet of him that was suicidal. This side of Conrad was not familiar to Zanna or myself. His delicate petite Korean girlfriend told me that Conrad confided in her that he wanted to take up a more dangerous hobby each successive year until he ultimately found one that would take his life before he turned thirty. I told that story to Zanna. She was unfamiliar with this slant on Conrad's mental state. We believed that he enjoyed his life although he was reckless with the narcotics much like the rest of us. I remember one of Samuel Becketts characters said something to the effect that 'Life is a bowl of cherries.' It would be accurate to say that Conrad seemed to have less reason than most people to go hang himself.

Unconsciously perhaps, I sensed my own life's energy wane. At heart, I was an artistic collaborator growing weary of seeking new associations with lesser artists than Conrad. This was one facet of the meaning of that odd word 'entropy,' both physical and metaphysical. Imagine the 20th century deprived of the gifted wonder of Picasso's life and genius. Out of necessity now, I built a photo studio into my live-in cliff side hideaway up at the top of Echo Park Boulevard. I hadn't planned to use it for photo shoots initially but it turned out to be a perfect little studio space that could accommodate set building, a rock group with three, four, five members and all that it entailed to pull off a group shot. I was wearing too many hats stacked a dozen deep. All my hats, Maureens hats, Conrads hat. Shoot speed, work harder, that was my plan. I locked myself into a tunnel vision of possibilities. I was unable to see that my threads were unravelling.

I met a lady, beautiful, refined and offbeat, who typically dressed like a collision between a Christmas tree and Marie Antoinette. At my first sighting, she appeared in the crowd at the P*NK Magazine super party. She looked like no one else on the planet earth. I began seeing her around the late night haunts and curiously walking around on Hollywood Boulevard during the daytime. I even pointed her out to Zanna one day as we drove by her walking up Wilcox Avenue. She was bizarre, with elegant beautiful features and she applied her make-up in a manner that transcended extreme. I was smitten and followed her around nightclubs to the extent that I managed to meet her. She was freshly exported from England with a pleasing soft spoken upper crust speech pattern. She said to me that she had come to Los Angeles, Hollywood in particular to become a TV star. She said that she had hoped that if she wore fashions of her own design and dressed up in character, as I have attempted to describe, that a film or television studio would hire her onboard to do a kind of Lucille Ball style sitcom or movie. Also, she told me that she was an errant member of the British royalty, something like a countess or a duchess. Even with my experience at a British art college, I never gained a knowledge about the different echelons or ranks of British royalty. This young lady's wealthy family was unhappy with her behavior and they completely cut her off financially. Overcoming these obstacles, she stubbornly persisted and made her way through America on her own. Her name was Eppie, short for Euphemia. Eppie never anticipated that the Hollywood show business industry would show absolutely no interest in her whatsoever. She wasn't alone; she made friends with punk rock girls.

I went over to her apartment with some frequency to watch her sew once we had become familiar to each other. Without all her gear and make-up on, just as a plain Jane, she was naturally quite beautiful. We had no sexual relations but not for lack of effort on my part. I may have even resorted to prayer in a desperate attempt to influence any higher powers that would lend an ear over to my way of thinking.

"Please God. Make Eppie fuck me."

I sincerely hoped we were to have sexual relations and our interactions appeared to be moving favorably but not swiftly in this direction. In her presence, I began to be concerned that I now smelled like methamphetamines. Sometimes, when a person is addicted to the chemical, it seeps out through the pores in the skin and gives off a characteristic odor. I suspected that I sometimes emanated from my skin the rank smell of a laboratory chemical. Stinking effluvia was a despicable characteristic that I found repugnant in Andrew Wolfram, former boyfriend of Kitten and scion of good English blood. No matter how sharp-witted was his tongue, his penetrating malodorousness worked its case against him. Was my body now plagued by amphetamine reek which went hand in hand with other probable strong body odors brought on by less frequent bathing caused by interrupted sleep cycles? I asked Zanna. She said that I usually smelled nice but that I should wash my clothes more often.

Eppie was occupying a small studio apartment nearby to Sunset and Wilcox, down by a block or two. I lured her up to my spider's lair, the Echo Park studio, and took photos of her all dolled up. Being a photographer was fun. She didn't doll up like a Playboy Bunny; she dolled up like a pop art historical anachronism from the 18th century with an extreme overdose of Revlon drug store and punk rock make-up. As far as her film or TV career went, she rode a bumpy slow ride to nowhere. Her starship tilted over and fell to the concrete on the launchpad prior to final countdown. She soon realized that Hollywood wasn't ever going to be interested in her much the same way that the eccentric film director Paul Roman came to that same realization in not so small brutal increments. Eppie found work at an elementary level in The Industry, primarily working as an extra in films and TV. That's usually shit awful work for little money. In addition, she sewed products for local fashion designers. For whatever the reasons, she was overlooked, misunderstood and unappreciated both in fashion and as an actress. I had no way of knowing if she was a competent actress. Besides, how far does acting ability generally take a person in Hollywood, crowded with mansions built on nepotism? For her sewing, I suspect Eppie was paid sweat shop wages by L.A. fashion designers who had worked their own way up from the bottom. She was scarcely making ends meet and her conservative family, of course wasn't sending her two pence to be a strange kook in Hollywood. For her own entertainment Eppie would hang out at the Hollywood punk shows with the other wild ladies like Tina Tupelo.

Eppie, after I had known her for few months revealed that she had brilliantly deduced, Sir Arthur Conan Doyle style, a genetic connection between me and a blond girlfriend of hers. "I think I know your sister." she said. "Do you have a sister who lives in Los Angeles named Shannon?"

"I have a sister named Shannon. I haven't seen her for a few years. She probably still lives in Los Angeles."

"She's friends with Spider Black. Do you know Spider Black?"

"Sure I do. I love that guy. He's one of the funniest people I have ever met in my life. He has me in stitches. He hangs out all night at The Zero; sometimes he brings his saxophone in there and plays until the sun rises."

"We've worked as extras on several films together, your sister and I."

"That's interesting but I don't really see her. We don't get along. We aren't close. I had a fucked up family in some indefinable sense. I don't want to bore you with it. We were never brutally beaten or sodomized. We were Dr. Spock babies. Blame Dr. Spock. Did you have Dr. Spock babies in England? Something went wrong."

"Shannon and I have been very close friends. She had that boyfriend Henry who died of a drug overdose. Then she began dating this guitar player guy."

"Henry died? A drug overdose? That's hard to believe. He seemed so squeaky clean, almost wholesome. He had that actor's air about him. No tattoos. Generic good looks. Even Henry was a drug addict? Maybe he wasn't into drugs at all. If he shot up tomato ketchup or mustard, he would've dropped dead, immediately, on the spot. I only met him briefly once but then I talked to him again recently. He was riding a motorcycle up Hollywood Boulevard and he saw me and he pulled over and stopped. We talked for a few minutes. Damn. He was a real nice guy. That's shocking. So where is Shannon now? Is she still living in L.A.? Not that I want to see her. I don't want to see her. I'm serious about that."

"She moved to Las Vegas last year and she was working as a cocktail waitress. She met a guy there, a kind of Saturday Night Fever dresser, if you can believe that. He works for one of the casinos. She seems to be happy with him. He has money and she's been able to quit waitressing."

"You can't miss your jellyroll with a Saturday Night Fever styled man. The BeeGees are forever. I was never compatible with her boyfriends."

"I wanted to ask you something."

"OK. Ask away."

"Do you think that your sister would ever steal from someone?"

"Steal?" I said. That question took me by surprise. Instantly, an image of Shannon running out the back door with my mother's metal lock box flashed across my mind's eye. I felt I should answer honestly. I thought it over briefly, watching Eppie sewing by hand. "Yes. I am sorry to have to answer your query with a yes. She might steal. Why do you ask?"

"Several months ago, last year before she moved to Vegas, she invited me out to dinner. We were out for only two or three hours. When I came home my apartment was burglarized. I had some family gold heirlooms and diamond jewelry and some cash money taken. I thought that possibly Shannon lured me out to dinner so that her new guitar player friend could break in and take my things when he knew I was away. He would accurately have known, give or take a few minutes, how long I would be away from home. Do you see what I'm getting at? The timing is so unusual."

I sat there silently while Eppie sewed, thinking and imagining the scheme and the scene. Eppie never looked up from her sewing. Then I spoke what I believed to be the truth.

"If you're asking me if it's possible that Shannon might have done that to you, I would say that it is possible. She might be capable of an act like that."

This stab at honesty was my big faux pas, foot-in-the-mouth, penis guillotine, blunder, death knell, snafu with Eppie, short for Euphemia. A chill came over the room. The new Ice Age began now. Eppie had transferred her contempt for the jewelry thief over to me. I had better odds now of fucking Nancy Reagan doggie style on the floor of the Oval Office with Ronald Reagan standing by, looking on, wearing a black crotchless latex jock strap and patent leather high heeled shoes. Needless to say, I never prayed for sex again.

Mickey Mike met up with me at a Circle Jerks performance at Club Lingerie in Hollywood. After the show we headed off together to a party down where Vine Street changes its name to Rossmore Avenue, at The Ravenswood, reputed to be the classic old Hollywood haunt where Mae West kept an apartment. Coincidentally, the classic El Royale Apartment high rise a few hundred yards south on Rossmore is an old Hollywood Deco style structure that makes the same claim. By Hollywood standards, a classic old building with plenty of white marble and vaulted ceilings, The Ravenswood of the '80s was open to a casual lifestyle which included dogs and kids running in the hallways, a shaky quaint noisy intermittent elevator, plus beautiful high maintenance women with a high tolerance for swank wild late night parties. We exited the herky-jerky elevator at the sixth floor and bopped on down the hall where we entered an apartment emitting amplified sounds through the door of 'The Gun Club's' *Sex Beat*. Nice apartment. Thick old walls. There was a bald woman possibly in her very early twenties standing on a sturdy wooden dining room table in an interior dining room. She was announcing that it was her birthday or some personal occasion and she was thanking everybody in attendance for a wonderful year in Hollywood. She was one damn good looking bald lady, young and erotic, dressed up in a punky feminine way. The new trend at the punk oriented nightclubs was for the girls to wear only black undergarments as clothing, with the addition of a leather belt and shoes. As she spoke eloquently on the table-top, I imagined her naked.

Mickey Mike began casually fingering his way through the record collection. After 'The Gun Club' album played, Double M put on a new 'Tex and the Horseheads' album, then he went into the kitchen with a friend to find a drink. Mickey Mike often carried narcotics filled syringes around tucked in his pockets, so maybe he worked his way down to the bathroom. I found an old heavy chair and leaned up against the back of it to better observe the convivial group encircling the beautiful one standing on the table. I kept myself separate because my demeanor was not of a convivial nature, not ever really. Moving about the room was another extraordinarily pretty girl, short tawny hair, a petite 5'1". She seemed very much at home, so I figured the two for roommates. We talked for a few minutes over the din.

"Why are you standing over here all by yourself." She asked me.

"Oh, I was just people watching and thinking about billboards. The unseasonal heavy rain and winds over the last two days has caused a lot of the billboard advertising to peel loose around town. I guess that's not something that you would really ever notice."

"You have a strange obsession."

"Well that's true, I do. There's one up on Melrose that's almost entirely peeled off. It's one of those giant billboards, the ones supported on the huge metal pipe structures the size of telephone poles. I want it. I want it really bad. It's got a Camel cigarette advertisement. A pair of lovers smoking cigarettes with some ad copy. I can't figure out how to get up there and get it. I'm afraid of heights. If I get three feet off the ground I get scared. I'm a big chicken. I sometimes imagine that I plummeted to my death in a previous life. I thought that maybe I could rig up a long pole with a hook and pull it off. Just pull it down."

"What would you do with it when you got it? Roll it into a giant cigarette and smoke it or use it for wallpaper?" she laughed.

"I've got this little photo studio up in Echo Park. I want to take it up there and cram it in my alcove and try to shoot photos of some bands in front of it. I bet that just the lettering alone is a foot high. The images would be on a giant scale and you could see the printers separation dot screens."

"I'll climb up there and pull it down. I'm not afraid of heights." At that point, I looked her over up and down. She was a petite sexy knockout. Understand this, I'm not making up pretty or beautiful girls for a spicy narrative. Misguided mastur-bators will have given up on this erotic tale by this point. The girl was beautiful.

"No way. The ladder steps that are built into the poles don't start until fifteen feet up. It's too dangerous and you're too damn pretty and feminine."

"Don't tell me no. I can do it easy. If you can get a ladder to get me up to the first steps on the pole. I'll do it, really." The thesaurus at dictionary dot com has a long list of adjectives and nouns for a sexy five foot one pretty girl pushing nineteen, appealing, darling, dishy, a looker, a lulu, pulchritudinous, an eyeful, foxy, seductive, tantalizing. None of them are adequately descriptive. This girl was simply a perfectly beautiful female, a living sex fantasy. She had all of these lovely charms plus she wanted to perform some elevated acrobatic vandalism for me. This was a good night.

Clarissa was her name and she did, in fact, live there with the girl performing on the tabletop. They occupied this two bedroom apartment and Clarissa went off to her room to put on some bluejeans and athletic shoes. I rounded up the connoisseur of raucous behavior Mr. Fun, Mickey Mike, located in the kitchen telling jokes with several people. We figured to go pick up a ladder that was in the carport down below my studio on the cliffside.

Without vainly attempting to imitate, Mickey Mike was a dead ringer for the 1960s era Keith Richards but now two generations younger; he always got pissed off if anyone mentioned they were look alikes. I would have made this observation earlier on in the narrative, but upon first introduction we had caught Mickey Mike with his pants down and I thought it better to hold off on the description. This was Mickey Mike's fabulous period of guitar stardom on the stages of L.A. To sum him up for you, should the reader be a remedial parser like myself, Keith R, guitar flash, enormous penis, multiple drug addicted, not just a trivial Mr. Fun but reigning King of Fun, there you have his person in a nutshell. He had become a huge nightclub draw, a hot ticket. We used his amp equipment van hoping it would hold the rolled up great damp paper billboard in addition to the ladder, and still have room for the three of us on board. If a black and white rolled by during the act of vandalism we were cooked goose flesh.

Around 3:30 am, Clarissa climbed the ladder, then scaled high up the metal pole to the billboard platform so casually and with such agility and speed, she could have been a featured star in The Flying Wallendas. She moved swiftly across the aerial platform, then down tumbled the giant image. Mickey Mike and I rolled it and pushed it into the van. The entire maneuver took all of five minutes. We three drove it up to Echo Park and unloaded it and put the ladder back. Perfect. It was late at night. Double M took his leave. He was fucking a lady singer who was another musicians girlfriend and she was waiting for him in a warm bed in Studio City.

Clarissa stayed with me in Echo Park. She was stunningly beautiful naked, still a teenager. From the bed, we lay on our backs and stared at the roots growing through my ceiling because the house was so overgrown with vegetation like ivy and creeping vines. We fucked and laughed and played in candlelight. Eerie lonely sounds of the departing freight trains' moaning horns, crawling mile long night snakes moving out of Los Angeles from the vast central city yards carried into the room. The sounds of the Night Ghost, the all night hobo ride to Northern Califrnia. They were the same freight trains that Jack Kerouac rode as the indigent beatnik dharma bum literary king two, or was it now three, generations earlier. My cock was a slippery granite rock and human juices were flowing. It was a good night that rolled on into a great night. Whoooo! Whoooo! Big trains rolling and tumbling through the night.

I never used a condom, not ever. Call me lucky I guess; never had I contracted a venereal disease, with the exception of the aforementioned crablice which need no more discussion. Clarissa was too damn foxy to screw with a rubber hood wrapped over my lucky dick. She climbed that tall waxed pole with great agility and joy. I most certainly was willing to risk a horrible death by sexually transmitted disease to go flesh to flesh with her, commingling warm nectars. Mass media warnings blew away on the invisible winds. We discussed neither disease, protection nor pregnancy. She told me she was legal age sexually. In reality, instantly I forgot to think about it at all. We wanted sex and we took everything that we wanted. She fucked me and then she fucked me harder and deeper again. Although AIDS was killing people, primarily gay men and intravenous drug users, protection obsession became the Generation X phenomenon of a later era when the terminology for HIV was introduced into the culture. It was always my experience that punk rockers from Generation One fucked raw and natural. You could bet the pink slip to the new Porsche that down the road in Studio City, Mickey Mike wasn't shaking his ass in bed with his platinum blond sweetheart after rolling on a condom. One night Kitten told me that she'd already had eight abortions and she was nineteen.

A few days later I took photographs of Clarissa in the studio, not naked or naughty photos, just simple portraits. I am fascinated by great portraits. When I was in London I made several trips to The National Portrait Gallery. I especially enjoyed the Jacob Epstein sculptural bronzes, the portrait busts not his modernist style. On the other hand, I took naked photos of Kitten in Echo Park on more than a few occasions. Clarissa showed the proof sheets to her mom who lived high up in Beechwood Canyon. The roads get narrow and twisted up there as they approach the elevated crest where the famous H-O-L-L-Y-W-O-O-D letters are ensconced on the hilltop. Later that week they invited me up to the mom's house and I went over and had some tea and cookies and we talked about the proofs and made small talk. Clarissa and her mom both seemed to like me. It always surprises me when any person doesn't appear to dislike me on sight which is a most common reaction. In time, I learned to take it as it comes. Curiously, that appalling first impression hasn't improved much as I've aged, even though I have avoided the prison system. Clarissa's photos looked great through a lupe. I promised to make mounted blow-ups of a few selections.

Clarissa told me that she spent several years growing up in New Zealand living with her father. She said that her dad was a former pop music rock star of the 1960s.

I said, "I don't want to know who he is right now. I really like you just as Clarissa here and now in the present. It's not that important to me. Maybe tell me another time. You being a star's kid isn't why I like you."

It wasn't an eloquent statement. She was surprising worldly for a teenager. She knew the bartender at The Frolic Room on Hollywood Boulevard on a first name basis. He regularly served her up free Long Island Iced Teas. She behaved like she owned the place, not just that bar but the whole damn city. They knew her at Dan Tana's. It was fun to watch her operate. She got in free everywhere in Hollywood which meant she had an edge on me. I got in free almost everywhere but solely within the domain of punkdom.

Ian Wright approached me at the casa in Echo Park in the garden. He rarely descended the outdoor cement steps leading below the house to the studio and almost never knocked on the door. My rent was always paid by the due date. I could tell by his uppish stride that he was displeased with me. "I really can't have dangerous people running around my house." he gushed. "They were running around outside the house waving guns screaming that they wanted to kill you." He stared at me grimly.

"Who was doing that? That's bullshit Ian. Nobody wants to kill me. I don't know what the hell you're talking about. If you're going to complain about me, find something real to complain about. Were they killing me for love or money?"

"My boy could have been here. He stays here on weekends. They might have shot my boy by mistake."

"Who might have shot your boy? Nobody is shooting anybody. There's nothing that I can do about this because I don't know what the fuck you're talking about."

"It was The Vandals. They want to kill you."

"The band? The punk band? They don't kill people. They've never been up here. They don't know where I live or anything. The Vandals wouldn't come up here."

"It was The Vandals. I'm sure of it. You have bands up here all the time."

"I don't have a polite response for you Ian. This doesn't seem based in reality. You're mad at me for something I didn't do."

"Well, if it happens again. You'll have to leave. I can't have my boy in danger."

"I'm not worth killing Ian. Think about it. Only a fool would shoot me. I'm not worth the cost of the bullet. Shoot that stupid cartoon moose, Bullwinkle, that's what I'm worth dead. I'll say a prayer for you Ian, because television is destroying your mind."

He walked away. Ian sniffed lines of cocaine regularly. Cocaine can make a person paranoid and edgy. He was my height, my age and he'd inherited this house to live in. I liked to think that I was the more handsome man. He repeatedly emphasized that his ex-wife was an Encino snob, whatever that is. According to Ian, people from Encino were wealthy snobs. Following his line of thought, along these lines, it is a fairly certain hypothesis that a secure wealthy white lady from an upscale white community would never want to own a casa Tijuana in a predominately Latino neighborhood near downtown L.A., nor would she ever come to visit Echo Park, even in an armored truck. This castle was all Ian's, one hundred percent. To my disappointment his ex-wife never once showed up.

It was after hours at The Play, a habitual all night hideaway for nocturnal individuals, and I was standing around. It had an illegal bar that served until sunrise. Mickey Mike was approaching me with a bounce in his step. He was carrying a putting iron golf club and he had a golf ball palmed in the other hand.

"Dubba M., Mickey Mike. I was admiring your putter. You can never practice too much golf."

"There's a group of us who play out in Griffith Park once a week. It really is fun."

"Well, it's a gentleman's game now isn't it. Those of us who lack refinement and skill, keep to miniature golf. Have you seen El Duce in the other room? He's rolled and wrapped up top in an American flag with his pants off down below. He's got some huge monster giant gonads. I should put them on the cover of my magazine. You may want to check them out just for scientific curiosity. Maybe National Geographic magazine would be interested in his native genitalia."

"Say, I think we may have scared your landlord, Ian Wright. He's a little bit uptight isn't he? I want to apologize if we did."

"That was you? You tried to kill me."

"We didn't mean to scare him, we meant to scare you. Rocky collects weapons. He has machine guns, hand grenades, all different kinds of guns. Me and Rocky and Sawtooth Bob were hanging out and I said 'Hey let's go scare Ronnie. We'll pretend we're gonna kill him.' So we took these guns and went up to your place.

They were real guns."

"I heard about it. Ian was pissed off. But I am too cunning for small time thugs."

"Rocky brought a fully automatic Thompson sub-machine gun. They call it 'The. Street Sweeper'. It's awesome man. It has one of those round magazines that hold like a hundred bullets. I had a .44 magnum caliber pistol like Dirty Harry and Sawtooth Bob brought an Arkansas Toothpick. That's a hillbilly fighting knife that's got a blade fifteen inches long. We looked awesome. We knocked on your door and shouted 'We're gonna kill you Ronnie! Come out of there. We hate you and we're gonna kill you!' But you weren't home, so we ran around the outside of the house shouting 'Ronnie we're going to kill you!'"

"Ian thought you were murderers."

"Of course, they were real guns but they weren't loaded man. We made sure they weren't loaded. But when we ran back into the car, Ian came down the back steps and Rocky shouted, 'The Vandals are going to kill Ronnie Kale.' Then we drove down the back way because Rocky's studio is in Frogtown. Do you know Sawtooth Bob? He's a funny guy. He's missing a couple of teeth. He plays harmonica for me sometimes."

"Yeah, sure I know him. Ian was scared for his life. I just said that to Ian I wasn't at home. Don't blame me."

"I'm sorry if we got you in trouble man."

"Ian said 'They could have killed my boy by mistake'. Forget it. I don't have a problem with it. I don't care. The place has roots growing through the ceiling. I still have the office at Hollywood and Las Palmas. It's actually a better place except the vibes off the boulevard lead me into strange kinds of trouble. Do you know that Ian has a reel to reel tape, the wide tape not the skinny cheap stuff, of a Big Billy studio recording session. He's a beautiful singer. He's as good as any blues singer ever. It's an amazing recording and it'll never come out. Billy and the band can't agree on any of the legalities. And Gerardo refuses to sign his name to any contract of any kind. They still are having fistfights with each other."

"Look over there. Here comes Ian." Still holding his putting iron, Mickey Mike walked over to him and apologized. It looked like Ian was giving him a lecture on civil responsibility and gun safety. Then Ian took Mickey M's photograph with a wild looking punk girl in his arms. That was the kind of photography that Ian did, semi-candid images of people on the scene in Los Angeles. He had a conflict of interest going this night; he wanted to lecture Mickey Mike but he wanted to snap his photograph because he was a celebrity guitarist. Ian knew he could sell the photo on Monday to a newspaper gossip column. Ian came over and talked to me briefly. He was placated, even happy. Heck, I coulda blown up his house with a pipe bomb.

I formulated a plan to attempt to photograph a punk band a night for two weeks up in Echo Park. That meant building a new set each day then shooting photos into the late night. I used the cigarette ad billboard, hacked down a hillside of tall bamboo and dragged it inside, spray painted squiggly graffiti shapes on scrims and plywood, built flimsy structures, dragged in discarded toys, mix-matched a zillion variations of objects trouvé. I loosely borrowed from Conrad Miller's graphical book of tricks when it suited the situation.

Poor Conrad was buried, not cremated. Apart from the spiritual mumbo-jumbo, I was at times subjectively disturbed at the thought of him quiescently interred underground on that vapid graveyard hillside. Stiff, bloodless and cold he lay imprisoned underground in a dark lonesome hole for eternity or until Los Angeles slides into the ocean. Likewise, you and me, my friend, we're waiting next in line, whether we court death or shun it, to be taken in sacrifice by the demiurge. Nobody really gives a crap if and when you go unless you're leaving them money. Get a window seat and try to fuck the cute stewardess in the toilet.

Crammed with art stuff from set constructions, the studio took on a magical surreal air. Musicians became excited when they arrived. There was a buzz going around L.A. about my use of strange sets and techniques.

There was no telephone installed up at the Echo Park studio because I didn't want one. Upstairs at Ian's there was one, possibly two telephones, but I would have to be in the throes of a heart attack before I would climb the cement stairs and knock on his front door to ask him for the use of his phone. He had showed me his collection of two hundred empty cocaine glass vials on my previous visit upstairs. So what.

"Can I use your telephone Ian? It's just for a local call. My heart is fibrillating. There's a blood clot in my brain. And I'm kind of in a hurry. I've been shot, here and here. Here's five dollars. That should cover any charges."

I enjoyed being cut off from the world when I was up there. This self-imposed isolation from modern communication links meant that I necessarily drove back to Zanna's and over to Clarissa's nearly every day to make telephone arrangements for the next evenings shoot.

For a month or six weeks I had been spending nearly all of my free time with Clarissa. We became pretty tight. Zanna was being worked like a coal miner doing double shifts at Worldwide Films. She didn't have time to miss me. The vainglorious newly empowered Israeli entrepreneurs were launching multiple film campaigns for Hollywood movies that weren't even in production, dozens of film campaigns. Many of the scripts were as yet unwritten. The trade papers were filled with Worldwide Films' colorful promotions for films that were in various stages of unreadiness. Ultimately, only a few campaigns were for actual new movies with real movie stars. Worldwide Films did create several major hit movies from their formula for low budget productions making for sweet profits accumulating astronomical multi-digit numbers. This pumped up marketing strategy gave Worldwide Films the appearance of a major super studio launching an enormous amount of product. Zanna's in-house gang did all that promotional work.

Old-timer movie stars and famous directors gave Zanna wild gifts of appreciation. She had a major career for a woman in that era, but she was enmeshed in a corporate burnout scenario which extended from the corpulent ruling twosome up top, down to the unimportant little people. Gratuitously, I was on salary there for nearly a year. Again, Zanna hired me and fired me in the space of a week. The termination paperwork was lost in the business office. I continued receiving checks. Certainly, it wasn't my responsibility to complain. It was so difficult to say no thank you to free money. Worldwide Films sent me payroll checks and I immediately cashed them. After several months riding on the gravy train, I insisted that Zanna cut off the checks out of fear of Uzi retribution from the Israeli mafia. When Zanna first got the job, I rode up the elevator to the fifteenth floor with a poorly dressed fat man whom I assumed was the janitor. I am a good judge of character. That fat janitor was the crazy creative idea man driving the film production. He owned the company and he wrote many of the scripts. His partner was an accountant, the bean counter with the magic abacus. They created Worldwide Films.

He would yell at Zanna in marketing meetings. "This is not red. When I say red, I don't mean this piss shit red you geev me. Red is blood red! I want blood red! All my life is little people like you telling me what is right! You leetle people do not listen to me. I am right! Geev me what I want! Geev me blood red! Here! Here! Here!" He stabbed at the graphic image with his finger.

When the sequence of photo sessions was finished, I took three, four, maybe even five days off and slept over at Zanna's. Clarissa's place was too busy with lively human party traffic for a long sleep. Clarissa didn't have to work for a living and she and her roommate had a gaggle of friends. I watched cartoons and 1960s TV re-runs and then slept another day and another and another. Hawaii Five-0, Bonanza, Gilligan's Island, Popeye, Smurfs, Laugh-In, Rocky and Bullwinkle, Mannix. I spent one whole day where I shaved and scrubbed myself and washed my clothes. Late afternoon, I connected up with some friends in Venice who happened to deal methamphetamine. They had multiple careers. My friend Terry and his girlfriend Severina. Terry, another guitar player friend was currently on tour with his band 'Shrivs' and bubbly brash Severina did the honors of dealing methamphetamine by the gram. She was the blondest person I ever met short of being an albino. Her eyelashes were white blond shading intense blue eyes. She talked rapidly and her sentence logic always curled around in humorous quirks and non sequiturs and she would laugh at her own remarks. She made me laugh.

I hadn't been over to Marcos for a short time, partly because I had acquired even yet another speed dealer Donny, a friend of Kittens. Donny had long hippy style hair and he wore primarily green army surplus clothing. He would come over and sit on Zanna's couch for two days at a stretch, like an immovable object. Sometimes I wasn't up for a long visit. Donny wasn't annoying, he would mostly sit in one place and stare with a sinister demeanor. He was anchored so securely to the leather couch, I can't recall him even taking a bathroom break during his visits.

"Last night me and Donny were skin-popping." Kitten would say with delight. "You should see his kitchen. Last week Jester threw a jar of mayonnaise against the wall and it exploded all over everything. And it's still there stuck to the wall stinking. No one will clean it up." Jester was Donny's roommate. That alone may have been the reason that Donny spent days at a stretch glowering on Zanna's couch.

I came back from Venice and then went over to Herbert's studio to look at the results of his latest P*NK Magazine photo shoots. He said last week that he was going to try to arrange studio photo sessions with '45 Grave' and a new girl group who self-produced their own recording, a 45 single, that obsolete format recording with the big hole in the center. If you feel any nostalgia for 45 rpm records, you know that you're an old fart. Those girls were one of Maureen's finds although Maureen had moved on perhaps to strange new territory. Planet Maureen or something equivalent.

"What's the name of their band?" I asked.

"I don't know. I mean they don't know. They don't know yet themselves. They said they might call the group 'The Bangs'. But that could all change. I have their single on tape, two songs. Have you heard it? It's two sisters and two of their girlfriends. I like it. It's not punk music. It's '60s pop."

"I was working for two weeks straight on up in Echo Park and then I spent the better part of last week sleeping it off. I haven't heard anything new." Herbert played the songs for me. "It goes against my grain Herbert because it isn't punk rock. It's pop. Really great pop. But I don't have a problem with it. I think I love it."

"Let me show you the photo I shot of them."

"You da man Herbert. This means I don't have to go through proof sheets." Herbert had them nailed; 60s-ish pop clothing, mini-skirts, low camera angle giving a monumental look to their girlishness, raw industrial background.

"That's pimpin' hot shit Herbert. It's totally perfectly hot."

"'45 Grave'. I'm still working on them. They have to show up over here all at the same time ready to work. I'm not that far along."

Herbert and I talked and schemed about going out to the San Fernando Valley to photograph an eccentric artist, one who worked with pen and ink. We concluded that we might surprise him by showing up at his front door with a camera at 7 a.m. Catch him in his pajamas with an erection. I went back to Zanna's, ate rocky road ice cream and slept again in front of the TV with the sound low so Zanna could sleep. About noon the next day, I rode the '52 Ford on up to Echo Park. It had a new rebuilt transmission, the second one I had put in.

I pulled into the carport below the house. It was a hot day. 'L.A. is a desert city.' People always tell you that when you complain about the heat. The cement steps wound through the foliage and up to the landing giving access to the bottom part of the house. There was one window in my studio overlooking the cliff, the 5 freeway and Frogtown, with the backside of Mt. Washington in the distance. Leading up to the window was the ladder from the carport maybe twelve feet high traversing the vertical cliffside covered in lush ivy vegetation and leaning up against the side of the house, touching at its highest rung the bottom of the white trimmed window sill. I noticed that the house siding was done entirely in brown shingles, a detail I hadn't perceived before, being so entirely self-involved. A burglar, I surmised. I climbed the steps to the landing and found the front door was locked. I turned the deadbolt on the steel security door and then unlocked the original brown painted wooden door. It was a one doorway, one window studio.

There was Clarissa, her head resting strangely sideways on the low glass table in front of the couch. Dead. She was wearing blue jeans and bare above the waist. Her body was on the floor wedged between the couch and the table. Her stench was vile. I stopped. Her eyes were partially open with white slits like her eyes rolled up. Her mouth was open. There was a dried puddle of drool on the glass below her mouth. A yellow jacket wasp made busy, crawled into her mouth, crawled out of her mouth, flew around in a circle and landed on her chin. She had a syringe bent in the crook of one arm that twisted down to the floor. I first thought of a heroin overdose but she wasn't blue; although I had never seen a heroin overdose, so maybe skank users didn't die blue. Beautiful Clarissa.

She wasn't high on my drugs. It wasn't my syringe. My syringe was hidden in a tool box under art supplies in a clear plastic bag. I went over and retrieved it. It was so overused that the needle was crooked like a corkscrew and the plunger wouldn't push down unless I put a little vaseline on it. One night alone, I saw that it was squirting out vaseline when it pumped down to the bottom and I became frightened that I was injecting vaseline into my bloodstream. Vaseline came out of the needle like a micro toothpaste stream. So I hadn't used it for three weeks. I put the old crooked syringe in my pocket and locked the place up. The wasp ruled the roost.

I didn't alert Ian or attempt to use his telephone. He could have smelled the dead body through the floorboards but he always had cocaine up his proboscis. I was dazed with shock and fear. I got in the car, drove it down the back overgrown hillside where the road narrowed to one lane as it threaded along the cliff. At the bottom, I drove to the 5 freeway access. I headed off in the wrong direction. It took me north instead of south through downtown. I tossed the syringe out the car window into the 5 freeway heavy truck traffic and then exited at Griffith Park. From there I made my way over to Zannas on surface streets. The driving seemed to take an eternity. The faster I wanted to go the slower the traffic dragged.

I wanted to cry. I tried to cry. I couldn't cry. I can't cry. Maybe I'm shallow or numb. Maybe I don't feel the human emotions in the correct sequence. Kindness, sadness, grief, remorse, anguish, happiness, love, anger, all come out screwy at the wrong time. With me a bad experience gets internalized and digested slowly through the tissues, deep into the knotted back muscles and neck. Maybe I shouldn't be thinking about my feelings when someone else is dead. Maybe I am emotionally defenseless, taking pain down deep where it can do the most long term damage. Little Clarissa died. Ian was going to evict. Her mom. Her mom loved her.

"He has temper tantrums." My dying mom told Zanna.

I finally arrived at Zanna's flat. I called Zanna at work and told her what happened. We discussed the removal of illegal drugs. Zanna had none. I put the speed purchased from Severina in an envelope, put a stamp on it and mailed it to Kitten at the post office a block away. I certainly wasn't going to flush away good drugs if it wasn't absolutely necessary. I telephoned Ian and put him on short notice so he wouldn't have time to do anything stupid. I told him to hide his drugs if he had any on hand, the cops were going to be visiting the house in thirty minutes or less.

"Why? What's happened?"

"Just do it Ian! Shut up and do it! The cops will be up there in a half an hour. There's a dead girl downstairs. Don't go down there until the cops come or you'll be involved in a murder investigation. Don't go down there." I hung up on him. He was a wild card. He might tell the cops that 'The Vandals' killed her.

I called the police by getting the number of the downtown L.A. police station from telephone information. There was a dead teenaged girl. I told the cop on the phone that I would meet them up at the house. I said I was at a pay phone and that I would drive up to Echo Park in ten minutes. When I pulled my car up to the Echo Park house there was already a black and white out front, up top by the front door. The hilly road up there wound in front of the house and then U-turned around under the back side of the house. A uniformed cop was talking to Ian outside the front door. Ian pointed at me as I drove by. There goes the perp! They both took a good long look. I drove around below to the carport and parked. What a fucking mess. I walked up the back steps where I met a police officer on the landing. I handed him the keys. He handcuffed me and sat me down on the cement steps. He instructed Ian to stay up top or he too would be handcuffed.

Clarissa's car wasn't around, I wondered how she got up here. She definitely expected me to return sooner than later. It was four or five days that I hadn't seen or spoken to her. I had taken myself out of circulation. More police arrived. A paramedic. Then came the detective, Sherlock. A real big guy, white shirt and tie, six foot four, muscular, losing his hair, alert, inquisitive, controlling.

I had told my story to the uniform. I repeated my story to the detective. They called for the Coroner. The detective said that I wasn't yet under arrest. He wanted to talk to me at length downtown. Now. I could drive myself but if I didn't show up in thirty minutes he would have a warrant issued for my arrest. He mentioned possible murder charges, corrupting a minor. I told him that I wasn't up here with her and that I could basically prove that I was at home on Oxford Street for nearly a week. The girl brought her own narcotics and spike and climbed in the window. She was uninvited. I didn't murder anybody and I didn't supply the drugs.

The detective wanted to discuss the facts in a controlled environment and I assumed with a tape recorder. I told him that I would talk to him freely without an attorney. He wanted to know if the girl was involved with the punk band 'The Vandals'. I told him that Ian was an idiot. That comment didn't go over too well. He released my handcuffs and told me to report to the front desk downtown. The officer there would have my name sent up to homicide and the detective would come and get me. I had trouble finding the police station even though I knew where it was. Then I got charged five dollars for parking.

The tall muscular detective was both overbearing and cordial at once. His questions were incisive and they cut at me from surprising angles. It was my salvation that I was well rested and straight as an arrow for these sessions. It was probably my being on a secret mission from God to publish a Punk magazine that saved me from culpability. I explained what I did for a living, the tacky tiki diablo loco graffiti themes in the studio, the cigarette billboard, my abundant supplies of liquor and beer for the bands, the 50 cans of aerosol spray paints and most importantly my relation to the deceased girl.

There was the dual mystery touching on how she arrived there on the relatively remote hillside; and from whom had she acquired the narcotics on which she overdosed with a hypodermic syringe. I was unable to supply the homicide detective with any information on those two questions, or where she acquired the disposable syringe. Detective Sherlock let me go home but not until he invited Zanna down for an interview. He told me not to make any contact with Clarissa's mom or her girlfriend roommate. Zanna arrived and I departed. We passed each other at his office door. She looked at me somberly.

I was a free man for two days so I stayed indoors at Zanna's. The big shot inquisitive detective Sherlock called me the morning of the third day. He wanted to talk with me mano a mano tete a tete in his office again, now. On the way out the door I heard Ian's voice on the answering machine. He was leaving me a message telling me to clear out of his house if I wasn't in jail already. I met my detective after lunch hour. One o'clock. More grilling.

"Did you supply Clarissa with the hypodermic syringe? Can you tell me where Clarissa may have purchased those drugs we found on your table?" His questions were impossible.

"I don't have a syringe and I don't know what the hell she was taking. Street drugs. I'm guilty of publishing some crap, you know that. But I don't know what drug she was using. Party drugs. What killed her? Drugs are everywhere. There are a hundred bars and nightclubs and shows on any one night in L.A. nowadays. Generally, people overdose from heroin if they're gonna die. Clarissa partied all over town with movie stars and with punk rockers. She knew everybody. She was a kid. She loved to party. She probably took all different variety of substances. She wasn't an addict. She liked to have fun. She was troubled. Many youth are fucking troubled. Listen, I don't shoot up little girls and she broke in up there." That was the best response I could rally in the face of a possible murder or manslaughter charge.

"At the time she died, Clarissa had methamphetamine on the glass table and in the pocket of her jeans, in the syringe and in her bloodstream." He paused, looking into my eyes behind my thick eyeglasses. The detectives penetrating eye contact dissected me like a power tool drilling through my brain. I vainly attempted to cultivate a studious appearance for my interrogations, my hair was soft and natural, no cheap teased hairspray. This day, I wore a long sleeved blue plaid flannel shirt. No use having him stare at my tattoos. "And sulfuric acid compounds common to automobile electrolyte, more commonly known as battery acid were found mixed with the methamphetamine, inside the syringe and in her bloodstream."

"What? Someone put battery acid in speed! Excuse me." I closed my eyes.

"Enough that she might have bled to death if it was inhaled into her sinuses. Her injection of that garbage into a vein put her down hard. The entire gram she carried was poisoned to kill."

"I don't believe it. That's sickening. What a horrible way to die." I opened my eyes. My eyelids were heavy and sticking together. I had a migraine headache starting up.

"We're investigating Clarissa's death as a homicide Mr. Kale. We want the seller. Believe this. When we find the person responsible, he or she is looking at a murder charge. There is a killer out there or a deadly prankster."

"You can't catch'em. Someone probably just gave it to her for free. She never had to pay for much of anything. Here, I took some photographs of her last month in Echo Park." I pushed three photographic prints across the table. "I'm sorry sir. I don't have any more information. I was at home sleeping off a hard couple of weeks work."

"We have you Mr. Kale. Are you an amphetamine abuser?"

"I have already answered that question. I have no record of drug abuse, drug arrests, drug possession or selling drugs in any state in the Union. I don't sell drugs. I try to be a good boy but I'm no angel. I've got problems, read my magazine."

"I want the dealer. Clarissa's mother and father want this dealer found and taken out of circulation permanently. Now get out of here. You run on the same party circuit. Provide us with more information when you can. We'll be in touch with you. Stay in town. These are serious charges. The party is over Ronnie."

I stayed clean another several weeks out of paranoia of police surveillance. The L.A.P.D. drew blanks about Clarissa's contacts and whereabouts on the eve of her death or murder. Her bald sexy roommate must have given big detective Sherlock a snow job because she knew plenty more about Clarissa than I knew. As the weeks rolled by, I felt myself submerge down into an obvious conscious mental depression by slow increments. Under observation, the cops might have found me shuffling to the convenience store to purchase cigarettes and a Penthouse magazine with the purposeless gait of the walking wounded straggling around the grounds of a mental hospital. I should have become somewhat inured to unhappiness, taking into consideration that I had probably suffered from depression unknowingly since the age of six when the angelic phase of my being expired gradually and the tantrums began in earnest. People who suffer from depression can be severely depressed and not be aware of their condition. That may have been my perennial condition.

It's my own personal bias, but I always avoided and sidestepped psychologists, psychiatrists and psychotherapy. Physical therapy was plausible but mental therapy had never been an option for me. Like a backyard gardener, I prefer to do my own digging around inside my struggling little dendrites and synapses. Soon after she left her teenage years, Shannon became an enthusiast for psychotherapy. There wasn't a great deal of progress made in her case over the years that I noticed from my layman's point of view. From my perspective, people continually involved with various mental therapies never discover the person within despite the intervention from outside professional assistance. Then again, the seeker may discover that the person within is simply a miserable wretched creature not a sparkling diamond in the black coal. If Shannon looked within, she would surely find poodle excrement.

Consider the torture therapies, electro-shock, various techniques for lobotomies, cold baths; used in conjunction with sedative drugs like Thorazine or Prolixin creating in effect chemical lobotomies, these techniques have not been uncommon among mental health professionals. Keeping this under consideration, I decided that it would be best to let time heal my wounds. Let the professionals employ their skills on other minds who actively sought out their expertise. My mental mess was going to remain my own, a dark dirty labyrinthine maze leading down to the lonely sociopathic monstrous moaning minotaur.

I dropped off three framed photographs of Clarissa up at her mothers house; leaned up against her front door around midnight with a saccharin commercial sympathy card expressing sincere regrets in gentle platitudes. It was my coward's way out. If Clarissa's mother had wanted to see me, she would have telephoned me at Zanna's.

After several weeks I began to slip-slide back into my old lifestyle. Drugs and clubs and bars and bands. The new issue of P*NK Magazine was printed and I was taking care of my distribution duties. It should have been a great time to be social, riding the wave of enthusiasm from the new issue. Most of the original punk rock crowd from the late 70's had dissipated for a thousand and one reasons. That was one more small depressing detail in my overall frame of reference. I moved my publishing activities back into the Hollywood and Las Palmas office.

Terry and Severina, and Donny by way of Kitten were my current crystal meth connections. Donny refused to deal with me directly now because he thought the police were following me everywhere. I owed Marco and Royal a thousand dollars for drugs on credit so I wasn't buying from them. That's not such an enormous amount of money in the big scheme of things. I told this to Kitten one night when I was picking up several grams of meth from her apartment.

She said, "You owe those two guys money. Oh my god! Don't tell me this.

Ronnie wake up. Those are the wrong two guys to owe money. They break your bones if you cross them. I know from experience they can get nasty. Then they finish you. Royal fucked up pencilpud Irish Red. You were dating his girlfriend dontcha know. You must be crazy."

"Dating whose girlfriend?"

"That Clarissa girl was Royal's girlfriend. She dumped him."

"She was not."

"He thought she was."

"Oh man. That's weird that this is the first I've heard of it. When was this?"

"About six months ago maybe. They had a short fast one. Then she ran."

"Yeah but I only met her a few months ago. That woulda been after Royal was history. I can pay Marco back the green now that the magazine is on the stands."

"Royal followed her around so bad that she had to move. Dontcha get it? He got scary on her. He's a way narly prick. She moved out of her apartment and got a roommate from Sacramento, that foxy slimeslit babe with the bald head and they moved into that big white expensive building together, down below Vine Street and Melrose, The Ravenswood. Fancy place. It has a 24 hour concierge at a desk."

"You don't think Royal OD'd Clarissa with battery acid meth. That would mean that she was still talking to him."

"You didn't hear it from me. He probably meant it for you and she took it. Maybe he didn't care which one of you he got. You didn't hear it from me twinkiedick. Some philanthropist sure spoiled your hard on."

CHAPTER 16

I phoned Marco from a phone booth. Now I was cautious about police phone taps and surveillance. He picked up the call, no mechanical answering device.

"Yeah."

"Marco?"

"Yeah, what do you want?"

"This is Ronnie. I'm gonna send you a check for the money I owe you. Can I get your street address and zip code just to make sure it goes to the right address."

"I don't want a check. This isn't a grocery market. Make it in cash, and add ten percent for late charges. Just slip it under the front door in an envelope. Don't mail it."

"OK. You'll have it tomorrow."

"If you say so. It's been several months. Too long." He hung up.

On Hollywood Boulevard in my office, I conceived of a double issue, double the P*NK Magazine, double thick, more color, more writing, more art and hopefully more advertising. I had run into a girl from my art college, Ricarda, who expressed an eagerness to hustle ads. She was conspicuously short which is not a bad thing in itself, somewhere under five feet, and in general appearance moderately unattractive, which was emphasized by her dull conventionality in fashion. Prim. When she went out to court clients, she wore a woman's business suit purchased from Bullocks department store or Robinsons and she looked like a fashion don't, just slightly ridiculous. From the clients point of view, she didn't meet the immediate expectations of a salesperson from a notorious punk publication and she exhibited surprisingly demure manners.

I had once sold an expensive full page ad to a nay saying record exec by rolling around spasmatically on his office floor crying "Please please please. Without this ad I'll die here on your carpet!" Ricarda's approach was perhaps a little too far in the other direction.

On Ricarda, the power fashions never looked adequately powerful. She was the advertising equivalent of a physically small police officer wearing an oversized uniform. Ricarda struggled. She sold an insufficient amount of advertising space over several weeks time and then by that point, she was rapidly wearing down by attrition. When we saw her flailing, Zanna and Kitten teamed up with her to pursue some clients. They helped her along considerably. Zanna even hired Ricarda to work part-time freelance as a junior graphic designer at Worldwide Films. Ricarda settled in there, joyfully wielding her T-square, a little too conveniently for my liking.

I had forgotten about the waterbugs loitering in the men's rooms at Hollywood and Las Palmas; goddam cockroaches on steroids that were at home submerged in a pipe full of piss and then were able to leave their liquid medium to walk adroitly on land; in addition they appeared to have a set of capable wings aptly equipped like large exotic grotesque flying beetles. Equipped for land, air and sea (pee), this was an advanced inner city creature. Thanks due to Charles Darwin, no doubt. This time around, I learned that it was a grave error to paint them with aerosol insect killer; Black Flag or Raid had the same effect. After spraying a big one from close up, maybe nine inches, it turned on me in a face to face confrontation and adopted a battle stance. Rapidly moving forward, stepping high with military goose steps, it revealed hideous spiky legs; with wings fully extended, it ran at me and chased me out of the room. My skin was crawling and rippling with shivers and goosebumps of fear.

The tightly knit punk scene formed around the original Masque had long ago vanished from Hollywood Boulevard. Now there was an all night diner hangout about two blocks to the east that cultivated an intense white trash scene, but no musicians or artists, just trash. Kings Palace, up near Argyle where I had once seen NYC's 'Suicide' perform, had become an Indian Restaurant and then that was reinvented and transformed into a punk rock music club adopting the same name as the restaurant, Rajis. It was fun and crowded and noisy but it lacked the social impact which the Masque had in its day. To its credit, Raji's had a wall near the bar lined with colorful pinball machines that provided many including myself with a reason to keep living another week.

I was toying with the idea that the double issue P*NK Magazine might be my swan song to underground publishing. Punk was giving way to other styles. Cable music television was forcibly burying the Los Angeles creative originators whom I held dear. The TV video generation created by music television was borrowing the hardcore punk stylistic nuances without the content. In addition, punk gestures of themselves seemed to have grown clichéd and impotent through repetition. The essence and the power of the punk rebellion was to be found inside the songwriting of the punk bands. Their radical appearance increasingly became simply a part of the general American visual milieu but the songwriting from those early bands remains today radicalized and potent. If you switched musical genres entirely and grabbed an earful of Grandmaster Flash and the Furious Five's hit song 'The Message', there was a similarity in rebellious attitude to punk coming from African-Americans. More to the point, original punk music, first suppressed then reprocessed, was disarmed and broadcasted out through cable television in bright commercial packaging twenty four seven. The commercial media manipulations performed on the hippie generation had become accelerated and more perfidious in the punk era.

The Ramones, the greatest original punk group, remained essentially an underground band, globally popular, supremely influential but mass media pariah dogs, the real deal. In a seeming contradiction, the American punk music scene itself was bigger than ever and growing. Maybe too, I was simply wearing out. Big industry money was the true old God same as the new God. P*NK Magazine never worked the angles the slimeball execs played in the record industry game. This was underground publishing. Inevitably, it had to be short lived.

MORE BUG TERROR IN HOLLYWOOD: I was writing about two-thirty (Chinese dentist time) in the morning wired on amphetamines believing myself to be inspired. I went into the men's room. Peed. Met the Incredible Hulk of Waterbugs coming out of the pee drain, a bullish self-confident bug. I remembered that someone had told me in a bar that waterbugs (what those creatures are named in common parlance) are generally attracted to humans in a friendly sort of manner. I found that notion disturbing and with that in mind rushed out of the bathroom. Back writing about 3 a.m., I felt a rustling in my hair. I reached up and found that the jumbo skookum waterbug was perched on top of my head. I felt it with my nervous hand. Possibly it was reading the page that was scrolling in the typewriter. I sprang up vertically in a high jump knocking over the typewriter, the table and the chair. Screaming, really screaming, at maximum lung power volume in the middle of the night. Heart pounding from adrenaline accelerated by crystal meth, I spun in dizzying circles looking for the bug.

Panting heavily like I had run a mile, there was no bug around to be seen. My heart was hammering. Maybe it had used its wings and taken flight by air. The incident may have been a tactile error of misinterpretation by my fingers, possibly my imagination, but I couldn't settle down all night. Then, searching for the waterbug, I found an errant girl friend's pet snake. A runaway teenage girl had given me her pet snake in a small glass aquarium to keep for her while she was homeless and it had escaped the glass cage. I was never so happy to encounter a snake. No prickly spiked legs and wings and pincers, I picked up the sleepy little snake with beige stripes and put it back in its glass home.

Due to my malaise and unhappiness, I purchased a large quantity of LSD from a lady I knew in San Francisco. As a hobby, she collected the hallucinogen in its blotter form. Different batches of blotter acid were and still are I assume, typically imprinted with fascinating psychedelic graphic artwork. She had an extensive library of the blotter sheets. She collected it ostensibly for its unique imprint of artwork. She framed entire sheets of one hundred doses and she would hang the framed pieces on the walls all over her house. Her LSD portfolio was remarkable and quite famous in a secret way because it was illegal. Tina Tupelo once told me that she held the job as the person who dosed the LSD onto the blotter sheets. Put that on your resumé.

I wanted to feel happiness again and I knew that LSD was at least good for positive sensations that lasted for ten or twelve hours at a stretch. Also, I was cognizant that the drug graced the user with a certain universal religious awareness which I felt was being sucked out of me by Hollywood Boulevard. Acid Zen. The FBI would deny it, but it's real. I could have chosen to study Zen Buddhism like the contemporary composer John Cage, but I didn't have the free time at this point. This was a hurry up kind of happiness which I was seeking to achieve. A positive rapid jump start into the sci-tech mutated future. Acid and virtual reality minus the Disney themes. Borrowed William Gibson visions of booting into new worlds.

While I was up in San Francisco, my LSD lady took me to The Deaf Club. It was a punk rock night club that was run entirely by deaf people. The club owners and all their employees were unable to hear the loud guitar music and drums but they appeared to enjoy the social ambience of the crowd. I was certain that the deaf were experiencing the rhythmic sounds and percussion in a visceral manner. Some employees, perhaps were only partially deaf. There were paper tablets with pencils at the bar for ordering drinks. I had fun, knew many of the musicians up there, then soon returned to L.A. with my booty.

On my short San Francisco trip I even forgot to get morose about my dead parents which is an intrinsic reason I stay away from the Bay Area. Landmarks recall my childhood. There are of course magnificent landmarks there. My quirky relatives permanently alienated by my sister lived both in San Francisco and Marin County; and then another sad memory was that both parents croaked in that white painted Stanford Hospital a decade apart. They died, they expired, they croaked, they kicked the bucket, they checked out, they passed away, they rode low budget cremations to the end of the line in this material sphere, they were carried into grace and freed of their worldly sufferings by the hands of the Lord. And then, curiously, their spectres were, years later, murdered viciously in my dreams, night after night, although not every night. Some nights I never slept. Some nights they were allowed to rest.

When I returned to L.A., the big kicker happened. I began taking the LSD daily in addition to my amphetamine use; some days taking more of one chemical than the other, although it's difficult to equate the two. Zanna claimed that I had the biggest methamphetamine habit in L.A. In the 60s, the underground head publications had always warned against the duo. It was common knowledge among stoners that speed plus acid was a freaky mix of chemicals. Amphetamines were known to create bad LSD trips. They certainly intensified the experience. I noticed that after a week of continuous LSD use that the hallucinations ceased. From frequent repeated use, the chemical had lost almost entirely the potent hallucinatory effect that it had initially. Consuming LSD after an even longer extended use of several weeks, the drug just became mildly uplifting to my moods, barely noticeable. I increased my daily dose to ten doses of LSD some days, maybe twenty doses on other days. A dose being one perforated detachable square from the blotter sheet. Individuals commonly consumed one dose per trip.

I enjoyed walking up to the Chinese Theater on Hollywood Boulevard at 5 a.m., wearing my Ray Ban sunglasses, and waiting for the first tourists to arrive; then the next small group would straggle in, and the next until by 8:30 a.m., the whole area was already crowded with excited tourists. They arrived from all over the world. As the morning progressed they rolled in by the busloads. My favorites were the Japanese. They showed such delight on their faces. The Japanese, most of all, appeared to believe they were somewhere fantastic. Even the American tourists themselves did not disappoint with their unabashed enthusiasm. Marilyn Monroes tiny shoe print. Beautiful! R2D2, C3P0. Awesome! During this period of time, I showed up there daily, early in the a.m., like clockwork, and observed.

This arrival of the first tourist, became to me like a religious event, a ritual with rules and customs that must not be violated. In accordance with this etiquette, I never spoke to a tourist, never touched a tourist, never altered the path of discovery of a tourist, or attempted to capture their rapture with a photo snapshot. Within my own code of dress, I attempted to keep a low profile. I simply stood there, morning after morning, having stayed up all night, as unobtrusively as possible, stoned on LSD and methamphetamines, wan and expressionless, wearing wraparound RayBan shades, black engineer boots, blue jeans, a black leather biker jacket and I witnessed the coming. The endlessly flow of tourists was fantastic. This was not an actual religious pilgrimage the tourists were on but it seemed so precisely similar in essence. Here was a day-to-day manifestation of the early primeval power of the mass commercial entertainment film, television and radio mediums. As time progresses they increasingly rule over us like Supreme Deities. Hi-Def. Broadband.

The daily stream of tourist crowds was massive and never ending. The tourists never suspected that someone would come to that spot solely to watch them. After stepping into the footprints and measuring handprints with the film legends all around the courtyard, the tourists would drift up Hollywood Boulevard looking at the stars names and icons beneath their feet, soaking in the full effect of The Hollywood Walk of Fame. Curiously, many of the Hollywood Boulevard businesses were failing. Lucille Ball cookie jars and tea cups, James Dean T-shirts, Three Stooges dolls, heavy-metal headbands, T-shirts and belts could be found for sale in store after store. Perhaps the struggling souvenir stores needed to diversify the variety of their chachkis and make them more contemporary, religious or pornographic. No one wanted my opinion.

The less fortunate of the tourists, saddled with a regimented militaristic tour guide, were forced immediately to return to their tour bus and depart for another tourist destination. In truth, there was nothing much to buy on Hollywood Boulevard but tourist crap. Well, to be completely fair, there were a couple of great book and poster shops available dealing with the subject of Hollywood movies; and a block away was a Hollywood Wax Museum which was inferior to another Hollywood themed wax museum located to the south of Los Angeles. In the wax museum outside of L.A., the viewer could actually look up a sexy waxy Nancy Sinatras mini-skirt and see her white feminine scanty panties reflected through a mirror placed on the floor. How thrilling that was. There was a Pussycat Theater two blocks east of The Chinese Theater, soon to be made obsolete by the home video market for porn, that had posted on its marquee either 'Deep Throat' or 'The Devil In Miss Jones' year after year. No handprints, imprints of any kind or remembrances for Linda Lovelace at the Chinese Theater.

Ultimately, observing the repetitions of the emotions of the tourists upon their first arrival, their wandering excitedly around the theater courtyard in a frenzy of discovery, the group photographs, and then their eventual meandering away, sometimes with their group and sometimes simply paired in twos, observing the unending predictability of their reactions made me feel Godlike. I would then walk back to my office by late morning. Sunshine made me feel ill. Still in the habit of avoiding the Brown Cowboys at the shoe shine stand, I preferred entering the building from the keyed side entrance on Las Palmas.

On Saturday night, Monifa came over to visit me. I'd know her since she was fifteen years old, back when she played guitar in a teen brat punk band. She was a sweet African-American girl, still a musician, now maybe eighteen or nineteen. She enjoyed eating imitation crab meat with melted butter. Monifa stayed overnight. She took LSD with me although her dose was only a single blotter square, it was potent. We talked all night. As it is accustomed to doing, the unstoppable sun rose. Sometimes that annoyed me. It was too bright in Los Angeles and it meant that all the people would begin rushing around. Hurry. Hurry. Well, this was a Sunday and the rushing was subdued. Monifa and I were relaxing taking in the new day. In fact, we were hanging our heads out my second floor window at the corner, overlooking Las Palmas Avenue and the intersection with Hollywood Boulevard at around 7 a.m., I was explaining about the idiosyncrasies of life in this uniquely positioned office, at this busy and sometimes entertaining corner in Hollywood.

First and foremost, I explained that this was the ideal perch for the Hollywood Christmas Parade and the lesser known St. Patricks Day Parade, omitting the anecdote about Black Dick and his racist graffiti. The office had a pizza parlour just below and the Las Palmas Newsstand was located conveniently across the street. The Newsstand appeared unchanged except for the vintage of the cars from the way it appeared in the famous *on the run* scene of the 1949 film noir classic 'Gun Crazy'. I recalled also how a movie company was shooting a car chase, explosion and shoot-out scene for a movie in the middle of the night on Hollywood Boulevard just two weeks previous. Another Saturday night there was a lonely Christian evangelist who preached at the top of his voice until five in the morning across the boulevard on the street corner where the Gold Cup Coffee Shop once was.

On yet a different morning, I walked out into the hallway through my office door around 6:30 a.m., timing my exit to precisely when the coffee shop on the eastern corner of Las Palmas and Hollywood opened up. I walked right into the middle of the filming of a 'Stairway Up to Heaven' episode, a current television show. They were shooting in the hallway just outside my door. There had been no warning notices given out by the building management. The crew had never made enough noise during the night that I heard them setting up equipment. I stumbled out in front of the running cameras, the crew and actors, tweaking on my happy drug mix. Cut! From behind my sunglasses, I saw famous TV stars with their jaws dropped open so that I could view their dental work. Salvador Dali would have loved this moment especially if I was carrying a pet aardvark. My sudden stardom surprised the hell out of me as much as the entire cast and crew. I wrecked the shot but maintained my dignity and outward composure as a scruffy professional office rat.

There was only one possible subsequent inference to draw as I shuffled downstairs to get my coffee and donut. This was not my opportunity to be 'discovered' accidentally as new Hollywood talent. When I returned the cast and crew were all waiting around for me counting minutes and seconds. They were friendly as they might have been to Charlie Manson. I was clearly as high as an unbalanced space satellite. That's all right, I paid rent and wasn't on their payroll. I said my hellos, shook a few hands, dished out a few compliments and then went back into my office. At the risk of setting an unpleasant tone, I had two shit pissed off TV stars blocking access to my office door. Big deal. None of them was a Dirty Harry or a Charlie's Angel. Plus, the crew was blocking the door to the men's room.

Monifa and I were laughing about this misadventure and the allegorical morality themes of that particular TV show while we were hanging out the window enjoying the morning air. We watched inattentively as a 1960s Chevy pick-up truck pulled up alongside the curb and parked. I noticed that it had a flying falcon or hawk crudely spray painted on the passenger door. It was a faded blue truck with non-matching faded green doors and some patchy paint spots but no dents and all the chrome was intact. A well dressed man got out of the truck then turned toward us. I was shocked by his supernatural appearance.

"Do you see that guy Monifa? What is that? It looks like a demon or a devil. Can you see him? A devil."

"Oh my god!" she said. "That's scary. I saw something like that once before."

"That's not a human and it isn't some dopey actor."

"That guy is real but I don't know what it is."

This being appeared to be completely evil. A dybbuk, diablo, hellion, Evil One. It was either a he or an it. It irradiated evil. It boldly walked in broad daylight. He walked across the street and walked into the coffee-donut-pizza-burger place which occupied the open corner on the east side of Las Palmas at Hollywood Boulevard. This was where I got my usual early morning coffee and donut. When it was open to diners, the restaurant had no front doors, just iron roll-up grates which they opened and closed coinciding with business hours.

"Watch this." I said. "He's walking in there, and they won't notice a thing wrong with him. He'll change his appearance to look like a human." He disappeared into the interior. It was operated by a young married Korean couple who never seemed to get along. They were always fighting.

This was the only time in my life where I completely panicked. Fear overwhelmed me. I ran screaming around the room. "He's gonna kill us. He knows we're here. We've got to escape." I threw open the office door and ran up the main building hallway where they were recently filming 'Stairway Up to Heaven' a few weeks earlier. No heaven here today.

I screamed! "Monifa let's get out of here. Hurry up Monifa! Run!"

I ran down the stairs located in the center of the building leading to the ground floor entrance at the Cowboy Brown shoe shine stand. It was early Sunday morning. The shine stand was closed and the building itself was chained and barred shut at the wrought iron gates. I ran up to the bars leading to the Hollywood Boulevard sidewalk and shook and pulled at them in a hopeless frenzy. Then I turned around and ran to the rear door. It too was barred shut.

I screamed in fear, "Oh shit. We're trapped. We can't get out. It's gonna kill us in here!"

Monifa who had run after me said, "It's going to be OK Ronnie. I don't think it's come here to Hollywood to get us today." I was completely wild-eyed.

"Let's go back and see where it goes when it comes out!" I whispered. I turned around and ran upstairs and back into the office. Good luck that it was a Sunday and early in the morning. The Brown Cowboys would have chased me out of Hollywood. This was just the kind of behaviour that they needed to witness to get me tossed out permanently. We ran into the P*NK Magazine offices and looked out the window. There it was again, exiting the restaurant with a cup of coffee in its hand. And no, it didn't have a claw.

"Look, when he gets past the threshold of the iron roll-up gates he'll change back into a demon." The demon walked across the street carrying his cup of coffee. It was the most terrifying horrible sight I have ever seen. This anthropomorphic spawn of hell exuded omnipotent overpowering evil.

"What is it Monifa, is it the devil? Why is it drinking coffee on Hollywood Boulevard?"

"Why not. Devils can drink coffee too, just like humans." She said. "I know I've seen that thing before."

"It's not a white devil. It looks darker." I observed.

The malevolent being entered the pickup truck. The Chevy truck engine kicked over and the old pickup made a U-turn and rumbled back up Las Palmas toward Franklin. It rolled away and gradually disappeared from sight. My personality was irreversibly altered.

"We both saw that in the plain light of day. There was no vagueness about it." I asserted.

"I saw it too. It was scary." Monifa stated wide-eyed.

About an hour later I took Monifa home to her cheap apartment off of Santa Monica Boulevard and drove myself over to Zanna's. I told her what I had seen in a trembling voice. She laughed at me and dismissed it as just another wild night.

There was a demon on the cover of a Marvel comic on the black glass table top in front of the black leather couch.

I said, "It looked like this!" holding up the comic book. "Its face looked a lot like this drawing of a monster Zanna." She said that I should get some sleep and that there were fresh groceries in the refrigerator. Then she went to work. Because of Zanna's disbelief, I revealed no more about the continuing progression of my unique visions to any other ordinary human.

Looking through my same eyeballs, this was the same world that I had been born into, but I was seeing it from within a completely new reality. From my preternatural experience with Monifa, I had gained unique permanent insights and enriched perceptions not commonly sensed by most human beings. I was at a point of rapid ontological growth where I felt that I had the ability to perceive phantasms and demons that other ordinary individuals could not see. My mind was awhirl with medieval gargoyles, demonology, the suffering of Poe, exorcisms and biblical prophesy, hallucinations, parallel spiritual dimensions, and flotsam and jetsam from Mario Bava's 'Black Sunday', Lucio Fulci's gothic horror 'The Beyond' and H.P. Lovecraft. I read up on ancient witches Mother Shipton and Isobel Gowdie, and the living San Francisco satanist Anton Szandor La Vey (1930-97).

I believed that I could see the essences of evil and good fluidly moving through this world as on a breath of wind. The powerful demonic influences were able to gain a grip on hapless persons and then capture and destroy human souls. There was a devil walking the city streets arm in arm with mankind dealing out malevolence and destruction. From what I could deduce from my firsthand empirical observations, my Devil was an Old Testament styled demon, similar in many characteristics to the one from the Book of Job.

Over the next few weeks, I continued dosing myself with methamphetamine and LSD and the purity of my visions improved dramatically. My observations drew me to the conclusion that our world and beyond, in fact the entire universe, all of creation, was involved in a desperate cataclysmic struggle to the death over morality, Good versus Evil. Good Wrestlers versus Bad Wrestlers. Good Food versus Fast Food. Good Driving versus Bad Driving. Good Politicians versus Bad Politicians. Good TV versus Bad TV. Good Mommys and Daddys versus Bad Mommys and Daddys. Good People versus People possessed by Evil. Every passing thought or fancy of every individual contributed to the outcome of the whole in eternity. If the Evil conquered the Good, the universe itself would be annihilated entirely through insurmountable destruction. Every personal act was a piece of the infinite mosaic puzzle leading to universal annihilation or holiness and salvation.

Mostly, almost entirely, I was now able to see through the disguises of the many of the Agents of Evil working on earth. I never saw directly any angelic forms or energy but I believed that I was driven by their Powers. I felt them to be the imperative driving me toward a new course of action. In non corporal ethereal forms, destructive nefarious demons attempted to enter into the souls of humans. The evil in the eyes of the possessed couldn't be dissembled or hidden from my unerring perceptions because the eyes are, as everyone knows, the windows to the soul. There were of course exceptions to the rule, such as blind people and other individuals with disabilities. Pinheads, for example, which were rare.

Unlike other common men, I had seen a genuine sinister infernal Devil in the flesh walking the streets of Hollywood, boldly in the harsh light of day, brazenfaced and cocksure of its power. I believed that I needed to move against it. As my situation progressed in the space of a few weeks, I came to believe that I was the leader of an elite clandestine L.A.P.D. police force empowered to track evil and destroy it. This secret cadre had been empowered by the United States government and its written Constitution to use ultimate force, should we need it to remove the more dangerous demonic threats to humankind.

These Special Officers communicated solely via Telepathic Messages. At great personal risk, we kept all knowledge of our unique mission hidden from the day-to-day common policemen and women, so that we would not risk exposure of our Crisis Action Force to the general public and the media. My own enhanced state of perceptions came and went, in and out of my mind by degrees, but my overall directions were perfectly clear. I was now tracking local Demons. Every small part contributed to the good of the greater universe. Although I attempted to maintain the appearance of business as usual, I had stopped my work publishing P*NK Magazine immediately with the initial appearance of the malevolent creature drinking coffee outside my offices. Had it dropped a small but powerful sinister talisman inconspicuously below my office? Now I was worried about evil pixie dust. Shit. That's fucked up.

Monifa was lost. The next time I saw Monifa, she was on the television. My girl pal Monifa had made the local evening TV news. She went down in person to a prison facility in Southern California where she was waiting to meet with a serial murderer who had terrorized the Los Angeles community with brutal slasher killings, a criminal who was obsessed with satanic emblems and drew them in blood at the scenes of sacrificial death and murder. She told the TV news reporter that she hoped to marry this serial murderer. She was a young woman in love. Seeing Monifa on the news absolutely convinced me that she had been adversely affected by the creature we had viewed that Sunday morning.

When I digressed from publishing, I began making compulsive colorful drawings of fiends, hellions and spectres. All varieties of Beelzebub, Mephistophles, Lucifer. Then I painted this demonology directly onto the fourteen to eighteen foot high walls in the major two rooms of the office. I mixed spray paints, acrylics, gouache and oil paints. It was a fantastic looking environment. My mural illustration skills were simply amazing. A pure vision of Hell, although I imagine Ronald Reagan's proctologist viewed similar visions. I cropped my teased hair in favor of a skinhead. I also initiated the Top Secret Coca Cola Can Project for the Telepathic Police Cadre. Using my moniker 'Liverhead' as a code name, I undertook an important new high risk hush-hush priority one operation.

One afternoon, I made a bizarre crazy remark to a large muscular African-American man while waiting in line in the 7-11 store near Zanna's fourplex. He turned back and looked down at me and then he ran out of the store. I felt I was gaining in power. I have never been able to recall exactly what it is that I said to the young man. It was a strange offhand remark that contained a reference to the game of golf, shooting a birdie, and inserting a long tubular metallic driver handle end up into his rectal orifice by a foot or more. My comment and demeanor took the big fellow by surprise. He may have been troubled by the narrow five inch strip of beef liver taped to the crown of my head with surgical tape. He forgot to take his items on the counter. Several people in the store turned to me and stared.

I made a necessary trip to the hardware store picking up a metal file, a variety of tapes, sealants, glues, band clamps, rubber plumbing connectors and plastic pipe connecting parts of different sizes. Then I went to Pep Boys automotive and bought a couple of oil filters. Back at the office I went to work filing the front sight off the barrel of the revolver, then fitting the pieces together taping, sealing, gluing and clamping my chosen variety of makeshift items tightly, whatever fit where it was needed, culminating in a Coca Cola can which I had filled with the insides of the oil filters, heavy steel wool and epoxy sealant. It took me about a week to build the structure onto the barrel of the .38 Smith & Wesson, a home made silencer.

While the glue was drying on the .38, I set about collecting the clothes I would need to dress myself up as a punk girl. I had trouble walking with the spike heels so I settled for a pair of orthopedic black nurse's shoes which I picked up at a second hand store. Tina Tupelo helped me round up most of the items so that I looked correct stylistically. Short tube mini-skirt, a girlie tank-top, bra, panties, make-up, a handbag, the works. She was great. She didn't question why I wanted to dress up as a punk girl. The platinum blond wig, I took from Zannas closet. It fit perfectly. She never wore it. It had bangs and then straight hair down to the shoulder.

When I was at Zannas one afternoon that week making preparations, Conrad's former girlfriend, petite Korean and extremely pretty, showed up at the door with her new girl pal. Prior to his subterranean entombment, Conrad had two girlfriends, the one he lived with who had moved to New York City after his death and this one, his outside Asian girlfriend Jane. I knew Jane better than his number one girlfriend.

"Hi Jane." I said, surprised to see her. "C'mon in."

The two of them marched inside. "Can I use your bathroom?" The caucasian girlfriend asked imperiously.

"It's down the hall to the right." I said.

She went off down the hall and Jane followed. "I think I left some of my clothes here." Jane said. Jane went into Zanna's bedroom and walked immediately into her closet.

"That bitch stole my clothing. I know it's in here." Jane shouted.

This was highly unlikely if only one took into account the height and overall physical size differences between Jane and Zanna. Zannas clothes began flying out of the closet and onto her bedroom floor. Jane was inside the closet going through her clothing in a frenzy. I hurried down the hallway in time to see the girlfriend standing in front of the toilet casually vomiting like an open fire hydrant. Heroin, I thought.

"Let's go down to Melrose Avenue or something and get a coffee or just hang out." I said. "I want to get out of here Jane. We can come back later." I had to get them out of Zanna's apartment before it was trashed and Zanna's clothing, jewelry and make-up items were stolen. Through my experience wrangling intoxicated punk rock bands at photo shoots and interviews, I had learned to keep the mood elevated and to shift the crazies in the desired direction. To my surprise it worked with these deranged women and we three filed casually out the front door, which I double locked. We all got into Janes beat up Jap economy car which was parked at the curb and drove off, with me occupying the rear seat. Edna was peeping at us through her front curtain. This was just a bump in the road, nevertheless these junkie women were fucking with my epiphany.

"Let's just go back to my apartment." Jane's girlfriend ordered more than suggested. I don't recall her name so she can be named Ms. P, which is an abbreviation for Prostitute. This friend of Jane's was so obviously a hardened prostitute heroin addict. It's not easy to overlook those two avocations combined in one lady. She opened her small nine inch by six inch handbag and no less than forty hypodermic syringes burst out of it. Ms P had some difficulty cramming them all back in after she located her lipstick which was washed away by the vomit. I was hoping to be back at Zanna's in one hour but now this had become a digression from my suggested short drive to Melrose Avenue for a coffee. Ms. P lived in a studio apartment off of Fountain below the Sunset Strip between Fairfax and La Cienega, one of those buildings comprised of around twenty units, two stories tall with a small cement courtyard containing two or three struggling plants; built in the 1960s, square, boxy, and flat roofed with thin walls, painted white with grey trim, a typical Hollywood luxury apartment for meager incomes, with the familiar overhead ceiling style with sparkles.

We were in Ms. P's apartment for a couple of hours. She spent her time on the phone setting up a narcotics pick-up with a first interlocutor and then in a series of shorter calls with a central supreme madame, she booked an important job which included Jane. Jane seemed intimidated and servile, not with me, but towards Ms. P.; Jane was behaving like a neophyte in the profession. A heavy invisible chain linked Jane to the bossy lady, Ms. P., and Petite Jane was noticeably strung out exhibiting characteristics of heroin addiction. Jane had shaky hands. Strangely, she was behaving in a freakish manner that paralleled heroin addicts as they were commonly depicted on television police dramas. Life imitating TV imitating life. As a dedicated methamphetamine addict, I held their heroin addiction in some disdain. My buddy Mickey Mike was different; he took speed or he went with the heroin, he didn't seem to care much either way.

I only wanted to get back to Zannas but the time passed by relatively quickly. The two women were so screwed up that their presence was in many ways entertaining. Ms. P was self-assured, confident and dominant. Jane's personality had undergone some extreme detrimental changes since the death of Conrad the previous year. Previously, with Conrad, she was effervescent and fun-loving with sparkling Asian eyes. Currently, she was a beaten down bitch dog. She was so changed that this was the first time that I didn't want to fuck her on sight. So much of what makes a person attractive and sexy lies in the mind. Jane's mind was on the run rolling down a sewer sluice pipe.

We three were sitting on the bed. I noticed again the ceiling, comprised of glittery flaky snow-like material, only now I was counting the sparkles in binary numbers versus decimal number systems. It impressed me that the bed was made up with a decorative fitted bedspread. Ms. P again had her purse spilled out and she was sorting through a pile of syringes, make-up items, keys and cash. She ordered Jane to get herself cleaned up and ready for a busy night at the Crown Aventura Hotel in downtown Los Angeles, a modern high-rise hotel, expensive and classy. Jane immediately made herself busy with her clothing, hygiene and make-up. They were hired to work a businessmen's party after a convention.

"You got an extra dress and a wig because I could use a few extra dollars? I can work the sloppy drunks. Hit'em on the head with an ashtray or a TV and take their wallets. I'll stack their bodies in the closets." I couldn't get a laugh or even a wry glance from either of them.

During my attempts to make upbeat small talk that afternoon, I noticed that Ms. P had thus far exhibited no sense of humor whatsoever. With all those syringes spilled out on the bed, I remarked to Ms P, "I've heard of guys shooting up in their jugular vein to get high faster."

This was the only time she exhibited any enthusiasm toward me in casual conversation. In fact, she and I were by now both wondering what I was doing there in her apartment. I wanted them to give me a ride back to the Z-pad and Ms. P was figuring how to ditch me.

Her eyes opened wide and she looked into my eyes. "That's nothing. The guy upstairs, Dennis," she pointed up at the ceiling for emphasis, "he shot up heroin directly into his heart."

"Into his heart? No. He did not. That's impossible. First off, the needles aren't long enough." I pointed at her disposable syringes. "You couldn't do that because they just won't reach."

"Oh he did it. He got a long needle and he stuck it in through his chest." she replied straight out.

"So what happened to him?"

"He had a heart attack."

"Ouch! So he's dead."

"No he's not dead. But he's doing better now. He's upstairs recovering. He's much better now than he was." She began systematically packing her small purse and urging Jane to hurry up. Nevertheless, despite her urgings, when we left the apartment, the sun was down. We entered Janes car in the same configuration as before; Jane was doing the driving with me in the back seat. She was so small behind the wheel, barely able to look over it. Curiously, Jane wore a scarf arrangement over her head not unlike the manner peculiar to Muslim women. It may have simply served to protect her hair styling but it also obscured her eyes and face, if it was bruised. Ms. P gave Jane directions which took us a short distance east along Fountain Avenue and then we parked on a side street. Ms P jumped out of the car.

"I'll be right back." she said.

She walked across the street and disappeared behind a row of hedges concealing either one or two red brick apartment complexes. Ms. P could have been good looking if she cleaned up, lost the waxy complexion and a few conspicuous open facial lesions covered over by make-up. She shot up in her legs and feet. After at least an hour or ninety minutes passed, I convinced Jane that she should walk across the street and seek out Ms P.

"She's probably nodded off removing her Tampon. She may not wake up until midnight or later." I repeatedly coaxed Jane who was physically trembling in fear of Ms. P's ire and from heroin withdrawal. Jane got out of the car and ran across the street and disappeared behind the hedges. Another hour or ninety minutes passed. Eventually, the pair of them appeared from behind the hedges and walked to the car. They both climbed into the car. Stoned (skanked?) on heroin. Ms. P showed an obvious disappointment to find me still occupying the rear seat.

"We're really late. We've got to hurry." Ms P said. She turned to me and said, "We don't have time to take you home. You have to get out of the car now!"

"You're going to have the worst fucking night of your life starting right here and now. Take me back home now or we're gonna ride the terror train to hell." I had seen inside her purse. She wasn't carrying a gun or a knife unless there was one in the glove box or under the car seat. If they didn't drive me home I was going to crash the car. Ms. P had figured that out.

Ms P looked at me coldly. "Take him back. Hurry up."

It was after midnight when they dropped me off on the curb outside Zannas. I hurried in. I wanted to clean up the vomit in the bathroom and the mess in Zanna's closet. Zanna was at Worldwid Films, still working. With the mess cleaned up, I drove up to Hollywood Boulevard and parked in the lot behind The Pioneer Spirit Building.

Upstairs, I began laying out my special operations items in an orderly manner, the women's clothing, the surgical tape, my contact lenses, the weapon with the improvised silencer. I realized that the weapon needed to be transported in a briefcase of some kind so that the silencer wouldn't get jostled. It wasn't a compatible shape with my women's purse. I switched from the purse to my portfolio briefcase that I sometimes used to carry my camera, film and a lunch. Tomorrow I would begin sub rosa stalking Marco and Royal by parking up the street and watching their movements from a safe distance. I borrowed uncle Leo's antique binoculars from Zanna to use as a visual aid.

Sitting inside the '52 Ford for several hours at a stretch was not at all unpleasant. The interiors of earlier model American cars were conceived to give the rider the comfort and space of a small cozy room. For the first few nights I wore everyday clothes. I observed the coming and goings of the main players as well as the carefully paced arrivals and departures of their discreetly selected customers. Not that this was even slightly unfamiliar territory to me. I had been in and out of that apartment two or three nights a week like clockwork over the past few years, until I accrued the debt I mentioned.

The speed addiction added some regularity and order to my life. That was one positive side to it. Then the bad boys refused to extend my credit beyond a thousand dollars. Well, it was initially a crummy two thousand dollar debt which I had paired down to a thousand and then I couldn't pay that off for several months. They became unsocial, but I didn't expect to get my arms broken in an alley behind a nightclub. On TV, the sucker needed to owe his bookie at least twenty thousand dollars before the hoods were sent over to knock his dental work onto the floor. I was safe.

I knew everything about Marco and Royal and I knew nothing as I have told you. Marco was an extremely social creature and he loved to be seen at nightclubs and chic secret after hours clubs. Royal wasn't social in that way but he kept himself busy enough that he might show up anywhere unexpectedly. He moved about to different patterns, an outcast's outcast he was. Obviously, they did a cash business. Someone had to handle that aspect of their work on a daily basis. Marco couldn't be watching their money from a nightclub and they didn't make the kind of income that could be reported to the IRS. I figured Royal wasn't manipulating the tax books at night but he was handling some large amounts of cash and quantities of narcotics that needed to be safely and routinely concealed and transported. It was laughable to imagine those giant hands holding a sharpened number two pencil and writing small decimal figures in a ledger book. The most likely situation would be that they kept a heavy safe somewhere in that duplex and then did the same at various other remote less trafficked secure locations. I ruled out the use of a loose floorboard and a fake wall socket. That's just too amateur.

I knew that Marco and Royal were criminals in the sense that they were professional dealers. It was their sole line of work. As a user of narcotics, I wasn't at all familiar with the day to day working methodologies and practices of the professional drug dealer, so I watched them from my car with binoculars. I noticed that Royal went out later than Marco, sometimes with a girl, sometimes alone in a cab. If he went with the girl she had dark hair styled like Bettie Page, she drove a new model large black Lincoln. I was always partial to women with Cadillacs of any color. Royal was unaccustomed to doing frequent after hours nightclubbing. I knew because I had rarely seen him out at one of those joints. He stayed in the apartment between midnight and two, either solo or with his lady friend before he left. Royal went through many women, sometimes they died. I wasn't familiar with this new sugar lollipop in the Lincoln, but I never paid Royal much real attention.

I'm not sure how many nights I watched out there. Enough nights. On a friday evening when there were several kool shows around town with big name out-of-town groups, I dressed myself up. I heard that Nick Cave was supposed to play and also I knew that Stiv Bators was hanging around in town just to party. Marco would be sure to want to catch up to those scenes.

I went up to the office. With surgical tape, I strapped a narrow strip of fresh beef liver onto my shaved head. This was my lucky talisman, uniquely mine, a primitive visceral preparation derived likewise from the ancient Greeks as well as from modern genocidal African gunmen before a battle. Then came the blond wig, placed on my head over the securely anchored animal organ meat. I had shaved my legs and chest. Spackled the pig with Revlon. Contact lenses. Then on with Tina Tupelo's girlie clothes. Among other qualities, I lacked enough of an ass and hips to be a sexy chick and my tits were a bit lumpy under the bra. Apart from these small details, I was well disguised. Figure this, after 2 a.m., I looked like a foxy woman to a fat stupid lonesome drunk.

I might at least make it as new competition for the black transvestites that regularly worked the Hollywood Walk of Fame neighborhoods and for some odd reason those same trannies drifted down onto Western Avenue near Zanna's fourplex. We were on familiar terms. They always waved to me because we saw each other in both neighborhoods all the time. Now here was I, me one of them. Good to be somebody else. I is another person. Like Rimbaud. Adrian Piper. Theater and the Plague. Artaud. Anton Szandor La Vey. Scorpio Rising. Invocation of My Demon Brother. Lucifer Rising. Bobby Beausoleil. Killed Gary Hinman. Detective Sherlock. Book of Job. Devil Black John. Francis Bacon. Screaming Pope. Frances Farmer. Lizzie Borden. Liverhead Woman. Black Widow Spiders. Shoot Poison Speed. Four On The Floor Murders. Spahn Ranch. Barker Ranch. Cease To Exist. Chemical Lobotomy.

"Never console yourself into believing that the terror has passed, for it looms as large and evil today as it did in the despicable era of Bedlam." That quote from Frances Farmer looped obsessively round and round in my mind.

I carried a tackle box and a portfolio briefcase and put them in the car. I put some extra gas in the trunk. Some pizza and sodas and water, cigarettes. I was one well-equipped transvestite. Then I drove down to my stalking grounds, parking on the street east of Marco's duplex where I could see the front door clearly and beyond the lights emanating from the Fairfax Newsstand. And then I sat there with binoculars in my lap.

I brought a can to piss inside the car so I wouldn't have to be walking around the neighborhood. A guy can piss in the alley and no one cares but a girl not. Then I waited and smoked cigarettes, super-wired on speed, acid-buzzed. I had a cheap tape recorder and I played rock tapes that one of Zannas boyfriends made for her to listen to at work. I had dozens of them in a shoe box. I was nervous but brimming with overconfidence and a sense of controlling all time and space. The strange looking Flash Gordon Raygun, 3 live bullets in the .38 with the Coke can attachment on the end placed in the briefcase on the passenger side floor. Telepathic Cadre Agents in plain clothes walked by on the sidewalk. All the most experienced agent assassins were in place waiting for the right moment to cue me into action. I saved more speed and acid for later; that was the tactical plan. Wait for the telepathic go signal.

Around 11:30 p.m., Marco left in a cab with two sexy women. I waited another twenty minutes or maybe more. Opened the briefcase, removed the few unnecessary art supplies, then padded the gun back in place with crunched up newspaper and a blue cotton shop rag and closed the case clicking the latches. I had pencilled a verse fragment by Poe and clipped that to my visor. *"Death has reared himself a throne in a strange city lying alone far down within the dim West, where the good and the bad and the worst and the best have gone to their eternal rest."* I rhymed the ancient moribund words aloud. Then 'The Dead Boys' came alive from the tape recorder. *"Ain't it fun when your friends despise what you've become."*

I punched the tape recorder button to off. I checked my face in the rearview mirror and renewed my lipstick. I got out of the car, straightened out my mini-skirt and tank-top and picked up the briefcase off the seat. Time to move. The front door to their duplex was in an alcove with a tiled stairway leading up to the second floor apartment. Never once in the two or three years that I had been routinely going to Marcos had I seen any person use those stairs to access the upstairs. If Royal opened the door my plan was to shoot him quickly. If he figured out what the deal was and slammed the door in my face before I nailed him, then I was a dead man. He surely would hunt me down and kill me at his leisure. Be the hunter or die the prey.

My dad taught me to shoot a pistol and a rifle. When I was a pre-adolescent kid, I was already a dead shot with my dad's .38 revolver but only if I used it with single action. That means cock the hammer first, then pull the trigger. If I used double action, the stress of pulling the trigger to cock the hammer caused my wrist to bend to the right pulling the pistol off target. Using single action, I could hit a beer can or a bottle at twenty yards at the age of twelve.

I approached the alcove, opened the briefcase on the grass shaded in the penumbra of the lighted doorway and removed the gun. I stuffed the blue shop rag in my belt behind my back, then placed the briefcase in the garden plants next to the four steps comprising the entrance stairs leading to the alcove. I knocked on the door firmly and then backed up against the smooth stucco wall so that if Royal answered, he couldn't grab me immediately and kill me with his enormous hands. If a girl answered, I would either run away or calmly ask for Royal and then go inside and shoot him. Whatever felt right at the moment. I cocked the hammer. This was the point of no return. My heartrate accelerated. Feel no fear.

I waited. No answer. Then I heard the footsteps from inside crossing the polished wooden floor. Heavy boots. A man. The door opened. There, Royal stood in front of me sober, in a white sleeveless T-shirt, blue jeans and black engineer boots, a huge man, muscular and cruel. Suddenly I was frightened. I held my left hand with red painted fingernails over the gun which was nestled below my tits in my right hand so that only the Coke can would be visible.

"Who is that? *Liverhead?* You fucking faggot. What do you want?"

Funny he should use that nickname. I became frightened by his size and pulled the trigger prematurely. Tut! He grabbed at his ear in reaction and then looked at his fingers which were painted with a small amount of his blood. I recocked the hammer.

I thought, "Hurry up. Silencer worked. Must be the steel wool that I glued in with the oil filter stuff." Then Royal made one big mistake. He pulled out his balisong and shook it into a knife dagger with lightning speed.

"I'm gonna cut your heart out you faggot piece of shit and throw your pussy in a dumpster."

That was my break. I aimed. His cocksure big huevos knife move took a fraction of a second too long. He had the edge for an instant if he'd just jumped on me. The appearance of the Coke can and the lack of a loud report were misleading him, making him only partially cognizant of the lethal danger. I squeezed the trigger again. The gun pushed firmly against my hand like an old friend. Tut! The second bullet hit his chest on the left side. My eyes were locked staring into his eyes, the windows to his miserable soul. His windows showed me that he knew he was dead before he crumbled to the floor. He was looking directly at my face when the .38 caliber lead bullet ripped through his upper chest. The bullish malevolence in his posture got cancelled out by a sudden change in perception, an inward vision. Big Royal was commanded now by the greater reality, the internal vision of his new master, death. Snake eyes dead man. He dropped suddenly, his massive torso and head falling back into the apartment onto the polished wooden floor giving off the sound of an uncommon double thump, the left leg crossed uselessly under the right.

A bullet in the heart, you drop dead, guaranteed.

I knew deep inside that he was a dead man but I was nonetheless totally scared as hell of him; afraid that he might still grab me and kill me with his massive hands and limbs. I climbed into the threshold of the door. His hands and jaw twitched frenetically, some kind of rapid uncontrolled nervous system response to a barbaric life extinguishing wound. The balisong was resting innocuously on the floor five inches from his left arm. I again cocked the .38, positioned the Coke can silencer firmly against his upper torso so that it was pressed up under his sternum, aimed at his heart muscle with no bone to impede its progress

"Thugs die better with Coke. Dontcha know that Royal?" I fired again. Tump! The gun pushed back against my hand. His torso jerked. The bullet ripped through his body and appeared to penetrate into the fabric of the couch against the back wall. Double dead. Ruined his T-shirt. Splattered destroyed human tissue sprayed out of his upper body across the floor behind him. No more bullets. That was three. Royal was no longer present behind the vacant eyes. No need to keep killing a dead man.

Standing over him it crossed my mind that I could piss on his face. Suddenly jolted, I saw a half-naked girl with long black hair run swiftly out of the bathroom and streak across the hall titties bouncing, wearing only a purple g-string. She startled me. I couldn't be sure if she cast a glance toward the door. I concluded that she did catch a glimpse of the scene. And oh shit! Royal's boot was protruding out the door. I had to put the gun down outside the door on the rubber doormat outside, then heft his colossal leg up bending it at the joint; then slither back out pulling the door firmly shut before the booted foot slid back across the door jamb. Outside, I realized that I forgot a detail. I pushed the door back open a few inches, reached around and pushed in the button lock on the handle and wiped it over with the greasy blue shop towel. I wiped the outer door knob.

"Happy trails. Piece of Satan shit." I murmured. I had a short bastardized quotation prepared to recite from the Book of Revelations but now I had to move quickly. Besides, I forgot the words in the heat of the moment.

Judging by the lack of noise from within the apartment, Royal was still alone in the room dead on the floor. I grabbed the gun, accessed the briefcase in the garden plants and as I was walking east I slid the weapon into the black briefcase. There was no blood on my clothes or hands. Hell, his heart had stopped pumping, it was ripped to shreds.

I turned left at the first corner and walked halfway up the block and then stopped. Adrenaline was dominating my actions. This was ridiculous behavior. I crossed the street in the middle of the block and doubled back. I was going to walk straight to my car. Odds were good that the girl wouldn't follow me. She was inside the apartment stoned on either heroin or methamphetamine or ecstacy. Partially dressed. Barefoot.

When she discovered that Royal was murdered, she would be afraid to alert the police or to draw the attention of any neighbors because of the large quantity of narcotics they held in there. She would be confused and scared. Would the killer return? This was the definition of a bad fucking date. No one but me planned for there to be a murder tonight. This girl may have been the woman from the Lincoln but there was no black late model Lincoln parked nearby.

She was beautiful, sexy, stoned and she had only two safe options open to her. Leave the dead body, lock all the doors and go seek out Marco in the feverish Hollywood nightlife or sit there alone with the dead body and wait for Marco to return home; sit there with the doors securely locked and the murdered drug dealer she was fucking, lying on the floor. Clearly, she would want to get the hell out and catch up to Marco. No one with their senses intact could stand to sit alone with a bloody corpse and wait it out. If she ran to anyone but Marco, a girlfriend for instance, she risked involving a witness to a legal nightmare of narcotics possession and murder.

I am thinking as I walk. Marco comes home and finds his half brother shot dead on the floor. Possibly, Marco is informed beforehand by the girl I saw inside, who catches up to him at a nightclub. He suspects everyone. If the girl catches up to him, he keeps her with him and loses his date so as not to involve his date as a witness or accomplice. Back at his duplex, he has a problem. Marco has a Royal Problemo. He can't call the police because he lives an illegal lifestyle. He possesses a quantity of drugs and drug money within the duplex which needs to be removed. Cops know where to look for hidden items. He's going to jail, the state pen, if the cops come over to his apartment. What do you do for a living Mr. Marco? That question alone leads him into trouble. In addition, Marco is stoned, oh so righteously.

Marco won't have a way to immediately get rid of the narcotics because he trusts no one except Royal who is so completely dead. His narcotics are his livelihood. He will need to hide the narcotics away then move Royal's body to another location or vice versa. Just how sentimental is Marco with his own ass on the line? Perhaps he would be willing to make do without proper funeral arrangements. If Royal's body was found in a dumpster, Marco would still be interrogated, searched and found culpable of something by the police. Time is an issue. Royal is going to stink soon. He's a big piece of unrefrigerated meat. A murdered half brother is tantamount to an unsolvable puzzle for Marco. He will be much too busy sorting things out to worry about the identity of the murderer at the door for some time. Maybe it's a cleaner fix for Marco to kill the girl, dump her with Royal. There were probably a couple dozen people, maybe many more who desired to see Royal depart from this earthly orb in some horrible manner. I am thinking that Marco's best option will be to decide to bury the body in secret out in the desert. He's going to want to get rid of the body immediately. No body, no death, no investigation. Royal is too damn big to start chopping up into pieces to put into a freezer. Besides, Marco would have to buy a huge freezer. And then maybe a lot of things.

I walked to my car and got in, took off the blond wig, wiped off the make-up with paper towels putting the discarded items into the tackle box. Best to avoid driving on Hollywood Boulevard on a friday night. There were metal-flaked low-rider cruisers out on parade and following them were the cops whose job was to chase the cruisers and anyone else remotely suspected of cruising. Harley-Davidson bikers, tourists, the whole scene would be unwinding around 12:30 a.m. I brought a change of clothes, blue jeans, a black sleeveless t-shirt, a tartan flannel shirt and high top Chuck Taylors Converse basketball shoes. I changed in the rear seat and emptied out the can of piss in the gutter. The Ford was already full of gas. I drove ahead onto Fairfax Avenue passing slowly by the apartment, recently the scene of a sudden grisly death, and followed Fairfax Avenue up to Franklin where I could cross over Laurel Canyon and then catch the freeway out of L.A. I made my way to the 5 north. Morbidly, I ate some candy to celebrate, two chocolate candy bars, a Baby Ruth followed by a Snickers. A sugar rush is good for driving. I put on a Mink deVille tape and drove into the night. The wig went out the car window in the pass near the Vasquez Rocks on the 14 East. I left a murder mystery behind me. Just like Raymond Chandler and Cornell Woolrich. Except I was the murderer, an anti-demon special agent, a G-Man. A demon slayer given covert authority to kill by the United States Government.

It was 3:30 or 4 a.m. when I pulled off the road onto the shoulder of hard sand on the outskirts of Darwin. I got out of the car. It was warm wearing a sleeveless T-shirt even at this hour. I went around to the back of the car and opened the trunk; pulled out two red one gallon plastic gasoline cans, two road flares, a roll of duct tape and a small flashlight. I locked up the car all around and avoiding the township entirely, hiked directly into the moonlit field of sand, home to dramatic joshua trees, spiky chollas, creosote bushes, coyotes, various rodents, reptiles, arachnids and insects. I hiked around the north side of the abandoned mining projects. A distant intense crescent sliver of white light, the fragment of moonlight illuminated my way. In time, I crossed over the peak of the small rocky hill, descended to the rudimentary dirt road then came upon the darkened station house.

Since I had visited with Marco, the house had been fenced in all around, encompassing approximately two acres of land, with a twelve foot high chain link fence topped with barbwire but the new gate was left unlocked; the deadbolt hadn't been installed yet, there was just an empty hole. I wore the duct tape around my wrist like a bracelet and the flares were riding together in one pocket. I walked around to the back of the house, taped a flare to a gas can giving it an estimated fifteen minute burn time until it melted the plastic gasoline container and exploded. I had already added a half quart of motor oil to each gallon of gas to make it more viscous. I read once that adding oil was a good technique to employ when concocting recipes for molotov cocktails. I struck the road flair alight and climbed up on the old wooden railing that ran along the eaves of the back porch and pushed the volatile contraption up onto the rooftop. I found an old broom and used it to push the gas container much further up onto the roof. I taped the second flair to the remaining gas can and lit it with the friction cap and leaned that device against the back door on the wooden deck. Then I walked away from the old house.

I was already over the top of the hill descending toward my green Ford when an orange glow emanated from the far side of the hill. By the time I made the car and started the engine, the glow was bright and festive. Sparks were rising into the night sky. I made a U-turn and drove away from Darwin, having never entered the town. When I reached the end of the Darwin slip road at the intersection of the main two lane highway between Lone Pine and Death Valley, I turned to look through the rear window; there was a constant orange glow irradiating skyward from the direction of Darwin, at the convergence of the old road with the horizon. Turning right, I headed the old Ford east toward Death Valley. I hoped to arrive there by sunrise. Somewhere that night, I stopped on the shoulder of the highway entering into the Panamint Valley alongside an unnamed dried up alluvial wash. I placed the .38 with the silencer in the sand and rolled a large rock over it. I remember the absolute anechoic silence of the barren desert landscape and the gritty sound of the rock moving and the dome of stars overhead. That gun is probably still there today thick with rust and corrosion. How many people did that one weapon kill before I buried it? How many of the dead were possessed by demons and how many innocents?

I drove into Death Valley as the sun was preparing to rise. At Stovepipe Wells General Store I pulled up to the gas pumps and turned off the engine. It was an hour later when the store opened its doors. The day was already a hot one, a scorcher. My plan was to pass through the desert before the full heat of the day. Death Valley has a forbidding appearance like that of a hostile alien planet. I filled up the tank with high octane, bought some cigarettes, barbeque potato chips, a Coca Cola six pack and three gallons of water.

Death Valley appeared to be entirely devoid of plant and animal life except for tourists, some travelling in RV trailers and others parked their cars and slept at the motel across the highway. I drove south passing Furnace Creek Inn situated conveniently beneath the Funeral Mountains and speeded freewheeling on down the long two lane highway leading to Baker, the little town famous for its giant thermometer. At Baker, I gassed up and then headed back toward the toxic Los Angeles basin where so many millions of people choose to make their homes and live their lives. When I arrived at Zanna's, it was approaching noon and I went inside and climbed into bed and slept with my clothes still on.

I always turned on the TV as I slept. I watched the news that night. The 11 o'clock News described an arson fire in an isolated California desert community in which two people died. A thirty five year old mentally retarded man Derek Thompson and his twenty nine year old wife who had Down's Syndrome were killed. Derek Thompson's wife had a name, Sue. Their destroyed bodies were found fused together and incinerated in the ashes beneath the charred wreckage of a two story wooden framed house. The suddenness of the inferno caught them unawares. They were the caretakers of the destroyed property. Fire investigators stated that evidence indicated that they were sleeping in the building at the time of the fire although they kept their own home located also in the town of Darwin. Investigators indicated that they found evidence of incendiary devices in the rubble.

Derek Thompson and his wife Sue were burned alive as they slept, burned to death, barbecued, burnt toast, flame broiled, cremated crispy critters, FUBAR (fucked up beyond all recognition), viciously murdered in their sleep, freed of their handicaps and lifted from this world into grace by the loving hands of God.

Zanna came home about midnight. I took a shower and got back into bed. When she got into the bed I put my arm around her and held her close to me. I imitated the rhythm and pacing of her breathing and soon we both fell into deep sleep. I stayed in bed at Zanna's and slept continuously in front of the TV for six months. For the next two years, I became a recluse. My circumstances could possibly be termed as a breakdown in my mental, physical and personal life. The world, which I scarely had conquered, immediately forgot about me. There were so many other ambitious music publications, exciting videos and new media formats vying to catch the viewers attention. Events move swiftly in Hollywood and I felt that I was never really missed by anybody, except uncle Leo. He invited me over for lunch.

... ❧ ...

EPILOGUE OR EPITAPH: "Hello Kitten. Hey, this is Ronnie. Could you do me a favor, one that doesn't involve getting any dirt under your fingernails and it shouldn't take any time. It's just little look–see type of thing."

"Ronnie I haven't seen you for a while and I think I want to keep it that way."

"Just listen. Do you know the bald sex bomb that used to room with Clarissa? You must know what clubs she hangs at. I want to know if she drives a new black Lincoln, the big new expensive model. And does she wear Bettie Page wigs sometimes when she goes out late at night?"

"Ronnie I don't want to be involved with anybody getting hurt. My brother is a Hell's Angel in Sacramento and I hate the violence. Please Ronnie. I don't want to be involved in this."

"Kitten, I'm not going to leave the house or hurt anyone. For my piece of mind, if you can find out these two little details, I can put my mind at rest about the murder of Clarissa. Friends need to look after friends. Even after they're dead. I just want to know if it was one of them or both of them that did it."

"Ronnie I can't promise you anything. I'll find out. But you have to promise not to hurt anyone."

"Kitten, I'm studying computers. Did Zanna tell you that?"

"No."

"It's my new line of work. Kitten if it was you instead of her I'd try to find out. Maybe I can send the cops an anonymous note. It's a rotten way for a pretty girl to die. She was a teenager."

"Ronnie! Ronnie! Stop it. You are not hearing me. Listen carefully. Marco is still in business in Hollywood. He's only moved to a fancier place and he has a new partner, another big thug. The girl...the girl drives a new black Lincoln and she wears wigs. That's her style. Sometimes no hair, sometimes fancy hair. You're in way over your head. These people will kill you if you get within their line of sight. Marco doesn't think you're capable of killing a housefly or you would already be dead. Everybody thinks that your magazine failed and you had a mental breakdown. The bald girl is Marco's girlfriend now. Go study computers. Stay straight. Stay alive."

*****

TO THE L.A.P.D. — This book does not contain the confessions to any past unsolved crimes (murders, shootings, arsons, narcotics infractions).

Written in Hollywood, Studio City, Lincoln Heights, L.A. County–USC Hospital, and Ridgecrest, California.
1980-2004. ©Bruce Caen

ACKNOWLEDGEMENTS: Trouser Press dot com. La Polt Law, Dina LaPolt. The dedicated nurses, interns, and doctors of L.A. County-USC Hospital who took me from Emergency Intensive Care back to good health through a long illness. They aid an endless stream of indigent humanity. A prayer for Elliot Smith who died in L.A. County-USC Emergency at the moment I was released. Dr. Eric Roberts. V.Vale. Joel Wallach. Piz. Suzanne Gardner. Scott Greiger. Mark Gash. Fred Tomaselli. Lyn Mayer. Jonathan Rosen. Mad Marc Rude. Maxine Miller. Alice Klarke. Craig Shannon. Penelope Spheeris. Dave Grave. Dave Arnoff. Donna Bates. Billy Barminski. Roger Doucette. Anthony Mostrom. Ramones. Gary Panter. Carol Lay. Raymond Pettibon. Andrew Maben. Monica Rex. Joe Potts. Michael Morrison. Bill Bentley. Gary Lloyd. Edward Colver. Mike Mollett. Minimal Man. Gary Leonard. Ewa Wojciak. Claude Bessy. Billy Shire. Doug Martin. Ronn Spencer. Christopher Sullivan. Dee Detroit. Kerry Colonna. Melanie Nissan. Harry Kipper. Jules Bates. Edit De Ak. Mavis Humes. Georgia Michaud. Carla Rajnus. Wenden Baldwin. Robin Ghelerter. Dreva & Gronk. Lane Smith. Lezle Stein. Miles Forst. Edgar Allen Poe. May Zone. Mikal Gilmore. Mike Martt. Stanislaw Sobolewski. Ariane Bazin. Bob Seideman. Richard Duardo. Shawn Kerri. Georganne Dean. Linda Giorbino. Gary Hirstius. Los Angeles Free Music Society. Tom Recchion. Survival Research Institute. Target Video. Murielle Cervenka. Ron Michelman, attorney. Posh Boy. Harry the Dog. Kim Fowley and Rodney Bingenheimer. West Coast U.S.A. Punk Rock bands, musicians and fans, past, present and future. Free independent artists and musicians around the world.

SUB-HOLLYWOOD —— BRUCE CAEN

YES PRESS INC.